# The Wolves of Ragnarok

Nick Steuver

contained in the material herein, is the sole responsibility of the reader.

Any copyrights not held by publisher are owned by their respective authors.

All information is generalized, presented for informational purposes only and presented "as is" without warranty or guarantee of any kind.

# DEDICATION

For Fish.

Heee.

# CONTENTS

# Prologue

"Loki, son of Farbauti, son of shadows, son of tricks and schemes, you have been found guilty and your punishment is nigh."

The one-eyed man stood straight as a post at the base of the mountain and let the night wind blow his charcoal cloak around him. Odin held his dark, wide-brimmed cap tight against silver hair that rustled around his shoulders like a thousand needles warping and melting together in a hot forge. Freya watched him carefully. Fury peaked its way through those stony features in small muscle spasms and an uneven curl to his lower lip. That stiffness in his muscles was a desperate attempt to hold himself from strangling the man before him.

The wind screamed through the trees that surrounded them in their tiny clearing. The starless night stared down at their gathering. Freya caught a glimpse of a pair of yellow wolf eyes that disappeared immediately in the dark behind branches fanned with green needles. The sharp scent of the blood clinging to the animal's mouth came to her through the aromatic spruce, a recent kill that was all too familiar to her. But the wolf wouldn't dare come any closer than the edge of the trees.

Loki glowered at the old man through hollow eyes, his body twisted into a position that made him look almost boneless in the grip of a massive man with a thick, red beard. Thor wore his fire openly in his eyes and held the short shaft of his hammer close against the twisted creature's throat, muscles bulging and quivering, ready to smash the shaft inward and crumple his prisoner's airway. Thor's mouth was strained in a snarl he didn't bother to hide.

"By your trickery, good Balder was slain." Odin said. His single eye became a ruby as he said the name. "And by your coldness, he remains with Hel. You will never be forgiven for your treachery. You will be bound until the end of time."

Odin dragged the tip of his index finger through the air. He drew sharp corners and loops that Freya could only see for a split second, shimmering with the faintest golden light before they disappeared again. There was a grumble in the earth as three massive boulders rose from the ground beneath Thor and his prisoner. They were jagged and glossy black, unnaturally called forth from a world that even Freya didn't know. Only Odin had paid the price to obtain that knowledge. He gestured to the stones.

"May the world of men wipe you from memory. May loneliness gnaw at your heart long after you forget love. And may the angst of meaningless words wrap you in a prison of your own lies." The old man turned his head sharply to a man behind him, who carried a golden horn at his side and had skin inlaid with golden flecks. "Heimdall, bring the bonds."

The bonds were taken out, and Freya bared her teeth in a smile at the sight of them. They were entrails, not ropes. She could see dark veins and strings of raw fat that knotted their way across the bumpy surface as Heimdall carried them.

"A son of yours is dead and serves as your binding," Odin growled, "so that you will feel your loss against your skin until all memory has gone."

The Aesir were fierce with their justice and Odin had no mercy. Thor held Loki in that twisted position as Heimdall knelt with the grotesque knots in his hands to bind him.

As soon as they touched his skin, Loki lurched violently. "Which son did you kill, Odin?" he screamed. "Which son? Are those Vali's guts or Narfi's?"

"Narfi's," Odin said with a dead calm. "Slain by Vali, as his eyes yellowed and his humanity left him."

The wolf at the edge of the trees howled and Odin's eye darkened. The one-eyed man's cloak had already blown mostly away from his warrior's tunic, and he had to rearrange his grip on it to keep the increasing wind from plucking it off his shoulders. Freya's skin prickled at the cold and she felt that familiar drop in air pressure. A storm was on its way.

Loki writhed and cursed as Heimdall finished tying the knots and fastened the grisly bonds to the rocks. As he moved, the entrails stretched. Then they twisted. Then they yanked back on his limbs as if alive. Loki screamed vengeance on the Aesir and their entire world, screamed that he would destroy what they had built and plunge everything they cared about into cold, unthinking entropy.

Then he was suddenly quiet as the deep blue of his eyes turned soot black. He smiled at the man who had bound him, a sickening smile that nearly split his face.

"I will enjoy your death most of all, Heimdall. You and I will meet on Vigrond."

"You and I are finished," Heimdall replied.

"He speaks the truth!" a grayed woman spat from Odin's side. Frigg rarely spoke of the future. She generally kept it to herself, to Odin's eternal torment. She was trembling with rage as well, for it was her son whom Loki had murdered. "The truth from the liar's mouth, for once. This day is the first mark of *Ragnarok*. When this wretched creature is freed, the world will tremble. You will fight and kill each other when the last battle comes, Heimdall."

Heimdall looked at the man bound with the entrails of his own son. His eyes took a golden gleam as he studied him. Finally, he shrugged. "If it is destiny, it is destiny. But I will give you no mind until then."

Loki dragged his lips across his teeth in a grin. "You

will mind, old friend. You will suffer for this day."

"*You* will suffer," came Odin's voice, laying heavily across the air with the weight of his hatred. "When the end comes, you will shed many tears. If you had only shed the one—"

"Enough," came the voice of one who was usually silent, a calm voice that cut through the wind and the voices. Tyr gripped the hilt of his sword with his lone hand, as he always did, but his voice was tense and impatient. "Finish it, Odin."

The old man nodded and closed his eyes. He gathered his cloak to conceal his tunic and straightened his hat so that the brim cast its shadow over the eyeless half of his face. He wrote another symbol in the air and a serpent appeared, shimmering as it came into substance from whichever realm Odin had drawn the rocks. The snake calmly extended itself outward so that Heimdall could take it.

"This snake will be your tormentor," Odin continued at last. "It will drip its venom on you and you will suffer with every drop. May it bring you mania, that you will always feel the fever you have caused the rest of us."

Heimdall carried it back to Loki and positioned the serpent on a branch so that its first drip of poison fell on Loki's forehead.

The world erupted in an earthquake so violent that the trees around them barely held the ground by their roots. Loki screamed, and that scream echoed across the mountains to cause avalanches so heavy that they could bury entire towns. Each time he writhed, the world shook with him. When it had subsided only a little, he struggled at the bonds and glared at each of them in turn. He forced a crooked grin. "Who transformed my Vali to murder his brother?"

His eyes demanded an answer, but no one spoke. Odin met the creature's eyes with his one; that it was singular only increased its ferocity. Loki's eyes darted among all of those present, until finally they rested on Freya.

"It was you."

"It was," she replied.

He bared his teeth at her with an odd kind of peace, his eyes still darker than the sky above them. "*Fimbulwinter* will come. You will fight it, but it will come." He writhed in advance under another growing drop of venom. "Love will forever bleed dark and gritty in your heart and I will hide you from time itself." He paused. "You will know madness as I know it. All your power, and you will be helpless to use it. I give you these gifts, my lady."

Freyr stepped forward and Freya stalled him with a look. The beautiful, blond man nodded at her.

"You don't frighten me," she said as she hefted her spear. "Prepare yourself well for Ragnarok, Loki. If you do yourself the honor of a good fight, the last word you hear will be my name."

The drop of venom fell on Loki's face again and his shrieks racked the earth around him, but his tormented eyes, now blue again and wide with agony, did not leave hers. They promised vengeance, and despite her outward bravery she wanted to shiver. Thunder cracked in the distance, that unbidden storm approaching. Fimbulwinter, he had promised. Three winters with no spring and summer in between. The frost giants were undoubtedly on the move already. Freya tightened her grip on her spear.

***

The Israeli air was dry and seemed to move with the lines of sweltering heat rising from the baked ground, creating illusions of darkness over the dirt that disappeared when one started to walk toward them. Mirages, just the way they happened in stories. The rocky earth split in places for lack of rain to keep it smooth and here and there a sickly plant struggled for its life out of the cracks.

"You know what causes mirages?" Gordon Prince said as he looked across the landscape and adjusted his white hard hat.

Gordon's business partner, Paul, raised an eyebrow.

"The sand's heat is transferred into the air above the ground. Hot air refracts light that comes through cold air, and it refracts the image of the sky to your eyes. Blue, like water. The hot air moves upward to mix with the cold air when it gets hot, making the blue seem to wave just like actual water beneath the wind." He grinned and nodded into the distance. "So if someone were to walk across that piece of sand over there by that actual lake, they would appear to be walking on water."

Paul looked to where Gordon pointed and smiled. The Sea of Galilee lay just beyond them to the south, just far enough away that a mirage made the body of water seem significantly larger than it was.

There was a deafening snap as a cloud of splinters and dust danced its way to the top of the excavation site. The crane dropped the large chunk of wood a few feet away from the now-open doorway.

"They said I was crazy," Paul said, grinning like an idiot. "They said we would never find it. They *laughed* at me, Igor!"

The darkness of the entrance was almost a complete black. Gordon was focused on the darkness inside, which should have been more visible with the sun beating its way through the new opening.

"I don't see the big deal." A soldier, whose name Gordon hadn't bothered to learn, stared into the dark opening as he spoke.

Gordon would have done without the soldiers if he had the choice. Their sponsor had insisted, political unrest of the region and all. Gordon wished they would at least shut up and let him have his moment.

Paul took the gracious approach to the soldier. "There's a very real chance that this is Balder's tomb."

The soldier said nothing as he looked down the incline roughly carved into the desert's face.

Paul continued. "Balder was the Norse god of light, the son of Odin and Frigg."

The soldier was silent. He stared into the doorway of the tomb, still shrouded in shadows despite the dust being almost completely clear.

"When Odin and Frigg received a prophecy that Balder

would be killed," Paul said, "Frigg took a sacred oath from everything in the world, living or not, that it would not harm her son."

Gordon imagined the wintry queen demanding a promise from a rock. He smiled when he imagined her getting it.

The soldier didn't ask any questions. He didn't ask how a god could die and Gordon was annoyed that Paul didn't get to explain. Norse gods were interesting precisely because they were mortal, unlike gods in most other mythologies. Because the gods could die, they could be tragic heroes instead of comic relief. When Balder became close to immortal through his mother's actions, the gods all had a good laugh trying and failing to kill him.

Paul did get to explain that, for whatever reason, Frigg didn't bother to get her promise from the mistletoe. Loki, the trickster god, carved the mistletoe into an arrow and tricked Hodur, the blind god of darkness and Balder's brother, into using it. Hel, the goddess of the underworld, offered to raise Balder from the dead if every creature in the world wept for him. Only Loki refused, and Balder stayed dead. Odin burned his son's body on a funeral pyre atop Balder's dragonship.

"Sounds like Loki was an asshole," the soldier said.

Paul smiled. "That sums it up pretty well. He tricked the god of shadows into murdering the god of light."

Gordon nodded. Loki tricked night into murdering day.

The soldier shook his head. "If the body was burned,

what's in the tomb?"

Gordon turned and looked at the soldier, raising an eyebrow. Maybe the man was listening after all.

"Mythologies become what they are over time," Paul said, "but they're based on something real. The most fearsome of gods could have been built on famous warriors or ancient tribal chieftains. The man who became Balder the god might be buried here."

Gordon and Paul left the soldiers and the two men made their way down the incline to step past the ruined door. Inside, the darkness seemed to swallow the light from their headlamps, expensive as the lamps were. That, Gordon knew, was nonsense. His eyes were still adjusted to the bright light of the desert. There was enough light to find their way around, and that was what mattered.

Pillars were toppled and were lying shattered on the stone floor. Basins where fires might have been lit for sacrifices were smashed, and Gordon thought he saw the grease of sacrificial animals still glimmering on them. In stark contrast to all of this, the statue at the far end of the temple behind the altar was fully intact and upright.

Gordon's headlamp couldn't banish the fuzziness around the edges of the sculpture. Through the haze, he could see a man's face that was decidedly pointy as it emerged from the carved black stone. Pointy eyebrows hung over eyes that were piercingly sharp despite being carved centuries before. A wicked grin split his face in half to reveal a set of blocky, too-large teeth, the razor sharp corners of the mouth seeming to stretch progressively farther toward the long, pointed ears even as Gordon stood looking at it. The man was robed and his arms were crossed in front of him. His feet were positioned perpendicularly, a foot apart.

Impatiently.

"If this is Balder's tomb," Gordon said after a long time, "why does it contain a monument to Loki?"

There was a sound behind them. A scraping of a footstep against the sandy stone, perhaps. Gordon spun on his feet and squinted into the darkness. The dark seemed thicker now though, somehow consuming even more of the light than it had before.

"What's the matter?" Paul said.

Gordon didn't turn his attention away from the darkness. Something was there. He let the silence linger. "Didn't you hear that?"

"I didn't hear anything."

"Something moved," Gordon said.

He was sure he had heard something, but the light revealed nothing at all. The sound came again, stretching across a longer length of time. It sounded more like the low growl of a large dog.

A bead of cold sweat glided down between his shoulder blades. The feeling of dread was thick in his chest, and he could not shove it away. A panic attack? A heart attack? He debated briefly on whether he had taken his baby aspirin this morning or if he had left it in his pack.

"I'm sure it's fine, Odin," Paul said.

Gordon stared at the man, whose features were no

longer illuminated by the light that struggled through the space between them. "What did you call me?"

Paul's blurry outline walked next to the statue and rested its elbow on Loki's shoulders. "I said it's fine, Odin. Fenris is still chained."

Fenris, the wolf large enough to swallow the world whole. The low growl returned. It was deep, the vibrations crawling through the floor to touch Gordon's feet. There was no sharp bark, only the constant grumble like the motor of some distant and massive machine.

"Paul," Gordon said, "the joke's over. Whatever you're doing to make this—"

"My joke on you was played out a long time ago, Odin. It's time to end it."

The darkness swelled and Gordon turned to see that the doorway had disappeared, removing whatever illumination the desert sun had tried to offer. Gordon couldn't see Paul's face, but he imagined the man was grinning and he couldn't understand why. The more he stared, the more Paul began to look like the statue next to him.

The ground beneath Gordon's feet shook and his headlamp winked out.

"And so he sets a fire, to sear his soul and purge away all that stands in his desperate path, to forge his focus and save the ones for whom he walks his bitter road. Now his illness, cured in flame, sails away on tendrils of smoke until the heavens weep for all he loved. 'We march to Ragnarok,' he says to no one as he hefts his mighty sword. 'Behind us, all we were, before us, only bloody battle. You carry lightning in your eyes, my friend, bolts as numerous as grains of sand. Your burden is nigh, the last to die, for there is fury in my hand.'"

—*Scrawled onto a wall of the last temple of Loki before the world burned.*

# Chapter 1

## PRELUDE TO REVELATION

The bowl of shrimp was the size of one of those plastic baskets that Jeremy's mother used to collect his laundry when he was a kid. It tilted at a precarious angle on a pile of napkins to catch drops of condensation forming on the outside of the bowl, forming a lopsided centerpiece on the pink-clothed table at the front of the conference room. As he passed the bowl in favor of the crackers and spreadable cheese ball, he felt a masculine hand pat him on the shoulder twice and linger until he turned around.

"You must be Jeremy Coleson," said the owner of the hand. "Kyle Dark."

Kyle was four inches taller than Jeremy and more than four years younger, with the fragrantly moussed hair and consciously shaved face of a business major newly freed from the frat house. Looking at him, Jeremy was irritated to become aware of his own slight stubble and poorly-controlled brown mop. Somehow, Kyle was now standing between Jeremy and the snacks.

The silver shirt and skinny black tie really demonstrated, Jeremy was sure, that this kid was a self-starter who knew style. Kyle's eyes lit up as he saw someone familiar in the cubicle area and, rather than leaving to speak to them, opted for a game of charades through the glass window that separated them while Jeremy tried to decide if it would be rude to simply walk away.

When Kyle was done, he opted for whatever corporate networking strategy employed too much eye contact and leaned forward slightly, extending his hand to Jeremy. Consciously suppressing the urge to comment on the fact that the name ought to belong to the mild-mannered alter ego of a comic book hero, Jeremy completed the circuit of the handshake. Kyle's squeeze was a little too intense and Jeremy had a weird feeling that he was being challenged in some subtle way. He shrugged his shoulders, admittedly slumped in comparison to Kyle's, and slowly made his way around the man and toward the snacks.

"A man of few words," Kyle said. "I get that, man. I like it."

Ah. Kyle was in sales. He'd probably been to some recent seminar and emerged transformed, convinced that every stranger out there was, in fact, an invaluable connection that he had yet to make. It was probably the same seminar that had told the company's executive board that these office parties for interdepartmental mingling were necessary to the growth and prosperity not only of The Company, but the Great United States Herself. Jeremy's plate was now full of crackers, so he grudgingly turned back around. Kyle sucked the end of a shrimp from its shell and placed the empty tail on the tablecloth.

"I hear your team got assigned the new software contract for the Army," Kyle said in the middle of a wet round of chewing. "That's a pretty big fish."

Jeremy shoved a cracker in his mouth. As he spoke around it, a crumb made a break for freedom and rode his breath until it landed daintily on Kyle's tie. "We've taken on bigger projects. There's just a lot of red tape involved in this one. You know government stuff."

In truth, he hadn't even met his team in person. Most of them were lucky enough to telecommute, leaving Jeremy the pleasure of working mostly alone in his cubicle. On top of that, his part of the project was pretty minor. After his last promotion, he did only bits and pieces of coding to fill in the gaps where one of his team members had a problem. Otherwise, it was a matter of stitching things together and sending it off to the testing team. But none of that was worth telling the salesman who was positive he was going to be a CEO someday.

Kyle nodded and proceeded to make too much eye contact again. "Make sure you do a good job on that one, man. I'm the one who got that contract, and it wasn't easy. You're on vulnerability management?"

Nope. But Kyle had most definitely taken a seminar lately which left him absolutely convinced that putting his own personal touch on every sale all the way through to delivery, including speaking to every single person who worked on the project, would be the key to owning his own mansion someday. The man bobbed his head and spoke again before Jeremy got a chance to say anything.

"So as a personal favor to me," Kyle said, "would you check over the thing once or twice before you hand it in just to make sure everything is money?"

Something in Kyle's pocket started rapping. Kyle pulled out his smart phone and tapped it a few times, smiling at a text message and bobbing his head again. A part of Jeremy wanted to tell Kyle that, asshole, *money* was a noun and not an adjective. A bigger part of Jeremy decided that this conversation should only go on as long as it had to, and anything detracting from that objective was probably the wrong thing to say.

"Sure thing," Jeremy said as Kyle turned to the snack table.

While Kyle's mouth busied itself around another shrimp, Jeremy crabbed left and ducked forward, tucking in his repeatedly blousing dress shirt and giving the crab and duck again to another business associate before finally finding his way to Beth.

Jeremy's wife was talking to a brunette with librarian glasses who was gesturing with her long nails and talking feverishly into the face of her new conversation partner. Beth's eyebrows seemed to be making the same dash toward her scalp that Jeremy was making away from Kyle, and he saw her fingers make small movements as if she was resisting the urge to smooth her olive-colored dress, conservatively cut in a square neckline that didn't quite plunge far enough to show cleavage. The light caught Beth's blonde curls as she tossed a few over her shoulder and offered a reverse-engineered cackle of a fake laugh.

"Hey, Prince Honeycakes," she said when she saw him. "Peggy here was just telling me that you're one of the nicest guys in the office."

He raised an eyebrow as a small smile tugged at his lips. One of Beth's favorite games was called *Pet Names In Public*. Make up something ridiculous and the other person has to try and top it.

"Hey, Princess Snuggle-Pie." He turned to the other woman, wishing slightly that he hadn't agreed to play the game every time Beth decided it would be fun. "Thank you, Peggy."

Beth smiled and politely told the brunette that it was nice talking to her, waited for a count of five so that she was out of earshot, then turned to Jeremy. "You want to get the hell out of here, don't you?"

Jeremy shrugged. "You kidding? I'm finally starting to catch on. I was just thinking I should check out some of these success webinars they're e-mailing around the office. They might really help me increase my adjusted gross—"

"We're getting the hell out of here," she said as she grabbed his hand. "And you're never saying the word *webinar* again."

"Do you think it's alright to be the first couple to leave?"

She dragged him to the elevator, smiling pleasantly at Karen the administrative assistant and matching her melodic hello with a similarly chipper goodbye. When she hit the button, he grinned at her and squeezed her hand.

"I thought you wanted me to play the corporate game a little," he said. "*Let's go sleaze it up and get you a promotion.*" He squeezed his voice into a high-pitched tone. "'*Don't you have a jacket that fits?*'"

She squeezed his hand back. "I know what I said. Fuck the promotion."

The elevator dinged and the doors opened. Beth dove inside, yanking his tie like a leash, and pressed her full lips to his. Jeremy realized he was still holding his plate of cheese and crackers,

She raised an eyebrow and looked up at him, her smile deepening. The light glossed across her brown eyes and made a reasonable impression of a starry sky. "Well, you're welcome to stay and finish your crackers." She leaned in as she kissed the corner of his jaw and whispered in his ear. "Or you could take me home."

"Yep. That."

Beth grinned at him. "You know it's your birthday today?"

"No, it's not." He thought for a moment. "Oh." He honestly couldn't remember what the date was.

The corners of Beth's smile stretched toward her eyes and she tossed her head back with a short cross between giggle and shriek. She recovered and met his eyes, then put her hands behind his head, dug her nails into his neck and kissed him again. She smelled vaguely like sweet basil and Jeremy wondered if it was a perfume that he had bought.

"I have a surprise in mind for you," she said.

Home was a half-hour's drive away to the tune of Beth's howling and laughing rendition of every radio song that she happened to think was ridiculous.

"Just let me get a few things ready," she said when they got inside.

Jeremy watched her go and sat down on the couch. He blew through a few channels on the television, passing by several reality television shows and a documentary on the Loch Ness Monster. He had seen the documentary twice, even though it was one of his least favorite ones. Jeremy was more partial to science and history than he was to urban legends and bogeymen.

"Brittany Michaels, twenty-four year old pop princess turned out-of-control partier, has outdone herself. The singer of the latest hit single 'Scandalous,' a far cry from her earlier, innocent-image material, had been arrested for a third offense of drunk driving after having her license suspended in early June. More at eleven."

Jeremy flipped the channel.

"If Senator Ali becomes the President of the United States, our country is in for changes that I don't think it's ready for. He's the first candidate for the presidency who's *ever* said outright that the wealth of the country needs to be redistributed. The media has painted this socialist as America's Messiah, and he's going to destroy our entire economy."

Political talk shows. Jeremy put his hands behind his head.

"I think that's taken way out of context," the man on the opposite side of the debate said. "What he meant to say is that there's a wide gap between the rich and the poor that cannot be bridged without government involvement. Right now, the actual statistics show that upward mobility is next to impossible in lower socioeconomic—"

Jeremy was too late to find out the man's name, so he decided to name him Boris.

"Well, that's exactly what redistribution of wealth means!" said the first man. Jeremy named him Penelope. "Taking money from people who have earned it and giving it to people who haven't."

"We're not talking about redistribution," Boris said. "We're talking about the American dream that's been denied to so many Americans under President Pearson. And I think it's a stretch to say that the super-rich have *earned* their—"

"Taking money from people who have earned it," Penelope repeated. "Redistribution of wealth. Socialist. Marxist. Hates hardworking Americans and probably Christmas. That's what we can expect from Senator Ali."

You could always tell what the slant was of a political talk show, because the speaker who was inclined toward that slant always just spouted off a couple catch phrases as if they proved his argument, usually interrupting enough to prevent a full argument from the other side. Liberal or conservative, it was invariably the one who held the dominating viewpoint of the show that was the bigot. Maybe it meant that the *actual* slant was the other direction.

"Hey," came his wife's voice.

He turned off the television and turned to look at her. She wore a cute, little girl smile that looked like she was on the verge of spilling a big, juicy secret. The gown she now wore was his favorite crimson, hanging from her left shoulder as the neckline slashed down and beneath her right arm. She grinned and twirled, mahogany eyes searching his face for approval. They found it as Jeremy stood and embraced her, laying a gentle kiss on the side of her neck as he pulled her close with a hand on the small of her back.

"My husband," she said.

"My wife."

Her breath smelled minty and Jeremy wished he had also brushed his teeth instead of watching politics, since his breath probably smelled like cheese. She didn't seem to notice as she took his hand. "Come on."

Jeremy wondered if he should have noticed the picnic basket on the counter earlier, or if Beth had prepared it while he was watching television. She led him outside and spread a picnic blanket on the front yard, smoothing every wrinkle and taking off her shoes before they sat down. He kissed her cheek and she snuggled toward him, and he felt the odd moistness of his own kiss press into his skin.

"So," she said as she sat up and pulled a bottle of wine and two glasses from the basket. "Tell me a thought."

He raised an eyebrow as she opened the bottle and poured. "I wish I had used mouthwash before we came outside."

"Eh." She handed him a full glass. The ruby wine was almost black in the faint moonlight. "Tell me a better thought."

He swirled his wine in the glass so it came as close to the brim as possible without hopping over. "I hate my job."

Beth smiled. "I hate your job too. I don't think I could stare at a computer screen for two hours, much less eight."

He smiled and swirled the wine again. Beth dug into the picnic basket and retrieved a Tupperware container. When she opened it, a layering of fresh mozzarella cheese and tomatoes peaked up at him. Ribbons of basil dusted the top like autumn leaves and it was drizzled with a dark reduction. The smell of sweet basil brushed his nose again.

"For my husband," Beth said, handing him the container. "The only man I know who forgets his own birthday. I've got three more containers in here, since I figured you wouldn't like the food at the party."

"I hope you—"

"If you ask me if I spent too much on the food, I'm going to slap you."

He took it and kissed her again before digging in with his fingers. She offered him a box of plastic forks and he took one, setting it down on his lap and opting for the finger strategy anyway. The sky was less than starry with a blanket of clouds over it, but it was August in Ohio and that meant it could change any minute.

"Are you bored?"

He looked at Beth. Her eyes were just a little glossier than the had been. "No. What? No, not with you."

She breathed a sharp gust of a silent laugh through her nose. "I mean in general."

"God, yes."

"Me too. Want to move? I wouldn't mind Miami for a while." She made an approximation of a wink at him. She always had to try so hard to make a wink work, and it usually just looked like an eye spasm.

"I thought you *liked* Podunk."

"Of course I *like* it," she said. "But that doesn't mean I couldn't use an adventure."

"I want one too," he said with a smile. "Let's go build us a castle in Europe and find ourselves a dragon to slay."

"We'll have to take swordfighting lessons," she said. "And learn to ride horses."

"I thought you hated horses." He clicked his teeth together and made a shocked face as he held up his hand with one finger bent to look like it was missing. "*They're the biggest assholes on God's Green Earth.*"

"Yeah," she said. "Fuck horses."

"Well, it's the twenty-first century. Maybe we can ride motorcycles instead."

"My knight in shining black leather." She wrinkled her nose. and stood up to make a mock bow at him. "I pray you take this favor," she said, handing him her panties.

"When did you—"

She leaned forward and kissed him.

\*\*\*

"The testing team found another bug," Mr. Douglas said as he tossed a folder over the cubical wall and onto Jeremy's desk without slowing his walk. "I'll need this one taken care of before you leave today."

Jeremy opened the folder and read the report. It urgently warned Jeremy that there was probably an issue with the coding, possibly the JavaScript section. If anything from this system actually used JavaScript, Jeremy could have understood why they paid these guys.

"I'll take care of it," Jeremy said to nobody. "It won't happen again."

He dusted some crumbs from his keyboard, still there from yesterday's peanut butter and banana sandwich. Three cubicles away, Karen answered the phone.

"*Good* morning. Why yes, he's *actually* on another call right now. Can I have him call you back? Okay then. You have a *great* day."

Beneath the bug report, there was a short envelope with his name scrawled in the front. He opened it, wondering why someone on the team would bother sending him an enveloped letter when an e-mail would suffice. The paper inside was crumpled and browned as if it had been written long ago, tossed in a compost heap, washed off, dropped beneath a sink and found again years later before being placed in the envelope and dropped in the folder. It was written in the same furious script. One word.

25

*Heimdall*

"*Good* morning," came Karen's voice again.

Jeremy stared at the paper. It was delightfully unhelpful, with just a hint of something useless.

"*Absolutely*," Karen said. "It will be my *absolute pleasure* to put you through."

What kind of idiot sends a one-word letter? He put it aside and brought up the code on the Army project. They were calling it VIGROND, an acronym that he probably wasn't allowed to understand on pain of security clearance paperwork and extensive drug testing. All necessary and proper, of course.

"*Good* morning. I'm *very* sorry, but she's not in today. Can I put you through to someone else on her team, or should I have her call you back? Well, I can *certainly* do that. You have a *great* day."

He scanned the limited lines of code in the section that had thrown an error while doing, well, the report didn't say. The set background of the program was black and the print was blood red, which seemed a little dramatic to him. But the color settings were trapped in parts of the code that were blocked by an encryption and he didn't have the pass code, so dramatic it would stay.

"*Good* morning. Why *certainly*. I'll put you through."

He rubbed his eyes with the heels of his hands. Someone had typed *HAHAHAHAHA* in place of actual code in one of the reference files. Maybe even the same asshole who had left him the note. He imagined someone setting up the joke thinking it would be elaborate and genius, then botching the execution entirely by trying to be more subtle than necessary. He pulled up his browser and ran a search for Heimdall, trying to at least give the poor guy's joke a chance before he replaced the reference file with his backup.

"*Good* morning. Why, how *are* you, Mr. Roland? I'm *wonderful*, thanks for asking! What can I do for you? Well, *certainly*! Just a moment!"

Right. Thor's friend from the comics. Or Heimdallr, the watchman of the Norse gods with gold teeth, who apparently spent a lot of time sitting on a rainbow and drinking mead. Either way, Jeremy didn't get the joke.

"*Good* morning."

He closed the browser and tapped at his keyboard until lunch. Somehow, he managed to write five hundred words in a report to Mr. Douglas about what was essentially a typo in the code. Of course, that e-mail needed editing so that he didn't look like a moron to his boss, but he saved that for later. In the meantime, he fired off a number of e-mails to his team members who were probably sitting at home in their underwear. He retucked his dress shirt in his eternal war against blousing.

At lunch, Jeremy picked at his salad in disappointment. The lettuce leaves were already turning brown and releasing a small amount of mystery liquid onto the paper tray below. He dumped the entire cup of ranch dressing over top of it and scraped what he could from the sides, listening to the conversation of the two men sitting several tables behind him in the otherwise empty cafeteria.

"I just watched this crazy documentary," one of the men was saying. "Apparently, there's a secret code in the Bible that confirms the 2012 end of the world thing."

"Those are the same idiots that told me not to go into programming," the other man said, "because my career wouldn't exist after Y2K. Screw 'em."

Jeremy grinned around a bite of shitty salad.

"Yeah, but apparently Hebrew words also act like numbers and if you add them all together, or divide them, or something, you get a date for the end of the world."

"I bet. And the Mayan calendar stops the same year. Here comes the Rapture."

"Well, the Mayans predicted all kinds of stuff, right?"

"Yeah," Jeremy said around another mouthful, "but did they predict that Brittany Michaels would get another DUI? Because I did."

The two men fell silent and Jeremy realized he had accidentally responded to their conversation in a voice loud enough to be heard. He poked furiously at the salad, making a cherry tomato into a fearsome adversary as it used his pile of dressing against him. The men resumed talking in voices too quiet for Jeremy to hear and he felt his face flush.

When he got back to his desk, he had another bug report waiting for him. An urgent e-mail invited him to a meeting tomorrow with Mr. Douglas for his annual evaluation. Also, Karen's computer was acting up and she was *so* glad he came back because she needed help *right away.*

\*\*\*

"I know I'm late again, Beth," he said as he walked in the door with a pile of mail from outside. "It's been a long day. I'm apparently not as good at my job as I think I am."

"We're at war, Jeremy."

The soft voice came from the living room, where he found his wife laying on the couch and watching the evening news. Beth didn't watch the news. Her eyes were fixed in a kind of trance vaguely directed at the screen and she didn't look at him as he walked toward the couch.

"Elizabeth Ruth Asher-Coleson, there's always a war." He only used her full name when she was being silly, and it usually helped ease the mood when said with a mock-serious tone. Despite the heavy-laden mock-seriousness, her face didn't change. He let his tone drop back down to concerned. "Iran?"

She nodded and Jeremy sighed. The political talk shows had all been calling the present situation in the Middle East a ticking time bomb for years now, but each time the morons who served as the hosts had been wrong in labeling every small event in the United States government as the certain trigger of impending doom. Lately, it was the presidential candidate of Arab descent, a second-generation citizen who had risen to the American Senate and who was now winning in the polls for the upcoming election. If he came too close to becoming President of the United States, warned the talk show hosts, Israel might get nervous about its future. The first Arab U.S. President might not back them as others had, and their well-being might depend on making an attack while the alliance was still strong with the outgoing President, entangling the States into war before a new leader could change foreign policy.

With all the talk shows calling Iran an "impending threat" because of their nuclear research program, forecasted to be capable of producing a nuclear bomb sometime in, oh, a dozen years, a new war was almost certain to happen sooner or later.

But according to the anchorwoman as Beth turned up the volume, the first move had not been made by Israel. Perhaps the Jewish nation's intentions were predicted by some Arab leaders rather than just a few sensationalist morons on television. Or maybe it was just strange timing and had nothing to do with American politics or Israel's intentions, but Iran had bombed an Israeli biomedical equipment factory and had potentially released dangerous, world-ending materials into the Mediterranean Sea. Story on that later tonight.

The civilian and military death toll of the bombing had caused Israel to declare ware on Iran with full backing from the United States.

None of this would matter to Jeremy if Beth's younger and only brother wasn't stationed in Israel. She had staunchly disagreed with Damien's decision to enlist and had heard little from him in the ten years since. Jeremy had only met Damien at their wedding, and the man had been vague about his role in the military. Jeremy didn't even know which branch called Damien one of their own.

He put his hand on the back of her neck and rubbed gently. "He's going to be okay, Beth."

The anchorwoman smiled pleasantly out at them from the television. "To those affected by this terrible tragedy, we offer our deepest sympathies. Next up, are your hands as clean as you think they are? Samples of a certain brand of hand sanitizing solution have been shown to contain traces of Ebola. Is your health at risk?"

Jeremy wrinkled his nose.

"Let's go out," he said. "Whatever you feel like eating."

He took the remote and turned off the television. Beth stared at the blank screen for a few seconds and then nodded. He put his arm around her as they stood up, felt her frame melt into his, and kissed her cheek. The cool wet on his nose told him that she had been crying before he got back and had just barely failed to get rid of all the evidence before he got to the living room.

***

"Wilbur, you lag behind any farther and we're going to leave you to fend for yourself."

Damien jogged backward, looking through sun-closed eyes at the double-file line moving next to him along the rocky terrain. Wilbur Thorton was in the back, struggling as usual about three paces behind the rest of the group. Fucking new guy.

Wilbur was the only one Damien called by his first name. It was such a wimpy name, and Damien thought it perfectly characterized the skinny man. The newest recruit to Damien's training camp, the man could barely run a mile. How he had managed to get contracted in, Damien didn't know or care.

But Wilbur was here, six weeks into training, and the kid was going to get somebody killed or captured if he was even close to a real op. Beheading didn't sound too bad as ways to die went, but Damien would be damned if he came to that by Wilbur's fuck-up. He pounded his boots into the sun-baked ground and bared his teeth.

"Yessir, Captain Asher," came Wilbur's answer between heavy breaths.

"*Hut*, two, three, four!" Damien yelled as he kept pace with the man. "Move your ass, Wilbur."

"Yessir."

Damien Asher wasn't officially a captain. He wasn't officially anything, as far as he was aware. He was private sector, contracted in by the same man who had recruited Wilbur, and his job was to turn guys like Wilbur into stone.

"Mark time, march!" Damien barked.

Every man in the line took one more step and then marched in place, the toe of each foot coming two inches away from the sand and the heel coming four. They marked time to an imaginary drum cadence, the cadence that would be playing if it wouldn't announce their presence to any small band of insurgents that might wander by. Having moved ahead, Damien jogged back to where Wilbur was marking time and exhaling labored breaths.

"Wilbur, I want you to give me fifty right here.

Position!"

The kid's eyes widened but he didn't look at Damien. He was picking up something, at least.

"Yessir."

Wilbur dropped to his knees and pushed himself forward onto hands laid directly beneath his shoulders, straightening his legs so that his body was almost completely in line.

"Straighten that body, Wilbur."

The kid did his best and his posture improved slightly. Damien nodded and glared down at him.

"One!" Damien barked.

Wilbur went down and up, keeping his body in line but shaking slightly in the elbows.

"Two!"

Wilbur went down again, touching his chest to the ground momentarily.

"Three!"

The kid lowered himself to the ground and back up again. This time his elbows didn't just shake. They wobbled. Damien kept counting. He counted to five, then ten, then fifteen. But when he got to eighteen, Wilbur's arms shook so much he looked like he was doing an impression of a chicken and grunted as he lopsidedly brought himself back to position. Damien sighed loudly enough for the whole unit to hear the whistle in his throat.

"Wilbur," he said, "are you telling me you can't do even twenty fucking push-ups?"

"No sir," Wilbur said. "I can do them."

"Then let's see the snap to them, goddammit!"

"Yessir."

Despite his chicken arms, Wilbur managed to make it to fifty. Damien could feel the heat bearing down on him, but he very deliberately ignored it, a skill he had learned over the many scorching days in the Israeli desert. The hottest part of the day was fast-approaching, and he wanted to get at least another mile in before it came.

"Let's go, gentlemen," he barked. "Another hour to go. Jogging again at my order. Resume, march!"

They pressed forward, facing the sun. When Damien judged they had gone another mile, he would order them to set up camp and they would rest and hydrate for fifteen minutes before running combat drills. As he ran, he scanned the dunes for any movement that might indicate an ambush of some kind.

\*\*\*

Damien stood outside of a tent near the center of the camp. It was cooling down now outside, and the sweat on the back of his shirt was starting to get cold. Whenever he moved, it pressed against him and sent small stings of chill through his body.

"Come on in, Asher."

Damien came inside and saluted briefly before the Brigadier General dismissed the formality with a sweep of his hand. Warren Leonard was the man who had recruited Damien when he was thinking about enlisting as a soldier, doubling the salary he would have received from the Army and putting him in position to actually have an effect on what happened out here in the desert. Damien did his best to keep rank in mind when speaking with his superior officer, but the General didn't care much about formality.

The General was seated on the thin blanket stretched over the otherwise bare ground to act as a floor, surrounded by pages of notes and maps containing various degrees of detail. There was no furniture in the room, just a sleeping bag and an old camp lantern strung from the ceiling with a shoelace. The lantern bobbed back and forth as the wind jostled the outside of the tent, making the General's shadowy silhouette dance this way and that on the floor.

He regarded Damien with dark eyes before looking back down at his papers. He scratched his white beard. "How's the new kid?"

Damien shook his head. "Terrible, sir."

The General smiled without looking up. "Well, so were you."

"Yes, sir."

Warren shook his head. "Enough of that. Call me *sir* again and I'll have you guarding an embassy in France."

Damien nodded.

"We have a mission." The General picked up a file folder and held it out for Damien to take. "It's a nasty one."

Damien took the folder and opened it. Missions were rare for Damien, who spent most of his time training men for missions in other parts of the world. As he scanned the document inside, he felt a storm begin to howl in the back of his mind. "We're going to bomb Iran?"

Warren Leonard nodded. "Somebody wants to send a strong message."

"Yes—"

"Don't call me sir. Tell me you can get this done."

The storm screamed in Damien's brain. He grabbed it and tossed it into a dark cell with no windows. There wasn't room for debate. "I can get this done."

The mission was to plant a nuclear bomb on the outskirts of Tehran and level the city.

"Select two men for your team. This is need-to-know for them, of course."

Damien kept his features hard as stone. He had withheld information from his men before, but never regarding civilian casualties.

"You'll be posing as converted Muslim men making a pilgrimage to Imamzadeh Saleh, in Shemiran." Warren pointed to his map. "That's just north of downtown Tehran, so you'll have a good reason to be in the city. Once inside, you will rendezvous with two spies who will introduce themselves as Bonnie and Clyde."

Damien stared at the General.

"Speak freely, soldier."

Damien slammed his thought into the dark cell along with the storm. He shook his head. "No need, sir."

Warren ignored the honorific. "Asinine code names aside, they're some of the best-placed spies we have. Bonnie in particular is an old friend of mine. They've already taken care of security for your arrival and will be the men who get you out of there afterward. Come here tomorrow with your team assembled."

*** 

"You have to get your feet up *high*!"

Damien heard the voice as he left Warren Leonard's tent.

"Come on, Anderson! Show 'em how it's done!"

There was a smacking sound, followed by the cheering of a group of men. Damien followed the voices. If circumstances were different, he would have smiled.

"Your turn, Wilbur!"

All the men laughed as Damien walked between two tents and watched them from the darkness just outside of the lantern lights.

"Come on, Wilbur!"

The man speaking was Victor Lyon, the private who had come in just a few months before Wilbur. Unlike Wilbur, however, Victor had been nearly ready from day one.

Victor pushed Wilbur forward, toward the man wearing a set of the heavy body armor. That was Charles Nolan, maybe the heaviest man in the entire unit. He had been here the longest, but his heavyset frame never seemed to shed all of that weight. Damien watched, knowing the game they were playing. Hell, Damien had played it when he had been a new recruit.

Wilbur backed up a few steps, eyeing first Charles, then Victor. Victor was urging him forward, but Damien couldn't tell whether it was true encouragement or whether this was all a joke.

"Might want to back up a few more steps, Wilbur!" came a voice from the crowd that Damien didn't quite recognize.

Wilbur did as he was told, to the wild amusement of some men who almost fell over laughing. Wilbur's face colored, visible even in the dim light of the lanterns, but he locked his eyes on Charles and positioned himself. He charged forward and jumped, landing a kick directly on Charles's chest. But Wilbur, without the weight the other soldiers had, couldn't build up the momentum required to knock Charles over. He fell to the ground, grunting as he hit the sand that had been packed and hardened by the constant heat of the sun and the trampling of soldiers' feet in heavy boots. Victor burst out laughing in unison with Charles, and within half a second all of the other men joined in. Wilbur lay there in the sand, pathetically clutching the shoulder that had taken the force of his fall.

Then Victor saw Damien, just barely visible as he emerged from the shadows, and he fell instantly to attention with his feet together and hands at his sides.

"Sir," Victor barked without hesitation.

"Sir," came the startled bark from the others.

Even Wilbur was standing at attention now. A tear ran down his face. Damien narrowed his eyes at the man.

"As you were, men," Damien said. "Lyon, get Wilbur up to speed. Enough dicking around. Lights out in an hour."

"Yes sir," Victor barked, snapping into a salute before

breaking attention.

Damien made his way back to his tent. That storm in the back of his mind had been muffled to a small whisper, buried beneath duty. His men relied on him. Warren Leonard relied on him.

A small envelope waited on his pillow. It had no address, just his name written on the face of the envelope in a handwriting that looked as if the sender had been under torture while scratching out the letters. Mail was delivered in the mornings, so the envelope's appearance meant that someone had entered his tent without permission. He opened the envelope and took out a crumpled, dirty piece of paper.

> *The Captain said to the crocodile,*
> *"Take my hand and stay a while."*
> *One-armed prince, I know your fate.*
> *I set your execution date.*
> *The dog approaches; you hear its call.*
> *You are mine when at last you fall.*
> *Captain, my captain, even in death.*
> *Your flesh is mine, to forsake the rest.*

Beneath the verse, there was a line of prose.

*Practice your begging, Tyr. Do not disappoint us on Vigrond.*

Despite the cryptic nature of the last line, Damien's

stomach lurched. Tyr. He traced the three letters of the word with his eyes and told himself that a threat like this should be reported to the General. Someone was playing a joke that was out of line.

Damien stared at the letter for a long time. He didn't report it.

He killed the lantern and laid himself gently on his cot, trying to empty his mind. He imagined himself gliding along the smooth surface of a massive lake, a crystal mirror that extended past the horizon. Damien looked down into that imaginary water and massive yellow eyes stared up at him from below. Each of those yellow irises was the size of a man's head. Damien floated past them and upward through the air, toward a small island that appeared ahead.

On the island, he found himself standing in a dense forest. It was cold and the snow flakes that occasionally touched his skin were almost warmer than the air itself. Then a wolf, massive enough to own the eyes that had stared at Damien from the water, snarled at the group that gathered around it. Its jaws, large enough to swallow a car, snapped twice at the air and set themselves into a grin that was almost human as it towered over the group.

"Another chain," the monstrous creature rasped through its exposed teeth. "Bring another and I will break it."

"There is only this one," an old man said to the beast. He held a thin band of metal that took on a strange coloration in the moonlight, reflecting colors that belonged in the sunset rather than the night. The man's silver hair danced in the wind beneath his dark cap. "If you break this, you are truly a god among beasts."

The wolf's grin seemed to deepen, but it shook its massive head from side to side in refusal when it saw the chain that the old man held. It looked thin enough that a child could snap it in two. "I'm not a pup, Odin. My pride is not so great that I cannot recognize a trick when I see it."

"It is no trick," the old man replied. "We've tried every metal and you leave us defeated. Break this, and we will worship you. Fail, and we will mock you. I give you my solemn word that you will go free after."

"You lie!" The creature snarled as it stepped uncomfortably close to Odin, putting its face close to his.

The old man glared back at it. "You cower."

The beast roared. "Your words are worthless, Odin, solemn though they might be. Put your hand in my mouth. I will release it when I break the ribbon or you remove the binding. Refuse my offer, and I will tell the world your cowardice. The Aesir will forever be known for the terrified little children they are."

"I will do it," Damien heard himself say. "It is only sport." It was a lie, he knew. But the trick must be played. He felt fear grip him as the giant wolf turned its head to meet his gaze.

The wolf stared at him and something deep within Damien knew that its name was Fenris. In that gaze, Damien saw something beyond the contempt it had shown Odin. Its eyes were a little wider, a little more trusting. It laid on the ground, its body uprooting a handful of large trees as it pressed against them, and rested its massive head on the ground in front of Damien. Gaze fixed on him, it opened its jaws slightly.

Damien heard himself take a deep breath and flexed the fingers of his hands. He stepped forward and placed his left hand inside the open jaws of the terrible beast, smoothing his features to stone calm as well as he could. Fenris gingerly clamped his teeth on Damien's wrist, tight enough to prevent his escape but careful not to hurt him. He could feel the wolf's hot breath on his skin.

The others wrapped the ribbon-like chain around the animal's limbs, binding them together in front and behind it so that it would not be able to stand without breaking the bonds.

"It is set," Odin said. He smiled.

Fenris stretched his legs and thrust them about, as he had before under the bonds that could not hold him, but the ribbon held. The wolf's eyes widened in fear and anger as he fully realized what foolishness had overtaken him, that he had sacrificed his own freedom for pride, and those angry yellow gems narrowed again as he resumed his stare at Damien. Odin and the others barked an unpleasantly jovial laughter, but Damien could only manage a defiant grin through the torrent of bile that churned inside of him. His heart squeezed fists full of blood through his veins as his eyes leveled on the wolf's teeth.

"You will pay for this," the thing growled around his outstretched hand. "You will pay."

Fenris's massive teeth clamped together, crushing Damien's wrist. Then the wolf's head jerked only once, claiming Damien's hand. Damien pulled back in agony, pain flashing through his arm and shoulder like lighting, and stumbled backward into the closest tree to avoid the snapping jaws as the beast tried to tear at the rest of him. When he was out of its reach, the wolf howled at the sky and tossed Damien's hand into the air with its teeth before swallowing it like a pill.

Damien woke, barely containing a scream. He held his hands out over his face, heaving a sigh of relief when he saw both of them. His left hand felt numb and was slightly throbbing, but he was sure he was only imagining that. The letter had struck a chord with some gory movie he had seen as a child was all, even if he couldn't remember what the movie had been. Outside, it was still dark. His watch said that an hour had passed since he went to sleep.

Sleep came slowly, interrupted periodically with a vision of those cold, yellow eyes. They came with fear, anger, and most strangely, guilt. Damien shivered through the night.

***

Jeremy's head felt like someone had unscrewed it from his neck while he was sleeping, popped it into the microwave for a few minutes, and returned it to him. The last few drinks the night before had been a bad idea. He rolled over and draped his arm over Beth's waist.

She snuggled up to him, laying her head on his chest and sighing deeply. He stroked her hair, partly out of affection and partly to remove a few loose strands from his nostrils, and he sighed too. She felt so warm, so comfortable, that he really could have fallen asleep again. But if Jeremy stayed, he would be late for the third time this week. He kissed her gently and stroked her head again before getting up to get ready, stumbling toward the bathroom with his hands shielding his eyes from the light.

"Good morning. Yes sir, I'll put you through."

He was in fact late, but nobody seemed to notice.

Jeremy was grateful for the fact that the office was quieter than usual. It seemed Beth wasn't the only one who had taken the news hard. Even Karen was sapped of her usual pep. The sound of his feet on the carpet became the sound of a trudge through tightly packed snow in the silence. He passed Mr. Douglas, who didn't return Jeremy's nod.

On his desk sat the file for the VIGROND project again. He sighed as he sat down and booted up his computer. The bug report was as vague as the last. They were still sure that the program used JavaScript, so Jeremy sent their team leader an e-mail reminding him for the fifth time that it didn't. Then he scanned the code in the prescribed section, finding nothing. He checked the reference files. Nothing.

He stood up and got a cup of coffee before putting another hour into the search. Again, he came back with nothing at all. The hangover pounded against the insides of his head, and he took a break by thinking about Beth and what they were going to do for dinner tonight. It seemed to make her feel better when they went out, but she always insisted that he pick the place. He rubbed his temples as he thought it over. Chinese? But Beth had to be in a certain mood for Chinese. Any of the various family restaurant cheeseburger joints around would be too loud and crowded, especially if his headache held on into the evening like most of his hangovers did.

The cursor still blinked at him impatiently, and to keep from putting his fist through the screen he decided to get a drink of water. On his way, he thought about the note. No one had looked at him strangely or made any sign that one of them might have written it. He really hoped that it wasn't a joke someone planned to continue.

When he got back to his desk, deciding on Mexican for dinner and debating on exactly how terrible of an idea it would be to order a margarita, he spotted the problem with the code. Someone had replaced the number eleven with two lower case L's. He ran a quick find command through the whole program, discovering that someone had done this fourteen times across six files.

Well, someone was getting fired. He was just going to have to figure out who.

"Jeremy," Mr. Douglas said, passing his cubicle. "Just the man I was looking for. Let's go ahead and do your evaluation now."

Jeremy's boss continued across the sea of cubicles and down the hallway to the conference room without waiting for an answer. Jeremy shrugged and slid the bug report back into the file folder before getting up to follow.

"Jeremy, Jeremy, Jeremy," Mr. Douglas said when the door of the conference room shut and Jeremy sat at the table across from him. The man wrinkled his forehead and sighed through his hand as he tapped a pen against the evaluation form in front of him.

"Yes, sir," Jeremy said. It felt like an odd thing to say and he wasn't in the habit of calling anyone sir. But honestly, Jeremy's head hurt too much to come up with anything better.

"First," Mr. Douglas said, "I'd like to tell you that you're a hard worker and we appreciate that here. You get here on time and I don't see you screwing around during the day."

"Thank you very much," Jeremy said.

"Jeremy, I'd like to see you take a little more initiative around here." Mr. Douglas held an uncomfortable amount of eye contact while speaking. "Just this week, I've had to ask you multiple times to get in contact with the testing team for your software and work out these issues. There's currently a new bug report sitting on your desk."

"I know. I'm right in the middle of—"

Mr. Douglas waved a hand in dismissal of whatever Jeremy was about to say. "It wouldn't hurt to spend a little more time socially with other people in the office as well. You'll need those connections if you expect to continue your career at this company."

Jeremy stared at his boss. "Sure, I can—"

"Jeremy," Mr. Douglas said, "I'm marking you down for satisfactory competence and unsatisfactory work ethic, with no recommendation for a pay increase at this time. If you clean up your act, we can talk again in a few months."

"What an asshole," a voice said.

Jeremy started and looked around the room. They were alone.

Mr. Douglas, still staring intently at him, followed his gaze for a second before raising an eyebrow and leaning back. He bent his neck forward and nodded slowly like a condescending turtle. "I'm trying to help you out. Are we clear, Jeremy?"

"Yes," Jeremy said.

A person's shadow moved on the wall behind Jeremy's boss and Jeremy did his best not to look around to see who was casting it.

"Fuck that guy," the shadow said.

"We're clear, Mr. Douglas. Thank you very much. I really appreciate the advice."

As Jeremy left the conference room, he wondered if he might be having a stroke. He didn't mention it to Beth when he got home that night.

***

In the 1960's, when fear was high that Soviet troops might try to press beyond the Iron Curtain and nuclear winter was high on the list of things people worried themselves sick about, the United States armed troops on the borders between capitalist and communist countries with Davy Crocketts.

These were new kings of a new frontier, small rockets with nuclear warheads that would devastate approaching troops and irradiate the land so that it could not be inhabited again for at least forty-eight hours, leaving enough time for NATO troops to be mobilized. These were the smallest nuclear devices in existence at the time, the entire rocket no bigger than a man's torso and weighing only about fifty pounds. Technology had gone a long way since the Cold War.

The nuclear device that Damien carried in his backpack was a cylinder only twice the diameter of a soda can and about as tall. It could have weighed no more than ten pounds. The General had assured Damien that the radiation of the device was so well contained that he could use it for a pillow, and so durable that he could play football with it. Still, he was uneasy keeping it close to him. Every little tingle in his skin, every itch that came when a pore first began to release sweat, was a tumor popping out from his flesh. Every time a grain of sand landed in his eye, he was sure that eye was puckering in the first stages of melting out of his head.

And he would deserve all of that for what he was about to do.

Damien was just under a mile from the target location, accompanied by Victor Lyon and Charles Nolan. They had met Bonnie several miles outside of the city. The spy was tall and thin and had yellow eyes, which Damien found thoroughly unnerving after his dream. Bonnie had a grizzled beard and wore a purple robe that Damien didn't think anyone would confuse for an Imam's clothing. The man carried a golden scepter that he never allowed to touch the ground. Warren Leonard was right about the spy being well-placed, if he could walk around dressed like a king and manage to avoid the attention of the local population. Whatever Bonnie's influence was, he had used it to bring them through security and into the city with no problems.

They carried copies of the Qur'an and walked openly in the streets among the people, something Damien thought was overly brazen. But people in Tehran were similar to people in any large city. They bustled about their business without noticing others much. Occasionally, clerics or other officials would pass their group, but none even bothered to make eye contact. If they were stopped, they had been instructed to make completing their pilgrimage their obvious, highest priority. That kind of devotion would be unlikely to arouse extreme suspicion and would deter anyone not wanting to anger the extremists by standing in the way of a religious journey. It didn't look like that would be necessary at all.

As they covered the distance over the next half hour, Damien felt the storm in his mind begin to rage again. He made accidental eye contact with a young woman wearing a tight scarf that covered her hair. As she passed him, her dark eyes crinkled momentarily and her mouth formed a slight smile. Damien barricaded the walls around that storm and quickened his pace, walking closer behind Bonnie.

The spy led them into a nearby building. The inside was empty and beautiful. The blood-red carpet was embroidered with long runways of ornate patterns in gold thread. The pillars were spiraled with gold as well, and the ceiling was a kaleidoscope of blues, whites, reds, and yellows. It was a mosque.

"This way," Bonnie said as he walked to the *Minbar* at the end of the room.

They followed him up the stairs, then down into a small chamber behind the lectern. Here, in the tiny wooden room, Bonnie motioned toward a small stool on the ground.

"This," he said, "is where God will descend upon this nation with a sword of truth, a white-hot scythe that will cut the wheat for the bread of heaven."

Damien stared at him for a second before opening his pack and laying the small canister down on the stool. Bonnie's eyes gleamed when he looked at it.

"I was told that I would also be meeting Clyde," Damien said.

Bonnie's lip curled slightly. He adjusted his guard's uniform and clicked long fingernails against the gun at his side. "He is attending to other business."

Damien tried to imagine the General's voice in his head. This man was not a typical spy. He had the look of a lunatic rather than an agent. Prolonged deep cover could do that, but could he be trusted? Or was Damien trying to find a way to avoid his own guilt?

He looked at Lyon, then at Nolan. Neither knew what the canister was. "Both of you find cover out in the main hall. If you hear a struggle in here, I want you to find a way back to base and let the General know we've been betrayed."

They nodded and made their way out.

Bonnie smiled. "We have the same goal, Damien Asher."

Damien stared at him. Then, after a long moment, he reached beneath his shirt and removed the key from the cord around his neck. He knelt before the tiny altar and with shaking fingers slid the key into its slot in the canister. He turned it with a solid click and heard three light beeps as the storm inside of Damien threatened to unleash itself. He felt bile creep up his throat. The bomb was armed.

He set his watch for thirty minutes and then removed the key, putting it back on the cord around his neck so that it could no longer be disarmed. Bonnie stared at the canister in anticipation.

"I don't suppose you're going to stay here," Damien said. "And it's time for my men and I to leave."

Bonnie's lips puckered into a wolfish smile.

"Bonnie," Damien said. "Your orders are to get us out of this city. Now."

Bonnie didn't move. He just smiled at the bomb.

"Bonnie," Damien repeated.

Finally, the man looked up at him without relaxing his smile even slightly. His yellow eyes remained excitedly wide. "Your men outside are dead."

Damien walked to the doorway and peaked out into the main hall. The carpet right outside the door was just a little darker than he remembered, and a large, booted foot lay just on the edge of his sight. He couldn't see if its owner was dead or unconscious.

He grabbed Bonnie by his robes and pressed him against the wall. "If this is an ambush, you die next. You understand me? Then I'll barricade the door with your body and wait out the next thirty minutes. Do not doubt me."

Bonnie's smile deepened. "I don't doubt you, Tyr."

Damien released his grip only slightly, but Bonnie pulled his arms to his chest and broke Damien's grasp on him from the inside out. He landed three heavy punches just above Damien's navel.

His gut twisted and clenched against the force. As he doubled over, Damien tried to grab Bonnie's legs. But he felt the cold steel of a muzzle press against his ear and he froze.

"Sit down," Bonnie said.

Damien followed the order, glaring at the man as he did so. "I don't understand."

Bonnie raised an eyebrow, then pointed the gun at the bomb and fired three rounds. Damien grunted with a stifled terror and flung himself against the far wall, getting low to the ground as if it would save him. The world spun as he expected it to turn to ashes around him.

Nothing.

Clear liquid spurted from the canister and pooled around him. He thought of tumors and cankers and his flesh slowly melting as radiation poured into it. There was no smell. Did radioactive fluid have a smell?

Bonnie knelt down across the room, keeping the gun trained on Damien. He dipped one finger into the clear liquid and popped it into his mouth. Damien stared at him with wide eyes.

Bonnie smiled. "I think the word for this is *lemonade*."

Damien let out a sound he didn't know he could make, a high pitched whine that crept deeply into his soul and mocked everything he trusted. He reached out and tasted the liquid for himself. It was sugary and sour. Lemonade.

"Why?"

Bonnie shrugged and shot him in the shoulder.

As lighting bolts of pain collided with each other in Damien's deltoids and bounced across his collarbone and down his arm, Bonnie smiled one last time to show teeth that seemed oddly jagged. He crossed the room and kicked Damien in the face. Everything went red and then black.

# Chapter 2

## A MASTER'S ECHO

"You've taken astronomy. You know how they're formed in clusters from condensing clouds of dust out in nothingland and how most of them are going to burn out billions of years from now. But a billion years doesn't mean anything when *you're* going to burn out in a handful of decades."

James leaned against a tree and took another drag on his cigarette. He hadn't, in fact, taken astronomy. Whenever Alex had enough beers, he parroted the same facts about the stars as if he was saying something new. Right now, Alex was talking over the distant waterfall sound of his own urine stream hitting granite stone. Or was it marble? It was soothing, really. Droning about astronomy over the flow of piss. Awesome. James took another drag.

"And it's meaningless to say that you'll have nothing to show for it," Alex said as he zipped his pants and walked back over to the tree James was leaning against, "because who would you show it to? With all the stars up there, billions of them—*trillions* even—there's no reason to think that we're in any way special down here on our middle-class star's solar system. Who do we think is watching?" He was starting to slur.

Alex had long, brown hair that James would bet hadn't been washed in a week. James's brown curls were starting to rebel for lack of a haircut, but Alex seemed to be aiming for a Steven Tyler sort of grunge.

James didn't have the heart to tell his friend that he wasn't pretty enough for long hair, with a nose that pointed half an inch more to the left than the rest of his face and a chin that almost disappeared beneath a pile of skin when he gave the only genuine smile he knew how to make. Those perpetual bags under his brown eyes didn't help either. Women weren't exactly tripping over themselves to get to Alex. Usually, they would trip over James instead.

Giving exactly no shits about any of that, James grinned. "There's no reason *not* to think there's something watching, either."

Alex either consciously ignored that or just didn't hear it. He was shivering when he got back to the tree, but it wasn't cold outside. "It's downright *arrogant* to think that we're anything special in this goddamn massive universe."

"Well, you would know about arrogant," James said, handing his friend another beer.

"Hey man, fuck you," Alex said with a smirk as he took

the drink. "I'm an arrogant, cocky prick and so are you." He tilted his face down and shook his head as if trying to feel its weight. When he finally looked up again, his eyes were a little more red than they had been. "And I'm *not* arrogant. I just know where I stand. And what I'm trying to say is that if you look up at the stars, your standing suddenly gets pretty damn low. You're just a flash that goes by briefly and then you die, and what you do in the meantime barely even matters."

James took another drag and rolled this over for a moment. He held the smoke in his lungs and opened his mouth, then breathed out just slightly to let tendrils of thick white climb eerily out of his mouth and fade slowly into the night air. Then he destroyed what was left of those tendrils by blowing the rest of the smoke through them. Hard.

"I don't know that it barely matters," he said as he flicked his cigarette. He unzipped his pants and walked forward to make his own waterfall. "I mean, it matters to other people. We might just be a brief flash, but we can make a difference to the other flashes. Maybe that's all we need. You watched Barney and Friends when you were a kid, right?"

He let loose his stream and hit the stone in front of him. He traced the engraved letters: Irma Williams, 1912-1998. He really hoped this pissed the old woman off. If Irma reached up to grab his leg and tell him that he was a rude little shit, then they would have proof positive that there was something after death, that the conscious mind survived in at least some facet of existence. Even if old Irma decided to kill him, he would still know something was next. And if he knew that, death wouldn't be such a big deal anymore and Irma really couldn't do shit to him in any way that mattered. Damn, he hoped Irma wasn't smart enough to figure that out. The better revenge would be to ignore him peeing on her grave than to come after him for it. That was a disappointing thought.

"Yeah," Alex snorted after chugging his beer. "For every good deed, you matter to one person for a few minutes. But that disappears as soon as they're gone or forget about it. Hell, even if you spend your entire life becoming a saint, the records of the traditions of the Catholic church would be destroyed when the world ended anyway. Nothing you can possibly do will matter." He threw the empty bottle at another tombstone in the distance and opened another beer with his lighter before the crash of glass shattering against stone.

"Now you're just adding the 'lasting forever' clause to the definition of what matters. Good luck with that, man. I don't see the connection."

Alex lit up his own cigarette after another couple sips of beer. James shook himself and zipped his pants. He had a feeling Alex was done with that bit of argument.

"I wonder what death is like," he said as he walked back to the tree and popped the cap off another beer. "I'm not sure I can really imagine just *nothing*. What comes to mind to me is usually something like life with nothing in it. Darkness and silence and no sensations whatsoever.

Completely alone for all of eternity."

"I think that would be more like hell," Alex said as he downed the last of his beer and opened another. "I'm trying to imagine the way it would be if you extended that pause between lines of consciousness when you go to sleep and wake up without feeling any time in between. I don't think we have the capacity to imagine it. Might as well try to picture the entire universe at once."

"Maybe we're just thinking about it too much," James said. "I mean fuck, we're not supposed to be thinking about death the whole time we're alive. Think about evolution. We're supposed to be *surviving*, not dying."

"That's the thing, man. We're not *surviving* anymore." Alex contorted his lips around the word as he said it, a very strange expression to see in the dark. "We're festering. We're buying shit, or we're cheating on our girlfriends, or we're eating."

"My God, the eating," James laughed as he sat down against the tree. "I could afford to starve for a change."

"I have an idea," Alex announced loudly and dramatically, as if addressing the entire graveyard. He threw his half-empty bottle into the distance. James heard it crash to the ground as Alex continued in a manner of articulation that was much less eloquent than the words themselves, jerking his neck to clear a clump of long hair from his eyes. "Let's take an organism with an average life span of, say, thirty years. Then let's give it an obnoxious longevity, oh, say, eighty or ninety years at least. That way, instead of realizing that life is so short it has to be lived moment to moment, threat to threat, the poor fucker can spend its entire life in paralyzing fear of its eventual demise."

James laughed out loud and lifted his beer into the air. Fuck, he already had to pee again.

"A toast," Alex said, holding up his hand as if he was still holding the bottle. "To those of you who think you're worth something simply because you exist."

James threw his beer in the direction Alex had thrown his and stumbled back out to do another experiment on the afterlife. Another data point on their survey of whether peeing on graves would piss the dead off enough to give themselves away.

"Fuck, man," Alex said. "This is bullshit. God has some explaining to do."

James looked out at the stars, getting that itching in his legs that was really his fear that, while he looked up, Irma might actually grab him. As much as it would ease his curiosity and a lot of his fear, the idea of it actually happening scared the shit out of him. One of the stars moved toward another one, something he thought was strange until a red blinking light announced it as an airplane. The moon hung in the black, a half circle of light that drew James's eyes more than any of the stars could ever hope to do. He lit up another cigarette and stared at the embers as if they were about to whisper to him the answers he was looking for.

"I wish someone would come back from the dead and just tell me what's going to happen," he said at last. "That way I could look forward to a heaven or whatever else is there. Or lament if there's for sure nothing. Either way. I just don't want to fucking worry about it anymore."

"You remember my dad?" Alex said.

"Fucking hippie," James said, and lifted his beer in reverence.

"No shit man. Best thing he ever did, he said he'd let me know what happened, but I'm still at the fucking graveyard at two in the morning."

"Fucker."

"Three maybe? What the hell time is it?"

James checked his watch. The light-up, digital display almost blinded him. If it was that dark, he was surprised he could see the engravings on the stones. "Four," he said.

"Well," Alex said, "if there *is* something after and someone could tell you about it, it would be like spoiling the best Christmas present ever. It would totally ruin the whole mystery of it for you. The greatest mystery, and you would fucking spoil it."

"Yeah, that's true. But fuck, you know?"

"Fuck."

"Jesus man, I'm drunk. No more beer." James took another drag and looked back down at Irma's grave. For a split second his insides turned to fire as he saw what looked like a hand right next to his foot. But as the wind picked up again, it turned out to be only a strangely-shaped leaf. He laughed out loud and took another drag.

"Let's go, man," Alex said. "I've got class in the morning. You know I wouldn't normally care, but it's an exam. If I get less than two hours, you know I'm not even going to show up."

"Let's hit a couple more graves first," James replied with a grin. "Just to make sure they're really not going to do anything."

\*\*\*

"Fuck you," James said to both the ringing phone and the evening air as he woke up on the couch.

It had been years since the graveyard conversation, and he was still dreaming about it. He let the cell phone ring itself to death on the coffee table as he reached next to it and grabbed his pack of American Spirits. As he plugged one into his lips, he hummed a note in harmony to the buzzing air conditioning unit. Lighting the cigarette, he mouthed one more curse around the smoke escaping from his lips. The blood-orange tint staining the walls told him that the sun was setting.

A tiny growl made its way to his ears and he looked down at a tiny black face.

"Hey Blackjack," he said. "No worries, boy."

The pug had his paws on the couch and was inching upward as tall as he could, his tongue already slapping his nose as he tried to lick James's face. James smiled and picked up the little guy, all black with a streak of white down his chest like a small necktie. He set Blackjack on his chest and was immediately greeted with a thorough face licking.

"Alright, alright man," he said with a smile as he ashed his cigarette and lifted his face out of licking range to take another drag.

Blackjack snuggled against James's breastbone and James closed his eyes. When he felt he was in danger of drifting off to sleep again, he picked the dog up and put him on the floor.

His phone rang again. This time he picked it up.

"Jesus, Bob. I'm up."

"Well fuck, James," said the voice on the other end of the line. "Get your ass to the club. We have a meeting at nine, remember? At night? That just so happens to be in half an hour. My God, kid, I can't believe you just woke up."

"It's down the street," James said. "Relax."

"You're the one who wanted to be choosy about your films. If you're late, I'm saying yes to whatever Arnie is proposing."

"Do that," James said. "See how that goes for you."

"Fucking kid. Get down here."

Bob hung up. Bob Olscum, James's agent, was always a pleasure. He was damn good at his job, though.

Blackjack stared at him as if he were a dog biscuit the whole time he made coffee and put clothes on. The dog had strange eyes for a pug, just a little more like human eyes than they should have been.

"Master," James said in a deep, quick voice that could have been a cartoon character version of the dog, "I wasn't done with your bath." Blackjack barked and ran a lap around the living room, nearly knocking over the guitar leaning precariously against the wall and rushing up to

James again and pouncing on his foot in response to the attention. James smiled at him. "Master. I want you to pet me."

James rubbed Blackjack's head as the dog desperately tried to lick his fingers with his tiny tongue. His black slacks hid the thousand tiny black hairs that were undoubtedly hitching a ride on them. The red button-down looked professional enough, made slightly less so by the way he rolled his sleeves up to his elbows. He checked himself over in the mirror. His dark brown hair was still short enough that he could get away without messing with it much. He felt a tiny bit of stubble when he rubbed his face. Fuck it, he was pretty sure he didn't want this job anyway. He rubbed Blackjack's ears once more before grabbing his leather jacket.

"Later, guy."

The club was more of a lounge, with a real singer accompanying herself on the piano. The decor looked classy enough, with red velvet and mahogany strewn about like someone had tried to recreate a scene from *Who Framed Roger Rabbit*. Minus the cigar smoke, that was. Arnie had apparently chosen the meeting spot, but it was Bob who wouldn't be caught dead in the kind of place that charged a dollar to rent an ash tray to "cover the fines" of California's smoking ban. Grudgingly, James put his cigarette out at the front door.

"Sooner or later," came Bob's voice from a nearby table, "people just aren't going to pay for porn anymore. Make it as high quality as you want, and people are just going to pirate it. It's the wild west of fucking on film, gentlemen. So if you want to really capitalize, you have to go with it."

"We can DMCA the free sites into oblivion," another voice chimed in as James approached. The voice had kind of a broken Brooklyn accent, like someone making a shitty attempt at mimicking a crime boss they saw on television. "It worked for Universal."

James wished someone would tell the guy that they were in San Bernardino.

"We're not Universal," Bob said, motioning for James to sit down next to him. "We don't have a lobby that any sniveling Republican or pussy Democrat is going to want to be seen with. You want to keep making money? We brand the videos. Product placement."

"Oscar Meyer dildos," James said as he sat down. He ordered a Maker's Mark neat from the waitress who seemed to get there a little faster than he expected. From the sound of them, the other men had been ordering drinks all afternoon and she was expecting a decent tip out of it.

Bob scowled, turning his boisterous fortress of a face into a dried fruit. He leaned back and his massively broad shoulders squared imposingly against the man sitting opposite him. "Something like that. Look, magazines make all their money on ads." He paused and considered. "Made, I guess. But fuck, doesn't matter. You know what the most expensive ad in all of magazine-dom is?"

James smiled. "Magazine-dom isn't a word, Bob."

Bob ignored him. "It's the back cover of Playboy. Because when you set the magazine down on your lap to hide it from people on a bus, you *have* to see that ad. That page gets more exposure than a TV commercial, and you know exactly what your demographic is."

"So what?" the man with the Brooklyn-esque accent said. He put his hands behind his head, framing his chinless face with his thumbs pointed downward and pursing his pudgy lips.

"Thank you, darlin'," James said to the waitress as she set down his whiskey. As he picked up the drink, he noticed a phone number written on the napkin beneath. She smiled at him before walking away.

Bob looked at the napkin and shook his head. "So sell advertising spots that scroll across the bottom of the screen. Cheaper spots during the shitty banter at the beginning and more expensive spots during the makeout session and money shot."

"Why the makeout session?" Mr. Brooklyn asked in his shitty accent.

Bob rolled his eyes. "James, this is Arnie. Arnie, James."

James nodded and sipped his bourbon. Arnie reached across the table to shake his hand and James reciprocated with marked reluctance.

"We have a proposition for you," Arnie said. "I hear you're a little...picky about things. But I'm expecting a big payout for this one, so I'll make it worth your while."

James swirled his whiskey. "Lay it on me then."

"We're looking to get Gloria Blanche in the studio for a

little punishment, if you know what I—"

"No rape scenes," James said. "I believe I've been clear about this."

Arnie curled his lips slightly against his teeth. "It's not a rape scene. It's just a little bit rougher than what you're used to."

"Yeah, I don't do rape scenes."

"Look, we just really want to get Gloria in on this one. We've got some followers dying to see her roughed up. She's only on board if you play opposite her."

James cringed at the use of the word *followers*. "It's not my style, and I happen to like Gloria. If she's not going to do it either, good."

Bob cleared his throat. "You know James, I know for a *fact* that you've done a few masked scenes with her. You don't seem to mind getting into the ropes, so why not her?"

"That's a bit different," James smiled. "That was fun." He downed the rest of his whiskey, and not seeing the waitress, excused himself to the bar.

He could hear them continue their conversation as he pulled out a stool and laid his empty glass on the lacquered mahogany. The bartender made his way to where James was sitting momentarily, a handsome guy with his blond hair yanked to one side. James ordered another bourbon and the man gave him a lingering smile, which James returned.

"Pour me another, bartender, just to turn my head. So-co and lime, martini-dry; I'll take a wine instead."

James hadn't really listened to the singer until now, but she was excellent. Her voice was rough in exactly the right places: a rasp here, a belted single note there with no vibrato. Her fingers danced out a high-pitched, gliding phrase on the right end of the piano while she ground out low chords on the left with a rhythmic swing. He listened all the way to the end of the verse before taking a sip of his whiskey.

"You say you're in love, bartender, so prove it true. Cry me a river, build me a bridge, and by that time I'll be over it too."

James didn't realize it, but he had lit another American Spirit while watching her. Seeing it burning in his hand, the forbidden smoke curling in the air around him, he saw the bartender frown and start to walk over to him again. He put a hand up to forestall the blond and made a beeline for the front door to finish up, leaving a fourth of his drink behind.

The night air was getting chilly. He took a drag on his cigarette. Worth it, for sure.

He gazed out into the parking lot. Curiously empty. Was it Saturday? He chuckled and took another drag as he watched a tiny black bird flit from one lamp to another. The brick buildings surrounding the bar looked like they were about to be condemned, with large swathes of concrete crumbling toward their eventual resting place as piles of rubble. A thumping sound from the dumpster at the end of the parking lot greeted him as he noticed a bearded man sifting through the garbage.

"Got a light, kid?"

James turned and saw the door swing shut behind Bob, who bit the end of a cigarette and smiled at him.

"Sure." James dug into his pocket and pulled the Zippo from its resting place. He opened the lighter and snapped his fingers over the wheel, sparking the flame with the return of his middle finger in one smooth motion. He held it out and lit Bob's cigarette.

"That's an interesting one," Bob said. "What does it say?"

James flipped the lighter across his fingers once and then held it out so that Bob could read the script. "*Abyssus abyssum invocat.* It's Latin, for *Hell invokes hell.*"

Bob raised an eyebrow. "I don't think I get it."

James shrugged and flicked his cigarette butt into the darkness before lighting up another. "It was a gift."

Bob nodded, cutting the air with his cartoonishly brazen chin. He took a long drag and billowed a pillar of smoke that Moses could have appreciated. "So, no to Arnie?"

"Yeah," James said. "Arnie's a fuck."

The coughing laughter that burst from Bob was annoying. "Because it's porn, kid." He took another drag on his cigarette. "Don't get me wrong. You hold it and pop on time with the best of them. But unless you've got a following, and good luck with that unless you've got a pair of tits you've been hiding all this time, the real money is in the number of films you can pull off in a year."

James closed one eye as the smoke from his own

cigarette decided to kiss his cornea. "Yeah, but that dude's real scum."

"Well, we don't all want to grow old in a shitty apartment. Arnie makes a lot of movies."

James tried to find the merit in that argument. Nothing came to mind.

"I get it, kid. Don't do it then. I fucking hate Arnie anyway. That prick makes some of the sickest films I've ever seen, and most of my clients aren't nearly as picky as you are." Bob tapped the ash from his cigarette. "If the money's good enough, most people will do just about anything. Come on. I'm going in for another drink."

James put out his cigarette and they went back to their table.

"So," James said as the waitress brought a fresh round, "where is Arnie, anyway? Making some phone calls about product placement?"

Bob chuckled and sipped on his drink, some sort of vodka on the rocks with a lemon rind floating in it. "God no. That guy's about as interested in innovation as you are in money. He said he was going to pick up that lounge singer. Maybe he got lucky, because I haven't seen him since."

"Or maybe not," James said as the lounge singer sat down at the bar by herself. He nodded to point her out.

"Ha! I bet the bastard just wanted to look like he made it."

James agreed. The singer perched on the bar stool with her feet resting on the upper rung below, hugging the stool with her legs and arching her back in a stretch that looked strangely cat-like. The singer gave a slight smile to the bartender and he brought her a huge mug of beer. James was fairly certain they didn't serve that size here and wondered if it was her own glass. She downed half of it in one pull before setting it down and adjusted chestnut hair that had fallen from its haphazard fixture behind her head. Then she picked up the mug and downed the rest. The bartender refilled it without surprise.

"So?" Bob said, snapping James out of his little trance. "I haven't seen you get starry-eyed in a while. You like musicians, kid?"

"Shut up, Bob."

Bob chuckled. "I think her name is Angela something. It's on the sign out front."

Arnie slowly made his way up to the bar behind the lounge singer. He stood there for a minute, drunkenly experimenting with his balance and rehearsing a few lines, and then leaned up against the bar next to her. "Let me buy you a drink, baby."

"No, thanks," Angela said.

"No, really," Arnie replied. "I want to buy you a drink."

Angela didn't turn to look at him. "No, really. Thanks though."

James and Bob chuckled, loud enough to be heard.

Arnie stepped back, biting the inside of his increasing rosy cheeks. Then he seemed to drunkenly decide that he deserved more respect than that, pouting his lips in a gross

70

sort of protest. He steeled himself, muttered some curses that weren't quite audible to James's ears, and leaned in as he grabbed at the singer's wrist.

Angela flung her arm into the air, free from Arnie's fingers, and calmly set it back down on the bar. She took a swig of her beer.

Arnie's next curse grew in confidence. "You stuck up bitch." He made another grab for her wrist.

"Woah," James said. "Hey man, that's too—"

Angela turned and wrapped her hand around the man's throat. Arnie's drunk face turned piously to the ceiling as the singer dug her finger deep into the bottom of his jaw. She stood and swayed her hips slightly as they rotated, leading him in the world's slowest dance as he squawked something James didn't catch. The dance ended with Arnie pressed firmly against the bar, struggling with both hands on Angela's arm.

She fixed his hair with her free hand, then leaned forward and put her nose next to his cheek. Arnie made guttural noises and tried impotently to move as Angela sniffed his cheek, then his neck. She stared into his eyes and gathered her mouth to one side with a cocked eyebrow. Then, without another word and inspiring a crescendo of whining from Arnie, she leaned in and sniffed him again.

Arnie's pouting lips tried to form words. He stuttered out a "please" and dug his fingernails into her arm like claws as his face turned a shade of red that James thought might be equal parts embarrassment and oxygen deprivation. Either way, James didn't feel the need to help him out. He noticed the blond bartender grinning at him and flashed one back. Angela whispered something in Arnie's ear and he made a sound like a latex balloon rubbing against a packing peanut. When the singer finally released Arnie, he had tears streaming down his face and was frantically wiping at them as he darted out the door.

Angela sat back down at her stool and downed the last of her second beer. Then she laid a bill on the bar, nodded to the bartender, and left. James adjusted his pants.

"Fucker didn't pay his bill," Bob said.

*\*\**

Damien lifted his wrists, heavy for the thick chains that shackled them to the wall, and felt the swollen bruise that marked the impression of Bonnie's steel toe. He was in a prison cell with steel bars for walls.

The mission. All those lives. The General would deny any involvement in the mission, so Damien was, in the official sense, a terrorist. Although he had attempted to blow up the city with lemonade, so maybe there was an insanity plea on the table for him.

*Denial.* In the back of Damien's mind, the word built a summer home.

It must have been a sniper who took out Lyon and Nolan. Had the spy called Clyde been the one operating it? If so, he must have been hiding from the beginning. Damien didn't see someone sneaking up on his two best men in the five minutes it took to arm the bomb.

The bomb. He needed to find a way to get a message to

Warren Leonard. Someone had infiltrated their unit and now had the real bomb. Someone back at camp was a traitor and needed to be found.

Denial.

The cell was dark and smelled like urine. There was no toilet or even a bucket, so that shouldn't have been surprising. Through the bars, Damien could see Wilbur Thorton in the next cell. The man hadn't been part of the team. Had he gone AWOL? Had the camp been attacked? Damien couldn't see any other prisoners from his cell.

"Hey," Damien whispered.

Nothing. Wilbur shivered in the fetal position.

"Hey," Damien said aloud. "You alright, Will?"

Damien's face burned. He didn't know why he said *Will* instead of *Wilbur*. Maybe it just didn't serve any more purpose to mock the guy. Regardless, the soldier didn't answer.

Damien rested his head, a little less painfully, on the wall behind him and closed his eyes. Suddenly, everything he had done to torment the skinny man had been pointless and malicious. Wilbur being a harder man would not have saved them from being captured.

They had not been interrogated yet. That meant something, but the meaning was trapped in whatever cotton currently stuffed Damien's brain.

The door clicked and popped, the echo stretching into eternity before the door opened. A man in a fine purple robe stood in the doorway and a smile flashed across his clean-shaven face. His ornate scepter of gold and gems didn't touch the ground. As the man's robe shifted, Damien could see a small sculpture atop the scepter that he hadn't seen before. It was the head of a wolf.

Damien bared his teeth. "Hello, Bonnie."

The man's yellow eyes caught the light strangely for a second. He held his left arm up and gingerly brushed his right hand over the regal silk. "I truly do prefer you use a different name to address me."

"I bet you do." Damien kept his eyes leveled.

"I have a thousand names," the man said, closing his eyes and rubbing his close-shaven cheeks, "but I promise not to make you learn all of them. There is only one name you ever need bother yourself with again. I am your master, your owner, your godly benefactor." The man leaned forward. "I am Fenris."

Damien tightened his stomach against a short wave of nausea. He knew the wave was stupid and useless, so he smashed it back behind the cotton in his brain with an army of imaginary hammers.

*Denial.*

"I'm going to kill you," Damien said at last.

Fenris smiled again, his teeth shimmering white, and looked down at Will.

The young man was crying. Damien was sure that the sobbing came more than anything as an excuse not to look at Fenris. The robed man grimaced in disgust and poked the young man hard in the ribs with his scepter, knocking him over and changing Will's sobs to panicked, uncontrollable gasps. Damien watched Fenris with contempt.

Then Fenris pulled something dark and shiny from his robe and raised it in Will's direction.

The gun fired and Damien's shout only gave Will enough time to look up fearfully and receive a bullet hole in the middle of his face. Blood spattered the wall behind and Damien was on his feet before he even realized it, testing the short reach of the chains and shouting obscenities at the robed man.

Fenris put the gun back into his robe and smiled at Damien. Then he left, slamming the door shut behind him and leaving him in the darkness with the corpse of the man who had just been trying to control his sobs so Damien wouldn't mock him.

"Will," he whispered in the darkness, his voice nearly incapable of producing sound. "I'm sorry. I really am."

If he ever got out of here, he would bring word of Will's death to his family himself. And he would say Will, never Wilbur.

Denial.

He knew on a very deep level that he was never getting out of here.

\*\*\*

James put out a cigarette and frowned at the awful dressing room. The furniture was made of plastic like McDonald's, but molded into shapes that could have been a tasteful couch and coffee table if they weren't also nonstick. Even the dresser was plastic, just a larger version of a college dorm's space saver that hid a Fleshlight and half an ounce of weed under a pile of socks. Somebody was real proud of their decoration skills but couldn't afford a real couch. Or maybe it was designed by people who thought that porn stars just warmed up with a round of sloppy sex before a shoot. It seemed like a reasonable guess that the studio sponsoring the set of *Tit-tanic* didn't have the budget for cleaning stained furniture. But it came with a TV, so that was nice.

He looked at himself in the mirror. His tan was fading a little, but he was still serviceably bronzed. He could use a haircut, but lately the industry preferred men with slightly shaggy hair anyway. Muscular physique was always a requisite, but he had no problem with that. He looked very fit, when he tightened his gut just a little. Cliché, sure. But that's what sells. And a movie starring Ricky Jam was a good bet for reasonable sales.

"Ricky, let's talk."

The voice wrapped James in silk. A sharp, floral perfume hit his nose and his pants got just a fraction tighter. Gloria Blanche had that effect. She had long blond hair that fell down her back in a a pile of curls and lips cosmetically plumped and smeared red. Fierce eyes peaked at him beneath a fade of smoke she had painted there. Those blue gems widened slightly with intent.

James treated himself to a quick glance down her silver gown, cut low between her breasts and stretching just slightly to show off every toned curve. He didn't hide his lingering gaze as he traced the shimmering fabric over her dancer's hips and smooth legs.

She glided across the room on leather high heals. Watching her, he wasn't sure the way she moved was even possible, despite the ease at which she accomplished it. He smiled at her and winked, just to show her he wasn't too affected. Poker face. Besides, he would be a lot closer to her than this in about a half hour or so. Hell, he had been as close before.

"Sure babe, what's on your mind?"

"I wanted to let you know that if you go off script with me again, I'm going to bite you during the blow job scene."

James had to work very hard to stifle his laughter. In fact, he managed only to reduce it to a chuckle, lighting a small flame behind those beautiful eyes of hers. Last time they had worked together on the set of *The Bone Identity*, he had continually ruined her big, orgasmic moments by humming cheesy porn music beneath her moans. When she got louder, he got louder. The director had thought it was hilarious and the movie went out that way. It had become a parody of a porn movie.

Gloria crossed the space between them, dragging the fabric of her dress downward with her index finger to expose some of her pale, generous cleavage. She pushed herself against him and wrapped her arms around his thighs. She moved slightly and he could feel one fingernail delicately tracing a path that made him clear his throat. She smiled at what he hoped was only a slight change in expression.

"I can be very, very good to you," she said, looking

down at her hand as most of her finger brushed against areas that were expanding with blood. She brought those two beautiful oceans of blue to meet his and pouted those lips that drove millions of fans wild. "Even after the filming's done."

He smiled at her. "Take a joke."

She took her hand back and raised an eyebrow. "Fine. I'll get to look over the edited copy this time before it goes out anyway."

James lit another cigarette and offered one to her. She took it and high-heeled her way to the plastic couch. Her dress was cut even lower behind, with crisscrossing strings of silver caging her otherwise naked back. He could see a tattoo peeking out from the right side of her lower back, a playing card set at an angle and dimensioned so it looked like it was being dealt onto the table from a deck. The Queen of Hearts. She must have gotten it since *The Bone Identity*.

She tweaked her nose at the couch for just a second before gracefully plopping herself down. The couch squeaked.

James followed and lit her cigarette before sitting down next to her. Looking at her, made up and ready to go in that dress, he almost asked if she'd like a warm up before they went on. He didn't ask, partly because the anticipation was fun and partly because he didn't want to fulfill the prophecy that he thought the plastic furniture implied.

Gloria puffed the cigarette, which she held between the

distal knuckles of her index and middle fingers. She was the type of woman who wrapped her lips thoroughly around the butt, which James didn't think was conscious. Although it certainly could have been. He'd have been equal parts surprised and bored to discover that she meant it suggestively. Even so, James's eyes drifted to down Gloria's neck and between her breasts for what seemed like the hundredth time since she sat down.

James stood up and walked to his dresser, retrieving an ash tray and his deck of cards. Returning to the couch, he cracked the cards into a bridge twice and cut them one-handed.

Gloria raised an eyebrow and smiled thinly. "Are you going to show me a magic trick?"

"Jesus, no." James grinned and took a drag on his cigarette, letting the smoke fall delicately from his lips. "I thought we'd play a few hands so I don't bend you over the ridiculous furniture."

She smiled and put out her cigarette without finishing. "Hit me then."

He dealt five cards each and laid the deck on the plastic coffee table, which might have been part of the Fisher-Price Elegant Adult Living Room Set. They picked up their cards and James studied his. Three-suited, with a pair of nines huddling together amid a three, five, and ten. He set everything but the nines face-down on the table. Gloria set down two cards and pulled two from the top of the deck.

James drew three more cards. Another ten, a king, and

a four. Now he was four-suited, which was jack in poker. James's father had once told him that the King of Hearts was called the suicide king because he appeared to stab himself in the back of the head. Looking at it, he thought of Alex.

Gloria eyed him. "Are we betting?"

James debated on a joke. Then he shook his head. "Got anything in mind?"

"Sure." Gloria tapped her cards. "If I win, I pick the next scene we do together."

"Not Arnie's."

"Jesus," she said. "Not Arnie's. We're just fielding his offer to keep bidding high on other projects. I wouldn't mind you getting a little rougher with me, though."

James shook his head. "It's not my style."

"Will it be your style if I win this hand?"

"No promises."

"Fine." She laid her cards on the table. "Straight, Queen high."

"Pair of nines."

She smiled. "I'll give you a call when I find something interesting."

There was a knock on the door and Gloria's assistant slowly opened it from the outside. "Gloria? You've got five minutes."

"We're decent," Gloria said.

The assistant came inside. She was a young woman, hair woven into a messy bun on top of her head and thick glasses that exaggerated her eyes. She handed an envelope to James. "This was sticking out under the door."

"Thanks." James took the envelope and laid it on the table.

The couch squeaked again as Gloria stood up. "See you in a minute, stud."

James smiled and the two women left. He set his cards down and picked up the envelope. On the front of it, in a painfully hard-scratched handwriting, was his name.

The letter was written in the same furious handwriting, and addressed someone by a name James didn't recognize.

*The fire giants come for you.*
*Their king, he stirs in mourning wake.*
*Flee, my Freyr, my deviant boy,*
*Into the barren lands, and die.*
*There is no spring come next for you,*
*No birth or death, no spring or fall*
*Surtr will smile upon your corpse,*
*And shadows serenade your soul.*

The letter was unsigned, unmarked by anything that would allow him to find out who sent it. Maybe he would look up some of those references after filming time, but now he needed to get ready. He took off his robe and carefully buttoned up the ship captain's shirt and pea coat. He suspected his pants were not quite regulation, bright red and made of cheap leather. When he was finally ready, he stuffed the strange letter into his pocket and checked himself over in the mirror one more time before heading over to the shooting room.

He really did hope Gloria didn't bite him.

\*\*\*

You will pay.

The wolf's voice rasped in his head again and again. Those hideous yellow eyes burned in his skull. *You will pay.*

Damien pounded the back of his head against the stone wall. They had come to collect Will's body only a few hours before, having left it in the cell through the night and most of the day. He couldn't smell the stink of blood anymore, but that wasn't due to any cleaning on the part of his captors.

*The Captain said to the crocodile*, a small voice recited in his mind, *take my hand and stay a while.*

Crinkling in his back pocket was the folded poem in angry script.

The door to the cell opened to interrupt his thoughts. Fenris strode inside, wearing a golden robe and a matching *kufiya* tightened to his head with a crimson rope. His eyes were calm and he pursed his lips in a smile that split his darkly bearded face. Damien was sure that the beard was fake, but it was a good fake. Three guards entered behind, bearded men with assault rifles.

The assault rifles were Chinese Type 56, a copy of the Soviet AK-47 rifle. According to what Damien had learned from Warren Leonard, those rifles became popular after the Cold War and they saw action in almost every conflict since. Hell, he was even pretty sure that they were even used in movies. That left Damien with no clue who these people were, but the man who called himself Fenris seemed to be playing the role of their religious leader.

Damien felt a small bubble of something rise inside of him, riding a wave of anger. He bared his teeth at Fenris, wondering faintly if he was losing his mind. No sane person blamed a mission failure on a monster from a dream.

They brought him outside for the first time since capture. It was a rocky basin surrounded by hills in every direction, with no buildings except for the prison itself. A plain wooden table was set with two chairs. Warren Leonard sat in one of the chairs and nodded solemnly to Damien when he saw him. The other chair was empty.

Other prisoners were brought from their cells and forced to their knees alongside Damien.

Fenris glided in front of them, the sun reflecting on the golden sheen of his silk robe. "You have come to steal our land." His eyes narrowed as the men around him nodded. "There is greed in your veins, infidel, and malice in your heart. But God, in His brilliance, has turned your mischief upon itself. Your wickedness will be punished."

The robed man grinned and stepped closer to Damien. He put his ringed pointer finger to Damien's throat, scratching back and forth with a fingernail that was longer than those of most women Damien knew. The men who followed Fenris kept their assault rifles pointed.

Fenris whispered. "There is a price that must be paid. You know this, Tyr."

Damien stared into those yellow eyes. His hand throbbed again and he bared his teeth outright.

"You remember," Fenris said, baring his own. "At least some. That is good."

Damien's eyes locked on the soulless yellow gaze as Fenris dug the fingernail upward to force him to his feet. Fenris pulled his hand away and nodded to two guards who immediately stepped forward and held Damien's arms. They led him to the table.

"Struggle," Fenris said as they pushed him into the chair and one of the guards slid a key into the lock on Damien's handcuffs, "and every infidel prisoner dies."

Damien felt the cuffs slide away from his wrists, but didn't move a muscle. They led him to the table across from the General. Damien looked at his commanding officer in silence.

"These men see themselves as conquerors," Fenris announced to the small crowd, gesturing at Damien and Warren. "They are only common thieves. Let their punishment be a warning to every stinking pig who lays a hand on what is ours."

They laid a silver tray on the table between the two men. On the tray were two meat cleavers.

"You will have the honor of delivering the punishment to yourselves," Fenris announced. "No true believer will have to soil his hands with your disgusting blood."

Damien stared at the tray. Warren picked up one cleaver exhaled a long breath.

Stomach acid seemed to boil in Damien's gut and he

furiously screamed in his head for it to be quiet. He took the remaining cleaver in his right hand and laid his left on the wood. Fenris smiled.

"I want you to pay attention to what I do," Warren said in a low voice.

Damien blinked. A small stream of hope trickled into his mind as he thought about escape. With this many assault rifles pointed at them, he still had faith in his General. If Warren thought he saw a way out, Damien would make it happen.

Warren held the cleaver high in the air. Damien took a deep breath and did the same. His heart pounded as he stared into the General's eyes.

"You can do this," Warren said.

Damien's heart sank and he nodded.

"Now."

They brought down their cleavers.

Lighting bolts of pain shot up Damien's arm and he narrowly managed to avoid screaming as he looked down at his wrist. His arm trembled, but he wasn't done. He had cracked through the bone, but it wasn't yet severed. He brought the cleaver down again, hard enough to bury it in the table and free his arm with a crimson spray. The crowd around them cheered.

When he looked back up at the General, his head swam. Across the table sat a perfect statue of Warren Leonard, as if the man had been turned to stone by magic. Even the cleaver that the General had been holding was now made of gray rock, fused to the wrist that it had been in the process of cutting. Damien stared at the General's stone face, turned slightly downward and split nearly in two by an unnaturally wide grin. Colorless eyes stared at Damien and seemed to gleam with a hatred that seemed to match that of Fenris.

"God has judged the thief!" Fenris boomed. His voice cut cleanly through the cheering. "See how the wicked are punished! On this day, we bear witness to one of His miracles!"

One of the guards brought Damien another tray with bandages and he wrapped his stump, trying his best not to look at the severed hand on the table. He wrapped one of the longer strips around his forearm and twisted it into the tightest tourniquet he could manage to stop the bleeding, all while staring into the eyes of what was left of his leader. In the back of his mind, he knew he had cut through arteries, big ones, and that he should be worried. He was oddly calm.

Fenris stepped forward and stretched out his hand to take Damien's chin with his claws. There was fire in his eyes as he spoke just loudly enough for Damien to hear.

"You belong to me now," Fenris said. "I will decide who and what you are from now on."

# Chapter 3

## THE WAR COMES HOME

"Garm," Loki whispered, twisting the shadows around his desk like a silent movie villain twisting his mustache. "Have you ever read Sophocles?"

"No, Master." The guard dog stood behind him, tapping on his smart phone with human fingers and moving a few heroes from one cell block to another.

"Herodotus?"

"No, Master."

Loki picked an empty soda can from the trash next to his desk and loaded it into an old wooden slingshot. He pulled back the sling and fired the can into a model house constructed from piles of dollar bills. "Heard of the Oracle at Delphi at all?"

"No, Master."

"Worst thing a hero could ever do. Consult the Oracle, and you're fucked."

Garm was silent.

"King Laius went to see the Oracle. It told him his son would kill his father and marry his mother. So he tries to have his son killed. Guess what happens."

Garm stopped tapping on the phone. That saved the guard dog some time in the box, Loki decided.

"The baby is saved by some royal family in another city, and they raise him as their own. Oedipus grows up, consults the Oracle about his true parentage, and the Oracle tells him the same thing she told Laius." Loki twisted the shadows into a green football helmet and set it delicately on his desk, staring at it for a moment before continuing. "Of course, she leaves out the relevant detail that he's adopted. So he leaves the parents that he thinks are his and journeys back to his home city, which is all new to him, where he kills Laius the king and marries his mother without knowing shit about either of them."

"Yes, Master."

Loki sighed. "The point is, the Oracle is an asshole. She'll tell you something shitty about your future that will only happen if you try to avoid it. I'd love to meet Apollo sometime. He sounds like a real dick."

"Yes, Master."

Loki shrugged. "What news of the thunder god?"

"We've been watching him in his Maine cabin. He seems content with his typewriter and his wood chopping. He doesn't know himself any more than the rest of them."

Loki shook his head slowly. "He remembers more than most, but I bet he knows better than to tip his hand." He held up an envelope with a name scrawled on the front. "There are your instructions. Let me know when you have followed them. It won't be a letter for Thor, at least not directly. My memories might be black and white, but I remember how to dance with him."

Garm stepped forward to take the envelope and fell back immediately. "Yes, Master."

"Then do it."

The door opened again and the guard dog fled from the room. Loki spun two television sets from the shadows, old models with cathode ray tubes. On one, he watched a coyote paint a tunnel on a rock and a bird run straight through it as if it were real. On the other set, he watched a local broadcast about duck that had wandered out into a New York City intersection and stopped traffic for five minutes while it waited for half of its line of baby ducks to catch up. The anchorwoman promised a heartwarming story about what happened next. Loki lifted his hand, conducted an imaginary waltz for a moment, and snapped his fingers.

There was an eruption of fire in the background and the local broadcast became white noise.

\*\*\*

Jeremy sat on the couch with his arm around Beth, both of them staring silently at the news. Tears slowly made their way down Beth's cheeks, but she didn't make a sound. Jeremy drew a million figure-eights on her shoulder with his index finger, hoping that would somehow help. It didn't.

The field reporter on television wore a tan jacket and the wind blew her messy brown hair back and forth. Behind her, a hole was blown in New York City. Piles of rubble stretched into the skyline. Skyscrapers that had been slightly outside of the blast range bowed at strange angles as if their images were refracted underwater. Jeremy couldn't see the bodies at this distance, but he was sure they were there.

"Behind me," the reporter said, "you can see the aftermath of the most devastating terrorist attack in United States history. At 8:47 this morning, October first, 2012, terrorists detonated several nuclear warheads near Times Square. We don't have a full report on the extent of the damage at this time, but we can say for certain that much of the downtown area has been destroyed as well as parts of Long Island and New Jersey."

The camera panned, revealing the mutilated Statue of Liberty. Although the Lady was still standing, her crown and torch had been ripped away along with her extended arm and a large portion of her head. She leaned precariously toward the water as her remaining hand clutched her keystone tablet. Jeremy remembered learning that Thomas Edison once had a plan to make the Statue of Liberty talk when first introducing the phonograph. If he fulfilled his promise, the statue was supposed to be able to broadcast an official government message audible through northern Manhattan and across the bay into Staten Island. That seemed intensely creepy to Jeremy, who thought the next step would be surveillance cameras in Lady Liberty's eyes.

"As you can see, the Statue of Liberty remains standing," the woman on the television said. "This reporter wants to take the opportunity to announce to the world that America stands strong in the face of tragedy. As we stood on 9-11, as we stood at Pearl Harbor, or at the beaches of Normandy, we will stand strong. We will—"

With a series of snaps and pops that tested the speakers of the television, the statue crashed toward the water. When it came to rest and the waves calmed, only a small part of her wrecked robe was visible on the beach of Ellis Island. The rest sunk slowly into the waves as a thousand massive bubbles broke the water's surface. The reporter turned slowly back to the camera and took a deep breath.

"As you could see, the Statue of Liberty has just fallen. At this time, it is estimated that as many as three million people may be dead. Hospitals in the surrounding areas are already turning wounded citizens away because they don't have the resources to take them in."

Jeremy stopped his figure-eights on Beth's shoulder. "I love you."

"I love you too," she said without looking at him.

The week before, President Pearson had announced the first military draft since the early '70s. While Jeremy was too old for the draft to affect him personally, it wasn't a good sign for their standing in the Middle East or for Damien's safety. Jeremy had decided not to bring that up.

"I'm being told that we're getting a direct line from the White House. The President of the United States is going to address the nation. We will be ready after with a full analysis."

There was a corny animation with a flag and a bald eagle as they cut to the President at his podium. President Pearson glared down at the country, his eyes weighted by what Jeremy assumed was meant to be concern.

"Good evening," the President said. "This morning, America came under attack."

Jeremy began his figure-eights again.

"To the people of New York, I offer my condolences. I am pained at the loss of so many lives, and at the loss that so many families are now facing. My heart goes out to every man, every woman, and every child still waiting to hear from loved ones. I want to thank the heroes of the New York fire and police departments, whose tireless efforts have saved many lives in the aftermath of this tragedy. I want to thank the hospital employees as they try to save as many lives as possible. I want to thank each of you who have already donated money or food or clothing to help those displaced Americans who found themselves without a home only a few short hours ago."

Jeremy closed his eyes. He tried to picture the horror of that moment, when the mushroom cloud bloomed in the sky and a place so safe, so secure, so *American*, was turned to ash. What would it have been like for those people who saw nothing but fire in their last moments on Earth?

"At this time, I would like to offer a reading from Psalm twenty-three in the King James Bible. I hope that it will offer some small comfort to the families of those we lost this morning, as well as to all Americans in this moment of heartbreak."

At this point, Jeremy couldn't help but shake his head. Nothing like tragedy to inject a little bit of religion into politics. Beth closed her eyes and breathed deeply. It was a strange reaction for her, who had previously called gestures like this one obligatory political faith advertisements.

"*The Lord is my shepherd; I shall not want. He maketh me to lie down in green pastures; He leadeth me beside the still waters. He restoreth my soul; He leadeth me in the paths of righteousness for His name's sake.*"

Jeremy tapped out "The Battle Hymn of the Republic" on his leg and imagined it playing beneath the President's prayer, marching beat and all.

"*Yea, though I walk through the valley of the shadow of death, I will fear no evil; for Thou art with me; Thy rod and Thy staff, they comfort me. Thou preparest a table before me in the presence of mine enemies; Thou anointest my head with oil; my cup runneth over. Surely goodness and mercy shall follow me all the days of my life; and I will dwell in the house of the Lord for ever.*"

Jeremy hoped that Beth was getting some comfort out of this. Jeremy kept tapping. *He's gone to be a soldier in the army of the Lord. His soul is marching on.*

"This act of mass murder was intended to break the American spirit. We will not be broken. It was intended to corrupt who we are as a nation. We will not be corrupted. America is still the shining city on the hill. The world is waiting to see us come together, the way we always have.

"Nothing I can say will change the fact that you have lost so much today. Nothing I can say will change the fact that so many people lost their lives in the worst tragedy of my life time. But I can promise you this. I will follow the people responsible for this terrorist attack to the Gates of Hell, if I have to. There will be justice in our world. Thank you, good night, and God Bless America."

And there it was. At the end of all of it, the President called for war. Lord God sustain us while we manage to escalate the biggest tragedy in United States history into as much additional tragedy as possible.

The President nodded to the camera and turned to walk away down the hallway of the White House. The Secret Service followed him and Jeremy watched the same corny, eagle and flag animation as it brought him and Beth back to two local news anchors. The anchors decided that it was a powerful and moving speech. Then a correspondent in a skinny tie said that he was especially glad that the President had chosen to read from the Bible instead of bowing his head to political correctness. Another correspondent said that the President could almost certainly count on re-election with even the most moderate campaign, as long as he made sure to stay strong on the issue of terrorism. A third correspondent expressed the need for higher security, stating that we live in a terrifying time and we seriously need to consider how our right to privacy stacks up against a nuclear terrorist attack. Everyone agreed that these were all good points and that the families of the October First victims were foremost in their thoughts and prayers.

Beth stared at the television as Jeremy slowly lifted the remote control. He looked at her out of the corner of his eye as he hit the power button and the screen turned black. Beth didn't move. He set the remote down and touched her hand, and she adjusted her body so that she could rest solidly on his shoulder with her damp cheek pressed against his neck.

\*\*\*

James tapped his fingers on his glass of bourbon, adding his own counter rhythm to the beat of the drum set. It was a swing beat, played softly on the high hat and accented on the occasional offbeat with a tap to the snare. He watched Angela Bianchi, whose name he had made sure to read carefully this time, on the piano. Her fingers danced across the puzzle of black and ivory, painting colors out of chords as she sang. Behind her, a round, white-haired man danced almost romantically with a string bass while a younger man in sunglasses and a tweed Paddy cap tapped out the swing beats on a drum set almost at the back curtain of the stage.

"The real money is in the starlets," Bob said. "There are a shitload of movies, but the girls are the ones who draw the following. We can deal with the shift to free downloads by making sure that the starlets connect with their fans and bring them in for conventions. Hell, we get our starlets using Twitter and we've pretty much got the market cornered."

"Sure," James said. "That'll work."

This was one of the few bars without a television, which meant that James didn't have to hear about the bombing. Everywhere you looked, there was some feigned unity over an American flag. James didn't mind people coming together in earnest, but he was tired of being told that the terrorists won if he didn't stick around for the next in a long line of musicians giving their rendition of "God Bless America."

Angela flashed a pretty smile at the audience as she played. Not a scant crowd, either. It was unusually crowded at the club for a Tuesday night.

"I was going to take a flight to City this week and talk some business with investors," Bob said, scratching his cartoonish chin and leaning back in his seat. "I could have been there when it happened."

The City. It irritated James when somebody used that phrase to refer to Manhattan when they weren't anywhere near New York. It was like name dropping, showing that you knew slang from a city across the country. He took a bigger gulp of the whiskey and forgave Bob for the annoyance. Bob just wanted to feel like he had things handled. Using the slang while he was still in California was practice, not pretense. Still, James had the sudden urge to slap him.

Bob didn't take anything from James's silence. "Are you going to visit your family?"

James finished his whiskey. "I don't think so. That's one tragedy that can stay buried."

"It's a shame," Bob said. "How long has it been?"

"Who cares?" It had been eleven years.

"Look," Bob said after upturning his glass of vodka and motioning to the waitress for another round, "family is important. They might not even know you're alive."

"Thanks for that," James said. "But I'll just keep doing whatever the fuck I'm already doing, thank you."

"Up to you, kid. But I'm going to visit mine."

Bob's parents had a little house in Cleveland, up on shoreline of Lake Erie. Even as far as they were from the attack, they were already seeing some New York refugees. Apparently, many people were voluntarily evacuating other densely populated areas of major cities and even some of the major suburbs in fear of a second attack.

James gazed across the floor at Angela.

"You know," Bob said, "Arnie's afraid to leave his house. Whatever that singer whispered to him really struck a nerve."

James smiled. "What did she say to him?"

"He wouldn't tell me." Bob took a sip of his drink. "He said he was done making movies and I didn't ask any more questions. Poor guy wouldn't even look me in the eyes."

"Good riddance."

Bob took another sip. "They're talking about passing new surveillance laws for the Internet. They've never been able to do it before, but they can probably fear-monger their way into just about anything at this point."

"Well, that sucks," James said, nodding an appreciation as a waitress brought him another bourbon. She was the same waitress who had given him her phone number during their talk with Arnie, and she pursed her lips at him. He had forgotten about the piece of paper in his pocket until now.

"It's pretty serious shit," Bob said. "There's some anti-pornography stuff in the works too."

"Isn't there always?"

Bob shook his head. "It could change the way the business works, kid. Black markets are dangerous as hell."

James shrugged one shoulder and tilted his head to the side until the first three vertebrae of his neck popped. "Then we'll find a way to tell them to fuck off."

"By the way," Bob said as the waitress set his next drink on the table, "I got you a hell of a deal. You're going to like it."

"No rape scenes?"

"No rape scenes. But it's got just about everything else. It's a big group thing, but not with one girl and a bunch of guys. Just lots of guys and lots of girls. And a rooster, I think. Some kind of farm animal costume."

James laughed out loud. "What's the title?"

"Old Mack-Donald."

"That's awful. That's really fucking bad."

They clinked glasses and James took a sip. He took in the smoothness of the caramel liquor and for a brief moment fought the urge to see if he could light his breath on fire.

Angela finished her set and walked over to the table next to the stage to collect her tip bucket. The pay was probably shit here, so James had dropped a twenty dollar bill in the bucket. It wasn't the only twenty. James watched her rummage through the bucket and toss the contents in her purse, a little black leather thing that caught the light when she turned around. He surprised himself by averting his eyes when she turned his way.

\*\*\*

Jeremy parked his truck next to a car with a singular bumper sticker that took up nearly the entire bumper. *In case of rapture, this vehicle will be unmanned.* He pictured the empty car sailing down the highway and taking out scores of people like a missile, its gentle and loving Christian operator having vanished mid-trip the way the bumper sticker implied. Way to cling to the moral high road, assholes. He sipped his coffee and walked into the office.

Karen the administrative assistant was on a leave of absence. Apparently, she had several relatives in New York. Apparently, not all of them had survived. Jeremy didn't function well as a shoulder to cry on, and a part of him was at least glad that she wasn't there to ask him to be one. He was afraid he usually just looked like a sociopath when someone needed comfort.

Jeremy didn't have anyone outside of Beth. It insulated him from the tragedy, but he wished he could feel it the way Karen did. He wished he could feel it the way Beth did.

Beth didn't talk about it, but Jeremy was pretty sure she was spending most of her time at home thinking about Damien. She was eating less and watching television more.

Jeremy wished that he had an idea of when grief or worry turned into flat-out depression, and he wondered whether he should bring Beth to the doctor. His internet searches had turned up conflicting information, but he thought it might be getting to that point.

For now, he stared at the computer screen. Another bug report had led him to finding the entire word HEIMDALL hidden in six places. One of these contained the word on one line. The rest were spelled as if playing a toddler's game of Scrabble, in acrostics and diagonals backwards and forwards across lines of code. The problem was that each instance occurred in a different section of code, written by a different programmer. When he checked his old e-mails, he found that the original files sent to him hadn't contained it.

*** 

According to reports, the explosion had come from an array of seven bombs, likely hidden in different buildings around Times Square. The experts interviewed on the evening news intimated that this was the work of a large and powerful terrorist organization. One correspondent said that it was unlikely to be Al-Qaeda or another such militant Islamic group, because they were unlikely to obtain nuclear materials while under the heavy surveillance the United States already imposed on them. A second correspondent said that he had personally witnessed Al-Qaeda affiliates crossing the border with Mexico only a week before the attack, and that it was irresponsible to absolve the terrorist organization of blame without a full investigation.

The second correspondent called for the President to close the borders while Jeremy decided the correspondent was full of shit.

In the following week, it was also revealed that the Vice President had been visiting New York at the time of the attack. He was counted in the final total, nearly two and a half million people dead. The same was true of several prominent members of congress, old men whose names or politics Jeremy didn't know. The President made the announcement with that same sadness that Jeremy didn't trust, following with his new appointment to the position. Jeremy had never heard of the new Vice President.

Over the course of the month, HEIMDALL continually popped up in the code of the VIGROND project. Jeremy took the opportunity for a break from work and read more about the mythological character on the internet. Apparently, Heimdall the watchman god had superhuman sight and hearing. The god spent most of his time watching for the beginning of Ragnarok, the end of the world, and was supposed to warn all of the other gods when it came. Then he and Loki, who seemed kind of like the devil of the mythology, fought and killed each other. Jeremy still didn't get the joke.

The cafeteria television was on today, and the few people at the surrounding tables were fixated on the screen. Jeremy listened to the report in silence.

"For those just joining us, another cluster of nuclear bombs detonated today, November the first, in Houston,

Texas. The bombing occurred at 8:47 this morning, the exact time that the bombing occurred in New York just a month ago. Although the death toll has not yet been counted, the number of dead is estimated as high as half a million. While families mourn, groups of citizens around the country are fleeing major cities in fear of yet another attack. Cities around the country are increasing their police force and implementing heavy surveillance measures in their metropolitan areas. We are joined now by Los Angeles Chief of Police Fred Nielson. Los Angeles is the first city to implement a revolutionary, high-tech security system to protect the city. Thank you for joining us, Chief."

In the interview, the Chief of Police described a system of three thousand cameras being installed, peeking down every alley and dark corner in all of Los Angeles. These cameras would be monitored by the citizens themselves, as everyone with Internet access could view any camera at any time through the city website. This would allow citizens to patrol their own neighborhoods and take their safety into their own hands without tying up necessary police resources. When asked if this was a violation of the privacy of Los Angeles citizens, the Chief explained that what people do in their own homes is their business, but what went on outside the door was now everyone's.

Jeremy clicked his tongue. "I'm sure public access surveillance won't be abused." He wondered what would happen when they realized there was nothing stopping someone from setting the nuclear bomb in the privacy of their own home.

Mr. Douglas gave the office the rest of the afternoon off. Jeremy fought the traffic and hoped he got there before Beth heard the news.

*** 

Angela Bianchi didn't see the note in her purse until it was time to pay the taxi fare. She threw it into the small trash bag hooked onto the back of the driver's seat. There were usually more notes than tips in her bucket. Some were addressed to Angela, some to Miss Bianchi. Some were addressed to *Piano Chick*, some to *Sexy*, and sometimes just to *Bitch*. The one she threw away in the taxi was addressed to *Freya*. After years of performing, she didn't read them.

She counted out the amount on the meter. She thought for a moment and counted out a few more before handing the wad of bills to the driver, nodding to him before stepping out into the rain.

Her apartment was a converted loft rented from Babs and Booty Harris, an elderly jazz couple who had once headlined at The Blue Whale in Los Angeles. Their San Bernardino home had once been a factory where violins were handmade. While it was no longer in operation, the Harris couple had turned the factory floor into a musician's paradise. Display cases of violins, violas, cellos, flutes, saxophones, and clarinets were all open for free use. An Ignaz Pleyel grand piano, flown in from Paris and kept in perfect playable condition, sat in the middle of the floor near a drum set, string bass and tenor saxophone on a stand. While Angela was sure the other instruments were wonderful, the Pleyel was her favorite.

She opened the door and was met with a slow, gliding melody. *Love is now the stardust of yester—er—err—day.* A piano's higher register twinkled and danced while the string base pushed rhythm like a heart beat. Etta Jones held the notes in her voice with a deep elasticity, growing each melody in her vocal chords like a yoga pose. If Angela were intolerable, she'd have called Etta an influence. Calling her an influence diminished her. Etta was a goddess.

"Darlin'," Booty Harris said when he saw her, holding up his crystal glass in a salutation that allowed Angela to see the half-full olive skewer bounce from one side of his martini to the other. The man's white hair, gathered with a comb and tugged politely toward the back of his head, stood in stark contrast to his midnight skin. The black bow tie of his tuxedo was slightly crooked.

"Come on in and have a drink," Babs said as she straightened her husbands bow tie. She wore a shimmering satin green dress that hugged her still-impressive figure. Her gloves, long enough to cover her elbows, matched the shimmering green of her gown. Her long, black hair laid regally on her shoulders and her pearl necklace twinkled as she lifted her glass of bourbon.

"Why thank you," Angela said, giving a terrible approximation of a curtsy. "What are we celebrating?"

All three laughed at her curtsy and Babs gave one back that was only slightly more sophisticated.

"It's an anniversary," Booty said. "November the ninth, the first time we played at Taylor's Point."

Angela set her bag on a couch as she crossed the living room to the bar. She picked up the cocktail shaker, filled it with ice, and grabbed a bottle of Tanqueray. "Taylor's Point. I don't think I know it."

"It's a jazz club in a terrible little town south of Chicago," Babs said. "It's where Booty decided to learn the saxophone."

Angela added some dry vermouth to her drink, then shook and strained it into a chilled glass. She twisted a strip of lemon peel over the smooth liquid surface and dropped it in, raising an eyebrow at Booty. "You don't play the saxophone."

Babs chuckled loudly and put her hand on her husband's shoulder. "Oh, he's not that bad."

"I've heard you play," Angela said to Booty with a smile. She sipped her martini. "It's not quite embarrassing. Sax is not your thing."

Booty laughed. "True, the piano was my first lady. Sorry, dear."

"Not at all," Babs said. She winked at Angela.

Booty nodded with a grin at his wife. "But the saxophone had its allure at one point."

"So," Angela said, "you're celebrating the anniversary of a night that you decided to try out an instrument you never bothered to learn."

Babs and Booty smiled at each other.

"At our age," Babs said, "you have to make up for a

lifetime of *not* celebrating the things you should have. It's too late for a lot of people to do that lately."

The three gave a moment of silence as they thought about the bombings. Angela took a long sip of her martini.

They stayed up drinking and talking for another two hours before Babs finally took Booty by the hand and told him it was time to retire. Angela picked up her purse and made her way upstairs to her loft apartment, where she tossed it on a coffee table.

Angela grabbed the remote and turned on her stereo as she undressed down to her underwear and walked to the bathroom. It was whatever passed for a pop love song, the sappy, obnoxious kind that was sung by a guy with a voice higher than hers. She walked back out to her bedroom and turned the channel, flipping through stations until she heard a familiar voice croon deep and rich from the speakers. Angela smiled and hummed lightly, careful not to try too hard to mimic that sound. She closed her eyes and swayed back and forth to the smooth beat on her way back to the bathroom. Etta again.

She turned on the water and waited for a minute or two until steam started to rise from the shower. While she waited, she looked at her nearly-naked body in the mirror and turned to look at herself from the side. She looked at the slight bulge below her belly button and the minute sag of her breasts and wrinkled her nose. Was that a roll of fat growing under her chin, also?

Until now, she hadn't realized that she was tightening her mouth in one corner, causing her lips to to stretch toward one side of her face in a kind of twisted duckling smirk. She undid the expression and gave the mirror a view of her middle finger.

She washed and dressed, letting her mind wander note to note as the old song played. She thought about what it would be like to perform in one of the clubs where these women had sung. A massive grand piano in front of her, old-style, steel microphone hanging inches from her lips as she sang. The spotlight interrupted by the flow of white clouds from a hundred cigarettes, a smoke ring or two growing and disappearing into the air above the crowd. After every verse, she played with chords that had never been written down until finally the song was over and the audience clapped slowly and heartily. She smiled at them. Thank you, goodnight.

\*\*\*

On December 1, downtown Los Angeles was destroyed by another cluster of bombs. The bombing was executed at 8:47 in the morning, just like the others, and despite the police department's high-tech security system having been completed weeks in advance, the bombing was executed without warning. Jeremy sat in his living room and clicked through the news stories on his laptop while Beth slept next to him on the couch.

Within days it was reported, but not confirmed, that all three branches of the federal government had gone underground. The President was making weekly speeches at this point from what Jeremy imagined to be his secret lair, but it didn't calm the general population. Interstates were almost completely clogged with refugees fleeing major cities across the country. The only flights allowed in U.S. airspace were either military or by special permission as the nation and the world prepared for the possibility of nuclear war.

Riots broke out as the National Guard blocked interstate traffic to stem the flow of refugees. The news called the rioters 'anarchists,' 'radicals,' and 'atheists.' Arrests skyrocketed. Curfews were created and strictly enforced, especially in minority communities. Civil rights leaders across the country organized protests and racial tensions were stoked. Both black and white power groups gained momentum.

The economy began to implode. Unemployment rose to fifty percent and crime increased. Jeremy started to look into home alarm systems. Then he started to look into guns. Beth, emerging momentarily from her mournful lethargy, warned him that she wouldn't live in a house with a gun. As firearm sales increased exponentially and political tensions rose, Jeremy didn't buy one.

Some religious groups began to claim that the Rapture was at hand. Their followers soared to higher numbers than had ever been reported before, and these followers withdrew from an already shrinking economy to live by God's law and avoid the gruesome apocalypse detailed in the Bible. More mainstream religious groups claimed that God had removed His Protective Hand from the country because of its liberal policies on abortion and traditional marriage. The solutions proposed ranged from peaceful mass prayer to prison sentences and death penalties for the practice of homosexuality.

As police departments in major cities became increasingly militarized, more and more citizens decided that it was best not to leave their homes unless absolutely necessary. Food and water were rationed in high population, low income areas. Riots and arrests became more commonplace.

Before all of this, Beth had talked about holding a party for the end of the world on New Year's Eve. It was 2012 after all, and now Jeremy wasn't sure that the crackpots were wrong.

\*\*\*

Loki grinned at the television, watching news reports followed by commentary, followed again by news reports. It was amazing how many deaths could be glossed over in so few words. He smiled and flicked his eyes toward a display table against the far wall. On the table sat a horned helmet. As he smiled at it, the horns grew like saplings into the air. Of all the things he had ever had to do, hiding here while the action went on was the hardest. He was, after all, a showman at heart.

He snapped his fingers and the screen displayed an old man sitting in a prison cell. Gordon Prince rested his head on the wall behind him, a seamless black stone that had been grown rather than constructed. Loki had been disappointed when the old man failed to recognize it.

He whispered to the man's image on the screen anyway. "Hello, Odin."

The door to Gordon's cell opened and another one of Loki's prisoners was led inside. Damien Asher stood for a moment before sitting down against the wall opposite the old man as the cell door closed.

Damien's stump of a left arm was almost entirely healed. Fenris had taken his role a hair too far.

The old man stared at the soldier while Loki watched on the screen. "What's he calling you?"

Damien waved his stump at Gordon. "Tyr, the one-handed warrior god. You?"

"Ah." Gordon nodded. "Fenris does like to lay it all out in plain view. I'm Odin, king of the gods."

"Good for you." Damien said as he rested his head against the wall.

"You don't believe yet," Gordon said, "but you will."

Loki grinned.

"You know," Gordon continued when Damien said nothing, "you were the one who raised Fenris from a wolf pup. That's why he trusted you, and that's why he took your hand."

The soldier continued to say nothing.

"Suit yourself," the old man said. He winked at Damien. "I've been here for a long time. The only ones who survive are the ones who believe."

Loki's grin deepened.

\*\*\*

It was New Year's Day at 8:40 in the morning. Jeremy sipped his coffee and Beth leaned against him, her face expressionless. They both stared intently at the news. In seven minutes, the next attack was going to happen. Like a terrible monthly ritual, the people who remained in the downtown area of some city were going to die.

Chicago, Dallas, and Washington D.C. had all been evacuated, but news reports showed that there were many people who refused to be displaced. Mayors of major cities as well as many state governors held mass prayers for protection while staying safely out of metropolitan areas.

It was 8:45 in the morning and Jeremy took Beth's hand as he took another sip of coffee. The television anchors halfheartedly gave the morning headlines, painfully aware they would be interrupted at any moment. Racial tensions and police brutality cases were flaring up across the country. Was there a race war on the horizon? Full story tonight. As it turns out, green tea might not be very good for you at all and terrorists may even be lacing certain brands with lead. Protect your family, story at eleven.

"We have a breaking story," one anchor finally said. "At 8:47 this morning, January 1, the fourth in the unbelievable series of nuclear bombings has occurred in Chicago, Illinois. While the death toll is estimated to be much smaller than other cities because of evacuation, downtown Chicago has been destroyed. Sources tell us that —wait, another breaking story! Another bombing has just occurred in Washington D.C. "

Jeremy squeezed Beth's hand. Her eyes became glossy, but no tears rolled down her cheeks this time.

"Our sources tell us that both the White House and the United States Capitol have been destroyed along with many other historical monuments. This is a dark day in United States History, an attack that none of us honestly thought was possible. To tell us more, we have Washington correspondent Daryl Tannin. Daryl, thank you for being ready on such short notice."

Daryl proceeded to thank the anchor for the introduction, then went on to say that the Washington Monument was also destroyed in the blast along with the Library of Congress and Smithsonian Museum. When he finished confirming that it was, in fact, a dark day in American history, several analysts discussed their take on the newest attacks. They inevitably concluded that the government had failed miserably in combating the terrorist threat, that the country needed to beseech God for protection and forgiveness, and that it was time for America to reclaim its security and close the borders.

Jeremy turned the television off. The office was closed today, but he would have taken the day off even if it wasn't. The VIGROND project was under full review by multiple teams now, all certain that its implementation was going to stem the tide of terror. Jeremy wasn't interested in the extra attention.

There was a knock at the door. Beth shifted her weight to get up, but Jeremy put a hand on her knee and got up instead. He took a long sip of his coffee and blindly patted down his matted hair before opening the door.

"Good morning, sir," said a young woman. She held a crying infant to her chest and bounced up and down to comfort the baby as she spoke. Her tee-shirt and jeans didn't quite fit. "We lost everything in New York. Is there anything you can do to help us?"

"I'm sorry," Jeremy said. "We really don't have anything left to give. There's a church up the street and I think they're helping refugees."

"Sir, I'm sorry," the woman said. "But we're hungry. We've been going door to door here for three days and nobody will help us."

"I'm really sorry," Jeremy said, "but—"

"Sir, please."

"I really can't help you."

At this point, Beth was standing in the living room just out of sight, looking at him. Their bank account was overdrawn already and they were three house payments behind.

"Please, sir!" The woman held her baby tighter as she started to raise her voice. "We lost everything and we just need a place to stay."

"I already said no."

Jeremy started to close the door, but the woman put her foot in the doorway to stop it. As soon as she did, Jeremy reacted without thinking. He slammed the door hard on her foot, causing her to move it before he could close it again. A long string of obscenities floated through the air from Jeremy's mouth as well as the woman's as he slammed the door tight.

He sat back down on the couch and Beth sat next to him. He stared at the blank screen of the television in silence until they heard the woman knock on the door of their neighbor's house. Refugees routinely made the rounds in their neighborhood now.

Beth's lips pursed and quivered. A tear finally made its way over the ridge of her cheekbone and Jeremy wiped it away with his thumb. He wanted to tell her it was going to be alright.

The President didn't make any more speeches after the bombing in Washington D.C. Various political analysts speculated on the reasons. The President's direct line to the people may have been obliterated by the bombing. For instance, it was certainly possible that the emergency broadcast system the President had been using was located in the White House itself and therefore wouldn't have survived the attack. Other analysts decided that the President was certainly dead and that the remainder of the federal government, currently just as silent as the President himself, should begin succession proceedings. Still others started speculating that state governments were going to have to start taking on the tasks that the federal government could no longer perform, expressing concern about their lack of resources to do so.

Parts of the military were already being heavily incorporated into the police forces of state and local governments. As prison systems became woefully overcrowded, prisoners were shipped across the country to massive, newly-constructed detainment centers to await trial. There were voices who criticized this as a violation of due process as guaranteed by the Fourteenth Amendment to the United States Constitution, and those voices soon became residents of the detainment centers.

Curfew violators and protesters were arrested and detained indefinitely. Curfew violators were drafted into the military and sent overseas to fight various terrorist organizations suspected of the bombings. Protesters were never seen again.

On January 15, the Pentagon declared martial law. Several radio personalities decried the decision as one that was outside the authority of Pentagon officials, but the majority of news media wholeheartedly agreed with the decision. Those dissenting radio voices soon disappeared from their respective stations and the mainstream news decided that their disappearance meant that the free market had spoken.

On the morning of the seventeenth, London suffered its own bombing. Paris suffered one a few hours later.

\*\*\*

Loki danced in his horned helmet as he listened to the news on the radio. He stood atop his desk and danced a lone *Pasodoble*, thrusting his hands outward and digging his heals into the wood beneath him. He shifted into a moon walk that carried him over the edge of the desk, narrowly sticking the landing on the floor before stepping up onto an overturned chair and popping his way into a reasonable strobe dance toward another nearby table. He leaped from overturned chair to table in a *saut de chat*.

"To you," he said as he danced. "To all of you. It's been, I should say, an absolute pleasure to present my little production." He bowed, surrounded by the shadows that undulated against the walls like a flood. "An encore? You're too kind. I'll be happy to oblige, if you would do for me the smallest of courtesies." He grinned at no one in particular. "I'll need a volunteer from the audience."

He dug his heels into the table and spread his arms out wide like a magician introducing a new trick. "I am the angel of your darkness and stupidity. It's time to come out and play."

# Chapter 4

## A MANUSCRIPT AND A GLASS OF FINE SCOTCH

Andrew Stone added wood to the stove to combat the stubborn February chill. He placed a five-gallon pot of snow on top and watched as the snow began to sink slowly into the pot. He watched it make its way to join the pool of fresh drinking water that formed at the bottom. He watched the snow flakes on top fuse together and turn translucent before they sank beneath the surface of the water. As he watched the tiny icebergs take residence there and contemplate a change of phase, his stomach growled.

The kettle next to the pot of snow whistled. Andrew took the glass jar of coffee beans from his cabinet and poured a full cup into the grinder on the wall behind the stove. He ground the beans slowly, taking in the sharp bitterness in their aroma as he turned the grinder's crank. The fresh grounds collected in a ceramic mug, where they waited to be transferred to his press. He transferred them, then added some boiling water from the kettle. He swirled the press to form a hot slurry, then filled the press with more boiling water. At this point, he set the kettle on the ground and left the press to soak. He set a cast-iron pan on the stove and laid four strips of bacon on it to render their fat.

He returned to the press. He closed the lid and slowly depressed the plunger, dispersing the flavor and aroma of the grounds into the water. Then he filled the mug with his black coffee without bothering first to shake out the remaining grounds.

He went to the window of his kitchen and gazed out across the snowy forest surrounding his cabin. His eyes skated over the dunes of snow and danced across the branches covered in frosted pine needles. Inhaling deeply, he caught the herbal scent of the pines even through the smell of his coffee.

The bacon crackled. He set the coffee down on the kitchen table and took three potatoes and a grater from the cabinet, setting them down on the table as well. While he shredded the potatoes, he took periodic breaks to sip his coffee and listened for the crackle of the bacon to become the dull plunk that would announce it was ready to be turned.

When the bacon was finished, he transferred it to his plate and dropped the shredded potatoes, dried first with a towel, into the hot fat with a healthy few pinches of salt from a jar next to the stove. He held his hand over the pan to ensure that the heat was high enough, then bent low to put his nose an inch from the surface and catch the smell as the hash browns formed their first crust. He drank the rest of his first cup of coffee in front of the stove and poured himself another from the press, still chewing the grounds that had been at the bottom of his first cup.

He turned the hash browns, uncovering the golden-brown crust seared into the potatoes through the rendered bacon fat. Now that the pot of snow was mostly melted but was still relatively cold, he removed it from the stove and ladled some fresh water from the pot into a glass. This he emptied in three gulps and filled another, which he emptied in the same way. He set a cast-iron skillet on the stove where the snow pot had occupied its space.

Then he set his attention to chopping an onion and a few cloves of garlic on his wooden cutting board. He diced the vegetables and set them aside, returning to the pan and removing the potatoes from the heat. He added the onions and garlic to the pan, letting them fry in the remaining fat while he laid another six strips of bacon on the skillet. To these he added brown sugar as well as another healthy few pinches of salt. As the bacon sizzled, the sweet aroma of caramelizing meat made the hairs on the back of his neck stand up.

When the onions and garlic were fried to his liking, he returned the potatoes to the pan and mixed them with the vegetables. Then he crumbled the first slices of bacon and mixed them into his hash browns as well. Finally, he made four wells in the potatoes and cracked four eggs into them.

He covered the pan and turned the bacon caramelizing on the skillet. Within another minute or two, he called it finished.

He took a long sip from his coffee, then piled the hash browns, eggs, and bacon onto his plate and sat down at the kitchen table. He closed his eyes and took a deep sniff inches from his completed breakfast, nearly dipping his beard. He plunged his fork into the hash browns, finishing them and the eggs before consuming the caramelized bacon in a single bite and washing the whole thing down with a gulp that emptied his ceramic mug.

When breakfast was over, he washed his plate and scrubbed the cast-iron cookware with salt, returning both pan and skillet to their homes underneath the stove. He drank two more glasses of water and and poured himself another cup of coffee.

He left the kitchen and walked to his study in the next room. He looked at his stacks of books that lined the walls, piles of words that laid delicately on hundreds of thousands of pages. Some were glossed with artwork on the covers. Others were dusty and worn, hardback books with jackets long displaced. Andrew didn't organize the piles. Nathaniel Hawthorne sat atop James Baldwin atop Vladimir Nabokov. Homer and Virgil shared a pile with Sartre and Camus, Hitchens and Hume with Jules Verne and Fyodor Dostoyevsky. Ralph Ellison whispered encouragement to Mark Twain and Hemmingway quietly lectured Fitzgerald.

Andrew touched the spines of the books gingerly with

his fingers, his strong hands making only the slightest contact with Virginia Woolf and Grace Paley, touching Arthur Conan Doyle and Alfred Tennyson. He traced the letters of Stephen King's name, dragging his index finger across Bronte and Asimov and Dumas. The pages peeled from the souls of so many writers thrilled him, and he reluctantly left them to set his coffee on the desk and sit in front of his typewriter.

He loaded a piece of paper beneath the platen, rolled the platen knobs until the paper was in position, and slid the carriage as far the to right as it would go. The blank page cursed upward at him and he smiled back at it. The world was empty as he leaned back and closed his eyes to fill it.

The world in his head was far colder than the winter outside. The sun that lazily lit the snow in the forest around his cabin was absent from the world he now saw, but the moonlight crashed against ice and exploded across the frozen landscape as he bounded forward. Trees were replaced by rocky cliffs, menacing eyes looking down on him from their peaks. Icicles slowly grew in his beard and his fiery hair blew behind him in the snowy wind. He continued his run.

He ran faster, until the cliffs became a blur around him. He leaped over rocks and ducked beneath jagged branches that jutted from petrified trees.

Slowly, he became aware that he was being followed. He felt the presence, although the creature did its best to prevent his awareness of it. When he turned its head, he saw nothing. He barreled ahead, increasingly aware of the iron gloves he wore. It was the only iconic armor he wore here, breastplate dyed black and hidden beneath his cloak.

He leaped across a rocky ravine and into a dark forest that smelled of rot. Upon landing, he immediately banked left and cradled himself beneath the root of a massive tree, watching the direction from which he had come. Seconds hung thick in the air as they passed by, one by one, and he gazed into empty space on the edge of the ravine. Even the snow blowing in the merciless wind seemed to drift more slowly across the expanse of open air.

The longer he looked, the more he suspected that he had misjudged the direction of the threat. Images flooded his mind, encapsulating monsters of dripping claw and curled tooth that watched him just behind his own visibility. He saw smoldering pincers reach for his throat from the darkness behind him. He saw a twisted, shadowy creature with fiery eyes and slimy, scaled appendages. He felt its breath on his neck.

Then he actually felt breath on his neck. He twisted his forearm and stretched his fingers at his side, feeling an imaginary weight lift somewhere in the distance. The wind rushed around him as he leaped from his hiding place and a howl erupted from the roots below. His back slammed against the ground and snow crunched lightly underneath him, serving nothing to break his fall. The creature lunged at him.

As it launched itself through the air, he finally caught full view of the thing. Its eyes, bulbous and blood-shot, were framed in a hairless, ape-like face. Scaled spikes jutted from its back like a porcupine's and it reached for him with a thunderous shriek from its serpentine jaws. He arched his back and connected his feet to the creature's belly, launching it screaming into the ravine.

Before he could hear its body crash against the ice, he was on his feet. A low whistle pierced the roar of the wind and he gave a toothy grin at two more ape-like creatures that climbed out of the darkness between the trees. The whistle grew more noticeable and became a shrill crescendo in his ears until the sound was almost painful.

He threw his hand into the air and Mjolnir's short handle settled into his palm with an unnatural grace. One of the ape-like creatures threw itself at him, its mouth open to bare its needle-like, stained yellow teeth. His abdomen swelled with exertion and his belt pushed back as he swung the hammer. Thunder clapped once as it connected with the creature's jaw and collapsed the lower half of its face. The creature fell to the ground in a ruined heap.

The second creature studied him before making its attack. It lunged left and right, staying just slightly out of his swinging range. He locked eyes with it, daring the creature to make its move.

Finally, it barked twice and leaned forward just long enough that he shifted his weight to his left foot. Then it leaped to the tree on his right and launched itself at him. Caught off balance, Andrew swung the hammer as he felt claws drag across the ridges of his armor and tear into his cloak. As he landed on his side against the massive tree whose roots he had sheltered beneath only a moment earlier, the creature crouched low and gazed at him with a ravenous hunger.

As the creature pounced, he hefted his hammer and loosed it with every bit of strength his shoulder could offer. Mjolnir crashed against the creature's hind leg, sweeping it backward through the air toward the ravine. The creature struck the ground, bounced once, and launched itself back from the edge of the cliff on three functional legs. Andrew leaped forward to meet it in trajectory, thrusting his hand into the air again. Mjolnir screamed through the wind as it made its way back to his hand just moments before the creature's claws reached his throat. He brought the hammer down on the top of the monster's head.

Andrew landed on his feet as the ape-like creature plummeted into the ravine. He turned and saw the moonlight shrink to darkness over his path, indicating that his prey knew he was coming. He laughed out loud as he loped into the forest.

*** 

"I think I'm starting to understand Hannibal Lecter," Alex said.

"I doubt it." James ran his hands over the various culinary abominations that were the 'guilt free' aisle of the produce section. He picked up a package of *tofu pups* and turned it around in his hands. Their name might not have been an accident, he realized as he watched the things slide around in such an excess of liquid. God knew what the liquid actually was. They looked like animal fetuses preserved in formaldehyde on a biology classroom shelf. That seemed overly ironic. He pinched the middle of one of the fake sausages and swung the package lightly back and forth, feeling the weight shift awkwardly and suddenly like the solid bits in a carton of spoiled milk.

"Dude," Alex said. "Don't touch that."

James shrugged and put it back. Then he picked up another package. "Cheese alternative," he announced. "Cheddar flavor." He held up the pack of pale yellow tofu slices and pointed to the writing at the bottom of the label, in big black letters. "It melts!"

Alex wasn't listening. "It's Kantian ethics. You know, treat every person as an ends in and of themselves and not some means to a different ends."

"Hannibal is just supposed to be the Bogeyman," James said. "He kills people who irritate him. He's not enforcing some kind of morality."

"Sure he is. Say there are twenty people on a life boat that can only hold fifteen without sinking. What do you do? Nothing, if you're following Kant. You can't throw people off without treating them like a means to an ends. They have to go over willingly, if they do. Otherwise, everyone has to just sit on the boat and let it sink."

James poked a couple of the packets of fake cheese slices, watching the substance separate and then fill in the hole when he released the pressure. "No one's just going to let it sink."

"Exactly," Alex said. "But that's where the enforcement

comes in. When you lose that respect for someone as a person and are willing to sacrifice them for yourself, you don't deserve that respect from anyone else. That means the first five people who try to throw someone else off are the ones who don't get to ride the boat anymore."

"So what does that have to do with Hannibal?"

James picked up a package and pushed it into Alex's face. Alex stared at it. Inside the sealed container was what looked like a pile of preserved, dead worms.

Alex shook his head. "I had a vegetarian once try to tell me that if I was going to eat animal meat, I might as well eat human meat instead. She put her 'gotcha' face on and insisted I tell her the difference or throw my chicken sandwich away."

James took the package and jiggled it. "This is vegan spaghetti. What's it about regular spaghetti that vegans can't have?"

"Eggs. They can't eat eggs, man."

James looked over the specimen in his hands and shook his head. "Jesus."

"But that's bullshit," Alex said.

"Veganism?" James said, throwing the fake noodles back on the rack.

"What? No. Well, maybe. But I'm talking about what she said. Human meat and animal meat being the same thing."

James grinned. "What did you tell her?"

"Humans have that capacity for moral responsibility," Alex said. "They can respect each other in a way that animals can't."

"Some humans can't either."

Alex bared his teeth and raised his eyebrows twice in rapid succession. "Those are the ones who don't have that respect for other people. They're no better than the animals we eat, and that's why Hannibal has no problem eating them."

James laughed. "That's really sick, man. Dude." He picked up a jar of a gloopy, off-white liquid. "Isn't Thousand Island dressing supposed to be orange?"

"That's disgusting. But you get what I'm saying?"

"You might be onto something," James said, putting the jar back on the rack. "But Hannibal doesn't just kill people that lack that kind of respect. He kills anyone he just thinks is rude."

"So his moral compass is a little off. That's why he's a villain. But he's not *just* a villain, you know? He's got a serious point." Alex picked up a jar of pale-yellow French dressing, which James was sure should have been red. "Maybe dictators and soldiers who terrorize their people should be butchered and fed to them. That'd be a system I'd like to see. Cure world starvation and human rights violations in one shot."

"Now that's the right idea. Moral cannibalism." James fished through the refrigerated case. He reached behind the vegan spaghetti, hoping to find something more disgusting. "Are there eggs in spaghetti, though? I didn't think there were."

As he stretched his arm farther into the case, his fingers

brushed something bristly and covered in freezer burn. The scent of pine tickled his nose as he plucked a small branch covered in hearty green needles. He stared at it for a moment before looking up at Alex. When he looked, his friend was gone. The weight in his hand changed and he returned his gaze to see the wicked curve of a blade, dark blood oozing from the razor edge. He dropped it with a decided start and it shattered like glass on the linoleum.

***

"I'll tell you, all you got to do is look around," a voice urged through the tiny speakers of the small television set, "to see what happens when we give up on God. He gives up on us!"

James clumsily emerged from sleep as the man on the television spoke. He was on the plastic couch in his dressing room, holding a glass of bourbon that he could barely believe had stayed in his hand instead of crashing to the floor like the oddly fragile weapon in the dream. What the hell had that been about, anyway? He took a sip and looked at the man in the purple cleric's robe.

The man was tall and lean, giving the audience a wolfish grin and following it up with a somber scowl as he paced back and forth next to his podium. He clearly thought it was more personal and meaningful than standing where he was supposed to stand. Once in a while, he would grin at his audience and regard the camera with yellow eyes.

"We did this to ourselves," the man said as he paced and shook his head. "We did it to ourselves. We took God out of schools. We took God out of courthouses. We took Him out of our laws. Did we really expect that He was going to keep His hand of protection on our country when we allow—Lord, forgive us—*homosexuals* to walk around in the open with no fear of His wrath?"

James sipped his whiskey.

"Did we expect, when we gave women the right to kill their unborn children, that God would protect us from a group of people more devout than we are? America isn't the modern Jerusalem anymore. It's Sodom."

The man walked to the podium and tapped his fingers on the wood next to the microphone. The hollow sound caused the speaker to squeal for a moment before he continued talking.

"We did this to ourselves. I had an idea to fix this a long time ago, but I couldn't get it through Congress." The man smiled at the camera. "Maybe now you'll listen to me. Maybe now that Babylon is destroyed and you're hiding underground, you'll finally do things God's way instead of your own." He threw up his hands and closed his eyes, shouting. "Proud of your sin! Proud of your sin, and full of the filth of the homosexual agenda. If you hate God, He'll bring His wrath upon you. Maybe now you'll see that."

James took a long sip from the bourbon and rubbed his temples with his thumb and middle finger. He looked at the clock, finding with dismay that there was still half an hour to go before shooting.

"And the Muslims are more devout than we are," the man said. "Make no mistake about that. Those mushroom clouds might be a terror out of Revelation, but all God had to do was get out of the way. We're losing the devotion battle, and we have—pardon the *Hell* out of me—we have the Truth.

"The Way, the Truth, and the Light. That's what we have. They may be trying to bring Sharia law to America, but we don't have to stand for any of that. We can stop that horde and we can do it for His glory. We can secure His protection for us again. But we're going to have to make some changes."

James set his glass down and got up to dress. The rubber breast plate felt strange against his bare skin. It didn't scratch him, but it was molded to a strange idea of the human body. That meant it awkwardly cupped his pectorals and obliques as it tried to accentuate his muscles. He put on the plastic gauntlets and crimson robe, just a bristled helmet away from being the worst Spartan hoplite in history. The preacher on television continued his speech.

"So I have a message for you, secularists and sinners. If you don't want to shape up and start standing for God's laws, we're going to do it ourselves. Who's heard from the government in the past months? So we'll form a new government, one that glorifies God instead of some filthy lifestyle."

James stared down at the black leather mask in his hands. It zipped up in the front, leaving only a large hole for his mouth and chin and two smaller holes for his eyes. On the back, a golden pig was embroidered against the leather. He assumed that alluded to the pig in the other room, ready to film.

The film was going to include a real, live pig. That, as well as twenty-three women including Gloria, thirteen men, and a live snake. James smiled at the man on the television. He could rally his morality police all he wanted. Yellow-eyed bastard, poking his head out of the Dark Ages and deciding that the world would be a better place with just a little more hate, fear, and superstition.

James kissed his fingers and flicked the kiss toward the television. He imagined it splatting against the robed man's face like a blot of jism. "This one's for you, asshole."

***

Booty and Babs danced while Angela's fingers glided across the keys of the Pleyel. She blended melodies as she played, a little jazz with a little blues that led into a variation on a soulful tune she remembered without knowing its name. Once every few minutes, she played with just her left hand, grinding out chords in the lower register as she sipped a martini with her right.

She brought the melody to a close and paused before beginning again. The silence grew as the last murmurs of a resounding cadence were absorbed into the brick walls.

"I think I'm going to need a break," Booty said. He coughed lightly into his hand and made his way to the couch.

Babs and Angela joined him. Booty coughed again, harder. Then he exploded into a string of coughs, each one doubling him over just a little bit more than the last. When he was finished, Babs reached over and straightened the bow tie on his tuxedo. The woman had absolutely *insisted* that they hunker down in style.

Angela studied him. "That cough is getting worse."

"I know," Booty said with a grin. "But at this stage, I think we can assume somebody else needs that hospital bed more than I do. Besides, the phones are dead."

He coughed again, a singular bark that echoed across the factory floor. Babs patted his knee and excused herself to the kitchen. She returned with a glass of water, a twist of lemon floating in the top, and handed it to Booty.

"Thank you, darlin'," he said.

"You're welcome, dear."

"I think you should see a doctor," Angela said. "We can walk there if we have to."

Booty chuckled. "I don't think I'm in any condition to hike."

"But we can help you. We can—"

"I kept the door shut on a hundred refugees this week." Booty's face was solemn. "More than a hundred, because I was afraid that a few of them would hurt us. I'm not going to push through them, still offering *not-a-goddamned-thing*, just because I need something."

The resonance of his *not-a-goddamned-thing* yielded to a deep silence from all three of them. Angela wanted to stuff the old man into a taxi and bring him, complaining all the while, to the hospital. But it was dangerous out there, and for whatever reason, her cell phone was effectively useless after the Los Angeles bombing. They would have to go out and hope to get a taxi, simultaneously hoping no one saw them as easy prey. The odds of either were shit.

There was a knock at the door. Booty coughed again around a gulp of water. Babs rubbed his shoulders and shot a worried look at Angela.

"We're not getting that," Angela said.

Booty coughed. "Agreed."

The knock came again, louder and expectant. Booty glared at it and put his hand over his mouth. Babs took a nervous sip from her bourbon.

"We should barricade it," Angela said quietly.

Babs nodded. Booty gave her a long, sad look and loosed a string of muffled coughs into his hand.

***

There were two clean-cut men in black suits waiting for Jeremy when he got to his cubicle. One of them held an open manila folder. He looked down at it momentarily before studying Jeremy.

"Mr. Coleson?"

"That would be me," Jeremy said.

"We're going to need to have a chat with you."

They led him down the hallway into a conference room. A third man in a suit was already sitting at the table and didn't bother to look up at him as he walked in. He was rifling through another manila folder and had a stack of them on the table in front of him.

"Tom, this is Jeremy Coleson."

Tom finally looked up and nodded, then went back to rifling. Jeremy debated the merits of saying hello, then decided against it. Seconds crawled by as Tom carefully ordered the papers and closed the folder, setting it down on the stack.

"Have a seat," he said to Jeremy.

Jeremy did as he was told and one of the other men handed him Jeremy's folder. Tom glanced through it briefly and nodded to himself as the other men sat down next to him across the table. Jeremy put his hands together and turned his wedding ring over and over again on his finger, mentally preparing his resumé to fill the long stretch of silence. He wished he had cleaned the stale chips and soda cans out of his desk.

"Jeremy," Tom said, leaning forward over the stack of folders, "I'm going to level with you."

"Okay," Jeremy said.

"We're from the Pentagon. We're investigating some possible sabotage on the VIGROND file."

Jeremy said nothing as Tom studied his face. A person-shaped shadow on the wall behind Tom put its hands to its ears and wiggled its fingers. Jeremy did his best not to look at it.

"They're not from the Pentagon," the shadow said. "They're just here to mess with you."

"Now, we're not accusing you of any wrongdoing," Tom said after a long silence. "We're trying to get to the bottom of why this software hasn't passed even baseline security tests after six months of development."

"Don't give them anything," the shadow said. It danced across the wall and leaped over the heads of the men across the table from Jeremy. "But then again, they're not really looking for anything. They're kicking your tires."

Jeremy tried to ignore his apparent mental break. "Honestly, I couldn't tell you. We've been having issues getting the code right."

Tom looked down at the desk and tapped his pen. "Why don't you take the rest of the day off? We'll talk again tomorrow when we have more information on hand."

"They're going to send you to prison," the shadow said.

Jeremy strained and managed to continue ignoring the talking shadow. A small part of him thought that this whole thing—the talking shadow on the conference room wall, the magical reappearance of HEIMDALL over and over again in the code, and now an investigation by the Pentagon—was all some kind of elaborate, corporate stress test to see if he had what it took to become an executive. A larger part laughed derisively at the smaller part of him and declined the imaginary promotion in advance.

It was only 9:30 when he got home. Just walking from his truck to the front door, he apologized to three refugees for not being able to help them. The anger behind their eyes was gone now. Instead of reacting aggressively, they gave solemn nods and moved on to the next house. They shuffled across the street like something out of a bad zombie movie.

Beth was drinking coffee and watching cartoons on mute when Jeremy went inside. She grumbled at the animation, some woodland critter wearing soldier's camouflage as it performed various antics on a desert backdrop. Jeremy was sure it was hilarious with the sound on. With the sound off, it looked like an anti-war film that was more clever than effective. Jeremy was just glad she was sitting up.

"Well," Jeremy said, "I'm going to need to look for a new job."

Beth didn't turn around. "Oh yeah?"

"Yeah."

"That's okay."

He wasn't sure she had really heard him. She didn't even flinch when another knock on the door broke the silence. Neither of them made a move to answer it.

\*\*\*

Andrew laid his work face-down on the desk next to his typewriter. He cracked his knuckles and stood up slowly, then walked to the kitchen and added some more wood to the stove. He ran his hand along the remaining pile of split logs, tracing the splintered grain of one log as it slowly approached a knot the size of an egg. The pile was low.

The axe that rested against the wall next to the door was old and wore a little rust on its blade. It was a heavy tool with a four-foot handle and a head that weighed nearly ten pounds. The steel had long before lost its shine, but the edge was sharp. Andrew slung it over his back and went outside into the snow. There, he took a wide log from his wood pile behind the cabin and set it on the ground.

He took his time aligning his swing. When he swung

the axe over his head and slammed it into the wood, the log shattered into several jagged pieces. He broke those again with a few more swings, gathered up the newly-split wood into a neat pile, and laid the pile against the door before turning to get another log.

Something deeper in the woods caught his eye. He walked carefully, avoiding fresh and snapping twigs under the snow as he carried his axe. Within moments, his eyes fixed on what had drawn them: a shadow-covered face, unmoving against the wintry backdrop, stared at him with a frozen smile.

He approached the face. It was jet black, with a sharp-angled, tight-lipped grin that slashed downward from one ear and back up to the other. Its eyes, wide open and stark white, seemed to track him without moving as he approached. The smile seemed to deepen, but otherwise it didn't react as he came within a few feet of it. The figure that crouched in the woods seemed intent on staying there.

Andrew bent down and stuck his face an inch from that grin. He studied its eyes, which stared right back into his. He listened for breathing. There was none except his own. He looked for a shiver, a ruffle of clothing against the wind. Nothing. Andrew maintained eye contact with the three-dimensional shadow as seconds crawled straight on into minutes.

Something whispered in the back of his head. Andrew mouthed the words as they echoed across his skull, but kept his eye contact with the shadow.

*When the dunes of spirit lack oasis,*
*And redemption is as the sun dried moon,*
*Angels dance when our eyes are closed,*
*As we pray to them, fly low and swoon.*
*This is where we thirst for answers,*
*Quivering beneath hot dreams,*
*Approaching the ever-further well,*
*Approaching truth that liquid seems.*
*When, late at night, our eyes begin to close,*
*And we mouth prayers we can never know,*
*Dry tears fall to sleeping ground,*
*Dry with want of heaven's own.*
*We were wrong, my friend in all.*
*The lies we told are grains of sand.*
*Our inspiration to the world is lost,*
*And there is fury in my hand.*

Then the shadow's eyes grayed and cracked. The grin chapped and flattened, and its body turned to gray stone in front of him. Andrew kept his gaze on its eyes, then slowly nodded. He lined up his swing and brought the back of the axe down hard on the statue's face. It exploded into a million particles that swirled in the air around him. He frowned at the particles until they were swept away by the wind.

He repeated the chopping process with two more logs, then returned the axe to its home and brought the newly-split wood into the cabin. Then he poured himself another cup of coffee and sat back down at his typewriter.

The blank page once again became the snowy expanse of rocky, alien terrain. He held his hammer to the throat of a hulking creature bound to a massive tree. The thing stared at him through blood-red eyes and grinned an angular grin. Dark shadows crawled over its skin like a mass of black centipedes.

"Do it," the creature said. "Do it, Thor. My brothers know you are here."

Andrew smiled and tossed Mjolnir into the air. He held the giant's gaze, then leaped upward. He caught the hammer in midair and brought it crashing against the tree, shattering the wood as a thunderclap pounded the air around them. The tree fell and the giant struggled in vain against his binding as he fell with it.

"I have some questions for you," Andrew said as the giant looked up at him from the ground. "If you lie to me, I'm going to make sure your brothers find you tied to a fallen tree with this in your mouth." He pulled a massive apple from his pack.

The giant's eyes rolled in his head like a spooked horse. Andrew knelt down and rested his hammer against the giant's legs. It writhed as the hammer's weight sunk deep against its bones.

"I'll take your name, first."

The giant breathed deeply and the shadows on its face writhed. Horns sprouted from his forehead and he spoke through a rapidly growing, prideful smirk. "I am Scorn, Lord of Shame and Disgust."

Andrew nodded and tested his fingernail on one of the

creature's horns. It was as hard as stone. "Scorn," he repeated. "Still naming yourselves for what you wish you ruled over."

The giant glowered at him.

"Another gate has opened in Jotunheim. Where does it go?"

The shadows on the giant's face slithered and stretched across each other. They folded again and again, building volume and taking on the form of a new face. A white beard sprouted atop a previously hairless visage. An eye patch formed over a previously present eyeball. Odin's grizzled face stared back at Andrew.

"Enough of that," Andrew said. "Where does the gate go? Muspelheim?"

The giant laughed with Odin's mouth.

"Vanaheim?"

The giant bellowed. Then it quieted, its eye straining to see behind it into the woods as massive footsteps echoed in the forest.

Andrew leaned close and whispered into its ear as the footsteps got louder. His lips brushed the creature's skin and it strained to move away. "You've tasted giant before, haven't you? Is it pleasant?"

The giant struggled against its bonds.

Andrew smiled. "I'm sure it is."

The footsteps steadily became louder. Scanning the horizon, Andrew saw tree tops bend in the distance.

He stroked the beard of the giant, who still maintained Odin's face. "Sounds like a mountain giant to me. I've met a few. Hungry fellows. Much bigger than they get credit for. Much more cruel to their dinner."

Odin's face vanished as the creature slithered back to its natural form. "The gate goes to Midgard."

Andrew nodded. "There you go. Giants haven't warred against humans in a million years. What are they doing with the gate?"

The giant rolled its eyes in the direction of the bending trees. "I don't know. I honestly don't know. Please." It caught its breath at the next footstep. "Please!"

Andrew smiled at the creature. He lifted his hammer and opened his eyes. As his study replaced the dark forest and the warmth of his cabin replaced the chill of Jotunheim, he looked at the blank sheet of paper in his typewriter, waiting for his creation. He took a sip of his coffee.

\*\*\*

The phone rang.

James picked it up from the couch without opening his eyes. "Hello?"

"Jesus Christ, James. Did you just wake up?"

"What time is it, Bob?"

"Three in the afternoon. On a Thursday."

James rubbed his eyes and sat up on his couch. "That's great. But I was up pretty late last night, so unless you've got something important—"

"I just wanted to tell you that we're up to a thousand people for the rally."

"Well, that's great, Bob. When is it again?"

Bob paused for a long time before speaking. "James, this was your idea. Don't you remember? It's next weekend."

"Ah," James said. He vaguely remembered that had been his idea, but he was pretty sure it was whiskey-tinged in its inception. "Yeah, I'll be there."

"I'm worried about you, kid. You've been drinking a lot more than usual."

"Thanks for your concern, Bob. I'm really alright."

"If you say so. Try to hold it together. You said yourself, this is a chance to give the sex moralists the old 'go fuck yourselves.'"

James stood up and poured himself a glass of water from the sink. "You're right. I just need to clear this hangover first. Then we can get to planning more of it. You mind if I call you back?"

"Sure, James. Or I'll call you when I've got something else."

"Sounds good. Later."

James tossed the cell phone across the room and it barely landed on the couch. He sat down in his arm chair and downed his water in a few gulps before leaning forward and cradling his head in his hands. He decided against a cigarette. For once, the idea made him nauseous.

There was a knock at the door. James craned his neck backward and sighed, suddenly reconsidering the cigarette after all. He had only received a few refugee visits since the Los Angeles bombing, but each had been its own kind of heartbreaking. The first had been a fifteen-year-old boy with radiation burns who needed money for the refugee center. The center had started charging a fee for entry to cover expenses.

He decided not to answer. As the knock came again, he picked up his deck of cards and cracked them into a bridge shuffle. The knock came again. It was louder this time, pointed and quick. It was the kind of knock that expected to be answered and wasn't leaving until it was. James got up from the chair and shoved the deck of cards into the pocket of his slacks. When he opened the door, he was unsurprised to see three police uniforms.

The cop who stood in the middle of the doorway had a gut that ballooned through his work shirt and spilled over the front of his pants. His pursed lips took up residence just north of a slight crease that was clearly meant to be a chin. Salt-and-pepper stubble decorated his face like a light dusting of powdered sugar and cinnamon.

"Are you James Reynolds?"

James flashed him a grin. "Yes, sir."

The officer nodded to the other two men. "Mr. Reynolds, you're under arrest for production of illegal pornographic videos."

A tiny bark battered the air between them and Blackjack launched himself at the officer's feet. The chinless cop kicked the pug aside and pushed forward through the doorway, followed by the other two. As James put his hands out to protect himself, they grabbed his arms and forced him onto the ground. One of them pushed on the back of his head, grinding his face into the carpet. The smell of old cigarette ash and dust wormed its way through his sinuses as his arms were twisted behind him and cold steel pinched around his wrists with a series of clicks.

The chinless cop stuck his face next to James's ear and whispered. "This is for the dog, asshole."

The electric shock felt like a burst of a cold shower at first, tightening his muscles until he arched his back and a guttural protest broke free from his throat. Every part of his body itched and stung, as if he had been attacked by a thousand angry bees.

"Fucking pervert," another voice said.

James felt his muscles spasm and wobble as he laid on the ground. The shock was finished, but he still couldn't move. Then the cold shower rained on him again and his muscles clenched so hard that he thought they might actually rip from his bones. He heard Blackjack yelp as one of them tossed the dog into the bathroom and slammed the door.

***

Jeremy turned his wedding ring on his finger as he waited in the conference room with two more men in suits sitting across the table. Both had short, brown hair and chiseled jaws that were accentuated by their frowns. One of the men looked at his watch, then contented himself with studying Jeremy's face. The other tapped his fingers on the cover of Jeremy's file and gazed down the hallway through the open door.

Mr. Douglas had been arrested on Jeremy's way in. The man had shouted and struggled while being removed from the building.

Jeremy felt his phone vibrate in his pocket. Both men were staring at him now and he decided to let it go to voice mail. The shadow behind the men waved and Jeremy immediately wanted to leave.

"Jeremy," Tom from the Pentagon said as he walked into the room. "How have you been?"

"As well as can be expected," Jeremy said. He had absolutely no idea if that was the right thing to say. "How are you?"

"Doing very well." Tom sat down on the same side as the other men in suits and opened Jeremy's file.

"Very little," the shadow behind Tom said. It chuckled at its own joke.

There was a long pause as Tom turned page after page, making Jeremy wonder how much new material could be in the file since yesterday. Maybe it was just an interrogation tactic.

Finally, Tom pulled a piece of paper from the file and slid it across the table for Jeremy. "Jeremy, I'd like you to explain this to me."

It was a page of the VIGROND code. Across multiple lines, letters were circled in pencil. Always adjacent to one another even across lines, the same circled letters found over and over on the page spelled one word. The circles found it spelled upward and downward, left and right, appearing dozens of places on the page.

*H-E-I-M-D-A-L-L.*

"I really don't know how that happened," Jeremy said.

Tom shook his head, then leaned forward. "It seemed like an odd coincidence at first. Just some letters that kept repeating. Then we ran a search for the word HEIMDALL across the entire program. This only happens in the section of code you've been working on. It occurs seventy-five times."

"I'm not sure I—"

"There's also a back door written into parts of the code that you shouldn't be able to access. That back door shouldn't be there, but somebody decided to put it in anyway. I'll give you exactly one guess at what the password is."

Jeremy's heart raced. "I didn't put that in. I have no idea how all of this happened, but I didn't do it."

"We've been monitoring the entire process," Tom said. "No one else has made any changes to the code. When we found the back door, we searched your desk. We found this."

He pulled a crumpled scrap of paper from the file and slid it across the table. As his fingers left the paper, they revealed a single word in a furious handwriting. Heimdall.

"Help me understand, Jeremy," Tom said, "how you haven't built a whole lot of security problems into VIGROND for your own purposes, then delayed completion of the project until you could get your back door right."

Jeremy looked at the paper in silence.

Tom sighed. "Get him out of here."

"No, wait," Jeremy said. "I have to call my wife."

"We'll notify her."

"I'd like to call a lawyer then."

"I bet," Tom said.

The shadow tap-danced on Tom's head without the man noticing. Each tap was audible only to Jeremy and he felt the quick vibrations in his chest. "We both know they're not going to let you have a lawyer."

Tom started packing Jeremy's file away while the other two men stood up. Jeremy rocketed up from his chair, nearly knocking over the table as he dove for the doorway. One of the men grabbed at the back of his shirt, but he twisted his body and ran as fast as he could down the hallway. He burst through the door into the stairwell.

"Hello, Heimdall."

Jeremy stopped dead in his tracks as he looked down the stairs and saw a figure leering up at him from the landing below. The figure seemed wrapped in shadows, its skin a dark and dull gray that resembled no human skin Jeremy had ever seen. There was a glimmer of movement as shadows seemed to crawl across the figure's face.

The figure cracked loose a sharp bark of a laugh, its dark expression never changing and its torso oddly devoid of the muscle movements a laugh should require. It leaned back against the wall and the shadows seemed to smooth out any depth of its features until the thing became two dimensional.

"You're welcome to call me Loki," the shadow said. "At least, that's the name you can use for me."

The men in suits burst inside and slammed Jeremy

against the brick wall of the stairwell. The shadow laughed again.

"Please," Jeremy said as the cuffed his wrists behind him, "I have to talk to Beth."

"Sir," one of the men said, "you're now also being charged with resisting arrest. You're going away for a long time."

"They're not federal agents," the shadow said. "And you really should check out the legality of what that fucker just said. You know, when you have time on your hands."

"I just need to let my wife know what's happening," Jeremy said. "Please."

"Don't worry, Heimdall. Everything's going to be okay. You can still be her knight in shining black leather."

Jeremy writhed as the men struggled to drag him back into the hallway. As the door closed behind him, he heard that bark of a laugh again.

***

Booty coughed politely into his hand. Then he coughed again, a little less politely. Then he doubled over and fired off a round of choking hacks that made Angela and Babs cringe. When it was over, he wiped his chin with a burgundy handkerchief from his jacket pocket and took a sip of his martini.

"Sorry about that," he said.

There was a knock at the door. Without looking at each other, the three collectively pretended not to hear it.

Angela stood up from the couch to pour herself another

drink. The bottle of Johnnie Walker called her beneath its black label, so she set her martini glass in the bar's sink, picked up a rocks glass, skipped the rocks and poured the liquor neat. She dipped her finger delicately into the caramel alcohol and rubbed it on her palms, then cradled her nose with her hands and breathed in the bonfire smokiness of the scotch. By the time she made her way back to the couch, the aroma was only just beginning to dissipate.

Another knock. Angela looked up at the door, which now had a large wooden bookshelf resting against it. She smoothed her emerald dress, pulled from Babs's closet. Booty fought against another coughing fit as the knock came again and Angela sat down. This time, the knock was determined and assertive. Their response to it didn't change.

Silence laid heavily and uncomfortably between the three of them, like a winter blanket left on the bed in spring. Beneath it, Thelonious Monk danced across piano keys and crooned lightly from buzzing speakers set low. Angela sipped her scotch and gazed out over the factory floor below.

A pop rang out, followed shortly by a larger crack as a gust of wind and dirt ripped through the air. The door knocked the bookshelf clean over as it was blown from its hinges. Angela got to her feet and dropped her glass as Babs and Booty did the same.

Men in SWAT uniforms stormed into the room with guns drawn. Booty put his hands in the air immediately and four men brought the elderly man to the ground. They screamed at him to stay still and Angela felt her heart sink as one of them yelled at him to stop resisting. She let herself breathe when the shouting calmed to an odd silence and she and Babs kept their hands up at the instruction of men who kept their rifles pointed.

"Well, you're not what I expected," one of the men said, removing his SWAT helmet and looking at Angela.

"Fuck you."

"Just the same," the man said. He nodded to two of the other men, who lowered their guns and walked to her sides. They twisted her arms behind her and patted her down, their hands lingering on her hips. The man giving the orders walked toward her until he was only a foot away. He leaned forward, sniffed the air in front of her face, and licked his lips. The men cuffed her hands behind her back.

\*\*\*

Andrew picked up the stack of papers next to his typewriter and placed them in a leather satchel. He walked outside and hung it next to the front door of his cabin for pickup. He took a minute and watched as the sun hung low and massive over the horizon. Rays of light found their way through the snowy tree branches and shattered against the smooth piles of snow, crashing droplets of light in all directions. He breathed in the cold sting of the air and exhaled a hot mist.

He went back inside and took his bottle of Glenfiddich from the cabinet, running his thumb over the golden, embossed letters of the label touting the forty-year aging process of the single-malt scotch. He owned a single crystal glass and he filled it with the liquor before returning to his study and sitting down at his desk.

The aroma of honey and beeswax drifted to his mind as he brought the glass to his nose. Oak made its appearance next, and a subtle smoke that weaved its way into the crafted alcohol. Andrew bathed his mind in the aromas, each specifically chosen by the craftsman. The taste was smooth and sweet like honey wine, but grabbed his senses as if with firm handshake. As the sip cleared the back of his tongue, he let the warmth expand from his esophagus outward into his torso, slowly stretching out as far as his fingertips. He set the glass next to his typewriter.

From the drawer of his desk, he took a small mahogany box and set it next to the scotch. He unfastened the latch and opened the lid, breathing in the spicy sweet aroma of tobacco. He packed his small, wooden pipe and lit a match, lightly toasting the tobacco on top before lighting and breathing in the dark, nutty flavor. When the tobacco held a rolling burn, he pulled deeply and drew the smoke all the way into his lungs, already feeling the nicotine excite his senses.

His front door burst inward as men with rifles filled his cabin. He nodded at them as they entered, then took another sip of his scotch as they shouted orders at him. Though he offered them a glass and a chair, they seemed intent that he make his way to the ground. He finished his drink, set his pipe down on the desk, and finally obliged them.

# Chapter 5

## VIGROND WAITS FOR YOU AND I

Freyr danced on the grassy battlefield. He buried his sword into the belly of a frost giant, then yanked it out of the pale, blue-tinged flesh and leaped into the air, cutting its throat and sending it crashing to the ground. An army of Vanir, men and women, imperially lean and moving with thunderous grace, fought behind him. A massive boar, whiskers glistening as if dipped in gold, dove forward on his left and buried its tusks in the groin of another giant.

Yet another giant towered over Freyr, wielding an axe with a head nearly as wide as a man's torso. It drooled sleet that froze the lush ground where it stood and smiled with black lips as it raised its axe and brought it down in a murderous crash. Freyr dodged left and watched the axe bury itself in the ground, then lunged forward and grabbed the beast by its armor. Freyr cut its throat in the same fashion and propelled himself off the creature's chest into another, knocking it into the open, hungry jaws of the battle boar.

"A little slow today," came a teasing voice behind him as the giant screamed beneath the sound of bones crunching.

He turned and his breath caught in his throat, the way it always did when he took in Freya's beauty. She wore a scarlet battle skirt, made an even deeper and more beautiful red by the blood that drenched it. He was certain that none of the blood was hers. She smiled at him before she plunged her spear into another giant's chest and removed it as the beast fell and launched herself into yet another.

He smiled back at her before killing another giant of his own. "They are larger than they have been before, my lady. Are they the warriors of a more lasting winter?"

She bared her teeth while cutting the tendon of a giant's heal and slashing another across the face. "Not while my heart beats. And I think you can drop the formalities, my *lord*. It hasn't been that long."

A spear the length of two men sailed through the air at him and he ducked to avoid losing his head. The giant who had thrown it, at least twice the height of its brethren, drew a broad sword.. The bravest of warriors had already begun trying to bring it down with harpoons and swords, but it cut them down in waves as if harvesting grain.

"Glad to have you back in Vanaheim," he said to Freya as he looked at the creature and began planning his attack.

A flash of red caught his eye as his sister's battle cry

erupted in waves across the richness of the blue sky. It rose constantly in pitch and volume until it crashed headfirst into Freyr's eardrums and began again. The ground rippled as she ran, her feet not touching the earth itself but dancing lightly on the tips of grasses that sprang up to catch her as she planted each step. She charged in with her red hair trailing behind her, holding her spear high and sounding that battle cry over and over again. As the giant made a sweep with its massive weapon, she leaped to plunge hers into its heart.

It ignored Freya, instead turning to deflect her attack with its massive shoulder and cutting down scores of other warriors who ran across the field to attack it.

Howling his own battle cry, Freyr thrust his sword up over his head and led a large group of warriors to the beast. He narrowly dodged a sweep of the giant's broad sword, but some behind him weren't so lucky. He leaped forward and plunged his shining blade into the beast's leg.

Collectively, they hacked and stabbed at the creature's hamstrings until at last one leg began to buckle and the beast tumbled backwards to the ground with a hollow thud. It clawed the air in an attempt to find them, but it was in vain. They slashed at the creature everywhere they found flesh unmarked, and soon the giant stopped moving. It was only after the beast ceased to struggle and a strange rumbling started from inside its body, that Freyr noticed something was wrong.

"The other giants," he said. "They've gone."

"We've defeated their champion," Freya said, smiling

into the wind. "They've retreated."

"No," Freyr said. "Something isn't right,"

The rumbling grew deeper as the massive giant corpse shuddered. The beast's black lips parted, its eyes opened and it screamed a sound so bloodcurdling that Freyr had to hold his ears. Freya's battle cry was almost painful at times, but this was a torture he had not been prepared for.

Something small and white rose from the giant's mouth and floated in air as the giant screamed. It sparkled in the sunlight for a moment, spinning like a king's perfect gem on display to dazzle his kingdom. Then it exploded, a shock so powerful that it knocked both Freyr and Freya clear from the corpse. On his feet again in an instant, Freyr surveyed the land. Freya's body lay motionless at the base of the closest hill. He turned to fight the giant who had awakened, but the thing's eyes were now closed and it rested peacefully.

Freyr ran to his sister. She was breathing, but her eyes remained closed when he tried to shake her awake. Her skin took on the blue tinge of the frost giant flesh and she felt cold to the touch. As Freyr looked at her, the air in his lungs took on the chill of an approaching winter. They had been tricked.

He picked up the goddess and began the trek across the hills. Somewhere in the distance was a gate to Asgard, where Odin could save her.

James opened his eyes as the truck hit a bump in the road and his head banged against the window.

His hands were cuffed together in front of him and

shackled to a chain that wrapped around his belly. It connected James to the prisoners on either side of him. The black steel box that covered the chain between his cuffs dug into his forearms when he either moved or relaxed his arms too much. It had made sleeping interesting during the ride.

At this point, James had completely lost track of where they were. They had been periodically unloaded from the truck and given a tin foil bucket of unseasoned rice and beans, but that meal came at odd times of the day and James wasn't sure how much time had actually passed. After a meal, prisoners were allowed to relieve themselves under supervision by soldiers wearing cross patches on their collars and were patted down to make sure they didn't pocket any of the small pebbles that were often included with the beans.

The only light in the bed of the prisoner transport truck came from the few fluorescent fixtures overhead. James looked around at the other prisoners. No one looked back at him. They kept their heads down, staring at the floor or letting themselves nod off into a mournful sleep. Angela Bianchi rested her head against the wall on the far end of the truck, her eyes closed and her head bouncing along with the terrain. She looked beautiful in her shimmering green dress. He had yet to say a word to her.

He could feel the deck of cards resting in his pocket. For some reason, he had expected to be given an orange jumpsuit and lose everything that belonged to him.

Instead, he was still in his red button-up and black slacks. They had taken his keys and his wallet, but the cards and the strange letter delivered to his dressing room were apparently his to keep. If his hands were able to reach each other through the black box at his wrists, he would have cracked off a few bridges and a spring with the cards to give himself something to do.

The truck slowed to a stop, bouncing most of the prisoners awake and causing a few to let out a series of moans. James could hear voices outside the truck. The language wasn't English, but he thought he snagged a few phrases that sounded like it. When the lock snapped and the doors opened, he kept his eyes fixed on his feet and made himself look as drowsy as the other prisoners. It wasn't hard to do so.

Soldiers surrounded the truck and the prisoners were unloaded one by one. The single chain connected every prisoner at the waist and one soldier yanked hard on it to rouse any prisoners who were slow getting to their feet when it was their turn. Angela glared straight into the soldier's eyes and kept her gaze there as she passed. James mustered his courage and lifted his eyebrows twice in rapid succession when his turn came, flashing the soldier a grin.

Seeing the soldier, James thought about Blackjack locked in the bathroom of his apartment. How many days had the pug gone without food? How long could he go? He assumed that Bob would be back after the rally and would show up at James's place to see why he never made it. But when had that been? His mind reeled at the image of Blackjack pawing against the wooden bathroom door and whining, begging for food. James did all he could to put it out of his mind as he followed the line of prisoners.

He had been expecting a meal, but they were led out and away from the truck and toward what James assumed was their destination. It was a rocky clearing at the base of a massive cliff, which walled the clearing in a half-circle. The top of the cliff was thick with shrubs and vines and a massive waterfall crashed over the the top and dove toward the clearing below. The clearing and the jagged escarpment were bare, but a statue the size of a skyscraper and made of polished black stone held its arms out in a grand, welcoming gesture as it leaned backward and its mouth took in the entirety of the waterfall between serrated lips.

At the statue's base, other chained groups of prisoners were being moved toward it at gunpoint. James looked around and saw other trucks being unloaded. That welcoming gesture took on a more sinister charm as he realized the statue was a prison. The cold began to bite into his skin as the group moved.

"I'm not going over there," said a man's voice.

James felt a yank on the chain and turned to see the man, three prisoners behind him, who stared at the statue with wide eyes and planted his feet firmly in refusal.

"Please," the man said. "I didn't do anything. I don't deserve this. Please, just let me—"

A shot ripped through the air and the man fell, nearly pulling down the prisoners next to him by the chain. Soldiers shouted and surrounded the group, pointing their rifles. The man gasped for breath and blood soaked his clothes. The soldiers continued shouting until the prisoners on either side of the dying man grabbed his arms and dragged him, allowing the group to move toward the giant statue again.

James stayed silent.

\*\*\*

Andrew watched the clouds roll over the clearing as the group made its way to the massive statue of Loki. A small span of purple sky was occasionally visible, but everything else was a swirl of grays. The armed guards spaced the chained groups of prisoners apart on their way through the clearing, making sure that no group became large enough to become a problem. As they made their way to the prison, he frowned at the soldier who walked next to him. The soldier, just as tall as the rest of them, was still a head shorter than Andrew. The soldier stayed close but out of reach despite Andrew's restraints.

The statue of Loki emerged from the rocky ground at the waist, leaving the rest of it under the surface. Just below Loki's navel, a doorway the width of a house welcomed other chained groups of prisoners. As he passed through it, Andrew looked for some blemish, any crack or errant chisel mark in the smooth black rock of the statue that would indicate that it had been carved. He found none.

The prison walls were the same smooth, seamless dark stone. It was as if the statue had been grown like a tree rather than constructed. A glowing white mist hung thick in the air near the high ceiling, never dissipating the way it should. It was the only source of light.

His group lined up at a row of windows, one per chained prisoner like a ticket booth at an amusement park. Soldiers stood in between the windows, covered head to toe in riot gear with dark visors that obscured their faces. The soldiers unlocked the handcuffs of each prisoner and Andrew stared at them as they resumed their positions. It appeared that Loki wasn't worried about an escape once they entered the prison.

A man with a pleasant smile greeted Andrew at his window, gazing at him over a small computer screen, and Andrew could hear him speak through the half-moon hole in the glass at the bottom of the window.

"Good afternoon," the man said. He was wearing a white tuxedo with a red bow tie. The pupils of his eyes were dilated to the point that they almost obliterated his irises, leaving just a hint of blue bordering the black. "May I have your name, please?"

Andrew stared at the man.

"Sir," the man said, not relaxing his smile, "I can't let you through if I don't have your name."

"Andrew Stone," Andrew said.

"Andrew Stone," the man repeated. His fingers rolled across the keyboard and he nodded at the screen. "Andrew Stone. Ah, here you are. It looks like you're invited to our Royal Wing."

The man in the red bow tie tapped a few more keys and then stopped. Something was flashing and lighting up his ever-smiling face in yellow, then red. "It looks like you have a meeting scheduled. Better head on up!"

Smiling, the man in the red bow tie waited in silence as nothing happened. Seconds of nothing stretched on until Andrew thought that Loki was playing a joke on him. Then two soldiers approached and led Andrew into the stairway behind the windows.

The light-shedding mist above was closer to them on the stairway, and Andrew tried to see what it was composed of as he climbed upward. It hung unnaturally in the air and didn't ripple or sway in reaction to the wind created as the three men made their way through the halls. As he walked, the sound of the waterfall that flowed into the statue's mouth reached his ears. It sounded distant, as if it were running right behind the walls of the passage.

The stairway forked, curved, and intersected with a dozen other passageways as he climbed. Then it reached a peak and the stairs began descending, spiraling downward until it reached a low and began climbing again. All the while, the soldiers led Andrew in the direction he was meant to go and that unnatural mist lit their way. The sound of water became a constant.

Slowly, the number of intersections with the staircase dwindled. Within a few more minutes, they were following a long, straight corridor ending in a single doorway. A gnarled man stood in front of it, staring at a small device in his hand through one uncovered eye. An opaque silver eye patch glistened over his left eye, oddly clashing with the white hair pulled tightly into a short knot on the back of his head. Several prominent liver spots dotted his temples and his cauliflower nose twitched as he tapped the screen on his device. When Andrew and the soldiers came closer, he glared up at Andrew through his uncovered eye, a brazen blue that reminded Andrew of a Siberian Husky's gaze.

"Thor," the man with the blue eye growled. "Welcome."

Andrew said nothing, but kept the man's gaze.

The man tapped a few more keys and the door behind him clicked open a crack. Black smoke oozed from the space behind it, then rushed back inward and was gone. The man with the eye patch motioned for Andrew to step inside. As he did so, the soldiers didn't follow. As soon as he passed through the doorway, the sound of running water stopped.

The glowing mist stopped at the doorway, leaving the large room only dimly lit. What light there was came from a lamp on an antique, rosewood desk at the center. The slight illumination didn't make it so far as the black outer walls, making it hard to tell exactly how large the room was. The black leather arm chair on the other side of the desk was empty as Andrew approached.

"Have a seat, Thor. I hope Garm was polite to you."

Andrew spun as darkness bulged behind him, then layered itself into a series of hard surfaces. The shadowy planes quivered and shed their darkness to reveal a mahogany dining chair with a red velvet seat and a back that was just as ornately carved as the lamp, with ribbons of gold inlaid across a floral pattern.

The empty chair on the other side of the desk swiveled and revealed an identical seat on its other side. The man sitting there wore a black vest and tie over a crimson button-down shirt. A black fedora with white pin stripes was pressed low so that the brim obscured his right eye. He held an unlit cigar in one hand, a full glass of caramel liquid in another. His full lips smiled beneath a dark pencil mustache.

Andrew's stomach tightened and he smiled. "Hello, Loki."

The fedora-wearing man nodded. "Care for a smoke?"

Andrew's pipe appeared on the desk in the same way that the chair behind him had, shadows bending and folding as the dark wood arose from the desk and grew into the familiar object.

"Clever," Andrew said as he sat down.

A tin of tobacco grew in place next to the pipe and a bottle of liquor appeared next to that. It was Andrew's Glenfiddich.

"Please," Loki said.

Andrew picked up the pipe and packed a pinch of his tobacco into it. He tamped it down looked up as Loki struck a long match and handed it to him. He toasted the tobacco and lit the pipe, taking a long pull as he savored the taste he had assumed would not touch his lips again. Loki poured a glass of the scotch and slid it across the table.

"To family," Loki said, holding his glass up for a toast

and locking eyes with Andrew. "May we always meet again."

Andrew stared at him. They held eye contact for a minute as Loki held his glass in the air. Finally, Loki tightened his mouth and broke eye contact for just an instant.

"To revenge," Loki tried again. "May it always be served at its proper temperature."

Andrew took a sip of his scotch without lifting his glass to meet Loki's. It was the real thing. Loki shrugged and took a sip of his own drink.

"I wanted to let you know," Loki said as he lit his cigar, "that your rations are going to be tripled."

Andrew stared at the man over his pipe. "That sounds about fair."

"Thank you for not making a fuss with the soldiers."

Andrew grunted and took another sip. "I'm here for one thing."

"I know. But I can't give him to you."

"I didn't ask you to." Andrew took a few puffs of his pipe. The smoke curled around their silence.

"I have to ask," Loki said. "You put a stack of papers in a leather satchel for me to find."

"Yes."

"They were blank."

"Were they?"

"Yes. Why?"

"Just a joke, I'm certain."

Loki threw his head back and laughed. It was the

voluminous laugh of someone too eager to display understanding. "You're lying."

"I'm sure I wouldn't know."

They locked eyes again. Andrew felt his face slowly creep into a smile. Loki's smile dissipated.

"I really am sorry for what's about to happen to us," Loki said at last.

Andrew lifted his glass. "I am too."

They clinked glasses and sat in silence for a long while before Loki had the soldiers escort Andrew to his cell.

*\*\**

Jeremy could feel the cold stone floor on the back of his head and on his arms. The handcuffs and chains had been removed, but the dull throbbing in his back told him he'd stayed in the same position for a long time. He opened his eyes and stared at the ceiling, listening to the faint sound of a waterfall rushing somewhere behind the walls. That sound might have been comforting in another setting, like the sound of rain hitting the trees outside while he and Beth slept in their bed, but it made Jeremy feel claustrophobic as he laid in his cell.

The man at the strange front desk of the prison had told him that he was going to the Royal Wing. Actually, he had said that Jeremy was *invited*. A part of him wanted to know if that meant something. A bigger part didn't want to know. They had taken his wallet and keys and left him just the crumpled note that had landed him here.

Heimdall. Jeremy had been framed for tampering with the code. He didn't understand why anyone would do that, especially since most people at the company didn't even know his name.

"Someone should really call your wife and let her know that you're okay," the shadow said.

The walls were so dark that he couldn't see the shadow even in the light of the mist above, but it had followed him. There was a certain amount of insanity in that thought, and Jeremy didn't mind. He might be spending the rest of his life in here, away from Beth. The shadow was welcome to keep him company, as long as it took some of the blame.

Beth. The ride to the prison had taken days. He imagined his wife on the couch, waiting for the news that he wasn't coming home. He suspected that no one had called her.

They didn't have savings, and Beth hadn't needed to hold a job in years. Jeremy's stomach lurched and he tasted something sour. And there was her grief. What would happen now that she was alone? What if she never recovered? Would she lose the house and shuffle aimlessly through neighborhoods like one of the refugees?

"I would think so," the shadow said. "I mean honestly, that woman is one lazy, horrible piece of shit."

Jeremy sat up so fast the one of the buttons on his shirt popped. He couldn't see the shadow anywhere and he glared at nothing. "I'll fucking kill you."

"There we go, Heimdall. Now we've got a dialogue. You have no idea how lonely it is to be a god. You've forgotten all about that."

Jeremy ignored the shadow again and moved backward so that he could lean against the wall. He touched the thumb of his left hand to his wedding ring and rubbed the smooth gold, stopping when he felt a few tiny ridges. He had scuffed the ring while carrying some furniture into their house years ago, and Beth had convinced him not to have it repaired.

*A wedding ring needs some character*, she had said. *If it's too perfect, it looks fake.*

"Fine," the shadow said. "You and I aren't friends anymore."

The door opened and two soldiers led another prisoner into Jeremy's cell. He was a young man who seemed about fifty pounds lighter than Jeremy and looked significantly better in his white button-down shirt than Jeremy did in his. The man had the placid look of someone waiting for his name to be called at the dentist's office, even nodding in appreciation to the soldiers as they closed the cell.

"I'm Lance," the man said, looking at Jeremy through eyes the color of faded blue jeans. He walked across the cell and extended his hand. "Lance Hunter."

Jeremy shook it without getting up, grimacing at yet another name that sounded like something from a comic book. "Jeremy."

At least he wasn't going to have to deal with an insane cellmate. Then again, Jeremy had just been threatening a shadow. Maybe it was Lance who should be concerned.

Lance sat down and leaned against the wall on the other side of the cell. "Have you been here long enough to try the food?"

"Not yet." Jeremy closed his eyes.

"You okay?"

"Jesus," the shadow said. "Will you just go ahead and kill this guy? He's really bringing my mood down."

Jeremy opened his eyes and looked at the man. Lance had a little stubble creeping out of his face, but also had a few stubble-free patches on either side of his chin. There were dark circles under his eyes.

"I'm fine," Jeremy said. "You seem a little chipper for prison."

"I'll be cleared pretty soon. My wife is working with my lawyer to get me out of here."

Beth would be doing the same, if she had any idea where he was. Jeremy squeezed his eyes shut and pounded the back of his head against the black stone wall. Then he did it again.

"You sure you're okay?" Lance said.

"Fine," Jeremy said again. "So what did you do, break curfew?"

"Oh no, it wasn't anything bad. Nothing that would even be illegal if it weren't for some laws that are going to turn out to be unconstitutional. My wife—"

"Well, what did you do?" Jeremy wasn't generally one who steered the conversation, but if Lance kept mentioning his wife, Jeremy was going to strangle him.

"Well, I'm the editor of my church newsletter. I guess one of the columns was a little too political and I got arrested in all the confusion we've had lately. But it's a pretty harmless column, and as soon as things quiet down I can show that the first amendment still covers it and I'll be free to go."

"Lucky you," Jeremy said.

Jeremy looked around. There was a toilet and water spigot installed against the black rock, which Jeremy now thought about using so that Lance would stop talking. Then again, he thought the man might just talk anyway. The cell door had an open window blocked with vertical bars, which Jeremy thought might allow communication with other people in other cells. Maybe Lance could talk to one of them.

"So where are you from?" Lance said.

"Ohio."

"Neighbors, then! I'm from Indiana myself."

"Yippee."

"Hey," Lance said. "Cheer up, pal. Things are going to blow over once the people doing the bombings are caught."

"I'm sure they will."

The door to the cell block opened with a clang and a pack of footsteps trudged through the hallway on the other side of the door. Jeremy stood up and peered through the bars from the back wall as soldiers led a man in a disheveled, red button-down shirt and a woman in a shimmering green dress into the cell across from Jeremy and Lance.

Though the man and woman looked like they had been on a date when they were arrested, they didn't look at each other.

"Hey," Lance said to the couple. "I'm Lance."

"Hey," the man said. "Fuck you, Lance."

***

Over the course of the night—Jeremy thought it must be night anyway, but the odd light from the mist that clung to the ceiling never changed—two more prisoners were brought to the cell block. An old man with a leathery tan like a cowboy was placed in the cell next to Jeremy and Lance. The old cowboy had buzzed white hair and wore an outfit of head-to-toe brown, which Jeremy suspected was the uniform in this prison. After a little while, he was joined by a tall, broad-shouldered mountain man with a red, well-groomed beard. The mountain man wore the same clothing and Jeremy wondered why he and Lance hadn't been made to change clothes yet.

The door to the cell block opened with a crash. It seemed more for dramatic effect than anything else, as Jeremy was pretty sure the door hadn't been so loud when he was first escorted inside. An old man with pulled-back white hair and a silver eye patch glowered into each cell and Jeremy heard him tap hard on something.

The smooth, black walls of Jeremy's cell shimmered and melted into the floor, leaving the metal door in an odd skeletal counterpoint to the sudden openness of the cell block.

Lance gasped and recoiled from the walls, but Jeremy watched them with a certain amount of relief. The shadow had mentioned that the walls were *optional* at one point during the night. Seeing them disappear like a magic trick gave Jeremy a small hope that he was more sane than he felt. Lance prayed just loudly enough for Jeremy to hear.

The man with the silver eye patch tapped on a smart phone and a wooden dining table grew between all of the prisoners. Chairs sprouted from the floor around the table and covered platters sprouted from the table's surface.

"Loki was afraid you wouldn't have much in common," the man said in a hoarse voice that was almost a growl. The man's bulbous, twisted nose twitched as he adjusted his eye patch before continuing and he gave them a smile that creased nothing but his mouth. "But you can take your meal together. Any seat will do." He tapped a few more times on his smart phone, which changed nothing else in the cell block, before looking back up at them. "My name is Garm, if that perks any memories."

Silence. The prisoners slowly stood and regarded him.

"Not much," Garm said. "That's interesting. Well in any case, you are invited to go by your royal or your peasant names, but Loki doesn't see any reason you that shouldn't know each other from the start."

Garm turned and looked at the man in the red button-down and the woman in the green dress. "Freyr and Freya. Welcome to the Forge." He turned to the mountain man and the old cowboy. "Thor. Odin. Welcome." He met Jeremy's gaze with his singular blue eye and nodded to Lance. "Heimdall. Beowulf. Welcome."

Then he turned and walked to the end of the cell block, toward the man still sitting in the corner with his eyes closed. He knelt to the ground and leaned forward, the way an abusive owner would approach a dog after beating it. "Tyr. Welcome."

The man was Damien, Beth's brother, and he was wearing the same brown uniform that the old cowboy and mountain man were wearing. He was missing his left hand, but he was alive. If Jeremy could tell Beth that they were both safe, everything could still be fixed. She just needed to hold on until they got out of here.

Garm stood up and tapped the screen of his smart phone a few times before smiling again at them. "Loki apologizes for the lack of dinner entertainment, but he hopes to accomplish some measure of that with the meal itself."

Jeremy stared at the man. Apparently, the weirdness of the prison check-in wasn't over.

"There's a process in the production of steel called tempering," Garm said. "A newly forged piece of steel is heated to an appropriate temperature for its use, then cooled. A hotter flame means that a piece of steel is more pliable and durable, like the blade of a good sword. A cooler flame makes it harder, but potentially brittle." He grimaced at them. "It's all a bit technical to explain to you while you're still recovering from your invitations. The point is, you are going to be able to watch us temper an army out of the guests admitted into this facility."

"You're going to try and brainwash us," the man in the red button-down said. He grinned and cracked a deck of cards into some kind of fancy shuffle. "Good luck with that."

Garm turned and looked at him, then bared his brown teeth in a grin. "You don't need tempering, Freyr. You're going to help."

"It's James," the man said. "And I'll be damned if that's the case."

"I still haven't had my phone call," Jeremy said.

Garm shrugged. "Loki will decide if that takes place. That's all for now." He took a few steps toward the door and turned around again. "Vigrond waits for you and I, my friends. In the meantime, let's try and by civil."

"It's *you and me*," the shadow said. "Garm is the fucking worst. I usually don't let him play the spokesman, and now you can see why. I also wouldn't hold my breath on that phone call. He probably won't even remember to tell me about it."

Me. Jeremy rubbed his temples.

If what the man with the silver eye patch said had anything to do with the VIGROND project that had been so interesting to the Pentagon despite being created by low-level corporate programmers, Jeremy's situation was getting worse by the minute.

They walked to the table and no one else heard the shadow's commentary. Jeremy, refusing again to acknowledge the shadow, took a seat next to Damien, who didn't seem to recognize him. Lance took a seat right next to Jeremy.

Jeremy lifted the cover of his dish. Slices of mozzarella layered with tomatoes and drizzled with a dark reduction spiraled around his plate. There was no dusting of basil. There was also no silverware. Jeremy set the cover on the table behind his plate, where it sank into the wood and disappeared the way it had come.

"*For my husband,*" the shadow said, pinching its voice in a poor impersonation of Beth's. "*The only man who forgets his own birthday.*"

Damien's cover revealed a bowl of ground, raw meat. He picked what looked like a broken sculpture of a finger out of the bowl and tossed it onto the table next to the spot where he rested his wrapped stump. It didn't disappear. Then Beth's brother plunged his right hand into the bowl and stuffed some of the raw meat into his mouth.

As Jeremy stared at the man's stump, Damien seemed to think he was looking at the stone finger.

"Loki likes to leave little messages wherever he thinks it's funny," Damien said. He chuckled. "*Bring me the pinky of Warren Leonard.*" He slammed his stump on the table and everyone except the old cowboy stared at him. Damien didn't seem to notice as he stuffed another handful of raw meat into his mouth. "Fucker."

The shadow laughed.

Jeremy wanted to ask if Damien knew who he was, but asking seemed dangerous. He turned to look at Lance, who was unwrapping a chocolate Easter egg from a large bowl in the center of his plate. Around the bowl, there were a dozen lamb chops.

"Do you want them?" Lance said, pointing to the meat. "I don't like lamb."

"Jesus," the shadow said. "Of course he doesn't. It seemed like a good joke at the time, but I had no idea that Beowulf was so wimpy."

Across the table, the woman in the green dress stared down at her plate. An elegant fork sat next a short aluminum can with a picture of a cat's face printed on the label. Next to the cat food, a small martini glass held a clear liquid with a piece of a lemon peel floating over the top. She sipped the martini and leaned back away from the table as Jeremy wondered what the funny message in a can of cat food could possibly be.

James, whose cover had revealed a burger and thick-cut fries, pushed his plate toward the woman in the green dress and nodded. She gathered her mouth to the side for a moment and took a french fry.

"Freyr and Freya," the shadow said, its voice heavy with mock-seriousness, "twin gods of beauty and fertility. Freya sings at a seedy night club these days and Freyr fucks on film." The shadow cackled.

The mountain man muttered quietly at the end of the table as he picked up one of three small balls of rice with a piece of raw, orange fish set delicately atop each. The old cowboy next to him took one of nine massive crab legs from his dish and dropped it on the larger man's plate.

Jeremy expected a comment from the shadow. He didn't get one.

"My name is Gordon Prince," the old cowboy said. He cracked a crab leg. "Years ago, I was an archaeologist. Here, I'm called Odin." He let the name hang in front of the group in the same way Garm had done, and finding none except Damien's nod, he frowned. "I sincerely hope that the rest of you come to live up to your names. We're either the Norse gods reborn, or we're going to die here."

"Or both," Damien said. His tone sounded mildly hopeful to Jeremy.

Gordon gave a solemn nod. "If we can't find a way to stop Fimbulwinter, that will be the case."

The mountain man took another one of Gordon's crab legs and cracked it open. The old cowboy stared at him in silence as he did so.

"Alright," James said, "the two of you have obviously been here too long. Either that, or you've been doing some very interesting drugs."

The woman next to him smiled.

"You're Freyr, the Prince of the Vanir," Gordon said. "You just don't remember."

James locked eyes with him. "And you're a crazy old man. Go fuck yourself."

"Freyr never did trust Odin," the shadow said. "Freyr was a hostage of Odin's after the Aesir-Vanir war. He and his sister are from a completely different tribe of gods."

Jeremy shook his head. He didn't like that the nonsense spoken by the shadow in his head played on what the old man was saying. He especially didn't like that it knew things about the mythology that Jeremy hadn't read in his internet searches. The term *Vanir* had come up, but it hadn't seemed relevant. In the long silence that followed, he scooped the mozzarella salad into his mouth and avoided eye contact.

Lance broke the silence. "What's Fimbulwinter?"

Gordon smiled, creasing the lines of his leathery face. "It's the last winter before Ragnarok, the end of the world. Snow and ice will come from all directions, and even the warmest places on Earth will freeze. People will starve and riot. Wars will be endless. Societies will collapse. Then the gods will stand on Vigrond and fight the last battle, where they will all die."

The group was silent. Then James broke into a high-pitched, tear-streaked laughter. Jeremy couldn't help but smile as the old cowboy's face fell.

"That's the most ridiculous thing I've ever heard," James said as he wiped his eyes. "People don't really still believe that kind of shit, do they? Most people don't even buy into that Christian end of the world bullshit in Revelation, and it's their own religion."

Jeremy saw Lance's nod out of the corner of his eye.

"Loki does," Damien said around a mouthful of meat. His smile, aimed at James, was slight. What it lacked in dramatics, it made up for in unnerving calm. "And here, Loki is God."

"Fuck Loki," James said, returning Damien's calm smile.

They ate the rest of the meal in silence, the rush of the hidden waterfall constantly tickling Jeremy's ears.

# Chapter 6

## FOR YOUR ENTERTAINMENT
## TONIGHT

PN500641T
Command: Follow Cyan.
040013G

Displayed on the inside of the soldier's visor, the words scrolled across the glass in yellow letters and stopped when they reached the far left of his vision.

The soldier followed the cyan glow that refracted from the mist through the visor. The stairs curved upward. They spiraled down. The soldier passed through a straight hallway into a six-way intersection and turned left to take another stairway downward. Six other soldiers met him at the destination cell block.

PN500641T
Command: Open door.
041213G

The words replaced the previous order, scrolling across the glass again.

He pressed his gloved palm to the panel next to the door. The door clicked and the soldier reached for the handle, but a grizzled hand reached past him and slammed the door open.

Garm adjusted his silver eye patch and tapped several buttons on his smart phone.

PN500641T
Command: Enter block.
041313G

Garm stepped into the cell block first and the soldier followed. As he passed, designations hovered over the prisoners' heads in his display.

With a tap of his smart phone, Garm opened the door to cell four, containing prisoners R1O and R1TH. "Odin," he said, "you've been invited upstairs for a meeting." He paused and tapped his smart phone again, opening the door to cell two. "Heimdall, you've been invited as well. I've been asked to find out how you like your bacon cooked."

***

Jeremy stared at the man in the silver eye patch as he was escorted into the hallway of the cell block. "He's making breakfast?"

"I thought it would be a nice gesture," the shadow said. "We're family, after all."

Garm looked at them, his grizzled face expressionless. He was waiting for their response.

Gordon looked at Jeremy and his lips visibly twitched as if he were fighting a smile. "Loki doesn't care how we ask for it. He burns it every time." He turned to Garm. "We'll take it raw."

Garm tapped his smart phone with a nod and the cell doors slammed closed. As they left the cell block, he tapped it again and one of the soldiers closed the door behind them by touching the palm of his glove to what appeared to be a scanner next to the door.

Jeremy didn't think the soldier's handprint could be scanned while wearing the glove, so it was possible that there was something in the glove itself that operated the lock. He remembered the small, personal electronic devices that had been issued to students when Jeremy was in college, used to unlock residence hall doors electronically after midnight. Despite everything that should have terrified him about the prison, he found himself wondering if the soldier's glove used a similar mechanism.

They were escorted down a set of stairs, where they crossed a straight hallway and proceeded up another flight of stairs that curved upward and to the left. The perfect black stone around them made Jeremy dizzy, seeming to swallow the light from the mist above. They took another stairway down and then followed a straight hallway until it dead-ended into a locked door.

The soldiers stopped dead in their tracks and stood like statues. Garm tapped on his smart phone and the lock on the door clicked open. It swung inward to reveal a dark room.

"Send one of the soldiers as well, Garm," said a voice from inside the room. "I may need to make a point."

"Yes, Master." Garm tapped the smart phone.

One of the soldiers snapped to life and walked forward into the darkness.

Jeremy was caught off-guard by the use of the word *master*. Jeremy had thought Garm was a high-ranking prison guard or even the warden, reporting to Loki in a bureaucratic sort of way. That had been Jeremy's impression of prisons in general, based on a documentary or two he had caught on television. Garm's word choice made him sound more like a slave than an administrator.

They entered the room and the door shut behind them without Garm's signal. In the massive space, only a small, wooden table and four chairs were made visible by a dim chandelier directly above them. On the table was a game of chess, the carved wooden pieces already arranged in a game. As they approached it, Jeremy could see that the only white piece left in the game was the king.

Black pieces cut off every possible move for the king except those that landed it in check, and Jeremy had dabbled in the game enough to know that the king couldn't legally do that. The white king, however, was not currently in check. According to the rules as Jeremy knew them, the game had ended in a draw if the last move belonged to the white king since it had no legal moves to make. That rule seemed strange, but it allowed a nearly-defeated player to force a stalemate and avoid losing if they were clever about it. If that wasn't the case here, the game wasn't finished.

"Oh, good," came a voice from the shadows. "You made it. I hope the guard dog was polite to you."

Fluorescent lights flickered and illuminated a white-walled kitchen with a blue, checkered border near the ceiling. A young man, skinny and clean-shaven with long black hair, stood at the stove and scooped piles of scrambled eggs from a frying pan onto three white, ceramic plates. He wiped his hands on the white undershirt that he wore, tucked the shirt into his torn blue jeans, and tossed some salt over the plates.

Jeremy and Gordon watched him. Next to the three plates of eggs, a fourth plate was piled with strips of bacon that had been cooked as black as the chess pieces.

"Clear that table off for me, would you?" The young man picked up two plates of eggs and stared at the soldier, who remained motionless. "Or stand there. I'm not getting the remote. Gordon, would you take care of the table?"

Gordon slowly stepped forward and started carefully picking the chess pieces off the table, setting them on the ground and keeping his eyes on the young man.

"Well, Chrissake!" The young man tossed both plates high into the air and gestured. Tendrils of shadows grabbed the chess set and flung it across the room. It hit the linoleum of the kitchen and pieces scattered across the floor. The young man caught the plates, swinging the one in his left hand sharply outward to catch an errant fork.

Gordon slowly backed away from the table.

"Sit," the young man said.

Jeremy and Gordon both did as they were told and sat next to each other. The soldier didn't move.

"I'm Loki," the young man said to the soldier as he laid plates down in front of the two seated men. "I'm honestly not sure how much of you is left in that suit, so I don't know how much you remember about me." He grinned. "But for what it's worth, I'd like to thank you for your service. I'd offer you a chair, but I'd need to find the remote in order to get you to sit down and it's not worth the effort. Besides, we have another guest."

The soldier gave no sign of comprehension.

"Abdul," Loki said as he walked across the kitchen and picked up the last plate of eggs as well as the plate of burnt bacon, "you can come out now."

The wall opposite the stove shifted and a dark, cavernous hole opened in the white surface. A man in a navy blue suit and red pattern tie walked slowly and warily from the hole to the table and took the third seat. He eyed Gordon and Jeremy for an instant before turning downcast and fearful eyes in Loki's direction.

Jeremy recognized the man. "President Pearson."

Gordon raised an eyebrow at Loki. "Why do you call him Abdul?"

Loki grinned. "I call him Abdul Loki in formal settings,

if that helps."

Jeremy shook his head. Gordon was silent. Loki sighed heavily.

"What the hell are they teaching you in America?" Loki set the plate of eggs in front of the empty chair and placed the bacon in the center of the table, leaving the space in front of the President empty. "Abdul is Arabic for *servant*."

Gordon's eyebrow lifted again. "So you named the President, literally, *servant of Loki*?"

Loki threw his arms up and whipped his wrists like he was about to conduct a symphony. "Because it would have been so much fun if he'd just played along! White, Christian President of the United States commits biggest terrorist attack in world history under an Arab name." He glared at the President. "But this one had to be strong-armed into it, so now that joke is no good."

Gordon leaned forward and rested his elbow on his knee. "How long have you been free?"

Loki twisted his mouth and bunched it to the right side of his face. "If I thought that was relevant, I'd lie."

Gordon turned his palms upward. "Everything is something."

The side-bunch of Loki's mouth looked like it was going to make an outright break from his face. He took a breath, cast his eyes to the side, and then his eyes brightened.

"Try the eggs!" He picked up a slice of bacon and crammed it into his mouth.

Jeremy stared at his plate. The eggs had no smell, despite the steam drifting toward his nose. For some reason, that seemed as strange to him as the magic hole opening up in the wall and the President of the United States watching them eat breakfast.

The three ate their meal in heavy silence for a moment as the soldier looked on and the President's face started to pout.

"You know something," Loki said around a mouthful of bacon as he popped a thumb at the President, "I didn't even need to threaten this guy into doing it. Not really. The right man at the right price tag, was all." Loki shielded his mouth from the President's view with his hand and spoke at full volume with a wink at Jeremy. "Banker."

Gordon nodded. "Seems like that's a story all to itself."

Loki shook his head. "It really isn't. I just politely offered to donate a reasonable sum to his opponent's campaign. Something that would help counteract all that accusatory race shit. This little guy jumped at the chance to avoid all that." He stood up and paced once around the table. "Well, that would have made an excellent addition to the joke, if he had just gone along with the name." He stopped and tapped out a syncopated rhythm on top of the President's head and then rushed back to his chair for another bite of eggs. "Fucker."

"I'm the President of the United States," Abdul said in a quiet voice. His eyes didn't leave the table.

Loki glared at him. "And you'll keep quiet or I'll rip your heart out, put a funnel on your head and leave your body in an apple orchard. You're starting to get boring, and that's an extremely dangerous thing to be." He shoveled more eggs in his mouth and spoke while chewing. "Eh, buck up, little guy. I'll see if I can find you a flag pin to wear or something."

Jeremy couldn't help his smile.

Loki leaned forward and and gave Jeremy a serious look, wrinkling the skin between his eyebrows and pursing his lips. "The joke on Abdul is just for me to enjoy, Heimdall. A whole lot of people died, and you should be concerned that it doesn't bother you if you want to play the big *hero* later on. It's not just big cities anymore, either. Just yesterday there was some nasty chemical stuff that turned a lot of small towns and suburbs to piles of goo." He leaned back and put his feet on the table right next to Jeremy's plate. "Honestly, I lost track, but I think the death toll was something like a hundred million. And that's not counting the riots and the race war that are going on now."

Jeremy's face fell and his stomach lurched. His lips couldn't form the question he wanted to ask.

Loki grinned. "What do you want from me? I'm the bad guy in this story."

Gordon and Jeremy were silent. The President reached for a strip of bacon and Loki slapped his hand. The soldier remained still.

Loki folded his hands behind his head and moved one leg, wiggling a foot invasively near Gordon's ribs. "We had an unsuccessful escape just this morning, old friend. I had to flood the halls and drown a thousand decent heroes. They just can't find their way through the maze if Odin doesn't work his magic."

Jeremy thought about the sound of the waterfall. He supposed that should frighten him, but he felt numb.

As if he had completely forgotten, Loki's gaze darted to the soldier and his eyebrows lifted. "Shit, where did I put that remote?" He stood up from the table again. "Look around, would you?"

Loki crossed the kitchen and rummaged through a few drawers. The President kept his gaze down but was darting the occasional glance in Loki's direction. Gordon watched Loki openly as he slammed open cabinets and checked under the refrigerator.

After a brief pause, he jumped into the air and clicked his heals. "Probably too much," he said in a voice that was just audible. Then at full volume, "But I think I know where that bastard is!"

Gordon stood up from the table and Jeremy did the same as Loki snapped his fingers. The table, the President, and the kitchen melted into the floor. The room was dark again for a moment, lit only by the chandelier, but the shadows swelled and grew into stacked shelves packed full of leather-bound books as more lights appeared above them.

The dining chairs morphed into large, cushioned seats covered in purple silk. Loki sat down and motioned for Jeremy and Gordon to do the same. Jeremy's head spun and he barely noticed that Loki had also replaced the white shirt and blue jeans with a long, olive green cloak with gold trim. Gordon looked at where the President had been, then back at the soldier.

Loki chuckled. "Oh, Abdul is fine. He just had to finish his lessons for the day. The soldier can stay."

Gordon looked around the room and licked his lips. "Your personal library?"

"Don't get excited," Loki said. "It's mostly just stories. Maybe I'll leave you a tome or two of real magic someday." He dug behind the cushion of his chair and picked up a smart phone. "Here's the remote. I very nearly forgot about your spy."

"Spy?" Jeremy stared at Loki, who turned the phone into three identical phones and juggled them for a moment before squishing them back together into a single device. Jeremy blinked.

Loki grinned at him and pointed to Gordon. "Always gathering knowledge." He motioned to the soldier and looked back at Jeremy. "A few of my guards mysteriously follow Gordon's orders when he gives them. He hides them well, but I can always find a few. How many would you say are your traitors, old friend? Ten percent?" He smiled. "More?"

Gordon was silent.

As Loki looked at the old cowboy, his eyes narrowed.

Silence. Gordon stared back at Loki in defiance. Jeremy's insides went cold and the numbness crept up his spine

"Eh, well," Loki said. "You can never have too much

chaos on the battlefield." He waved at the soldier. "Thank you again."

Loki tapped on the smart phone. Jeremy watched as the soldier drew his rifle, pressed the muzzle to his chin beneath the lower lip of his helmet, and pulled the trigger. The rifle cracked like thunder and black smoke poured from beneath the soldier's helmet for a moment before the body collapsed to the ground.

Sitting in the reading chair, looking down at the bleeding man on the floor, Jeremy felt nothing.

***

James watched Alex light his cigarette. It was dark on the roof overlooking the mostly-closed block of bars and shops, but as the flame winked on and off again in Alex's hand, James could see the dark purple slash of a bruise beneath Alex's swollen right eye. The bridge of his nose sported a puckered scab, shiny from a fresh application of ointment.

"Who clocked you?"

"Doesn't matter." Alex took a long drag and slowly unleashed a torrent of thick smoke that swirled and smiled in the air. It obscured his face and caught the light from the street lamp nearby, turning ghost-gray.

"Fine then," James said. "Hand me the pack."

Alex reached into his pocket and took out the pack of cigarettes. He rolled it across the backs of his fingers like he was about to do a magic trick before tossing it to James. James caught it awkwardly, flipping it up into the air by accident and catching it as if performing a single-object juggle.

He caught the lighter with less difficulty and plugged a cigarette into his mouth. "Did you start that short story for English class yet?"

"Started. Finishing is unlikely."

James lit his cigarette.

Alex was staring out over the buildings and running his fingers through his hair. "This place is such a piece of shit," he said, letting a large puff of smoke carry the words out of his mouth on the back of his breath. "We ought to ditch and go out to L.A."

James shrugged. "I'm good here for the moment."

Alex stood up and walked to the edge of the roof. "Come on, man. You can work in a restaurant there too if you really like it that much. And we could get some fucking writing done for once." He took another drag. "Real writing, not some shit for a grade in English class."

"Who clocked you?"

"Dude," Alex said. He didn't turn around. "My life has just been feeling like a color-by-numbers picture lately. Fill in the prescribed colors and get the pre-determined result. It blows."

James finished his beer and set the bottle on the ground. "Well, I'm out. You want to open the wine?" Without waiting for a response, he picked up the glass jug of white Merlot and twisted off the cap. He swung the jug out over his forearm, then lifted his elbow into the air with his lips on the edge of the opening. He glugged down what he considered to be about a glass. It tasted like grapefruit juice.

Alex finished his beer, crossed the space between them, and did the same. He wiped his mouth. "I've just got to get out of here."

"Well, fuck," James said. "Let's go then."

Alex handed the jug back to him. "Decided." He took another drag. "Dude, do you know why you're supposed to give a handshake with your right hand? I read about it today."

"No idea. And you need to tell me who punched you in the face. That's a score I'd like to settle."

"It's the weapon hand," Alex said. He took a long drag and coughed twice, holding his left hand to his chest. "Fuck."

"You alright?" James handed him the jug.

Alex turned it down with a wave of his hand. "Yeah, yeah. I'm fine. The right hand holds your sword, or your axe, or your mace, or whatever the hell you have. Shaking your enemy's hand tells them you're unarmed, so you're risking your safety in good faith. People who were left-handed were considered suspicious because they had to shake with their weaker hand to be like everyone else and kept their strong one behind. Fuck, the Latin word for left is *sinister*. There's no way that isn't on purpose."

James smiled. "As a left-handed person, how does that make you feel?"

"*Abyssus abyssum invocat*," Alex said with a grin. He finished his cigarette, hopped sideways to the edge of the roof, swung his arms like a baseball pitcher, and flicked the butt at just the right time to make it look like he was pitching a tiny fireball over the side. They watched the smoldering bastard sail into the night and blink out as it landed in a puddle. Alex looked at the puddle for a long time before turning around. "I wouldn't mind making wine for a living."

"I'd be up for that."

"Once we get enough money from writing, we could start a vineyard."

"Talk to me, man. Who fucking hit you?"

Alex took a drag on his cigarette. "You know," he said, "you're my best friend."

James took the last drag on his cigarette, crushed the butt with his shoe, and lit another. He handed another to Alex as well.

"You know," Alex said, "most people hate their lives. That's why retirement planning is such a big deal. They want to get to the finish line and start enjoying their lives right at the end, assuming they make it there."

"I know."

"I just never want to be that. I want to like my life the whole way through."

"Do you like it now?"

Alex took another few long pulls from the Merlot. "Sometimes."

James stood up and walked to the edge of the roof. He unzipped his fly and let loose, listening to Alex's silence overlay the light waterfall dropping into the alley beneath them. As he looked down into the alley, he heard a growl.

A creature with yellow eyes and gray fur stared up at

him. The wolf was joined by a second, then a third. They almost looked playful until the first bared its teeth.

"Dude, are you seeing this?" James looked over at Alex, who was just staring back at them.

Alex took a drag on his cigarette, the coal lighting up his face just enough for James to see the tiniest smile on his lips.

James opened his eyes in the prison cell. Angela was doing push-ups with her feet pressed against the far end of the cell so that they didn't slide on the too-smooth surface. As her green dress dipped low to the ground, James did his best not to look at her cleavage.

"I didn't picture you as the push-up type," he said.

"I know a few people who have done time. You lose your mind if you don't concentrate on something." She pumped her way through the exercise and stood up, narrowing her eyes at him. She walked over to the toilet and lifted her skirt, squatting over the seat without touching it.

James turned his head in the opposite direction and treated himself to a closeup view of the black rock wall.

"Oh Jesus," Angela said. She raised the pitch of her voice. "My hero."

James laughed, not taking his face from the wall. "I feel like I should apologize, and I'm not sure what for."

Angela laughed back. "Everything, probably. But that's okay." She stood and crossed the space between them, then looked deep into his eyes and put a hand on his shoulder in mock-reassurance. "I accept you for who you are as a person." She gathered her mouth to one side and raised the eyebrow above it, then sat down next to him and leaned against the wall.

Somehow, he got a very clear *fuck you*, despite the fact that she had chosen to sit next to him.

She sat in silence for a moment before extending her hand to him. "I'm Angela."

"James." He had almost forgotten that she didn't know him, having watched her perform several times.

"What do you do, James?"

"I'm an actor."

She smiled. "So you wait tables?"

"Porn."

Angela smacked the back of her head against the wall and cackled. Her laugh was one of the least feminine things he had ever heard, a screeching, oddly triumphant barrage of syllables that sailed through the air and hit his eardrums like Freya's battle cry in the dream he'd had a few days earlier. It sounded like her laugh felt to her like an achievement, and a middle finger to boot.

She looked him straight in the eyes. "I hope that's a good time, at least."

James grinned. "It is."

"So," she said, nodding slowly, "how did you get here?"

"New anti-porn laws. Apparently, the punishment is harsher than we thought."

Angela shrugged and a slow grin carved her face. "Well, you shouldn't have broken the law."

James shrugged, his smile deepening. "Fuck you."

She shrugged back.

"Alright," James said. "How about you?"

She rubbed at a stain clinging to the skirt of her dress. "I'm unlucky."

James snorted. "Fuck you twice."

"Hmm."

They sat in silence for a long moment.

James broke it. "Are you buying any of this mythology shit?"

"Not for a minute," she said. "These people are out of their minds."

The door to the cell block crashed open and the walls of their cell melted, leaving the doors as they had before. Garm made his way inside, followed by two soldiers. He glared at them with his singular blue eye and his mouth twisted into a sneer that James frankly thought was overacted.

"You've been invited to the arena," Garm said, his eyes lingering on Damien and Gordon for a moment before skating over the rest of them. "Loki has invited you to sit in the Royal Balcony with him."

The group was led upstairs, following one soldier and followed by the second. Then they were led down another set of stairs. They followed a straight hallway until it branched to the left and went down the loop of a spiral. Then they went up another winding staircase to end up pretty close to where James figured they had started. All the while, he could hear the faint sound of the waterfall running through the prison walls.

They finally found their way to a doorway where the soldiers stopped. Garm tapped his smart phone and one of the soldiers opened the door.

"Ah," came a voice inside the doorway. "Welcome, friends."

As they made their way inside, James saw a round-faced teenager in a purple toga and laurel crown standing there to greet them. The kid had a crooked nose and long dark hair that draped down the back of his head. As he looked over them with his hands on his hips, he grinned at James.

Gordon had mentioned that Loki could disguise himself as whatever he liked. Up until now, James had thought it was bullshit. As he looked into Alex's brown eyes, he wanted to crush Loki's skull with his fist.

"Fuck you," James said to him as they passed.

"Fuck yourself," the teenager said with a grin. "Ricky."

For the first time, James flushed a little at hearing his porn name.

The balcony held nine thrones, ornately carved from wood and inlaid with golden designs, upholstered in purple velvet. As James and the others were led out to take their seats, he could see that the balcony looked out over a massive amphitheater made of that same seamless, black rock. The stands were already packed with what James assumed were other prisoners. At the edge of the balcony, looming over the audience, there was a wooden podium that was just as ornate as the seats behind it.

The shouts of excitement were a roar, echoing from the ceiling and walls of the chamber and swelling to a thunderous volume. The stands of prisoners soared high above the battleground below, and a large collection of that same strange mist hung high above them. Above the mist, James could only see darkness.

"They like these shows," Loki said with Alex's mouth. He ran his fingers through stringy, dark hair and tucked a few errant strands behind his laurel crown. "Now that you're here, they're going to like them even more." He grinned and gestured to the thrones. "Go on! Take your seats and have a good time."

As they walked across the balcony, the crowd cheered. Each seat stood on a round, stone pedestal with the names that Loki had given them emblazoned on the front. James wanted to call the letters Gothic, but was pretty sure that was the wrong word to describe the embellished, decorative lettering.

Loki took his seat on the center throne, larger than the rest with LOKI carved beneath it in massive letters. He crossed his legs at the knees and put his hands behind his head, smiling at his audience. At his left, there were seats marked for Odin, Freyr, Freya, and Thor. At his right, the carved names dedicated the ornate chairs to Beowulf, Heimdall, Tyr, and Fenris.

Standing in front of the throne printed with the name FREYR, James heard the name barely pierce through the cacophony that came from the prisoners below. A low chant grew. Freyr. Freyr. They shouted it over and over again and he heard it clearly beneath the rest of the noise.

He looked at Angela, who stood in front of a pedestal

marked FREYA, and he wondered if she heard the name Loki had given her as well. Her eyes were closed and she took a deep breath before ascending to the throne. James heard another swell of cheers as she lowered herself onto the seat.

As James did the same, he felt he had accepted Loki's game in some tacit way. James was accepting the cards on the table knowing full well that Loki had given himself plenty of time to stack the deck first, and he didn't see anything he could do about it.

When he sat down, the chant erupted into a single declaration that rang clear in his ears over any other sound. "For Freyr!"

Similar swells came from the crowd as the others took their places, but none were clear enough that James could understand what was shouted. The other prisoners took their seats, filling every chair except one.

A man in a purple cleric's robe strode across the balcony, regarding them with yellow eyes and carrying a golden scepter topped with a small sculpture of a wolf's head. James recognized him as the *proud of your sin and homosexual agenda* guy from television, and he fought the urge to spit. The man gave them a toothy grin and sat in the throne marked FENRIS at Loki's right hand. The crowd cheered in the same fashion.

When James looked back toward the door, he could see Garm tapping his smart phone and scowling at the soldiers near the edges of the arena below. Through the haze of the moment, James wondered whether Garm had ever sat on a throne. If so, he wondered if Garm had a name before he became Loki's errand boy.

Loki flicked his wrist as if preparing to conduct an orchestra.

Fenris, despite having just sat, stood again and stepped to the podium at the edge of the balcony. The crowd of prisoners in the stands renewed their cheers with extra vigor. When the applause died down slightly, he spoke. "Welcome, friends."

\*\*\*

Jeremy stared out into the crowd as Fenris spoke. He scanned the massive stands, his eyes flitting across the sea of brown prison uniforms. If Jeremy was going to receive one of those, he didn't understand why he hadn't already. He squinted, trying to resolve the faces of the prisoners and find Beth's among them. He couldn't.

"For your entertainment tonight," Fenris said, gesturing grandly across the arena, one open palm while he gripped his golden scepter in the other, "we have something of a variety pack."

A shower of shimmering steel made its way through the air as a thousand weapons dropped harmlessly but dramatically from their hiding place above the arena to the empty space below. Swords, spears, cleavers, hooks, and even a few bows and quivers of arrows bounced and kicked up clouds of dust from the stone floor before coming to rest.

The crowd cheered. Lance, leaning so far forward from the chair on Jeremy's right that he looked like he might fall, stared down at the weapons as his face turned gray. In the throne to Jeremy's left, Damien stared straight at the back of Fenris's head. The seat on the other side of Jeremy belonged to the robed, scepter-carrying man.

"I'd like to introduce you to tonight's players." Fenris gestured wildly and doors on either end of the arena flung open.

A long string of prisoners was led inside from each doorway. Some of the prisoners walked with purpose, some shuffled in like zombies, and others pleaded with the guards but acquiesced under the gaze of a pointed rifle. There were hundreds of prisoners on the arena floor.

"We are also joined by the Royal Family, the personal entourage of your generous host. It's my understanding that they have just recently dined. Let's give them a show!"

Cheers rocketed to a volume that made Jeremy's throne vibrate.

"Before we begin," Fenris said, "I humbly offer a prayer."

The cheers fell to absolute silence.

"Dear Lord, we thank You for Your judgment on this world. We stand before You, wretched lives left to witness Your wrath firsthand. As You tear into our bodies, we open our souls to You. As You beat us, we become stronger. Trembling, we come to You cleansed of cowardice. We will be your army, Lord, soldiers of Heaven and Hel. Armed with Your Word, we will become giants of fire and brimstone. The time has come!"

Deafening cheers sliced through the silence. Jeremy

stared out over the crowd.

"Amen," Fenris said. He turned around and spilled a wolfish grin in Loki's direction. He turned back to face the crowd and set his hands on the podium, tapping his long fingernails on the carved wood as he waited for the cheers to die down.

"It seems appropriate at this point," he said, "that we go over the rules for our newest guests. The penalty for breaking the rules, we all remember, is steep."

The crowd moaned and laughed. Fenris's voice boomed over the noise despite there being no microphone that Jeremy could see.

"He who would save his life will lose it. No competitor may end the battle without shedding blood. If your weapon is clean when the battle ends, your guest status at this facility will be over and you will be executed."

A number of prisoners on the floor of the arena were already picking up weapons, feeling out the weight of them in their hands and even giving a few practice slashes in the air. They seemed relatively unconcerned about rule one.

"If you die poorly during battle, your guest status at this facility will also be over." Fenris leaned forward over the podium. "The Lord of the Forge requires valor, and a sniveling, pleading death will simply not do. A dead coward remains dead."

Jeremy shook his head. There was something nonsensical in that. Not that nonsense should have surprised him after his meeting with Loki, but the statement implied that people who were *not* cowards didn't stay dead.

"The final arbitration of either of these rules," Fenris continued, "is up to our gracious host. High Spokesman and Lord of the Forge, Francis Gelasius Loki!"

Loki smiled and adjusted his toga before standing from his throne. His face was different now, his bone structure rounded and his nose crooked, but his grin was the same as it had been when he had ordered the soldier's suicide. He favored Fenris with a handshake and turned to address the audience. He smiled out at them for what seemed like a full minute. Then he shrugged. "Let the game begin!"

Jeremy leaned forward as those who hadn't picked up weapons on the battlefield yet did so. Some were obviously veterans, rushing headlong into anyone nearby and dealing a series of heavy strikes. They fought without form, mostly hacking and stabbing their way through the crowd. Others took the more polite approach, doing their best to block the slashes from more zealous combatants. Those who stuck with that approach didn't last long.

As they watched, a man in a striped golf shirt pleaded with a burly prisoner wearing the brown uniform. The man in brown gutted him with a sword. As the wounded man screamed, his assailant held him by his hair and hacked at his neck until his head came free. It took a dozen hacks and Jeremy's insides ran cold as the man proceeded to hold the head, dripping crimson, up to the cheering crowd.

The fighter's glory was short-lived, as he then received the sharp end of a hook through his neck. The crowd roared with laughter and some even booed as he fell and his attacker ran to another fight.

After a moment, Jeremy noticed that Fenris was tracing small figure-eights with his long fingernails on the bandaged stump of Damien's left arm. Damien sat perfectly still and stared at the fighting below, leaving his stump on the arm rest of his throne and allowing the man to do it. Fenris tapped his fingernails rhythmically for a moment and then clapped as another man was hacked to pieces.

Small groups banded together and attacked as a squad. They surrounded other prisoners and hacked at them from all directions, making sure each weapon was shimmering crimson before moving on. Jeremy felt his eye drawn to the leader of one of these groups, a woman with platinum blonde hair that whipped around like a halo as she pulled her sword out of a man's abdomen.

She yelled at the other prisoners in her squad, shouting orders that Jeremy couldn't quite make out. They followed her without much hesitation and surrounded another small group. She shouted and a few members of her squad stepped forward to deliver death blows. In the next skirmish, she ordered different members to deliver the blows. Jeremy raised an eyebrow. The blonde was making sure everyone had blood on their hands.

The blonde barked orders and the group backed into a defensive formation. A dozen people formed themselves into a circle, facing down any would-be attackers with several sword points at once. She barked an order and the circle expanded, keeping its form but increasing the space between combatants.

"Why are they doing that?" Jeremy wondered aloud.

"It's less visible on the battlefield," Damien said without looking at him. "They look like easy prey as individuals, but they come together quick and kill as a group."

The slow smile that spread across Damien's lips as he spoke was enough to convince Jeremy not to ask any more questions.

After a few minutes, the prisoners below had broken up into groups or died trying. The groups that existed now held their ground and kept a solid distance from other groups. An eerie peace settled over the arena.

One circle suddenly made a break for the blonde's group. Three other groups descended on the attackers as the blonde's group defended itself. Within minutes, the survivors were all back in formation. The groups hung in little satellites slowly orbiting each other for a moment until Loki clapped his hands loudly and slowly.

The prisoners in the arena immediately turned their eyes upward and dropped their weapons to the ground.

"Friends," Loki said to the prisoners in the arena when the clang of bouncing metal subsided, "You have done well. You have earned your place here." He graced them with a darkened leer. "Except for a few of you."

The crowd cheered and thunderclaps of applause broke as seven shadowy tentacles descended from somewhere above the mist and gripped seven terrified prisoners by their necks. The prisoners clawed and struggled at the shadow nooses as they were plucked from the floor of the arena, legs kicking and faces pleading silently.

"Seven cowards," Loki said. "Seven whose time at this facility must unfortunately come to an end."

The seven prisoners continued to struggle.

"Let us pray," Loki said, "for the fallen."

The applause dampened to silence. Jeremy tried not to look at the faces of the hanging men and women. One door to the arena unlocked and swung open. In the silence, the echo of the door opening wafted by Jeremy's ear again and again. He stared at the open doorway while Loki and the crowd bowed their heads.

Slowly, a woman in chains made her way into the arena. The steel caught the light and Jeremy could see shimmers of it wrapped around her body, clasping her wrists and her feet and even shackling her neck. A bundle of chains extended behind her like a tail through the doorway, disappearing into the darkness behind. Her gown, a dirty white thing that contoured her lithe figure in silk and wrapped her shoulders in white lace, was only missing a long train and bouquet of pastel pink roses. For whatever reason, Loki had decided to make her wear a wedding dress.

She was a young woman, Jeremy thought, but she walked with a painful hunch and limped on her right foot. Her long, dark hair was streaked with white in places, and he could have sworn he could see part of her collarbone jutting out as if she were much older than she looked. The other side of her collarbone, however, was concealed behind youthful flesh.

The soldiers in the arena pointed their rifles at her as she made her way to the center. The terrified prisoners hung in the air above her and she stretched out her arms as far as the chains would allow. The shadow nooses brought the seven prisoners closer to her, their bodies already limp.

The shadows rippled and the woman flipped her wrists. A strange combination of gasps and laughter rose from the crowd as the slain began to stand. Stabbed and slashed bodies rolled in the dust and slowly stood up as the sagging bodies of the seven cowards fell into soft heaps on the ground nearby.

The man who had beheaded the golf player sat up with a start as the hook fell from his neck and the gaping wound began to close. The golfer, who had begged for his life before dying, didn't move.

The woman put her arms back at her sides and lifted her head to meet Loki's gaze. He nodded to her and she made her way back to the doorway, following her chains into the darkness amid the eruption of cheers from the ground.

Loki clapped again and the crowd gave both the victorious warriors and the reanimated slain a standing ovation. Fenris stood to offer a prayer before the prisoners were to be escorted back to their cells for a meal.

Fenris nodded solemnly. "Praise be."

"Jesus," James said from his throne on the other side of Loki. The word echoed across the arena the way Fenris's voice had, and the crowd erupted in applause.

# Chapter 7

## HEROES OF RAGNAROK

PN607291
Command: Follow Crimson.
221313G

The soldier followed the crimson glow coming from the mist above. The straight hallway ended in stairs curving down and to the left, then turned upward and took a slightly wider spiral to the right. He followed the crimson path through another straight hallway and down a straight set of stairs. At the bottom, he heard gunfire. He did not raise his rifle.

PN607291
Command: Follow Amber.
221613G

The soldier turned to follow the amber path and followed it until it stopped at a stairwell intersecting another straight hallway.

PN607291
Command: Stand By.
222313G

A round swath of rock sank into the wall and turned, drizzling water around its edges down the stairs. As it turned further, the flow of water became a jet that spurted from the circular recess and plastered the opposing wall before rushing down the stairwell. The soldier watched this torrent for several minutes as the stairway morphed and closed off, sealing the combatants beneath with just enough room for the chamber below to fill with water.

The soldier waited. The gunfire ceased.

After several minutes, the recessed circle of rock began to turn the other direction and shut off the flow of water. Below, the soldier heard the gurgle of water draining as the stairs reformed themselves.

PN607291
Command: Follow Burgundy.
225913G

The soldier followed the burgundy path down the stairs and through a straight hallway. The drowned bodies littering the hallway registered in the soldier's mind only enough to allow him to step over the ones that lay in his path.

He followed the burgundy path down another straight hallway and up stairs that curved to the left, then to the right. He followed it down three more flights of stairs separated by straight hallways until he received his next command.

*\*\**

Jeremy poked at his bowl of rice and beans with a fork. It was the same, tasteless meal that had been served to them on the trip to the prison, and that was alright with him. Sitting in the cell-block-turned-dining-room, eating beneath the glowing mist at the table with the people that Loki, who was either a god or a magical madman, called the Royal Family, he didn't think he had the stomach for food that was even the slightest bit more interesting.

As he grimaced around a tasteless mouthful, he watched the savage beheading again in his mind. He was sure he hadn't been able to see the eyes of the men in the arena, but he saw them clearly now. The man about to lose his head stared with wide-eyed terror. The man hacking at the other's neck had eyes wide with excitement. In those eyes, Jeremy saw a sickening joy that spread across the murderer's face in perfect consistency with a stretched, giddy grin. He heard the crowd cheer.

Unless they had all been drugged, the man calling himself Loki could do magic. Jeremy couldn't square that with anything he understood, but what concerned him wasn't what he had seen. What concerned Jeremy was that he barely felt anything when he saw those impossible things. If Loki was a god, the biggest issue Jeremy had with the idea was the he *didn't* have an issue with it. That thoroughly bothered him.

Across the table, James stabbed his fork into the bowl and leaned back in his chair. "Alright. Who the hell was the magic woman in the wedding dress?"

"That was Hel," the mountain man said, "the goddess of the underworld."

The mountain man had introduced himself as Andrew Stone, another name that belonged in a comic book. Jeremy was rapidly tiring of that. As he spoke, Angela glared and shook her head at him in silence.

"That's right," Gordon said. "She holds the power of life and death and dispenses it however Loki sees fit."

Next to Jeremy, Lance stared at his food without touching it. "Why is Loki doing this?"

Andrew swallowed a mouthful of rice and beans. "He thinks it's funny."

James shook his head. "How funny are gladiator games to Loki if there aren't any consequences? He just turned it into a video game."

Jeremy watched the beheading in his mind one more time. It hadn't been a video game for that man, who had stayed dead. A small part of him wished the shadow would speak up, just so that he could be distracted from that image.

Gordon nodded. "As long as the fighters in the arena continue to please Loki, they don't need to fear death.

Loki is setting up a bigger game and he needs warriors who fear cowardice more than anything else."

"Fine," Jeremy said, speaking up to banish the beheading from his mind, "but if he's flooding the prison and drowning everyone who tries to escape, what's the point?"

Everyone stared at Jeremy.

He felt his face flush. "It's something Loki said when he made breakfast for us. He floods the prison to stop escape attempts."

They sat in silence for a moment and the rush of water behind the walls made Jeremy's heart beat a little faster. He had been trying his best not to notice it since the meeting with Loki.

Gordon locked his eyes on Jeremy's and nodded slowly, tightening his mouth. "He kills prisoners who escape before he wants them to. He's God here, and he decides who comes and goes. When he thinks they're ready, he releases them."

"Then where do they go?" Jeremy said.

"I'm not sure," Gordon said. "Every time Loki lets a batch of warriors leave, he keeps me behind and puts me in a cell block with a new group."

Damien smacked his stump on the table and wore fire in his eyes when he looked at the old cowboy. "Tell them the rest."

Gordon stared back at him and his mouth tightened further. Their silence hung heavy in the air as the rush of water made its way back to Jeremy's ears.

Finally, Gordon spoke. "I've been fighting here for a long time. The order of events in the arena is always the same. Fenris leads a prayer that has elements of many religions so that it speaks to people of all faiths. The prayers change slightly, but the message does not. Listen to those prayers often enough before and after the battles, and you start to put your faith in Loki. He becomes your personal savior."

"More," Damien growled.

Gordon nodded. "The Royal Family thing is new. Whether we're really the gods or not, Loki is convincing his warriors that we are."

"What are we supposed to do with that?" James said.

"Until we can find a way out of here," Gordon said, "we follow Loki's rules. We aren't in a position yet to use whatever influence Loki has given us. If Loki sees us as manipulation tools, we don't have a choice in the matter."

James shook his head. "That's a terrible plan."

Gordon gave him a flat stare. "Then find a better one." He leaned back in his chair. "Remember the rules. We're going to escape, but in the meantime we need to survive. And when Loki claps, you stop fighting. He doesn't take it well when someone ruins his dramatic moments."

***

Angela glared at the back of the soldier's head as she and the others followed him. The soldier led down a set of stairs, turned left through a door set in a straight hallway, and took a curving stairway that spiraled upward and then downward. They took another straight hallway, turned left into yet another, then took a stairway upward again. That smooth black rock and dim light was starting to make Angela dizzy, but she kept her glare on the back of the soldier's head.

"I don't think I can do this," Lance said behind her.

"Then you're not going to survive," came Gordon's reply. "It's not an option."

Angela felt one corner of her mouth tug at her lips.

Their group approached a doorway at the end of another straight hallway and stopped while the soldier pressed his palm to the panel. When the door opened, echoes of cheers and applause brushed Angela's ears as they made their way into the massive, open chamber of the arena.

The ground was littered with swords and shields. Fenris smiled down at them from the balcony as the soldiers surrounded the boundaries of the arena. The thrones were empty, aside from the one occupied by Loki.

"For your entertainment tonight," Fenris said, "the Royal Family will demonstrate their mastery of the sword!"

Angela and the others made their way toward the center of the arena among hundreds of other prisoners. A concentration of the mist above shone light on them like a stage production and she felt the thrill of performance as the roar of the crowd climbed to a decibel level that noticeably pressed against her eardrums. If she'd had a piano and some following silence, maybe a cigarette, the violence-etched faces of the audience would have faded into fantasy.

"Before we begin," Fenris said, "I humbly offer a prayer."

Angela looked up at him. She could see those yellow eyes from where she stood. Her heart was beating faster, but she was oddly unafraid. In fact, a boiling edge of anticipation was starting to well up inside of her.

"By our lives," Fenris said, "let us shun cowardice. For Odin, we ride. For Tyr, we fight. For Freya and Freyr, and Thor and Heimdall. We call upon you, heroes of old, to grind us into dust and reform us in your image. Make us into giants and let us bleed vengeance so caustic it burns the world. We open our souls to you. Amen."

It was a very different sort of prayer, and Angela couldn't imagine it having an impact on anyone who didn't already believe in the Norse gods. Looking around at the pious, closed-eyed faces of the prisoners on the arena floor, it became obvious that they believed.

The others from her cell block picked up swords and shields from where they were scattered. She listened for a coughing fit in the silence of the prayer that might indicate that Booty and Babs were in the audience or on the arena floor. Hearing none, she quietly rationed her anger. She clenched her hand on the skirt of the green dress that had belonged to Babs.

As Fenris finished his prayer, Angela saw a man give her a wry smile as he swung his sword in a circle through the air. He was a head taller than her, wearing a white, button-down shirt that—oddly, considering the setting—

contained very little dirt and was complemented by a shimmering red tie. She ran her hand through her hair and smiled at him, daintily dropping her eyes and lifting them delicately back to his. He raised both his eyebrows up and dropped them in rapid succession. Her smile deepened.

"For our newest guests," Fenris said, "we should go over the rules one more time. The penalty, the rest of us will remember, is steep."

The crowd moaned and laughed the way they had before. Angela picked up a sword. It was heavier than she expected, but not too heavy. She picked up a shield, a wooden, blocky thing that was bound in a leather wrapper for reasons she didn't understand. As Fenris began to reiterate the rules, she shrugged and tossed the shield back to the ground.

James was staring at her.

"He who would save his life will lose it," Fenris said.

As he continued, Angela smoothed her dress and silently thanked Babs for not insisting that they hunker down in a style that required heels. The man in the red power tie was still smiling at her. Angela put her free hand on her waist and swayed her hips as she strode toward him, criss-crossing her steps to accentuate the catlike sway of her gait.

The man looked her up and down with a hungry grin she approached. "For Freya," he breathed.

Fenris introduced Loki again. Gordon's voice echoed in her head. Loki hated to have his moments ruined. Angela tightened her grip on the hilt of her sword.

"Angela," James said, starting to follow her, "we need to stick together. We need to keep our group tight so that—"

"High Spokesman and Lord of the Forge," Fenris boomed. "Francis Gelasius Loki!"

Angela thrust her sword forward through the red tie. Through the hilt, she felt the pop and scrape of the blade dragging through bone and cartilage. The corners of her mouth stretched her lips in an involuntary smile. She grinned at the man as he sank to his knees and claimed her sword back from his chest.

"FOR FREYA!"

The cheers of the crowd at the first death spoiled the silence and she caught Loki's glare as he looked down at her. She smiled at him as rejoined the others, holding her bloodied sword up and meeting Loki's eyes.

"Let the game begin," Loki said over the commotion.

\*\*\*

Jeremy stared at Angela as she made her way back to the group. His heart felt like it was going to leap out of his chest and he tasted stomach acid.

James was staring at her as well. "What the hell was that?"

"If Loki wants me to be Freya," Angela said, swinging her sword in a circle and looking out over the arena floor, "I'm not going to do it on his terms. I won't be his fucking tool."

"Form a circle," Gordon said. "Yell out if someone is coming your way. We'll need to disable them first so we can take turns on the killing blow."

Jeremy stared at the sword in his hand. "This is insane."

"Maybe," Damien said, "but you don't have a choice. Stay by me."

Jeremy looked up into the lights and the shouting faces. He watched as a man in the crowd pumped his fist into the air from the stands and accented curses with sharp movements of his reddening face. Jeremy thought the man might have been watching football or screaming a political rant at a pundit's smug television face. Was Beth in the crowd somewhere? Was she on the arena floor? Jeremy looked at the corpse that Angela had left behind only twenty feet from him.

Jeremy watched a large man bring his sword down hard on the back of a smaller man's head, leaving it embedded in his skull and leaning over to pick up another sword from the ground. The man caught Jeremy's gaze grinned as he ran toward them. A thrill of nauseous excitement shot up Jeremy's spine.

"We've got one," Jeremy said.

"Got it." Damien stepped forward from the circle and narrowly dodged the man's swinging sword. Damien dropped to his knees and dragged the sword across the man's heels with his singular hand. The man screamed and crumpled to the ground, legs kicking uselessly as they lacked the leverage to hold him up.

"Do it," Damien said.

The man groaned and sputtered into the dirt. His legs twitched and his ankles bled.

Jeremy stared at him. "I don't think—"

"Do it!"

Jeremy closed his eyes and jabbed his sword into the man's back as hard as he could. He felt it glide between ribs until it connected to the ground and Jeremy's sweating hands nearly slipped from the hilt.

"Good," Damien said. "Everyone has to kill."

Andrew pummeled another attacker with his shield and skewered his sword downward between the man's collarbone and neck. He smiled. That expression on his face was more than a little unpleasant.

From the corner of Jeremy's eye, he saw another group approaching. His heart sank as he saw a snarling brunette woman lock eyes on his. Damien saw them too.

"Hold," Damien said.

The groups clashed. A man carried two swords and swung them wildly at Damien. Damien stepped forward, ducked left and smacked the attacker across the face with the broad, flat part of his blade. As the man stumbled, Jeremy swung his sword and brought it down as hard as he could against the attacker's knee. Jeremy could barely breathe as the man screamed. His heart pounded the inside of his rib cage. He almost emptied his stomach.

"Lance," Damien said as he turned to fight another attacker. "Your turn."

Lance stared down at the groaning man, frozen. The sword in his hand bobbed up and down as he shook in place.

"Lance!" Damien said again.

A man and a woman careened toward Jeremy, both

wearing crazed smiles and flashing their teeth as they brandished their swords. Damien stepped in and slashed across the man's back, then buried his blade in the woman's shoulder. He ducked her desperate return slash and spun on his heels, leaving his sword where it was. He landed his palm squarely on the woman's face twisted his whole body, throwing her headfirst into the ground.

"Somebody get their hands dirty, goddammit!" he shouted, picking up one of the woman's dropped swords.

Lance stared down at the dazed woman and the man with the ruined knee. He didn't move.

Jeremy watched as Damien dove at Lance. Beth's brother dropped his sword, grabbed Lance's wrist, and threw the man, sword-first, into the abdomen of the woman now struggling to her feet. Lance's eyes widened and he screamed, a Wilhelm sort of shriek that rose to a mountainous pitch before cutting off in moral terror. The woman glared up at him until her gaze turned flat and she sank to the dirt.

Jeremy tightened his grip on the wooden shield, feeling his wedding ring cut into his middle finger, and bashed it into the head of the man with the ruined knee. The man sank to the ground, unconscious. For a brief moment, Jeremy hoped Beth was out there watching. The fear was dissipating. He was going to *survive*, goddammit, and he was going to find her.

Gordon's foe was a man roughly Andrew's size, dwarfing the old cowboy and bearing down on him with repeated, two-handed blows of a sword. Gordon held on with both hands as the attacker rained blows on his sword, old muscles bulging as he tried desperately to keep it up. Jeremy dove forward and stabbed the attacker in the chest. He stared into the man's wide eyes as he fell.

"I had him," Gordon said with a grim smile.

"I had him first," Jeremy said as he freed his sword. His second kill was easier than the first, but he still tasted stomach acid and his legs felt weak.

"Either way," Gordon said, "don't do that again. My sword is still clean."

Andrew crushed another attacker's throat with his own shield.

Gordon threw himself, sword held in both hands over his head, into a smaller man who narrowly ducked the old man's swing. They cracked swords against each other. Gordon dodged left, then right. Then his attacker spun and Gordon lunged, miscalculating his momentum. Jeremy watched as the attacker's sword wedged itself between the old man's eyes. Gordon collapsed, his sharp eyes running dull.

The crowd booed.

Damien leaped into the air and swung his sword wide, lopping the lower jaw from the face of Gordon's attacker. The man screamed and clutched his face desperately.

Damien looked around. "Who hasn't killed?"

They all held up bloody swords.

Jeremy stared down at the old, dead cowboy. A deep gash nearly split his face down the middle. Wide, gray eyes showed no signs of closing on their own, and Jeremy thought about fixing that until Andrew shook his head and pointed to the doorway that would give entry to the death goddess in a few minutes.

They reformed the circle. There were some tense moments of eye contact with prisoners in other groups, but the overall movement of the battle had stopped.

Clapping echoed from the balcony above.

"Well done," Loki said, smiling down at them. "Very well done. You have earned your place here. Except, of course, for a few of you."

The crowd cheered louder than they had during the entire battle.

Loki waited for the crowd to calm down before continuing. "I counted eight cowards."

"I counted ten!" came a voice from the audience. The crowd laughed.

Loki smiled darkly and the owner of the dissenting voice was lifted into the air by a tendril of shadow and tossed into the arena, where he was caught midair by another. The crowd went silent.

"Nine cowards," Loki relented.

Jeremy saw two fighters in another group with clean swords. They held each other and prayed as eight more tendrils shot downward. Two of those tendrils grabbed the pair and lifted them by their necks. Jeremy watched, powerless to help as they struggled for breath above him. After a few agonizing minutes of feet kicking the air, they were still.

"Let us pray," Loki said, "for the fallen."

The door closest to Jeremy's group swung open and Hel made her way to the center of the floor. The chained woman was still wearing her wedding dress. From his vantage point much closer than the balcony from which he had first seen her, Jeremy could see a strange skin condition that was attacking the left side of her face that made it look fifty years older than the right. Streaks of white weaved through her long black hair and her bright blue eyes shimmered with a hint of tears as she winced with every other step. As she passed Jeremy, she caught his gaze and he held his breath until she looked away. That look felt like a shot of ice water.

The woman lifted her arms and the nine dead prisoners floated above her. The woman's hair turned jet black and shimmered. Her skin smoothed she stood straight instead of hunching over. When she flipped her wrists, her hair lost its shine and turned gray all at once. Her skin became papery and her eyes bulged. Her chains shuddered as she almost fell over.

The bodies of the nine cowards dropped to the ground and the corpses of the slain men and women around Jeremy gasped and began to move. He looked at the two men he had killed, who stood and nodded to him before running back to their respective groups

"For Heimdall," one of the men said quietly.

That coldness in Jeremy's gut returned as his sense of guilt was stolen from him. Loki had called this a game, and it was already beginning to feel like one.

Jeremy looked down and raised an eyebrow when the

corpse of the man Angela had killed before Loki began the official battle remained still. She didn't look at the body.

Gordon coughed and slowly rose to his feet, the split in his face zippering shut, and he shuffled over to join the rest of them. The man who killed him also stood silently, his jaw now reformed, and rejoined his group on the other side of the arena.

Loki nodded at the woman and she turned, dragging her chains out through the same door. The crowd cheered and clapped, and Loki clapped with them. Then Fenris took the stand.

"Let us pray."

\*\*\*

James twirled a fork between his fingers. "So what's death like?"

Jeremy watched him for a moment, then went back to poking at his rice and beans. The metal bowl clacked against the wooden table and the fork scraped the inside of it in a way that made him shiver. He tasted the dish, teeth carefully crushing tasteless piles of mush. Something small cracked and he hoped it wasn't a bug.

"As far as I can tell," Gordon said, "it's not much of anything."

James picked a bean skin out of his teeth. "Great."

Jeremy scratched the back of his head and his hair squeaked. They had been led to a room full of showers after the battle, where individual stalls had formed themselves with the same architectural fluidity that converted the cell block to a dining room and back again.

The water had been hot, one of the odd comforts that was afforded to them in the otherwise cheerless imprisonment, and it had helped with the intense muscle soreness he had felt after the battle.

During the shower, he was struck with the image of the soldier's suicide again. For some reason, it bothered him more than the men he had killed on the arena floor. He could barely picture the faces of those men, and it had only been a few hours since the fight. In contrast, he could have drawn the pattern of black smoke emerging from beneath the lip of the soldier's helmet from memory. He could have reenacted the position of the soldier's body on the floor.

Although Jeremy had seen no one enter his stall during the shower, his clothes had been replaced with a brown prison uniform. On top of the uniform, there had been a razor, a mirror, and a small, wooden bowl of shaving cream. When Jeremy finished shaving, the razor had evaporated into thin air along with the bowl and the mirror. That kind of thing was becoming less disturbing.

Gordon scratched his chin, which was as free of stubble as Jeremy's. "It's interesting that Hel is Loki's prisoner, though. She's his daughter. Everything in the underworld is under her control."

Andrew nodded. "Capturing her is nonsense. They made a deal and Loki lied. I don't see another explanation. It also explains Garm's presence."

Jeremy looked at Damien, who stared silently into his empty bowl. The rest of them had been served the same meal, all poking at a tasteless heap of cheap nutrition. Damien had received another serving of raw meat, which he had eaten in just a few bites.

"Why does that explain Garm?" James said.

Gordon swallowed another mouthful of rice and beans. "Garm is Hel's guard dog. He works for Loki because his mistress is trapped here. The prophecies predicted that he would be freed from Niflheim, but he probably never thought he would spend his days in yet another prison until Tyr caught up to him."

Damien's eyes shot to the mountain man.

Andrew met his gaze. "It is prophesied that Tyr and Garm will kill each other in Ragnarok. All of our deaths are predetermined. Fenris will devour Odin. The fire giant Surtr will kill Freyr. Heimdall and Loki will kill each other."

Jeremy had already read that, but he didn't particularly like hearing it again. He was hoping that Loki was wrong about him. If prophecy was a real thing, he didn't want any part of it.

Gordon nodded. "If I know Loki, he's looking for a way around that."

Andrew uttered a sharp, low laugh. The group stared at him and he finished his bowl in silence.

"Freya doesn't have a clear role, unfortunately." Gordon looked at Angela.

Angela shook her head and shoved a pile of rice into her mouth. She was wearing a brown prison uniform as well, but she had kept her green dress and wore it tied around her waist like an emerald belt. "This is all insane. I don't care *what* we've seen. It doesn't prove a thing."

"That may be," Gordon said, "but I think Loki will be happy to prove it to you by the time this is over."

\*\*\*

You have done well, Garm. You may take an hour for prayer and reflection.

Garm tapped his smart phone and the door unlocked. He grabbed the handle of the steel door and pulled it gently open. The rich, dark stain of the wooden room greeted his eyes as he crossed the threshold. His desk, a magnificent mahogany, dominated the room. A cheap, aluminum cot rested against the far wall.

On the other end of the room, three candles surrounded a stone bust of a wolf. Its jaws grinned to reveal sharp teeth and jagged, rocky ridges created the appearance of matted fur. A mirror hung from the wall behind the bust.

One candle was burned nearly to the ground. The other two had never been lit.

Garm sat down in front of the bust. He touched his index finger to the middle of the wolf's snout and ran it back between the creature's eyes. He smiled at it.

Let us pray.

He let out a sob through his smile, a harrowed, trembling sort of praise that echoed in his throat. Then he massacred his cry with a dozen razor sharp breaths and squeezed his eyes shut as he forced that despair back into the recesses of his mind. His reflection glared at him with its one visible, pale blue eye.

Inklings of Master's Plan tickled the outskirts of his consciousness. Whispers of a thousand tricks and a million thoughtless soldiers barricaded him within the guard dog's identity. He would do as he was told. Master was a good master. Garm was a good Garm. Master's Yolk was easy, compared to His Sword.

You have done well, Garm.

Master was not going to throw him away. Garm was a useful Garm.

Let us pray.

Garm let out another cry. He lifted his silver eye patch and looked at himself in the mirror. The blue in his concealed eye was slowly darkening into blackness. He returned the eye patch and hugged himself, shivering against sharp winds that existed only in his memory.

He spoke.

*There is a dog; his name is Garm.*
*He raises every false alarm.*
*Given to shadow, and to the storm,*
*He feeds the fire with his scorn.*
*The Leavings of the Wolf, fears he,*
*Who rages there for all to see.*
*Shudder now, for when he dies,*
*Death will hide and gods will rise.*

# Chapter 8

## THE INCONSIDERATE DEATH OF
## JEREMY COLESON

"We'll need to get a crib and some baby clothes," Beth said, putting two fingers into the air. "*Ohmygod*, we're going to have to buy so many diapers."

Jeremy rubbed her back as she looked through the catalog. He brought his hand to the nape of her neck and toyed with a few curls of blonde hair that were hanging out of place in front of her ear. Then he massaged her neck with his thumb on one side and fingers on the other, eliciting a phlegmy sort of *heeee* from her lips along with a crinkly-eyed smile.

"You know," the shadow said, "it's interesting."

"What is?" Jeremy said.

Beth looked at him. "What's that?"

"Nothing," Jeremy told her.

"It's interesting," the shadow said, "that you never dream about your real self. Your dreams always center around her."

Jeremy felt a tickle in his throat, turned his head and coughed in the direction opposite Beth.

She flipped the page of the catalog. "How long do you think baby food stays good to eat? We should probably stock up, just in case, and it's cheaper if we buy it in bulk."

Jeremy ran figure-eights on her shoulder blade.

The shadow tap danced on the wall. "Just in case what? She's probably not even alive, much less pregnant."

"I'm probably just being paranoid," Beth said. She smiled at Jeremy. "You know, in case there's some big end-of-the-world thing that happens."

"It's a bit late for that," the shadow said.

Beth gasped. "Oh! Jeremy, we're going to need to get some of those shower cap things for his onesies."

The shadow emerged from the wall, a solid, dark figure with features like fluid onyx. It crossed its legs and fell backwards onto the couch on the other side of the living room. It put its hands behind its head and smiled at them. Beth gave no reaction to it.

"We'll need to come up with a name soon," Jeremy said. His chest felt like someone was stepping on it.

She crinkled her nose. "What about Jeremy Junior? We could call him J.J."

"That's awful," the shadow said. It gathered its mouth to one side in annoyance.

Beth grinned. "It's actually not that bad. I'm not

*suggesting* it or anything. But it's not the worst thing I've ever heard."

"Pass," Jeremy said. "Nobody's naming a kid after me."

Beth gave a staccato shriek of a laugh and turned the page. There were five models of strollers on the next page, each offered in at least three colors. One doubled as a car seat, but Beth had already ruled it out because of its low safety rating. She turned the page again.

A tear rolled down Beth's cheek as she smiled.

The shadow shook his head. "It's almost like you're trying *not* to remember being Heimdall. Is it because of her?"

Jeremy said nothing.

The shadow looked at Beth and raised an eyebrow. Then he arched his back and beat the couch cushions with his fists, crying in laughter. "That would be funny, but I'm not buying the sentimental explanation."

"We should think about getting a minivan or an SUV," Beth said. "They use more gas, but I think the safety ratings are supposed to be better."

"Eh," the shadow said. "It's not going to matter in a few minutes."

The shadow waved its arms and Beth stopped in the middle of turning the page. A few strands of her hair had been in the process of falling from behind her ear. Now they were suspended motionless in the air. The shadow stood up and crossed the space between them. It stuck its face in Jeremy's and sniffed.

Jeremy barely contained a fury that exploded within

him.

"I was so sure about you," it said. It breathed a heavy breath that bounced off Jeremy's face. The smell of nursing home halitosis announced its presence. "Maybe I miscalculated. What do you think, Heimdall?"

"Leave us alone," Jeremy said.

"Well, that's not an option. You're already my guest."

Jeremy lifted his hand and pushed the shadow's face away from his. Stubble scraped his fingers as he did. He wanted to split that face in two with a sword.

Beth didn't notice the movement.

"You should also consider why you never told her about me," the shadow said, standing up and crossing its arms. "I'm a little offended, if I'm being honest. If you don't tell her, I'm going to have to."

Jeremy didn't say anything.

"Alright," the shadow said. "Sweet dreams, Heimdall." The shadow pushed its face into Jeremy's again, rubbing its stubbly, smelly, pork-rind pudgy mouth against his cheek and ear. "I'll see you tomorrow."

The shadow disappeared and Jeremy looked out the window. The world outside caught fire and a wave of heat and light shattered the living room.

***

Jeremy awoke in his cell. Weeks had passed since he had first arrived at the prison. In that time, the shadow had mostly disappeared from Jeremy's waking life and taken to invading his dreams instead. More often than not, the shadow complained that Jeremy dreamed about Beth too much. Apparently, it found his wife boring.

Since his arrival, he had taken part in a dozen battles and lost track of the number of men he killed. So far, he had avoided dying in the arena. That was quickly becoming his only goal, to survive by any means necessary and find his way back to Beth.

Lance, on the other hand, counted his kills every night before bed. By virtue of sharing a cell with the man, Jeremy was painfully aware that Lance had killed twenty-three men and five women. Only two of those, a man and a woman, had been denied resurrection through Hel's magic. Lance prayed for forgiveness over those two regularly, even though Jeremy didn't think his cellmate was to blame. Jeremy, after all, couldn't remember how many of his kills had been permanent. Even so, Lance claimed to have memorized every detail of their faces.

Garm made his way into the cell block with a loud crash and tapped the smart phone, melting the walls. He gave them an arthritic smile, which received no help from his visible eye. "You've been invited to join Loki in the arena."

Following him through the broken tunnel of cell doors, they made their way up a set of stairs, down a straight hallway, and down a spiraling staircase that swung wide and upward again when they finally came to the bottom. A few more turns and they came to a doorway. They always seemed to take random passages until they reached their destination, and Jeremy suspected that the architecture changed every time just to make things complicated. It seemed like something Loki would do.

The roar of the crowd flooded into the passage when the door opened and Jeremy stared at Loki in his purple toga and laurel crown. Loki stared back at him with a gaze like a hawk's and winked, then gathered his mouth to one side. It was very similar to the expression that the three-dimensional shadow had made in Jeremy's dream.

They sat in their thrones and the crowd cheered. He heard the swell of a declaration from the prisoners over the rest of the noise. "For Heimdall!"

Fenris took the podium. "Welcome, friends."

Cheers and applause erupted again on cue. Fenris bowed his head several times to the crowd. He turned his head and grinned at Loki, who nodded without changing expression. Fenris always looked at Loki for approval, like a dog bringing him a newspaper or asking to play fetch with a tennis ball.

"For your entertainment tonight," Fenris said, "we have something a little different."

Cheers rose again, but Fenris patted the air on either side of him to quiet them down. Loki adjusted his seating and rubbed his temples. Something was different about the way he looked down at the crowd and fidgeted.

"Tonight," Fenris said, "our champions will each choose a foe from the battle field. Winner survives."

Loki flicked his hand as Fenris gestured, and a hail of weaponry shimmered through the air until it finally crashed to the ground. Swords, shields, meat cleavers, and hooks bounced and caught the light as they hit the dust.

"I'd like to introduce you to tonight's champions," Fenris said.

Jeremy leaned forward as he watched the prisoners making their way onto the arena floor. Jeremy always looked for Beth, but was never sure what he felt when he didn't see her. Numbness gripped him and he tried to focus on the match. This was a new kind of fight, not the free-for-all that they were becoming used to.

"Before we begin," Fenris said, "I'd like to offer a prayer."

Fenris prayed for judgment. He prayed for the Lord to make them soldiers of heaven, giants of hell fire, saviors of the human race. He prayed that the sins of the world would be washed clean in the blood of the ram. Jeremy wondered who in the crowd took meaning from the word *ram* used in place of *lamb*, which was the usual verbiage of Fenris's prayer.

"Amen," Fenris said.

James sat back in his throne and rubbed his temples as the cheers erupted again. He caught Jeremy's gaze and shook his head. Damien sat back as well, eyes on the robed man at the podium.

Fenris turned around and winked a yellow eye at Loki before continuing. Then he went over the rules. No clean weapons. Only one of you may survive. Only one opponent allowed this match, and multiple kills would be punished. Watch out for the tigers. The crowd laughed and moaned at that, gleefully rolling it over on their own tongues.

"Francis Gelasius Loki!" Fenris said, gesturing behind him to Loki.

Loki stood up and clapped. "Let the game begin!"

The prisoners picked up weapons from the ground. Some began circling each other immediately. Others lunged at the nearest victim. This tactic proved successful for some prisoners, who hacked their opponents down in a rain of blows without thought to defense. The early victors smiled happily up at Loki, following the rule not to take on a second opponent. Several bowed to him. One yelled "For Thor!"

Other pairs of sparring partners clashed against each other. Some duels were over quickly, while others involved long periods of ducking and dodging until one or both fighters started to get tired. At this point the duel was essentially over. As Jeremy watched, one man fell to his knees in exhaustion and shouted "For Heimdall!"

His opponent buried a cleaver in his head.

Jeremy saw Damien lean forward again as one duel came uncomfortably close to the line of guards surrounding the arena. The two men hacked at each other until one finally backed hard into a soldier. Jeremy winced, half-expecting the soldier to just shoot both of them. The soldier only stepped backward to keep his balance and returned to his former position, giving no other sign that he had noticed.

There was a growl and a jingle as a man and a woman fought each other with hook and hammer near the center, and a blur of orange and black shot out of the ground. The chained tiger leaped through the trap door beneath the dust toward the pair, who had come close enough to rouse it. It loped forward and pounced on the woman, sending the sound of her bones cracking to Jeremy's ears.

Another tiger bounded out from another trap door and roared as it swiped an ax-wielding man across the face, knocking him several feet across the stone and pouncing on him. The trap doors fell shut behind the massive cats, leaving them above to roar menacingly at the opponents of their prey. The survivors, panic-stricken at the fact that their weapons were still clean, charged forward and were devoured as well.

The crowd thundered with cries of happiness.

Three more tigers emerged from beneath the floor. Two burly men with hooks tried to take one of the tigers down, but their fantasy ended after two swipes of its massive paws.

After a few more minutes, the arena was dotted with individual fighters standing over corpses. Loki clapped his hands and stood up from his throne. As the fighters dropped their weapons and looked up at him, he didn't smile.

"Friends," he said with a solemn face, "you have done well. You have earned your place here. Let us pray for the fallen."

Jeremy raised an eyebrow. Loki hadn't counted his cowards, if there were any.

The crowd fell silent and bowed their heads. Jeremy heard fabric ripping as one of the tigers dug into its meal.

The moment of silence stretched on for ages, broken only by the scrape of tooth against bone.

"I have often struggled with doubt," Loki said, breaking the silence. "Sometimes, the silence consumes me unless I fill it. Sometimes, I have to fill it with fire and with blood. Other times, I can fill it with drink."

Jeremy stared at him. It wasn't even a prayer, just a strange moment of what seemed like humanity. Jarring as it was, Jeremy couldn't see the trick behind it.

Loki paused for a moment as he looked out over the silent crowd. "Sometimes our prayers go unanswered. I wish it weren't so, but sometimes there are no reasons why some of us live and some of us die. Sometimes we can only keep our course and watch those around us fall."

Jeremy scanned the crowd. Even from here, he could see some heads nodding.

Loki nodded. "Sometimes the dead stay dead. This is one of those times, my friends."

He let his words hang in the air, floating on the silence from the crowd. Jeremy looked at the corpses on the arena floor. He watched the faces of the victors fall from their satisfied smiles as they realized their opponents would not be rising from the dead. Some dropped their weapons. One man let out a shrill scream.

Others wore smiles that deepened when they caught Loki's meaning. One man in brown clothes soaked in blood lifted the hook and axe he carried in either hand as he kicked his opponent's corpse in the ribs. "For Loki!"

Loki turned and took his seat again without another

word. Fenris took the podium.

"Praise be," Fenris said.

Loki fidgeted on his throne. When Fenris turned around, Loki spoke just loudly enough for Jeremy to hear. "Clear the bodies. The Royal Family fights the next battle."

\*\*\*

The tigers were still out of their trap doors, lying lazily in the dirt as they watched Jeremy and the others enter the arena floor. One tiger looked at Jeremy as he passed it, staring at him with blue eyes that had an oddly human shape to them. It shook its massive head and licked a bloody paw. Jeremy was sure, however, that the trap doors were in different places than they had been when he had watched from his throne above. They were primarily on the outskirts of the arena now.

"For your *further* entertainment tonight," Fenris said from the podium as the cheers died down, "the Royal Family is going to war!"

The crowd erupted. Jeremy looked at the others. Damien was the only one who met his gaze, giving him a disinterested shrug. Gordon and Andrew were digging through clumps of weaponry, feeling sword tips and edges for sharpness with their fingers. Spiked shields had been dropped atop the weapons already littering the ground.

James and Angela had already selected their weapons. Angela held two meat cleavers, swinging them both in a circle with a flip of her wrists. James was holding a cleaver of his own, a spiked shield in his other hand. Both of them were scanning the other prisoners on the arena floor.

"On this side of the stadium," Fenris said as he gestured to the hundred or so prisoners who had just entered, "the Royal Army under Odin's command. Absolute obedience is required until the battle is over, and anything less will be punished."

Jeremy picked up a sword and a spiked shield.

Fenris smiled. "The challenging army may now enter the arena."

The door at the far side of the floor clicked open a similar number of prisoners were escorted inside. Each of these prisoners were clothed entirely in black, with grinning steel masks that had wide eyes painted around small holes for vision. Despite the fearsome look of their masks, several were clearly pleading in vain with the guards.

The crowd gleefully booed the masked army.

"The rules are simple," Fenris said. "One army survives. The battle is not over until the every warrior of the defeated army draws his or her last breath. Beware the tigers."

Jeremy tightened his grip on his sword as the crowd erupted again.

The opposing army selected their weapons on the other side of the arena. The tigers looked at them calmly, disinterested. The one with human eyes put its head down on its paws and appeared to go to sleep.

Loki stood from his throne as the noise lowered and Fenris took his seat. "Let the game begin!"

"Form lines," Gordon barked. "Shields front!"

Someone shouted "For Odin!"

"Cleavers behind!" Gordon shouted. "Gather weapons and prepare to throw!"

Similar shouts came from leaders in the masked army. Both sides shuffled their way to some kind of irregular formation and Gordon ran across the rough lines to straighten them out. Jeremy took his position on the front line, spiked shield squarely in front of him and his sword ready to jab. Gordon gave the order to hold and wait for the opposite side to charge. Seconds carried heavily into minutes as each side stared at the other. Jeremy wrapped himself in numbness like armor.

"Fine," Loki's voice rang in Jeremy's ears.

A dozen prisoners shot into the air from the floor of the arena, struggling in desperation at the shadowy tendrils that wrapped around their necks. The tendrils shook once, whipping the prisoners upward and then down hard onto the floor. Their motionless bodies bounced and cracked against the stone.

Loki's voice rang again. "Thirty seconds before twelve more cowards die."

"Hold!" Gordon shouted.

The crowd's cheer dissipated to a dull roar as the opposing armies stared at each other. Jeremy counted thirty seconds.

Gordon cracked another order. "*Hold!*"

The man right behind Jeremy was whipped into the air along with eleven other prisoners, then slammed hard to the ground.

The opposing army couldn't wait any longer. Someone barked an order and the masked prisoners ran headlong toward Jeremy and the others.

"HOLD!" Gordon barked.

A few in the masked army tripped and fell over the bodies of the prisoners who had already been executed by the shadow tendrils. The masked army continued over them without slowing. Gordon held his hand in the air, in line with the cleaver-wielding bunch. Jeremy felt a twinge of panic stir in the back of his head as he checked behind him to make sure no one there was holding a spiked shield. The front line was pushed back in a charge, wasn't it? All he had to go on were movies.

Gordon threw his hand forward. "Throw your cleavers!"

"For Odin!"

Cutlery rocketed forward from the Royal Army. Some hit opponents squarely in the torso, dropping them immediately. Others bounced on the ground and spun, taking off limbs. Even as a quarter of the masked army fell, the charge didn't slow. Jeremy stared at the wide, painted eyes on the masks. He remembered reading that those markings were supposed to look fearsome. Those wide eyes looked more afraid as they drew closer.

"Charge!" Gordon shouted.

The impact knocked Jeremy off his feet, sending him careening into the fifth line. The body that pinned him down was skewered by his shield, pressing it hard against

Jeremy's ribs. He strained to free himself as piles of men crashed into each other nearby. The smell of copper on the ground was thick.

A meaty hand reached under his shield and lifted it so that Jeremy could squirm away.

"There's more to do," Andrew said. "Don't die yet."

"Thanks for the advice," Jeremy said. He picked up his dropped sword and a nearby cleaver.

After the initial charge, the armies were back to skirmishing in small groups. Twelve more prisoners flew into the air and were struck down by Loki's shadows. One corpse bounced into Jeremy's path and he had to leap over it as he ran to rejoin the battle.

*\*\**

James chased Angela around the perimeter of the arena, keeping an eye out for overzealous, masked fighters. Angela had cut from the lines after the initial charge, once her cleavers were stained.

"Get back to the fighting," she said as she knelt to take the mask from a corpse. She lifted it enough to expose a man's chin, then stood up and ran to another body. She picked up a spiked shield as she stood.

"Yeah," James said. "I'm not doing that."

"Suit yourself," Angela said. She turned to a group of masked prisoners and yelled. "Babs!"

They charged at her.

"Jesus," James said as he stood next to her, facing them.

As the group charged, James dodged left and Angela dodged right. They ducked and slashed with their cleavers, hacking at their opponents' legs. One of the fighters dove at Angela, but she smashed her shield into his gut, driving the spikes into him. He collapsed.

When they were down, Angela checked under their masks. When she peaked underneath the third mask, James saw a clump of platinum blonde hair. Loki's shadows tossed twelve more prisoners to their deaths.

***

"Bravest of men," Damien shouted as he plunged his sword into a masked opponent. "Warriors of the Forge! Undead soldiers of Ragnarok, to fury!"

The prisoners around him cheered and shouted. Damien urged them onward, which wasn't difficult now that they had the superior numbers and were slowly surrounding the opposing army. He ripped his sword from where it was trapped and swung it over his head, gesturing with his stumped arm for balance to bring the sword down on another opponent's collarbone.

The masked army pushed back, surging forward so that Damien's group had to retreat slowly to the edge of the arena. Faceless guards lined the walls.

Damien killed two more fighters and barked more orders, until he found himself next to the soldiers. In the same motion, he tore his sword free from a falling warrior and plunged it into a guard's chest. He stared into the soldier's opaque visor as a gloved hand caressed the blade and went limp.

Another guard took two steps to stand in exactly the place where the other had died, standing over the armored corpse as if nothing had happened. Damien freed his sword and plunged it into this soldier's chest as well. Another took that soldier's place. He killed the third soldier and another stood over the three bodies.

\*\*\*

Twelve more prisoners flew into the air, some in the middle of fighting. Jeremy looked up at Loki, leaning back on his throne and staring up into the shadows above the arena. The battle was nowhere near over, and Loki didn't seem to be following any kind of rules when considering who to execute. He wasn't even watching them fight.

Jeremy refused to die that way, snuffed out meaninglessly because Loki was bored.

He shouted. "I challenge you, Loki. You want your fight with Heimdall? Come and have it!"

"Hello, Heimdall."

Jeremy turned and saw the toga-wearing god, smiling at him on the floor of the arena. Loki brandished a sword that glowed hot red, as if it had been pulled straight from a forge, and flew at him. Jeremy dodged left and met the first strike with his sword. Loki grinned and sparks flew as Jeremy lunged at him.

Jeremy swung again and again. Loki dodged and swiped with his own sword, parrying the attacks with ease.

It wasn't apparent to Jeremy's ears whether the crowd was silent, or if his pounding heartbeat was drowning out their shouts. Loki turned and smashed his sword into a cleaver that sailed through the air. Jeremy and Loki both turned to look at Andrew, standing ready with a cleaver in either hand.

Loki fought both of them at once, dancing from one to the other in a blur. "You're nowhere near ready for this fight," he said, stopping between them and grinning. "None of you are." Then he stopped in his tracks and turned to the edge of the stadium. "And what exactly do you think you're doing?"

Jeremy and Andrew looked in the direction that Loki was facing. Damien stood in front of a pile of a dozen dead guards. He stabbed another in the chest, forcing the sword through armor that Jeremy thought should have been harder than it was. The guard fingered the blade gingerly before falling to his knees, and another moved forward to take his place.

"Your soldiers don't fight back," Damien said.

"Well, of course they don't," Loki said. "Not right *now.*" He looked up at the stage. "Garm, get down here. Send for Hel."

Loki turned his attention back and dove at Jeremy. Jeremy lifted his sword and Loki swatted it down with his own. He tried to lift it again and Loki swatted it a second time. Then Loki spun and brought his sword down hard, pounding the weapon out of Jeremy's hands in a shower of sparks. He spun and cracked the broad side of his sword against the back of Jeremy's knees, searing his skin and sending him to the ground next to his blade. Tendrils of pain wormed their way through Jeremy's legs from the blistering welts. Loki spun his sword and gripped the blade without reacting to the touch of hot steel, then brought the hilt down hard on Jeremy's back.

Jeremy cried out and gasped for air. He picked up his sword and shook in agony as he turned his broken body to face Loki.

A shot rang out and Jeremy gasped again. His chest burned. Loki shrugged, tilting a handgun to the side for a moment, then aimed and shot him again. He shot him a third time.

The burning in Jeremy's chest became an inferno and he felt like he was trying to breathe underwater. The light of the arena dimmed and his vision tunneled around Loki's smiling face. His lungs ached as he struggled for air, but the world closed around him and his mind swam in darkness. He felt a fourth bullet tear into his forehead.

It was peaceful, here on Jeremy's couch. Beth was out somewhere, maybe the grocery store. She was safe. He could just get some sleep and he would make sure something funny was on television to take her mind off this whole Iran war thing. Right after this nap. Maybe something to eat first, if he could just summon the energy to go get a snack out of the—

The darkness lifted and he gasped with working lungs.

*\*\**

There was complete and utter silence in the arena. James turned in time to see Loki shoot Jeremy in the chest. He saw Jeremy sputter and gasp. Then he saw Loki shoot him in the face.

The door closest to them clicked open and Hel made her way into the arena. Loki tapped his foot twice and picked the woman up with his shadows, depositing her next to him rather than waiting for her to walk. He grabbed the chain that connected to her collar and yanked forward. She grimaced as Loki yanked again and gestured to Jeremy.

Jeremy gasped and coughed. He spat out some blood, but he no longer bled from the wounds in his chest. His face was whole again, the trail of blood evaporating from his forehead. Loki shot him another three times, let him die, and yanked on the chain until the woman cried out and Jeremy gasped again.

"Alright," Loki said as he turned to Damien. "I didn't put that much effort into the soldiers. They're *soldiers*. You wouldn't believe how cheap these guys are to make, and I don't even really need them. Here."

A dozen soldiers rocketed into the air. They didn't slow until they hit the ceiling. They plummeted through the air and slammed to the ground, kicking up a cloud of dust. As it settled, Loki shrugged again.

Loki looked at Damien. "I'd like you to kill Garm. Would you do that for me, Tyr?"

"Master?" Garm said.

Loki nodded. "Hurry up, then."

Damien turned slowly. As he started to walk, Garm drew a pistol.

"Now Garm, do no harm." Loki grinned. "We aren't to hurt our guests."

Garm holstered his pistol and nodded. He straightened himself. James could see his blue eye dim slightly, reflecting less light than it had just a second ago.

"That's a good Garm."

Garm's shoulders rolled back and he took a deep, calming breath. An oddly placid, smooth-featured expression settled on his face.

"Nice Garm."

Garm smiled. Damien pivoted his wrist to swing his sword in a circle at his side.

"That's a lovely—"

"Master?"

"Wonderful Garm."

Garm's eyes rolled in his head. His hand repeatedly twitched in the direction of his pistol, but he didn't touch the gun. Damien was only ten feet from him and moving at a full run.

"Master?"

The word stung James, reminding him of the voice he used with Blackjack at home.

Damien plunged his sword into Garm's stomach and ripped the blade free immediately. Garm's posture imploded and he leaned forward as Damien slashed across the man's neck without slowing, and a spray of blood sailed free. Garm clutched his throat and fell.

"Thank you, Tyr." Loki leaned over, picked up Garm's fallen smart phone, and tossed it at Jeremy. He grinned and addressed the entire arena with a booming voice. "Your freedom is at hand, if you can get out of here. Make it interesting."

Loki stretched his arms out in a grand gesture and

bowed to the prisoners on the arena floor. He locked eyes with James in the middle of his bow, raised Alex's eyebrows twice, and turned to stone. A perfect statue of Alex, bowing in a toga and laurel crown, grinned up at him.

Damien stared at the statue.

The crowd surged and James watched them make their way into the prison halls, knocking over the soldiers who stood like mannequins in their way. Andrew picked up a gasping, stumbling Jeremy and was joined by Gordon and Damien as they made their way into a nearby doorway without looking back.

James knelt next to the body of the masked warrior with platinum blonde hair and lifted her mask. The woman was beautiful, her eyes closed peacefully and her lips still containing the slightest pout. He pictured her in a silver gown taking a wet drag on the cigarette and laying down a royal flush on the cheap plastic coffee table. Had it been a royal flush?

Angela spoke from behind him. "Friend of yours?"

He thought about touching Gloria Blanche's face, then thought better of it. "Yeah."

"I'm sorry."

The masked army was gathering again in the center of the arena.

"We need to go," James said.

They ran.

# Chapter 9

## A SMUGGLER'S KISS

PN600657
Command: Follow Silver.
132414G

The soldier followed the silver path up the stairs and down a spiral, through a straight hallway and up another spiral.

"Hurry up with that, Jeremy."

The soldier continued the path up the stairs.

"Nothing's labeled. It's just dots and lines. Garm must have had this whole system memorized to be able to use it."

PN600657
Command: Follow Cyan.
132514G

The white path was replaced with a cyan one, and the soldier continued to follow that upward.

"Shit," one of the voices said from farther up the stairway. "We've got some company."

The soldier followed the cyan path between prisoner R1H and prisoner R1TH. He passed prisoners R1O and R1TY.

Prisoner R1O put a hand on the soldier's shoulder. "Stop."

The soldier followed the path upward, taking a left turn down another straight hallway at the top and descending down a straight staircase.

PN600657
Command: Follow Aqua
132714G

The cyan path disappeared. The soldier turned around and followed the aqua path back up the straight staircase, taking a right at the straight hallway and descending down the spiral.

"He's back," said prisoner R1O.

"Perfect," said prisoner R1H. "I think I'm getting the hang of this. Andrew?"

The soldier felt several square blows to his abdomen. The soldier grunted but did not defend himself. He continued to follow the aqua path, but his progress was impaired.

Prisoner R1TH landed blows to the back of the soldier's knees, bringing him down on the stone steps. The prisoner took the soldier's rifle.

"Sorry," prisoner R1TH said quietly.

"Me too," prisoner R1H said. "I'll need your helmet."

Prisoner R1O pointed another gun at the soldier and fired.

\*\*\*

Jeremy pulled the helmet from the dead soldier's head. The man's eyes were still open. Those eyes were jet black and Jeremy shivered as he looked at them.

"Some kind of magic?" he said.

Jeremy's voice echoed in the black hallway. For a prison break, it was oddly quiet. This was the first soldier they had encountered since the mass exodus from the arena floor. The only sound aside from their own was the constant trickle of the waterfall flowing within the walls.

"Brainwashing." Gordon closed the soldier's eyes. "Their pupils dilate permanently as a result."

"You've seen them before?"

Gordon didn't respond.

"But I'm okay to put this on?" Jeremy held up the soldier's helmet.

Gordon shrugged.

Jeremy cringed. Whatever it took. Loki had already decided against killing him and being done with it. He put on the helmet.

The display was in English. Jeremy hoped that was because the soldier understood English and not because it detected the native language of the person using the helmet. The latter wouldn't have surprised him at this point, and if it knew what language he spoke, Jeremy didn't want to think about what else it might be doing while poking around in his mind.

Above Gordon's head, the designation R1O hung in the air. Andrew wore a crown of the designation R1TH, and Damien the designation R1TY. Odin, Thor, and Tyr perhaps. Jeremy had no idea what the R1 stood for.

Jeremy looked down at Garm's smart phone. A blue dot connected to three surrounding dots with thick blue lines. As Jeremy tapped one of the outlying dots, the display shifted and that dot moved to the center, surrounding itself with a dozen smaller dots connected the same way. The helmet's display, to Jeremy's disdain, didn't indicate anything about the dots.

"Well, he's got these," Damien said. He held up three cylindrical containers. "Tear gas."

"Could be useful." Gordon extended a hand. "Give me one."

Damien obliged. Jeremy tapped dots on Garm's smart phone until the display changed.

PN600657
Command: Follow Ruby
133114G

The glowing mist above Jeremy's head changed colors and a path appeared, starting from his position and lighting his way in dark red. Jeremy tapped more dots until it changed again.

PN600657
Command: Follow Crimson
133114G

The ruby path disappeared and a slightly darker red took its place. Jeremy squinted and shook his head. "Why in the hell would you make the colors so close to each other?"

"Doesn't matter," Gordon said. "Can you use it?"

"I can get a lot closer than before. You want to give this a try?"

Gordon shook his head. "Loki gave that to you, and he probably had a reason for it. I'm making sure we're ready for his next trick."

"What do you think that will be?"

"Anything he wants."

Gordon leaned down and pulled off the soldier's gloves, putting them on his own hands. He and Damien searched the rest of the soldier's body while Andrew moved from one end of the spiral staircase to the other to watch out for more soldiers. Damien put the soldier's armor on himself, not once mentioning the fact that he was struggling with one hand.

Gordon finished his search of the body, finding nothing else useful. "Let's move."

They went down the stairs, took a right and went

partially down a long, straight hallway. Three doors marred the smooth black of the hall on the right side and Gordon pressed his gloved palm to the panel next to one of them. They ducked inside a cell block.

"We're here to help," Gordon announced, running from one cell to the next and unlocking the doors. "Get out of here."

Prisoners spilled out of their cells, doing their best not to look at Jeremy wearing the soldier's helmet. Some cells were empty and others contained almost a dozen cramped people. Those who had been in the most crowded cells did their best to spread out from one another as they poured into the hallway. Soon, the cell block was empty. Jeremy wondered how many prisoners had been in their cells while Loki asked Damien to kill his henchman.

"Let's get the other two," Gordon said. "The more we can release, the better. If Loki gives the order I think he's about to, we're going to need some cover."

Jeremy narrowed his eyebrows. Whatever it took. "We need to find the others. They're supposed to play some kind of role here, right?"

"Assuming they're still alive," Gordon said. "And that depends on what Loki thinks is funny."

"Great," Jeremy said. Any hope of predicting what Loki wanted at this point was gone after the way he had ended the battle.

They released the prisoners in the next cell block. The one after that was empty.

They made their way down the rest of the straight

hallway, up another set of stairs, and released some more prisoners. They found two more empty cell blocks up another spiral, then released the prisoners from one more at the end of a straight hallway, dead-ending their path.

"Jeremy," Gordon said, "we're going to need a way out of here."

"You're welcome to give it a try." Jeremy tapped another sequence of dots.

PN600657
Command: Follow Fuchsia.
133714G

Jeremy took the lead, following the fuchsia path in the mist over their heads. They backtracked up and down stairs until the path took them to an intersection with a downward staircase and stopped dead at the wall. There was a panel on it, but no door.

Gordon pushed his gloved palm to the panel and a circular piece of black rock rotated inward and the stairs melted the walls, replaced by a flat surface that closed off all but an inch of the exit. Water spilled out into the space, a small trickle that became a flooding gush. They heard a few screams below and they watched the water level climb back up through the small opening.

Gordon whispered something and put his palm to the panel again. The water continued to flow.

"Turn it off," Jeremy said. "Shut it off now."

"I'm trying," Gordon said. He put his palm to the panel

again, to no effect.

Minutes passed and Jeremy closed his eyes, trying not to listen as the screams and shouts for help became silence. He shuddered. Finally, the passage morphed into stairs again and the water drained.

Jeremy looked down at the soaked stairwell. "He wasn't kidding about flooding the prison if things get out of hand."

Gordon nodded. "We're going to have to be careful not to fall into one of those traps. We're going to need more gloves. Jeremy?"

Jeremy breathed slowly and clenched his stomach against a rumbling nausea. "I'll see if I can get a few more soldiers to come this way."

Damien surveyed the downward stairs, pointing to a drowned soldier. "There's at least one pair of extra gloves down there."

PN600657
Command: Press forward.
Standing Order: Kill them all.
LO 0140114

"Guys," Jeremy said. "We're going to have a—"

Gunfire erupted in the hallways, followed by a collection of shouts and screams that echoed over and over against the rock. Jeremy listened to the terror repeat itself and felt cold.

"Get down!" Damien shouted.

Jeremy hit the floor along with the others, half-expecting to be riddled with bullets as soon as he did so. Seconds crawled as he watched both ends of the stairs. The gunfire continued, but not in their direction.

They moved slowly, cheerlessly aware that another group of soldiers could be around any corner. Jeremy tapped the dots on Garm's smart phone, but the display didn't change. Loki had activated some kind of override on the entire system.

"He commanded them to press forward," Jeremy shouted over the unrelenting cacophony. "Where is forward?"

"To the bottom," Gordon shouted back. "He's pressing the escaped prisoners to the bottom so that he can drown them and start over with new ones."

"What does that mean for us?"

"He might not care anymore."

They ducked into an empty cell block and waited while Jeremy tinkered with Garm's smart phone.

\*\*\*

James and Angela ran ahead of a group of prisoners through the black rock hallways, listening to the sound of gunfire get louder and softer again as they moved. They had both collected a few extra weapons from the arena before fleeing, and James could hear the metallic clack of two cleavers bouncing with every step Angela took. They hung from the green dress she wore as a belt, tucked where she could access them quickly. They ran up a spiral and down a straight hallway, and corkscrewed their way through four other passages until they came to an intersection where yet another winding staircase cut across their path.

All the while, the rush of water in the walls tickled his eardrums.

"Which way?" James said as he passed the intersection.

Angela shrugged and pointed. "That way."

*Surtr will smile upon your corpse, and shadows serenade your soul.*

James stopped in his tracks. He looked around for Loki or Fenris as Angela and the other prisoners stopped with him, but he saw no one else in the black hallway. Were the lights starting to dim?

*Surtr will smile upon your corpse, and shadows serenade your soul.*

Fuck.

He ran forward and the others followed him up another flight of stairs and down another spiral. The gunfire was farther away now, echoing just a little less in the hallways. It grew louder as he ran, then softer. He wondered if the crescendo and decrescendo meant that the soldiers were getting closer or if they were on the other side of the wall.

The next corner brought them to a pile of bodies, some prisoner and some soldier. Judging by their distorted faces, he figured they had been there for some time now. The soldiers still had their armor and their rifles.

"We ought to take those," Angela said.

"I'm not wearing a dead guy's helmet." James bent down and shook a dead soldier's shoulder. "I don't think we're getting the body armor off these guys either—I think that's rigor mortis."

Angela took the soldier's arm and put a foot on his shoulder. It crackled as she yanked upward on the arm. Then she did the same with the other. "Now try."

He took the soldier's helmet off and threw it aside without looking too hard at the face. It smelled like someone sneezed rotting meat into it. He pulled the soldier's armor and tunic underneath over his head together, exposing the torso of the corpse but careful not to let that melted face touch the armor directly. Tunic discarded, he put on the armor while Angela and a few of the other prisoners did the same. It was tighter than he figured it should be.

There wasn't enough armor for everybody, but no one seemed to argue over who got what was there. James put on soldier's gloves and picked up a rifle.

*Surtr will smile upon your corpse, and shadows serenade your soul.*

"We really need to go," James said.

The gunfire became louder and Angela nodded. They ran again, winding through stairways and hallways until they came to another intersection.

Gunfire erupted and James cursed as bullets streamed through the winding staircase, hitting the walls and shooting sparks as the bullets ricocheted. Angela and the other prisoners were on the other side of the stream and everyone backed away to avoid being hit by a bouncing shot.

James dropped to the floor and aimed his rifle up the crossing stairway. He squeezed the trigger.

Nothing.

Bullets flew around him and he pulled the trigger again. Nothing. He looked for a safety switch but didn't find one.

"Piece of shit," he said as he pulled back.

"Keep going," Angela shouted. "We'll find another way."

"I'm not leaving." James said. He jumped back even more as a stray bullet smacked the wall next to him.

"Dumbass," Angela shouted back. She threw one of her cleavers lightly into the hallway and bullets ripped through the cheap metal. She motioned at the mutilated blade and made a horse face at him, tucking in her lower lip and exposing her upper teeth. She flashed an eerie grin at him. "Go!"

James went. He looked back before taking the next turn, but Angela and the other prisoners had already darted the other direction and were now out of sight.

*Surtr will smile upon your corpse, and shadows serenade your soul.*

He swatted the air around his ears and ducked down another spiral.

\*\*\*

Lance sat with his back against a dark wall, holding his stomach. Gunfire grew louder and then died down again in the distance, echoing forever in the dark hallways of the prison. Somewhere only slightly closer, something metallic was scraping against the ground.

Hot, dark red crept out from beneath Lance's fingers.

Despair washed over him in waves and he could feel another one beginning. He couldn't picture his wife's face. He couldn't remember the color of her hair or eyes. He couldn't remember the way her voice sounded when she hit snooze for the seventh time, telling the clock radio to get bent. In his memory, she scorned the radio in Lance's voice. Lance was having trouble recalling her name, but that may have been the blood loss.

He hoped Jeremy made it back home.

The metallic scrape drew closer. Lance wondered if he would bleed out or die from lead poisoning before whatever was causing that noise found him. Was lead poisoning from being shot a real thing? He had only heard about it in movies. He was sweaty and cold. Was being eaten by a tiger more pleasant than dying of blood loss? It would be more interesting, anyway.

To spite him, his heart pumped faster and he felt the blood pressure against his wet hands as the metallic scrape came closer still. He thought he heard a growl, maybe even a purr. He had heard once that tigers who were full would lay next to a wounded animal until they were hungry, since the animal wouldn't be able to get away and would stay fresh as long as it was alive. That sounded anthropomorphic to Lance.

He resolved to grin at the tiger before it ate him, one little act of defiance before he died. That would be the best way to go, certainly. At least he could stop being a coward right before the end. Hell, maybe he would even laugh. As he heard the first footsteps accompanying the scrape, he forced his lips into a grin and smiled up at his final friend.

Looking down at him, wearing a smile of her own, was the chained woman.

"You poor man," she said. Her voice was like silk.

His surprise didn't mar his expression, or so he hoped. He nodded and lifted his right hand from his stomach, pressing harder with his left to compensate. He gestured circularly, palm up, the way he imagined a magician would gesture during a bow to his audience.

"Does it hurt?" Hel asked.

"Not anymore," Lance said. "It did. Now it's just—" He cut himself off and finished the statement with a sweeping gesture over his body with his right hand.

She looked at him with differently colored eyes. The blue one had a youthful sharpness, but the other was gray and cloudy, diseased and useless. Half of her face seemed to be drawing life from the other, the smooth skin of youth blending strangely into the decaying flesh of the other side of her face. The chains that she wore bounced up and down on the ground as she shrugged, clacking rhythmically against the black stone.

"If I asked you to do something for me," Hel said, "would you?"

"I don't think so," Lance said. "I don't think I can trust you."

She smiled. The youthful half of her face seemed to bloom toward the dead half. Her nose became whole and her gray eye began to show the smallest trickle of blue.

Gray hair began to darken. "You most certainly can't. But would you do it anyway?"

"Is it going to kill me?"

As her face fleshed its way to wholeness and her hair became as shimmering black as the walls around her, she shook her head. "I don't think so. It will probably save you."

Lance dropped his smile and shrugged back. "Why not?"

She knelt and looked deeply into his eyes. He watched her dead eye take on the blue sheen of her living one. She studied him through them, turning her head like a hawk. Her face was not just youthful but beautiful, and she took his face in a smooth, warm hand. She smelled floral and pungent, but subtle like expensive perfume.

She leaned forward and pressed her lips to his.

\*\*\*

James carried his useless rifle in his left hand and a sword in his right. He figured at least some of the more violent prisoners would think twice about following him around if they thought the gun fired, and he could use the sword if he happened on anyone at close range. A cigarette would complete the ensemble nicely, he decided.

*Surtr will smile upon your corpse, and shadows serenade your soul.*

He twisted his wrist and swung the sword in a circle. That voice really needed to go away. It was a line from the poem he had received back in another life, before Loki had *invited* them all to his fun house. Back when he fucked for a living. He could feel that crumpled piece of paper in his back pocket as he walked. It was the first time he had noticed it in quite a while.

A spiral staircase became a straight hallway, which became stairs upward and then stairs downward. He had never thought a jail break could be so lonely. Despite the constant droning of gunfire echoing through the hallway, it had been at least half an hour since he had seen another person.

*Surtr will smile upon your corpse, and shadows serenade your soul.*

He shook his head. Same line, over and over again. Loki wasn't so proud of the rest of his verses, he supposed. He wondered if Angela had received a letter.

Angela was going to be alright. That woman was harder than he was.

He ducked down a straight hallway and up another spiral. At this point, he wasn't keeping track of anything. He wasn't even really convinced that the passageways weren't changing every time he turned a corner. Loki could probably do that, right?

"For the Royal Family!" came a shout ahead of him.

James flattened himself against the wall. He was pretty sure it wouldn't help, but somehow it still felt like the right move. The sound of gunfire pounded its way to his eardrums and he squeezed his eyes shut. Scuffs and grunts joined the gunfire and James decided his best bet was to get the hell out of there. He turned around and plunged down another set of stairs.

He ran up more stairs, then down another spiral. A single door greeted him right at the last step. He put his gloved palm to the panel and took a deep breath as the door opened and he stepped inside. The door clicked shut behind him.

It was pitch dark in the room and he clung to the outer wall as he made his way through. The smell of raw sewage and rotting meat crept into his nostrils, a strange barnyard smell of cut straw and dust following close behind. He held his sword and rifle, but he doubted there would be anyone hanging out down here. He felt pieces of straw under his feet.

Then he heard a growl and a metallic scrape. He heard the pat, pat, pat of large footsteps on the ground and held his sword ready. He remembered the tigers and wished the door wasn't dozens of feet behind him.

*Surtr will smile upon your corpse, and shadows serenade your soul.*

"Shut the fuck up," he said aloud.

He felt breath on his face. It was a hot, damp breath that smelled worse than the shit and rotting meat that had greeted James on his entrance. James thought to himself that walking right into a pitch dark room wasn't his best call. Then he prepared to die by wrinkling his face at that smell.

"Mow."

It was a deep, expectant statement. James hadn't been aware that tigers could meow. He heard the giant cat's weight settle, crinkling the straw beneath.

James heard the pat, pat, pat of another big cat making its way toward him. Then he felt the wind of the tiger in front of him turning its massive head. He felt the dust from the animal's coat tickle his nostrils and flinched when the tiger roared at full volume. The other cat pat, pat, patted away with a soft groan.

"Mow."

Seconds passed in silence, every one marked by a new gust of fowl air warming his face. The cat wasn't panting, but those massive lungs bathed him in breath until a bead of sweat formed on his forehead and traced its way down his cheek. Then the tiger's weight shifted again and the warm breath left him. He heard a dull thud below him as a giant head flopped onto massive paws.

There was a very reasonable voice that told him to back toward the door slowly. He was, after all, standing in a tiger's den. Despite that voice, he knelt next to the giant cat and set his weapons on the floor. The tiger didn't move, but it harrumphed and snorted in the darkness.

*Dumbass,* the reasonable voice said.

*Eh,* the less reasonable one replied. He was probably going to die anyway.

He reached out and touched the tiger's fur. It was soft and warm, and a little oily. He found the cat's ears, pliable and springy, and he ran his hand down its neck. Its purr was like a running car engine and it lazily pushed its big head against his arm, slopping some air in and out of its face with the force of its giant lungs.

He sat down and leaned against the wall behind him. It

was still pitch dark, but with the tiger cuddled up to him, he was less than concerned about that. But he knew he couldn't stay. He raised an eyebrow.

"Are you thinking what I'm thinking?"

The tiger didn't say anything. That, he probably should have expected. He reached around for the chain on the cat's neck. It was thick, with links the size of his hand, but wrapped around the tiger's neck once and not nearly as tightly as James would have thought was required.

Maybe Loki thought that it would be entertaining for the tigers to get free during an arena battle. Maybe he left open the possibility, just in case. Regardless, it didn't take much for James to slide the chain up and off the animal's neck. Its head immediately sought out his hand again, unleashing another thunderous purr.

James leaned in and smiled at it, though his eyes still hadn't picked up enough light to see the tiger's face. "You want to help me out?"

The tiger exhaled sharply and something wet smacked out of its nose and onto the floor. It purred again.

*** 

Jeremy pressed his palm to the panel and the door clicked open. Damien stepped in front of him and stuck the barrel of the gun into the opening, resting the rifle on his stump while his remaining hand held the trigger.

"Guess what."

"All roads lead back to the arena." Gordon leaned against the wall, took off his helmet, and rested his rifle against his leg.

The old man's head looked small poking out of his soldier's armor, his neck expanding and shrinking with heavy breaths like an empty, wrinkled balloon. Jeremy couldn't help but think he looked like a turtle.

Gordon used the pointed last few inches of a broken sword to scratch the finding onto the map he was drawing on the back of his soldier's glove. He looked like he would have fallen over if the wall weren't there to catch him. "Are they still waiting?"

Damien nodded and Jeremy peeked into the room. The masked army, stoically awaiting the next charge, was still huddled the center of the arena floor. A few turned their heads to the slightly open door, but made no reaction aside from that. Those permanent, steel grins and painted-on eyes were especially eerie when taken with their statuesque silence. The stands were empty, the spectators having left in panic to join the bodies piled in the hallways and staircases of the prison.

One masked prisoner walked in slow circles around the army. The prisoner was saying something to them, gesturing grandly, but said it in too low a voice for Jeremy to hear more than the occasional word. He heard *royal* and *swine* together, which seemed like enough.

Gunfire echoed in the halls behind them. It was getting closer.

"I don't think we should chance going back," Jeremy said.

"I don't think we can chance going forward," Gordon said. He picked up his rifle. "There's no reason to think the masked army hasn't been collecting guns as well." The old cowboy closed his eyes. "It can't end like this again. I can't do it again."

Jeremy stared at him. "So what the hell are they waiting for?"

Gordon opened his eyes and shrugged, reclaiming his composure. "They have orders from Loki. They're probably more afraid to disobey than anything else."

"Great." Jeremy tapped on Garm's smart phone. The lines and dots were endless, and Jeremy had yet to find a combination that would override Loki's order for the soldiers. That was assuming one existed.

The sound of the gunfire rocketed from a dull roar right into a deafening series of snaps and the four hit the ground. Damien kicked the door shut as he positioned the rifle over his stump and braced the weapon with his shoulder. The others all fell into some less-polished version of Damien's position. Gordon had proved to be a reasonable shot, but Andrew and Jeremy were basically there to fire off some extra bullets to distract while Damien did the killing. Jeremy pulled his helmet low over his head and the others followed suit, except for Damien. He had been less than enthused about the helmets, even when they had come across their fourth dead soldier.

They laid there in silence against the barrage of sound, watching the end of the hallway as bullets kicked dust and rock from the walls. Jeremy wondered exactly how much force a bullet still carried after it ricocheted from the rock. He tried to shove that thought out of his head. There wasn't anything he could do about that, except hope that the helmet he was wearing was made of something hard enough to take the force. Since a sword had pierced the soldier's armor without much of a problem, Jeremy found that doubtful.

"Now," Gordon ordered.

Andrew pulled the pin on a canister of tear gas and tossed it to the end of the hallway. Jeremy braced himself as thick smoke began to drift upward. It crept up the walls and along the floor at first, then swelled and became an opaque cloud that expanded faster and faster. Jeremy could already feel his eyes start to sting.

The gunfire became sporadic and interlaced with hacks and gasps as the smoke twisted around three soldiers staggering into the hall. Jeremy and the others waited for Gordon.

"Kill soldiers," Gordon shouted into the smoke. He had given the order to every group of soldiers they had encountered.

Jeremy held his gun ready to fire, but two of the soldiers stopped. They turned and shot the third, then turned toward each other. They raised their rifles and one soldier got a shot off before the other. The one remaining stood still and fired off a coughing fit that shook his helmet. Jeremy could barely hear it over the ringing in his ears.

Two of the soldiers had followed Gordon's order, just like Loki had said.

"He's alright," Gordon said, standing up and lowering

his rifle.

"I don't get it," Jeremy said, still crouched as he looked at the surviving soldier. "How do you get them to do that?"

"Doesn't matter right now," Damien said, standing. "If he's alright, we'll use him."

"Fine." Jeremy stood up. "What now?"

Gordon pointed to the hand-scratched map on his glove. "We're not going back. We tried all the intersections and it's just a big loop to another arena entrance that way. We go forward."

Gordon coughed and cleared his throat. Then he coughed again, doubling over and expelling air from his lungs until his face turned purple. Jeremy and the others coughed as well. Gordon wiped his mouth and squeezed his eyes shut, walking over to the door and putting his hand to the panel. The door clicked open.

"Charge!" came a cry from inside the arena.

"Great." Jeremy coughed. He looked at the other men and thickened his voice. "It was a pleasure working with you, gentlemen."

"Come on," Gordon said to the soldier, motioning frantically through the oncoming gas. "You go first."

As they entered the arena, Jeremy expected an onslaught from the masked army. What he didn't expect was that they would be running the other direction. But as he walked through the doorway, he was treated to the sight of a crowd of backs as the masked army charged a small group of unmasked prisoners at the other end of the arena. The defending prisoners looked at the larger army with resigned expressions, lifting their swords and halfheartedly returning the charge. All except for their leader.

Angela raised a sword high into the air and dove forward on the front line, stretching her legs and leaping into the air as she swung the blade in a wide circle. A handful of masked warriors went down. Then another. Her stained, green gown shimmered and bloomed over brown trousers as she killed scores of enemies. Jeremy thought it looked like a giant lawnmower was moving through the crowd, but there were so many fighters in the arena that they were starting to surround her.

Other prisoners shouted as they followed her into battle. "For Freya!"

"Kill only masked prisoners," Gordon said to the soldier. He looked around the arena. "And tigers." He looked at Jeremy and the others. "If you're not comfortable enough with that gun to avoid hitting Freya, because God knows what happens at that point, you should probably keep your fingers off the triggers."

The soldier fired and one masked fighter fell. Then another. Andrew threw multiple tear gas canisters into the masked army, bending more than a quarter of the fighters into a coughing fit. Damien joined in picking them off one by one with his rifle. Jeremy backed toward the door and gave the hallway another listen. More gunfire could be heard in the halls, announcing the approach of more soldiers.

"Gordon," Jeremy said, "we're going to have to deal with some more soldiers the way we came."

Gordon dove forward and started shooting his rifle into the crowd. Damien and Gordon's soldier followed. Andrew watched Gordon charge, looked at the doorway, then at Jeremy.

"I'll take care of it," Andrew said. "Find somewhere to hide."

"Get bent," Jeremy said.

Andrew raised an eyebrow and pulled his lips to one side of his mouth for a moment. He nodded and they ducked back into the hallway.

"There are a lot of entrances into the arena," Jeremy said when they were inside. "Soldiers or other prisoners could pop in anytime."

Andrew grunted and ran to the end of the straight hallway. He stayed in the intersection for a moment, tilting his head back and forth. Then he tossed the tear gas canister down a set of stairs before running back.

"Let's go," he said when he got back to Jeremy.

"Do you think that's going to cover it?"

Andrew opened the door. "Best chance."

Jeremy looked back into the hallway as he stepped into the arena. He couldn't figure out if the mountain man had done some kind of risk calculation or if he was saying they couldn't do anything else about it. Jeremy figured that should unsettle him, but it didn't. As a matter of fact, the idea of taking the sword from where it was tucked into his belt and joining the fight seemed exciting.

Gordon's soldier stood back from the crowd, firing one bullet at a time and taking out one masked warrior after another.

Damien and Gordon fired at close range, downing clusters of masked fighters and mostly managing to avoid shooting in Angela's direction. Enough masked fighters had noticed the small attacking force at this point that the masked army began to recede from Angela and move toward the others. Gordon and Damien fired at any fighters who tried to surround them.

By the time Jeremy and Andrew got to the fighting, the masked army was rallying a charge. Andrew routed it with a few more tear gas canisters, doubling over masked fighters as they gasped for air. A number of those went down in the subsequent barrage of fire.

Damien threw his rifle to the ground and drew his sword. "No backup clips."

Gordon tossed his gun as well. Jeremy and Andrew tried to back up and shoot at the masked fighters trying to surround them, but they rushed forward during the pause and the space around them filled up quickly. Jeremy turned and rushed to the center, pounding bullets into the opposing army and cursing beneath the constant, thunderous, crack, crack, *crack* of his own gunfire.

They were surrounded as they fought beneath the empty stands and the abandoned thrones, looking down on them as if invisible kings had assembled to watch them die meaninglessly. Jeremy squeezed the rifle's trigger again and the empty click was barely audible. He tossed it and drew his sword, and could see Andrew do the same. Damien hacked his way through more fighters and disappeared into the crowd, and it occurred to Jeremy that he may never see Damien alive again.

Gordon limped next to Andrew and nodded at Jeremy. The three stood alone against a hoard of Loki's masked prisoners, who closed in on them at a slow walk now that they had the advantage. It was strangely quiet beyond the ringing in Jeremy's ears. He heard metal bang against metal not far from him, but a little bubble of quiet surrounded Jeremy. In spite of his impending death, he grinned.

A roar shattered the quiet and a flurry of orange rose into the air. A tiger snapped its jaws at the masked prisoners and a swipe of its giant paw tossed three fighters aside like wads of paper into a trash can. James sat atop the animal's back, swinging a sword wildly and slicing through the masked army. His brown prison uniform was ripped completely open and his hair flowed behind him as he laughed. He roared with the tiger, an odd, strained yawp that mirrored the giant cat's bellow.

Some of the masked fighters broke and ran to avoid the tiger. Others surged toward it to fight, but the animal demolished them in waves as they took their fallen comrades' places. Those who had been slowly closing the distance between themselves and Jeremy's trio now turned their attention to the new threat. Jeremy and Andrew took the opportunity and lashed out, hacking their way into the distracted fighters and pulling back just as quickly. Gordon leaned against his sword, ready to collapse.

"For the Royal Family!" came a voice from the edge of the arena.

For a moment, it looked like the masked army was surging toward Jeremy and the other two men. After that, he realized they were being pushed forward as another army attacked them from behind. A few cracks of gunfire bubbled up from the clatter, and a few more answered them. Jeremy couldn't tell if the Royal Army or the masked army was firing guns, but he wouldn't have been surprised if he took a bullet at any second.

The tiger roared again and dashed across the arena. It loped through a doorway on the far side. Jeremy thought it might have been scared off by the gunfire, unsteadied by the shouts of its rider. Jeremy hoped that James was alright, but for now he had taken with him the most powerful weapon they had.

The frequency of gunfire grew. Jeremy lunged into the crowd, hacking his way into the masked army. He became and vaguely aware that unmasked fighters from Loki's Royal Army were beginning to outnumber the masked ones.

"We're winning," Gordon panted. "We need to follow James."

\*\*\*

The giant cat loped across the ground and James barely held on. His thighs ached with the exertion required to keep from falling over as those massive shoulders rocked back and forth, and his spine felt like it was going to leave his back of its own accord from the strain required to keep his balance as he swung the sword.

The tiger didn't mind him clinging to the scruff of its neck, which was good because his hand was curled into a claw of his own from the amount of forced with which he gripped the animal's fur. It occurred to him that he might be hurting the tiger, but it gave no sign of this and the thought was soon forgotten.

Gunfire grew in waves crashing down the black hallway, then made a decrescendo back to a percussive roar. The tiger brought him down a winding staircase, leaping over a firefight between a group of Loki's soldiers and a well-armed pack of prisoners. It loped up a straight staircase and down another hallway. Rock shattered next to James's head and he cursed.

"For Loki!"

Bullets pierced the air. The tiger roared and blood splattered the rock. Something slammed into James's shoulder, knocking him from the animal and sending him crashing to the ground. His head bounced with a snap against the wall and he tumbled down a spiral staircase against the soft, warm flank of the tiger. He leaned against it as the light above him started to dim.

"They're still coming," Alex said, leaning over him.

"No," James said, "they're—"

"You need to get up. You're bleeding."

His head bobbled. "You need to get out of here, man. Loki can see you."

"I'm not worried about it. Want a cigarette?" Alex bent down and extended a pack to James. "The tiger did his best, but he couldn't get you out. You have to do the rest yourself."

James shook his head. "You can't be here."

Alex shrugged and took one out for himself. He lit it with a heavy drag and slowly released a ribbon of thick smoke. James could smell the spiciness of the tobacco, some blend with which he wasn't familiar.

"For Loki!" came a faint shout.

Alex looked in the direction of the sound. "Fuckers."

"I don't get it," James said. "What's going on?"

"Roll it over later," Alex said. "You've got a whole bunch of fire giants headed your way."

Gunfire echoed in the hallway.

"That doesn't help," James said. His vision darkened considerably as he looked at his friend. "Fire giants aren't a thing."

Alex smiled. "Not if Freyr has something to say about it."

"I'm not Freyr."

Alex shrugged and took another drag of his cigarette. He looked for a long time at James, then took an even bigger drag. He managed a massive smoke ring with a smaller one inside as darkness overtook James's vision.

A meaty hand grabbed the folds of James's open shirt and stitches popped as the hand lifted him into the air. James struggled without effect as the hand slung him over a titanic shoulder. They moved forward. He drifted in and out of darkness, catching glimpses of skirmishes and death as Andrew carried him. Then he felt a chill, a pressure difference in the air.

"Checking out so soon?" came a cheerful voice. "We humbly invite you back any time you like."

James's eyes stung. He squinted against an invisible force pushing his eyelids together. The warmth of the sun cut through his chill and saw brilliant, deep forest greens and sky blues before the darkness overtook his vision again.

# Chapter 10

## AN UNLIKELY AUTUMN

The giant hall was filled with the stench of warriors, blood, and beer. Bold laughter ripped through the tatters of silence like wind through a ruined flag. Flutes and strings danced their way to flank and attack the sadness that waited just behind the eyes of those present. Beautiful women clad in silk ribbons danced hypnotically to the rhythm of drums and gave the men wolfish smiles, which were returned sloppily over precariously clutched drinking horns filled with strong brew.

Roasts of all kinds covered the heavy wooden tables. Surrounding the tenderly scorched joints of meat were freshly baked breads, crumbled cheeses, root vegetable stews, a host of egg dishes, and horns and pitchers of wine and beer. The men ate from wooden bowls, their bloodstained weapons leaned against tables at the ready, and drank deeply from cups that never ran empty.

Freyr carried his motionless sister through the center of the hall, where naught but the occasional glance fell their way. There was no concern for death in Valhalla.

At the head table, Odin blinked his singular eye and stood from his feast. He nodded slowly as Freyr approached, crinkling an old face creased with cruelty and sadness. The old man quelled the laughter that arose at his table with a momentary glance. Then he gestured and the contents of the table became airborne and crashed a dozen paces away. A goblet rolled another few feet and then traced a wide circle before finally stopping on a seam between two cobblestones. The men at the other tables didn't even notice the sound.

They laid Freya on the table as if she were the most fragile and precious object in the Nine Worlds, her arms folded across her breasts and her fiery hair claiming the table space in front of four men. Freyr grimaced at the dainty treatment, but it was necessary until they could figure out what had been done to her.

Odin looked down at Freya's blue-tinged face. "The battle went poorly, then."

The old man spoke softly, but the hall fell silent at his first syllable. The quiet hung heavy in the air like a soaked, infested blanket.

"Yes," Freyr said. "Do you know what is happening to her?"

Odin shook his head slowly and thoughtfully.

Freyr resisted the urge to chop the old man's head clean from his shoulders. "Do you know who can tell me?"

The raven Munin fluttered down and landed on Odin's shoulder. He whispered to it and it cawed back something rude that made Odin chuckle. Then his face creased with worry again. "I have an idea of who is responsible. I also have an idea of who can give her back to you."

"Speak truth."

A wolf growled from beneath the table. Freyr didn't bother looking at it.

Odin nodded. "The knowledge must never be spoken to those who understand. I will speak it to your sword, if you will agree to it."

Freyr nodded and his mind called out. His sword slid from its sheath behind him and sliced a circle through the air once before settling. When it settled, it hung midair with its point a breath from the old man's eye. Odin smiled and took the sword gingerly in his ancient fingers, crooning it to calm as he spoke words that Freyr's ears did not capture. Somewhere in the back of Freyr's mind, his shoulder ached. Then it tickled and stung, like something was trying to worm its way out.

"It is done." Odin let the sword hang in the air, suspended by its own magic.

Freyr's mind called and the sword sliced through the air again, coming to rest gently back in its sheath on Freyr's back.

"I'll need to borrow some of your men," Freyr said.

Odin shook his head. "These men wait for Ragnarok and I'll not call on them before. I recommend the living for a rescue, anyway. The dead don't have the empathy for it."

"Then I'll do without," Freyr said. "Will you keep Freya safe until I return?"

"Of course," Odin said.

The old man reached out his hand to touch Freya's forehead with his index finger. Before he touched her, Freyr's sword flew from its sheath and batted the hand away with its broad side.

"After all these years," the old man said with a grin that cut his beard, "you still don't trust me."

"It's getting late, Odin. And it's getting cold."

The old man nodded. "Truth spoken. The curse is one of ice, and it's the slow freeze that does the most damage to her body. If I hasten the curse, she stands her best chance to survive. It's up to you."

Freyr called the sword back to its sheath. "Do it. Betray me, and I will kill you."

"I think that would be extraordinarily stupid," Odin said.

"Think all you want."

Odin laughed, releasing a booming stretch of his voice that echoed through the silent chamber. He put his fingertip to Freya's forehead and her blue-tinged skin crystallized with slick ice. The frost that had been growing on her eyelashes bloomed into layer upon layer of a frozen tomb. Then Odin dragged his finger through the air and she disappeared, transported to one of Odin's secret chambers. When it was done, Odin regarded Freyr with a darkened eye.

"Your sword knows the way," he said. "May your travel be cheerless and your mercy nil."

"May your stomach swell and your mind darken," Freyr said. "May the Einherjar wait forever for their turn to fight."

Odin nodded and seated himself. As soon as he did, the cacophony returned. A man at the end of the head table ordered more roasts and egg dishes as Freyr turned and made his way out of the hall. As the doors groaned shut behind him, he put his index and middle fingers together. He kissed them and gestured the kiss into the winter air.

"Is that code for bumming a cigarette?" Alex said as he extended his pack.

Freyr looked at him. He looked strange in his jeans and gray tee-shirt, leaning against the wall of famed Valhalla over the backdrop of the pristine, cascading cliffs and waterfalls of Asgard. Alex blew a perfect smoke ring and imploded it by blowing hard through the center. Freyr took a cigarette and Alex lit it for him.

"Did you check out the writing prompt for English yet?"

Freyr took a drag and stared at the burning tobacco in his hand. "I didn't know we had one."

"You're going to hate it," Alex said. He crushed out the end of his cigarette against the wall, leaving a black smear on the polished rock. "You're going to hate it so much."

"What is it?"

Alex grinned and screwed another cigarette into his lips. He dipped his upper lip beneath his lower as he lit the cigarette and lifted his chin in mock-condescension as he recited. "John Lennon and his wife Yoko Ono held two *Bed-Ins* for peace during the horror of the Vietnam war. What does the term *Bed-In* reference, and why do you think this event is remembered as one of the greatest peaceful protests in history?"

Freyr stared at him. "What's a Bed-In?"

"It's like a sit-in, but for rich, white guys."

"I don't get it."

Alex shook his head. "You know sit-ins, where people sit somewhere as a protest and refuse to leave until they're arrested or they get what they want. They did it a lot to end segregation. Woolworth's in Greensboro and all of that. Some fucking diner that wouldn't serve coffee to black people, and the black people gave them the finger by sitting down and just not leaving."

Freyr took a drag on his cigarette. In the distance, a massive bird exploded with oranges and reds as it crossed the dipping sun. It banked and disappeared behind one of the shrouded mountains. "Yeah."

"Well, a lot of those ended violently. Fire hoses and dogs and beatings. Then there were lynchings. It was dangerous to be part of a sit-in, even though you didn't hurt anybody."

Freyr leaned against the wall next to Alex. Asgard was starting to look less familiar, and he knew he should be doing something about it.

"But John Lennon decides, hey, I can do a sit-in too. I mean, I'm not going to risk actually getting hurt or anything. But I can stick around and not leave my house for a few days. Fuck, maybe I'll just stay in bed. Tell those guys on the front lines that I really feel their pain. Yeah, I'm rich and could probably do something to save them directly. Yeah, I'm not taking any risk and this mostly looks like a publicity stunt for me. But I swear dude, *I'm doing this for you*. Like an angel." Alex took a long drag on his cigarette. "He fucking said they were like angels while they were having their fucking bed protest."

The cigarette in Freyr's hand went out. He motioned and Alex handed him the lighter. Freyr took a hard drag as he held the flame and the heat stung his nose. "Didn't he say it was a joke at some point?"

"Probably. John Lennon said a lot of shit. But if it wasn't meant to be taken seriously, why the fuck do it?"

"I'm not sure I'm buying it," Freyr said. "Not everything has to be taken seriously to be effective. Maybe it got people thinking."

Alex took the last drag on his cigarette and pulled two more from the pack. He lit them both at the same time and handed one to Freyr, who took it despite still having half of his own to finish. "Got them thinking what? That they can give peace a chance by staying in bed and think they're helping? Peace doesn't need a chance. It needs a fucking foothold."

"Didn't he help give it that?" Freyr said. He finished his cigarette and flicked the butt over the cliff, watching the tiny red glow sail out over jagged rocks and safely through the fog that obscured the water below. "A lot of people think John Lennon is symbolic for peace and love."

"Fuck what they think."

Freyr smiled. "Doesn't that mean he did something right? I'm sure a lot of people would have gone on being complacent with the war if they hadn't heard his music. Bed protest aside, he articulated some good things."

Alex turned around, unzipped his fly, and loosed a stream on the wall of Valhalla. Freyr thought this should bother him. It didn't.

"He articulated some really basic philosophy and wishful thinking," Alex said. "People who already agreed with him identified with his music, that's all."

"But didn't they rally around it and organize? That's some powerful shit."

"Yeah," Alex said, "right up through him writing *Revolution* and telling them to settle the fuck down and that he didn't want to be a part of it."

"I'm not sure that's what the song was about."

"Fuck, who cares? Point is, the guy did almost nothing except write songs and call himself a hero. Self-congratulatory asshole. I'm glad he got shot."

"Bit much."

Alex smiled. "Yeah, maybe it is. Hey, do you think I could do porn?"

Freyr stared at him. He waited for some cartoonish face to say that Alex wasn't asking for real. But Alex sucked his stomach in and put his arms out, looking down at his torso and then back up for approval.

"Why do you want to do porn?"

"Because," Alex said after another drag, "I could make a career out of a *fuck you* to people who say sex is dirty and you should feel bad for wanting it. You know, the hell fire types."

Freyr mulled this over as he blew an honest attempt at his own smoke ring, which came out a hazy blob that died an appropriately quick death. The wind was picking up.

"Sure," Freyr said. "I guess you could—"

Alex slapped him hard across the face.

Freyr rubbed his tingling jaw. "What the hell?"

"Don't you have some shit to do?"

"I don't—"

Alex slapped him again. "Don't you have some shit to do?"

"Fucking stop. What are you talking about?"

Alex slapped him a third time. "Don't you have some shit to do?"

James rubbed his jaw again. He could feel welts forming. "Really, I—"

"Wake up," came Angela's voice. "You're talking in your sleep."

Alex smiled and brought two fingers to his forehead in a salute. James opened his eyes.

Angela looked like she had showered and was now wearing a pale blue dress that tied at the neck and hugged her figure. She still wore the green dress as well, tied completely around her waist like a sash. Her hair, cleaned of the blood that had matted it in the arena, draped delicately over her bare shoulders. She glared at him through gemstones.

"Moron."

"How long have I been out?"

"Most of a day," she said. "It's hard to say how long, since Loki's care package didn't include watches."

He rubbed his face and felt several prominent knots at his temple. It wasn't until then that he remembered hitting the wall. When he was done, he saw a small smear of blood on his palm. He looked up and saw a sky that almost matched Angela's dress. A bird was circling the top of a sharp, mossy mountain peak in the distance.

"Am I—"

She slapped him across the face. "Fucking idiot. Oh look, you broke your stitches. Here." She steadied his face with one hand across his mouth and nose, barely far enough off center to allow him to breathe, and dipped a needle into his forehead. He felt a small tug and a tickle of thread on his cheek, but she was so gentle that he felt little else. "Riding a fucking tiger like you're in a kid's fantasy book. What the hell is the matter with you?"

James felt a drop of something warm roll down the side of his face. "It seemed like a good idea at the time."

She carefully finished the stitches and tied off the thread before cutting the needle free. Then she slapped him again. "Oh look, how clumsy of you."

"Jesus."

James tried to sit up from the uncomfortable cot, but she put a knuckle on his sternum and pushed down until he stopped. It hurt, but not as badly as her slap. It also felt strangely familiar.

"Cocky moron, risk-seeking bullshit dumb ass of a man." She went at him with the needle again, still infinitely gentle.

James smiled. He rolled his eyes around, trying to get a better picture of where he was. There were other people lying in other cots and a few more walking around the area and tending to the wounded. Some of the other people lying in cots groaned and whimpered. James remembered taking a bullet in the shoulder and it suddenly ached in confirmation of his memory. He tried to look down at it.

"You're fine," Angela said. "The bullet missed all the big vessels in your shoulder. We dug it out and you should heal fine. But you'll still be a fucking moron."

"That's nice of you," James said. "How many of the others are going to pull through?"

Angela shrugged her bare shoulders. "Some of them. They're much worse off than you."

Something sweet and floral caressed his nose and he gazed deeply into those gemstones. His chest tightened. "Angela, I think I—"

She slapped him a third time. "Let's not be stupid."

This time, he had to work his jaw slightly back into position. She started stitching his forehead again.

When she was finished, James sat up. He reached across himself to feel the wound in his shoulder, but Angela glared at him and he put his hand back at his side. If she was going to be this mothering, she could at least offer him a cigarette.

His heart sank as he looked around. Yes, they were outside. But just across the rocky clearing was the waterfall and, more importantly, the massive black statue of Loki bent backwards and drank from the waterfall like a spigot. The bird circling the distant mountaintop banked in the direction of the statue that had been their prison.

"Alright," James said. "So we escaped prison. Shouldn't we be moving away instead of setting up camp right next to it? Where the hell is this place?"

"Somewhere warm with lots of forests, if you want to check out the view over there. Gordon didn't say exactly where we are, but he's pretty confident he can get us home."

"And why in hell are we staying put when Loki could just send some soldiers outside and bring us back into his little fun house?"

Angela shrugged again. "We just left through what appears to be the only entrance to a prison owned by a guy with the power to do pretty much anything. He not only didn't stop us, but made sure we had accommodations on the outside. I get the feeling we're still at arm's reach for Loki."

James jumped as a shot knocked the bird out of the shining sky. He lurched to a standing position despite Angela's protest, body aching and head drowning in whatever chemical the brain released after a bodily trauma. "What was that?"

"Gordon ordered his soldiers to shoot any wildlife that came close to the camp," Angela said.

"Asshole." He looked around the rudimentary medical center. Lines of cots filled the area, most filled with wounded prisoners lying still and wrapped in dirty blankets. Several men and women paced the lines, checking pulses and listening for breathing. Others were still sewing up wounds or digging for bullets with tweezers. He rubbed his temples again. "Where did all of this stuff come from?"

"Loki sent one of those bow tie-wearing lobotomy patients after us with a cart of supplies. The buildings were already here, but Loki's man said that if we *must* check out early, we should at least accept his care package."

"What was in the care package?"

"Lots of freeze-dried food and bottled water. Changes of clothes. First aid kits. And some personal stuff. I think he left you a carton of cigarettes and a gas station pack of lighters."

"Oh thank God," James said with a cliché grin. "Where are those?"

Angela smiled back. "You have an office at the barracks."

"You've got to be kidding."

"Nope. There's a barracks, and that's not the worst part."

"What is?"

"It has forty-eight beds."

James stared at her and frowned. "I don't see the problem."

"All counted, fifty three people escaped from Loki's prison."

"And?"

"Three have died already from injuries. There are two more who aren't going to make it to the night. That leaves forty-eight escaped prisoners."

James stared. "I need a cigarette."

They made their way to the barracks, passing a few shelters where other prisoners were cooking dried food in pots over wood-burning stoves or washing clothes with those old washboards that James had only seen used by street musicians. The looks on the faces of the prisoners, free people now, at least ostensibly, were jarringly placid.

As they saw him, one yelled "For Freyr!"

"And they all do that a lot," Angela said.

James had to lean on Angela for most of the way, which she assured him was a sign that he should still be in bed. Also, moron, nicotine wasn't good for someone who had just had surgery to remove a bullet.

About a mile from the giant statue of Loki, they found the barracks. It was a rickety old thing on the ground against the far cliff of the rocky clearing. It must have been there when they were escorted into Loki's prison, but was far enough out of the way that the armed soldiers and massive, black rock statue had taken James's attention from it. It was a one-story building with one large chamber filled with beds surrounded by a narrow hallway connecting a number of small offices around the outside. Angela led him to his room.

When Angela had called it an office, James had been expecting something like a dorm room, or maybe even a one-bedroom apartment. What he had was a literal office, with a heavy desk of darkly stained wood and matching wooden walls. There was a chair behind the desk, nice black leather, and a few smaller leather chairs in front that were presumably for meetings. The desk had a little gold-embossed name plate, spelling *FREYR* in all capital letters over a dark background.

The desktop was empty except for the carton of cigarettes that Angela had promised. He tore open the carton, smacked a pack against his palm a dozen times and rested a cigarette between his lips. He didn't recognize the brand and the tobacco smelled a little spicy, with a background hint of something sweet that he couldn't remember.

"Lighters?"

Angela pointed to the desk again and James walked around to the other side. He pulled the black leather chair out gently and sat down, then opened the top drawer of three set into the desk to find an unopened pack of six cheap plastic lighters. He ripped open the package and lit his cigarette with a hard drag as he leaned back in his chair. He held the smoke, breathing in a little bit of air and expanding his chest. He exhaled the smoke without style, letting it mix hazily with the air around him. Then he dropped the ash from the end of his cigarette onto the floor.

He extended the pack at Angela. "You want one?"

She obliged him with a smile. She leaned forward and he lit hers, and she released her opening drag immediately and stared for a moment at the burning tobacco in her hand.

"I don't think we need to worry about lung cancer at this point," James said.

Angela shook her head and took another drag before sitting down in one of the chairs on the other side of the desk. "That's not it."

James raised an eyebrow, then dropped it and took another drag. They smoked in silence. James thought about Alex and the dreams about Freya. If Loki was to be believed, Angela was the same woman from his dreams. They didn't look the same, but similar enough that he could see the connection. Hell, he was pretty doubtful that he looked like the real Freyr. He wondered idly if Angela had similar dreams about Freya or if he was just losing his mind.

He didn't believe he was Freyr. At least, that was what he would say if asked. Those dreams were as vivid as the ones about Alex.

"The tiger," Angela broke the silence. "How did that happen?"

James shrugged. "I thought it was going to eat me and then it didn't. Then it let me pet it."

"So you climbed on its back?"

James made a shitty attempt at a smoke ring. "Yep. Probably a dick move on my part, but I figured I was about to die and it didn't seem to mind. What happened to it?"

"You were lying on its dead body when Andrew picked

you up."

He tried to shake off the bluntness, but it hit him like a knee to the stomach. He felt more grief for the tiger than for the prisoners who had died in the escape. He pulled out the middle drawer, which was empty. The mostly-full bottle of bourbon and crystal glasses he found in the bottom drawer were both reassuring and violating at the same time. The small revolver sitting next to them was less reassuring.

He poured two glasses and slid one across the desk. Angela nodded and dipped a finger from her cigarette hand into her glass, rubbed the liquor into her other palm, and flicked her wrist in front of her nose. She gathered her mouth to one side for a moment before taking a sip, then put the glass back on the desk.

"It's not bad," she said.

James took a gulp. She was right. It was a little sweet for his taste, but the burn was appropriate and the bitter smoothness made him forget that he was God-knew-where and up against fuck-knew-what. He took another drag on his cigarette, finishing it and dropping the butt into a third glass before lighting up another. His shoulder still ached, a dull throb that only occasionally announced its presence at anything more than a low rumble.

Gordon knocked on the open door, wearing dark jeans and a dark flannel shirt, and what appeared to be a brown cowboy hat made out of felt. His hat was pulled low at an angle, nearly covering his left eye.

The old man winked at him. "Good, you're up. We're

going to have to talk about a plan, so meet me in my office when you two are done in here."

James stared at the old man, who nodded to himself before making his exit.

"That's been happening a lot," Angela said. "He's just assuming we're under his command at this point."

"Fuck Gordon."

Angela blew a tendril of smoke that corkscrewed its way into the air before nearly freezing in place and drifting sideways, slowly expanding and dissipating. She waved her hand and the wind that followed cut the tendril in three pieces that drifted aimlessly away from each other. "I couldn't agree more, but he's still our best chance at getting home. Andrew is the only other one who seems to know what's going on and he rarely speaks. Damien just parrots what Gordon says and chuckles a lot at meaningless statements."

When James finished his next cigarette and freshened their drinks, they made their way into the hall and down to Gordon's office. The door was closed and there was no answer when they knocked. James tried the doorknob, but it was locked.

He put his glass on the floor, lit another cigarette and they waited. He found the deck of cards that had somehow survived the escape, gently decorated in dried blood, and dealt a poker hand to himself. The Queen of Hearts stared up at him and he thought of Gloria, packed the cards together again and shoved them in his pocket, and took a long sip from his drink.

When they had nearly decided to go back to James's office and wait for the old man to request their attendance again Gordon arrived with Damien, Jeremy, and Andrew. One of Loki's soldiers followed them silently, and James didn't understand why that wasn't a problem for anybody else. They just acted like that soldier was supposed to be standing there.

Gordon didn't apologize for their wait, but produced a key rich with rust and divots from his pocket, that he used to unlock the door. The old man looked at the cigarette in James's hand and opened his mouth as if to say something. Then he closed it and walked inside.

They followed. Gordon's office was the same as James's, but his desk had a pile of papers with scribbles and something rolled up in a dirty blanket. He had only one paper tacked to the wall behind the desk, a part-finished game of hangman that he was presumably playing with himself. The head, body, arms, and one leg were all drawn and none of the fourteen letters were guessed.

"Vowels," James said. "Try some vowels."

Gordon gave him a flat stare as he sat down behind the desk. James smiled around his cigarette.

"I think it's important," Gordon said, "that we know what we're up against. Loki hasn't always been a murderous psychopath. He was a friend of the gods for a very long time, but his constant tricks eventually crossed the line and they imprisoned him after he murdered Odin's son Balder. The imprisonment seems to have taken its toll on his mind."

James looked at the others. Angela had her mouth gathered to the side again. The men looked at Gordon without expression.

"In the stories, Loki is primarily a trickster. Sometimes he entertains himself at the expense of the gods, but he makes up for it. There's a story, for instance, in which Thor wakes one morning to find that Loki has shaved off his wife's hair in the middle of the night."

Andrew remained expressionless.

Gordon bobbed his head and smiled. "Afterward, Loki went deep underground at great personal danger to himself to ask the dwarves to create new hair for her. He played a trick, then made it right." He smiled. "Of course, Thor would have killed him otherwise. But that pattern is common. He plays a prank and fixes it when the gods get angry. He's less of an enemy than a friend who gets into lots of mischief."

"Fine," Jeremy said. "But if we're supposed to be the gods, why don't we remember any of this?"

"It's hard to tell how long he's been free," Gordon said. "I know he was messing around in my life before I ever found my way to the prison. He's probably been toying with your lives as well. He may even be the reason we're in this human form. His greatest trick ever would be to make the gods think they weren't gods."

Gordon sat back and watched their faces. James took a drag on his cigarette and the others didn't show much more emotion than that.

"Whether you believe it or not," Gordon said, "Loki

believes that we are the gods. His opinion is what matters. He's been testing the prophecies, seeing how much leeway he has to wriggle out of his fated death at Heimdall's hands." He looked at Damien. "When you killed Garm, you gave Loki evidence that there is wiggle room in the prophecies. Garm is dead and Tyr still lives, in direct violation of what's written."

James took a sip of his bourbon. "Maybe he's just wrong. Or insane."

Gordon shook his head. "If that's the case, we're all as good as dead already. We're alive because Loki believes."

Angela raised an eyebrow. "And if he changes his mind?"

"Then we die." Gordon shrugged. "But this is different. This is all different. I've never been part of a successful escape, and Loki has invited prisoners to escape before. We made it out because Freyr's luck allowed us to do so."

James shook his head. "He tried to kill us after letting everyone go."

Gordon smiled. "Loki doesn't know what he wants. You saw him in the arena before our last battle with the masked prisoners. His desire to survive is tempered by the fact that he's bored. We're his entertainment, and that gives us a chance to stop him."

"Alright," James said, "fine. End of the world and all of that, I get it." He pointed to the prison soldier, standing motionless and staring at them through the dark visor. "But what the *hell* is he doing here?"

Gordon nodded. He turned to the prison soldier.

"Remove your helmet."

The soldier took off his helmet and remained still, staring at Gordon through black eyes.

Gordon smiled. "This is Heracles. When I first fought with him in the arena, he was named Ralph. Eventually, he took the name Loki gave him."

James stared at the soldier. "He was a prisoner?"

"Until he wasn't."

Angela raised an eyebrow. "Why does he follow your orders?"

"Because I led him in the arena. My orders saved his life, and he got used to that fact. He's following me by instinct."

The group stood in silence. No one asked how many groups Gordon had commanded previously.

James wanted to double-check the color of his eyes in a mirror. "How did he end up like that?"

"I think it's the eventual result of Loki's prison," Gordon said. "You follow Loki's rules to survive. After a while, you stop thinking and you start following without question. When you trust Loki implicitly, he becomes your god. Whatever he does next, you stop fighting against it and accept whatever he plans for you."

Angela shook her head slowly, gems glaring at Heracles the prison guard. "So, the arena battles? The prayers? The guys in masks?"

Gordon tapped his fingers on the desk, letting silence hang in the room for a moment before speaking. James took another drag on his cigarette, releasing a pillar of smoke in Gordon's direction to spoil the dramatic effect.

The old man tightened his lips for a moment and spoke. "Everything teaches the prisoners that nothing is as it seems. The only constant is Loki's twisted sense of humor."

"Bullshit," James said. "Loki terrorized them. Why would they trust him now?"

"They only survived because it suited Loki. Loki has made their world so chaotic that he is their only constant. They're devoted to us now because he told them to be."

"Sure," Jeremy said. "But that was only in the arena. Why would they still be following it?"

"Because Loki never clapped to signal that the battle was over. As far as they're concerned, this is all just part of the game that Loki told them to play by following our lead in the arena. Fenris gave them clear instructions—they follow my command until it's over."

Silence hung in the air again. James resisted the urge to blow another pillar of smoke in Gordon's face. His whiskey was finished and he was going to need another drink if he was going to play this ridiculous game.

"So what's our next move?" he said at last.

"That's one reason I wanted to bring you together," Gordon said. "Especially you, Andrew. Loki sent these with his care package, and I want to know if any of you recognize them.

Gordon unrolled the dirty blanket on the desk, revealing a dozen swords with dark blades. Scored into the steel, if they were made of steel, was a border of deep tick marks that formed some kind of letters. James didn't recognize the swords, and that fact didn't surprise him.

"They're for scouts," Andrew said.

Everyone looked at the hulking man.

"Here." Andrew picked up one of the swords upside down, slammed it into the stone floor, and was gone. The sword, freed of its owner, stood up by itself despite the fact that only the smallest tip of its blade was embedded in the stone floor.

"Now here," Andrew said from the hallway. They moved to see him, standing huge in the hallway over a sword that was identical to the one in the floor of Gordon's office. It stuck out from the floor at the same angle. "They're good for transporting one person. If you can see it in your mind, you can go there. Pull it from the ground again and you're back."

They stared at him in silence.

"Loki just gave us the way to beat him," Gordon said. He licked his lips.

Andrew raised an eyebrow and stared at Gordon for a minute before continuing. "They're limited in nature. You have to return to your origin point on every trip, since that requires pulling the sword and planting it again. That leaves you vulnerable, since anyone can stand next to the sword and wait with an axe to cut your head off when you return. Or this."

He walked into Gordon's office. The sword in the hallway disappeared without even leaving a mark on the floor where it had been lodged a second ago.

Andrew carried the sword out into the hallway to join them again. "Anyone can pull it from the starting point, and that leaves you stranded. They're common enough that almost every army had them at one point. Then people forgot how to make them and started hiding them instead. There are thousands out there, maybe tens or hundreds of thousands."

James exhaled a pillar of smoke. "Well, that's terrible news. So we could have visitors anytime."

They looked at Gordon, who shook his head. "One problem at a time. Loki left us a crate with more of these swords than we have members of the Royal Army. For now, we need to put them to use. Andrew, I'll need you to lead the scouting team."

"No."

They all turned to look at the hulking man again. James gave a quick burst of a laugh.

"The prophecies will come to pass and I have my final battle ahead of me," Andrew said. "I'm also not convinced that you're Odin. You've recited stories, but you haven't said anything about the gods that can't be found in a library. I remember being Thor. I remember Loki as a friend and a family member, and I don't recognize you at all."

Gordon locked eyes with him. "I sincerely hope that you change your mind."

Andrew held his gaze. "And I'll rip your heart out if you're pretending to be something you aren't. We'll see if Fenris eats you whole, since that's Odin's fate. If he does, you'll have my apology."

"Suit yourself," Gordon said. "But we only have three prison guards, including Heracles here, along with thirty-nine members of the Royal Army. As far as weapons are concerned, we have ten working rifles and a few dozen gladiator weapons from the arena. If you're not going to help us prepare for whatever lives in those woods, we could be slaughtered at any moment. The prophecies don't guarantee us safety."

\*\*\*

James left the barracks alone and crossed the laundry and cooking areas again. The cooking pots released the smell of some kind of sausage stew with herbs that made his mouth water, but he needed time to think before he ate. He still didn't buy the Norse-gods-end-of-the-world thing, but he'd be damned if Loki's shadows and the magic sword didn't make a good case for it. The trickster god was real enough. It all just seemed stupid to him, playing out some antiquated mythical apocalypse.

And then there were the dreams. He needed another drink.

As he walked, he realized that the base wasn't the end of the waterfall. The stream ran across the plateau and down into a massive gorge. Deep greens from mosses and trees blended with the yellows and reds of leaves just beginning to turn, brought shining to colorful life by the sun as it sunk between mountain peaks. The peaks themselves had no snow, but a cap of grasses or mosses or some other plant that James didn't know. Another bird rounded a peak and ascended through the clouds that frosted a crystal blue sky. James hoped the bird would stay where it was.

"Hard to take in?" Andrew walked until he was next to James and lit his pipe. Then he surveyed the land with him for a minute. "I imagine it's tough to swallow. It must be especially hard for you."

"What's that?"

"The view."

James looked out and a part of him felt a spike of sadness. "Why *is* that?"

Andrew took a few puffs from his pipe. "Because whatever Loki is doing to bring about Fimbulwinter, he's already started. The leaves don't change color in Vanaheim."

Andrew gave James a pat on the back that felt like a thunderclap on his spine and walked back toward where dinner was being served.

"Wait," James said. "Vana-what? Where are we?"

Andrew didn't turn around.

# Chapter 11

## MISSION BELLS IN VANAHEIM

Jeremy sat at his desk and turned his ring over between his thumbs and index fingers, looking through it at the open doorway. He stared at the gold band, then spun it on the wood. It formed a golden ball that spiraled slowly toward him and fell off the edge, bouncing on his pants before hitting the ground. Jeremy got up and retrieved it.

"You haven't commented on my joke," the shadow said.

The dark silhouette was dancing on the wall of his office. He glared at it and slipped the ring on his finger. He felt the ridges and imperfections that gave the piece of jewelry, as Beth had pointed out, its unique character. Then he opened the bottom drawer and stared at its contents.

The top two drawers had been empty. The bottom drawer contained a single gold ring. It was identical to the ring on Jeremy's finger, scuff marks and all.

"That's because I don't get it," Jeremy said.

"Oh, come on," the shadow replied. "You should know this, Heimdall."

"I don't," Jeremy said. He ran his fingers through his hair and slammed the door shut. "And I'm tired of your jokes."

He thought about the macabre prison games. He thought about Lance, probably lying dead somewhere in those polished black hallways. Jeremy wasn't surprised that the number of beds in the barracks matched the number of escaped prisoners. It would have been easy for Loki to leave out the forty-eight beds and then moderate the number of escapees accordingly. A few too many? Hang them with shadow nooses. A few too few? Have a soldier release another cell block and kill off as many prisoners as required to get the desired number. It seemed easy to Jeremy.

He just had to think like a sociopath, which had become significantly easier than he ever thought it would.

A small part of Jeremy thought that, maybe, that emotional numbness growing inside of him was evidence that he really was a god. A bigger part of him thought that it came from the amount of death that he had witnessed, and more than that, having died and returned to life. If his lack of feeling was due to Loki's prison games, he was starting to understand what Loki was turning people into.

The shadow chuckled and tap danced. It made disappointed noises when Jeremy stood from his chair and walked into the hallway, leaving it behind.

Damien was in his office, scrawling a picture onto a piece of paper. His stump rested on the desk, holding the paper in place as he scratched back and forth with the other hand in what was only artistic shading by a technical definition. The pictures already fastened to the wall behind him demonstrated that Damien, despite his dexterity with a sword, couldn't draw worth a damn.

A wolf snarled at Jeremy from one of the sketches, its jaws stretched at an unnatural angle and clearly drawn atop a dozen other versions. Its eyes bulged like a frog and its fur was made from a hundred thick lines that stretched way too far across the page to represent the real thing. Jeremy squinted to discern a bloody cleaver from the chaos of another sketch, lines drawn at funny angles that might have been intended to look menacing and looked instead like they had been created by someone who was almost blackout drunk.

On the far left edge of the desk, sitting on top of a stack of other drawings, was a sculpture of a man's head. The head looked like it had been ripped from a larger statue, and its face grinned cartoonishly through a beard. It hadn't come in Loki's care package, so he assumed the head had been in one of Damien's drawers.

Jeremy knocked on the open door. "You alright?"

"Fine," Damien said, not looking up from his sketch.

"Gordon is getting some people ready to learn how to use the scouting swords. Are you in?"

"I'm taking a shift guarding the prison entrance."

Gordon had set up a large sign in case any more prisoners escaped, telling them that they would be shot on sight if they refused to put down their weapons. So far, no one else had come out of the prison.

"I see," Jeremy said, looking carefully at the man.

The drawing that Damien was currently slaving over was a hand, palm upward. It was significantly better proportioned than Damien's other drawings, but the fingers stretched out at pained angles and ended in long fingernails filed to points.

Damien stopped, smacked his stump heavily on the desk, winced, and continued in a flurry of less careful, less realistic slashes of graphite. The fingernails of the hand grew longer, curving at the ends. He drew the tiny hairs on the back of the hand, each way too thick and too long to represent what Fenris's actual hand had looked like.

Beth's brother lifted his head abruptly and met Jeremy's eyes. "What do you want?"

Jeremy surprised himself by holding eye contact. Damien's eyes were bloodshot and wild. "I need you to teach me to use a sword."

Damien looked back down at his drawing. "There isn't time for that. I'm not staying."

"What do you mean?"

"I'm going to kill Fenris, as soon as I find him."

He cursed and scribbled over top of his drawing, turning the hair on the back of the hand into wool and then some kind of hairy growth that blotted out the entire appendage. Then he whacked his stump on the desk again, took out one of the cheap, gas station lighters that James had been using and lit the paper without lifting it from the desktop. The campfire smell of burning paper tickled Jeremy's nose as the flames consumed what was left of the drawing, leaving a scorched patch on the wood.

Jeremy stared for a minute before leaving Damien alone. Before all of this, he had hoped that he could fix Beth's depression by reuniting her with her brother. Now, he thought that would only make things worse. All of that was assuming that she was still alive.

It wasn't fear or anger that gripped him at that thought. It was the same cold that had come over him when Loki ordered the soldier to shoot himself.

*** 

From her seat by the fire, Angela watched a few men swing swords at each other. They were calling it training, but no one seemed to be learning anything. The men just took turns attacking with slashes and jabs that missed of their own accord as often as they were blocked by an opponent. Two men had received deep wounds already this morning from blows that did hit their mark, but that didn't make the others think twice about taking a turn with the weapons. As one man saw her looking at them, he shouted. "For Freya!"

Angela gave him the finger.

They had dragged a few of the leather executive chairs from the barracks outside, where they looked incredibly out of place around the fire. Angela had a mild hope that this would annoy Loki, and was annoyed in turn by the thought that he would probably find it hilarious. She sipped from a glass of Andrew's scotch, a deep and rich flavor that dwarfed that of James's bourbon. But the bourbon had a rough charm, especially when tasted while looking at that stupid grin.

She heard footsteps crunch the grass behind her and smelled sausage and rice.

"My lady," James said, extending a bowl of food as she turned around.

One of the men playing soldiers landed a square hit on his opponent's shoulder, cutting deep into it like carving a roast. They laughed and the bleeding recipient made his way to the medical area for stitches and antiseptic, Gordon's rules. The old man had insisted that every "warrior" was needed for the time ahead, and that apparently required only the smallest of precautions. Their response had been a resounding cheer. "For Odin!"

Angela took the bowl and James sat down next to her, rubbing his own wounded shoulder. Andrew sat on the other side of the fire, whittling with a small pocket knife and unaware of a wood shaving resting comfortably in his wiry beard. She could see the curved outline of a long pipe emerging from the piece of wood in his hands.

She stirred her meal and took a bite. It tasted like what it was, freeze-dried sausage and parboiled rice with some overly salty seasoning mix coating every grain. It was better than the tasteless beans and rice inside the prison, but she was going to need an entire bucket of water to quench the salt thirst.

"So," James said to Andrew, "you remember your past lives, including Thor. What's that like?"

Andrew didn't look up from his whittling. He twisted the knife slowly, boring a hole into the wood. "It's like a mirror that falls over and shatters. When you try to put it back together, there are more pieces than there should be. I remember being Thor, and Thor remembers being other people, but not all of the pieces fit."

James grunted in response and lit a cigarette. He extended the pack to Angela and she waved it off. He extended it to Andrew, who didn't look up. Then he flicked the full cigarette into the fire and plunged a fork into his meal. Despite his excitement at finding the carton, he had been wasting a lot of cigarettes by smoking only the first puff and throwing them away.

A few more men picked up swords and joined in with the others. The man with the wounded shoulder sat a short distance away, pushing a needle through himself with more care than made sense for his level of self concern.

James looked up. "So why do you believe in the prophecies?"

Andrew paused for a second, then continued twisting the knife. "Because believing in them makes me stronger."

James pursed his lips. "I don't think that would make me stronger. It seems like the opposite of strength."

"Then don't believe them," Andrew said. "No one needs you to."

Muttering to himself, James stood up and walked toward the barracks. Angela watched him go, smiling at his back. It was interesting to see what flustered the man, since not much seemed to.

A breeze blew past them, colder than the previous wind, carrying a multi-surface cleaner smell of evergreens and rain. Angela leaned toward the fire to banish the chill and took another sip of her scotch. The cold didn't seem to bother Andrew.

"So what's Vanaheim?" she said.

Andrew stopped and met her eyes. Angela held his gaze, counting the deep wrinkles around his eyes that gave them a discerning look. She couldn't tell if he was weighing something about her or choosing his words carefully. Maybe he hadn't expected James to tell her what he had said.

He went back to his whittling before he spoke. "Vanaheim is a realm."

"Alright," Angela said. "A realm. Like a kingdom?"

"Yes, but also a world in its own. Separate from Midgard."

"Midgard?"

Andrew paused. "Earth."

Suddenly, she wouldn't have minded one of James's cigarettes. If he came back, she'd have to take him up on it. "Separate how?"

"Think America and Europe, separated by an ocean. Midgard and Vanaheim are separated by something like that."

"Alright. So we're in Vanaheim. What direction is Midgard?"

"No direction."

Angela pinched the bridge of her nose with her knuckles. Then she took another sip of her scotch. "So you know all of this, and you're deliberately being as unhelpful as possible."

He looked up at her again. "There are holes in whatever separates the worlds. Lots of them. Loki brought us through one of those gates to get here, which means that one is close. Direction, however, isn't something that applies to the gates. They lead where they lead."

"Do you know where it is?"

"No." He went back to his whittling.

She stared at him. "So you really don't care how all of this turns out?"

Andrew set the carving knife on his lap, folded his hands and looked deep into her eyes. "When we imprisoned Loki, we made him into what he is. Everyone wants something from Ragnarok. Gordon wants to stop it, and Loki wants to change it. I'm not here to play their games."

Angela sat back in her chair and sipped her scotch again as the fire crackled. In a way, she was glad that Andrew wasn't much of a talker. "I don't want anything from Ragnarok. From what I can tell, neither does James."

"Then stay the hell away from Gordon. I've told him enough that he should be able to avoid doing something stupid, but that doesn't guarantee anything."

***

"Just focus," Gordon said. "Imagine yourself standing

over there."

The strange sword tingled in Jeremy's hand as if it were electric. It was lighter than he thought it would be, much lighter than the swords he had used in the arena. The markings on the blade shimmered in the sunlight as he looked down at it. He pictured himself standing where Gordon pointed, then plunged the sword into the dirt.

The electric buzz filled his body and he winced as the world rose around him like an ocean, swallowing him whole. There was movement involved, but he couldn't figure out how as he felt himself tossed from where he stood. When the world sank and became normal again, he fell to the ground and fought the urge to vomit.

"Good," Gordon said. "It's difficult to land in a new spot, but now that should be easier. Pull it out and let's try again."

A crowd was beginning to gather around them. Gordon had said that would happen. The more people who were interested in becoming scouts, the better. Jeremy heard someone shout "For Heimdall!"

He was already getting tired of the Royal Army, who only seemed to be able to say one sentence.

Jeremy stood up and pulled the sword out of the ground. The electric sensation still happened, but the return trip didn't make the world lurch or knock Jeremy over. He waited a moment, then formed as clear a picture in his mind as he could. He tried to remember the perspective exactly, the distance from Gordon and from the crowd. As much as possible, he tried to *already* be there in his mind. He plunged the sword into the ground again.

This time, with the electric sensation came only a small lurch and he was there. Gordon clapped his hands and Jeremy plucked the sword from the ground, looking at them from his original location again. He grinned and performed the most half-assed of bows, bending mostly at his shoulders and neck.

Then he cursed himself for being an idiot as a swell of excitement exploded inside of him. He pictured standing in his living room, facing the couch where Beth had sat the last time he saw her. He tried to picture the color of the walls, some special kind of off-white that Beth had picked out when Jeremy had declined to give an opinion. He squeezed his eyes shut and dug the blade into the ground one more time.

Nothing.

He pulled the sword out and tried it again. Still nothing. Gordon looked at him with a raised eyebrow.

Jeremy pictured the spot across the grass again, stabbed the dirt, and he was there. He pulled it out and was back, then pictured his living room and stabbed the ground one more time. Still nothing. A small part of him was disappointed. A bigger part was numb.

They stared at each other for a long moment before Gordon shrugged. "We're going to have to set up a safe place for scouts to use as their starting point. It will need to be guarded carefully."

Gordon turned to the crowd. "Who wants to give it a try?"

He smiled as cheers rose. Everyone watching wanted to try the magic traveling sword. "For Odin," they shouted.

They took turns with the single sword, each struggling somewhat more than Jeremy had. Some couldn't stand that electric stab long enough to travel successfully while others couldn't even make the sword work. Gordon clapped after each success and did his best to encourage those who failed. Eventually, Jeremy and the others were scooting across the clearing, zipping back and forth between their starting positions and increasingly distant ones.

Somewhere in the middle of the training session, one of Gordon's soldiers shot down another bird.

They set up a scouting area between the barracks and the wall of the cliff surrounding the clearing. It was a roped-off patch of dirt with one of the three prison soldiers guarding it. After a few days, a number of members of the Royal Army were able to use the swords reliably.

The newly-trained scouts included Jeremy and Gordon himself. The other members of the Royal Family learned to use the swords as well, but declined Gordon's request that they join the scouting team. When Gordon declared it an order, they all issued a booming laughter that visibly disturbed the Royal Army.

\*\*\*

Jeremy stood on the cliff overlooking the escapee camp, hand on the hilt of the scouting sword. Behind him was an ocean extending toward the horizon as far as he could see. That ocean supplied the waterfall that fell into the mouth of the giant statue of Loki that had been their prison. The talking shadow didn't follow him up here, but as he looked at the statue, he was constantly reminded of Loki's presence.

Past the camp, the river formed by the waterfall divided into three large streams that themselves divided into dozens of smaller ones, all flowing downhill from one plateau to another before meeting again and flowing through a large canyon off into the distance. Mountains rose from the canyon walls, their forked and jagged tops covered in fuzzy greenery. Jeremy was starting to see farther, which came with implications he didn't think he liked. As Gordon kept reminding him, Heimdall was supposed to have superhuman sight and hearing. As the days passed, Jeremy was giving up the idea of his previous life being his only one.

As he looked out into the forest, he could see figures moving in the distance. These weren't Gordon's scouts. They wore rags that resembled skirts, and their gray, animal fur coats were slashed with pieces of red fabric. A crude, crimson lion centered an otherwise white flag that hung above the small camp.

As Jeremy looked, the people of the lion tribe seemed oddly familiar to him. They wore crested, wide-brimmed helmets that reminded him of the costumes that actors wore in documentaries about Spanish conquistadors looking for the fountain of youth. The helmets looked odd in combination with the fur clothing.

Jeremy pulled the scouting sword from the ground and was transported back to the roped off patch, where he stared down a rifle until the soldier lowered his weapon. It was amazing how little he was bothered by having guns pointed at him. Before all of this, he would have thought hard about the possibility that the soldier would have some kind of finger spasm and Jeremy's life would be over. Now, he looked at the soldier's dark visor and silently dared him to pull the trigger. If that happened, Jeremy thought Loki might just bring him back to life to continue the joke. Either that, or he would end up in the Norse underworld.

One way or another, he would find Beth. He wasn't going to give up that part of his old life. If she was alive, he would find her in Midgard. If she was dead, he would find her in Niflheim. Both seemed equally out of reach at the moment, but that would change.

When the soldier turned his attention to the other swords sticking out of the ground, caught in the grip of something beyond the dirt, Jeremy made his way to the barracks. Gordon was in his office, as Jeremy had expected. The old cowboy rarely left.

Jeremy knocked on the open door and Gordon motioned for Jeremy to have a seat without looking up. To his irritation, this reminded Jeremy of a meeting with Mr. Douglas. He did as Gordon gestured and examined the hand-drawn map on Gordon's desk as the old man sketched recently explored terrain. The cliff and ocean that Jeremy had just visited formed the edge of the eastern side of the map, with a large space extending about a foot of unmarked paper beyond it. The map grew slowly to the west, rings marking the edges of the plateaus and triangles marking mountains.

A number of tick marks indicated spots that scouts were made to memorize so that they could return at a moment's notice. Jeremy had only been to a few of these, much less memorized them. Gordon's orders for Jeremy had been to keep watch at the top of the cliff.

The river was carefully sketched between a few symbols that didn't symbolize landmarks. A lion, carefully outlined with one paw stretched high above the other, sat on one bank of the river. On the other bank, a bull pointed its horns at the lion. Farther downstream, a bear rested on its back with legs stretched stiff upward. Its eyes were exes.

Beyond that, deep within the forest marked by partial triangles that were drawn only slightly different from those indicating the mountains, there was a large Christian cross. The area next to the cross was circled three times and Gordon was sketching a long road from those circles that wound its way up the plateaus and toward the prison.

Gordon finally put his sketching pencil down and looked at Jeremy. "Any news?"

"The lion tribe seems to have a few hundred members."

The old man pursed his lips and went back to sketching. He drew the contour of the road carefully, marking spots where the forest around it became more or less dense. He marked places where the road turned sharply, drawing empty circles that Jeremy didn't know the meaning behind.

Jeremy tapped his fingers on the desk. "My sight is

getting sharper."

Gordon looked up at him momentarily, then leaned more deeply over the desk and continued sketching. "That's good. Get back to the cliff and keep me updated."

"Do you want me to go out with a scouting party?"

Gordon didn't look up. "No. We've already lost five men to animal attacks out there. Your sight is one thing, but the prophecies are clear that you kill Loki. That means that you hold the secret to stopping him, whatever that might be. If you get killed in an ambush or by a pack of animals, Loki wins."

The silence between them hung for about a minute before the sound of gunfire ripped it apart.

A crowd was gathering around the scouting area, where two of Gordon's soldiers kept their guns trained on a corpse sprawled across the rope line. The owner of the corpse had stumbled backward and taken a portion of the roping with him. By the time Jeremy and Gordon got there, the members of the Royal Army were whispering something about a barbarian army. There were a few shouts of "For Odin" and "For Heimdall" as they arrived, making Jeremy wince. The members of the Royal Army spoke among themselves, but their vocabulary became instantly limited whenever they saw Jeremy or the others from his cell block. They were another constant reminder of Loki's game, whatever it was.

The dead man wore a metal breastplate, shredded by the soldiers' gunfire into something that looked like a bloody metal vest rather than armor. The man's helmet, flat-brimmed metal with an inch-tall crest running from front to back, had fallen and bounced several yards away. His black mustache and hair were plastered against his head with some kind of ointment and a puckered burn scar marred his left cheek. The scar was circular, with triangular rays that made it resemble the sun in a kid's drawing. Next to the dead man, Jeremy could see the scouting sword that had transported him.

"Pull the other swords," Gordon ordered.

"That'll leave the scouts stranded," Jeremy said.

Gordon shook his head. "The chance is better that they're already dead."

Someone yelled "For Odin" and Jeremy gave them a sour look.

"Did he speak?" Gordon said to one of the soldiers.

The soldier shook his head.

At this point, Andrew, Angela, and James made their way to the scouting area to see what the commotion was about. Andrew picked up the dead man's helmet and turned it around in his hands. He looked at Gordon, then at Jeremy.

"We'll need to go through his effects," Gordon said as one of the soldiers stepped into the scouting area and pulled the two remaining swords from the ground. "Then we'll burn the body."

"We'll bury him with our own," Andrew said. "Trim his fingernails first. Hel is building her battle ship for Ragnarok out of the fingernails of the fallen."

Gordon stared at the hulking man. Andrew stared back.

Gordon pursed his lips and nodded.

James raised an eyebrow. "Well, that's disgusting."

When it was done, Andrew, James, and Angela returned to their fire. Jeremy followed Gordon back to his office to go through the dead man's possessions.

Gordon folded his map carefully and set it aside. Then he laid the ruined breastplate on the desk and the helmet on top of it. The breastplate was engraved with a bull that looked very similar to the one on the old cowboy's map. Gordon set a short black dagger with no markings at all next to a straight, thin sword with a cross inlaid into the hardwood hilt. He set down a small book the size of his palm and a crude pencil next to those.

"The helmet and breastplate have the style of a sixteenth century explorer," Gordon said.

Jeremy picked up the book and flipped through the pages. They were old and brown, lined with neat script. He saw some Spanish words, but had taken enough Spanish in high school to know that it wasn't the language used in most of the text.

Gordon ran his finger along the broad side of the sword, then scraped the edge sideways against his thumb. "The gates between realms have been open for a long time. If a group of explorers and their families came through, they could have established themselves. Given enough time, the ones who survived could start a civilization." He looked through the book. "It would certainly explain the evolution of their language. It would also explain the insignia."

Jeremy thought of the symbols on the map. The lion, the bull, the dead bear. The Christian cross. "They're from Midgard?"

Gordon nodded.

Jeremy looked at the sword and dagger. "Why don't they have guns?"

"Maybe they couldn't find their way back. Cut off from society, they didn't have the means or knowledge to make more powerful weapons. They were technologically advanced for their time, but they're obsolete compared to our modern world."

There was a long silence between them.

"We'll have to be on the lookout," Gordon said. "With one of their men gone missing, and them having captured or killed a few of ours, I suspect things aren't going to be peaceful between us. They've survived in this land for a long time without modern weapons, and there thousands of these people divided into different tribes. The Royal Army has a few dozen warriors and ten rifles, each of which contain a single, partially used clip of ammunition. That's a battle we won't win."

"Great," Jeremy said. "Then we need to get to a gate quickly. Have we found one yet?"

Gordon looked at Jeremy for a moment, then set the dead man's effects on the ground and spread his map out on the table. He pointed to the circled area around the cross. "There's a citadel here. I think it guards the gate that brought us to Loki's prison in the first place. The trouble is, it's massively fortified and much more modern than the tribe whose member we just buried. They have the same guns that were used inside Loki's prison, and the scouts have reported seeing a man with yellow eyes and a golden staff walking among the soldiers outside the walls."

Jeremy's heart sank. "Why the cross?"

"It's on their flag. Maybe it was a missionary group at one point, or a colonial expansion. It would make sense, if Fenris has been manipulating religions as part of Loki's plans, that a strong Christian outpost in this realm would be useful. It would let Fenris import weapons and prisoners into Vanaheim."

"Then how do we get in?"

Gordon leaned back in his chair. "I'm not sure we do. We certainly don't have the manpower to take the citadel by force."

"What about using the scouting swords to get inside?"

Gordon shook his head. "Even if that worked, we have no idea what's waiting for us inside. If Fenris is running the place, we can bet there's a trap involved."

Jeremy turned his wedding ring around on his finger. "Well, what then?"

"We keep scouting. There has to be another way."

# Chapter 12

## A LONELY VIOLIN

"For Odin," Ajax said aloud as he jabbed the ground with the scouting sword.

His mind calm, the picture perfect, he found himself standing between two massive trees and staring out over a plateau's cliff as the morning sun bounced across the river. He didn't pay attention to the curves of the river anymore, since Odin didn't ask for that information.

"What orders?" Achilles said. The Royal Warrior held the hilt of his scouting sword and fingered the trigger of his rifle with his other hand.

"We're to engage from the west."

Achilles nodded solemnly. "For Odin."

Another scouting sword appeared in the ground next to them, ethereal and dreamlike for an instant before becoming solid a moment later. David solidified next to it.

"What orders?" David said.

"We're to engage from the west."

David nodded solemnly. "For Odin."

The three pulled their scouting swords and jabbed the ground again, traveling to the scouting grounds and then some distance to the west, leaping to another cliff overlooking a swathe of paved ground. Several vehicles idled on the pavement, and near them, a block of soldiers stood motionless in the glare of the morning sun. The soldiers' dark uniforms shimmered with golden patches and they wore berets with an insignia that Ajax didn't recognize. Behind the block of soldiers, walls encompassed a massive stone fortress. A number of stone blocks were turned on their side, providing a texture difference to the surface of the wall in the shape of a giant cross. Odin already had that information.

"Let us pray," Ajax said.

David and Achilles bowed their heads, somewhere in the distance, Ajax could hear the soft tug of a string instrument. It danced gently, low enough that the army below didn't react. Odin had refuted that information, and so Ajax tried not to hear the music.

"He who would save his life will lose it. By our lives, Lord, delivered into the hands of the darkened sorceress, we reject cowardice in all its forms. For Odin, for Heimdall, for Freyr. For Freya and Thor and Tyr. For Loki and Garm and Fenris. For the wolves and the heroes, Valkyrie and the maiden ruins. Make us into giants, Lord. Let us bleed vengeance so caustic it burns the world."

Ajax prayed silently for forgiveness, in case he had

offended any of the gods with the verbiage of his spoken prayer.

The music grew slowly. They knelt and readied their rifles as one officer below lifted his face in their direction.

They stood and opened fire into the Army of the Cross.

\*\*\*

Alarm bells nearly drowned out the clash of steel against steel outside the castle window. Freyr grinned at the giant on the table, held there by the sword that hung gracefully in the air with the blade tip pressed firmly against the beast's sternum. Freyr had bound the giant's hands and feet at each end of the table, but that was more for effect than necessity.

"How is the spell reversed?"

The giant curled black lips around its teeth. "It won't be."

Freyr's sword pushed harder on the giant's breastbone, making the creature's eyes squeeze tightly shut for a moment before it hacked a feigned laughter. "You really don't remember, do you?"

Freyr pressed his index finger on the giant's breastbone, making it cry out. "You have a little bit to go yet, but not much, before the bone snaps."

The sword pressed harder. The cacophony outside had moved inward and Freyr could hear his men fighting in the hallway. More giants snarled as steel met steel in his ears.

Alex leaned against the stone wall and lit a cigarette. "Better hurry this up. I don't think we have much time on our hands."

Freyr leaned over the giant and looked into its pale blue eyes. "Tell me, or I'll bring your head back to Odin and see what he can extract from it."

"I think we've been over this," Alex said. He blew a cloud of smoke across the room and the giant coughed. "He's not going to tell you anything."

Freyr raised an eyebrow.

"Seriously," Alex said. He raised a fist and tapped his knuckle on the stone wall. It sounded throaty and deep, like knocking on wood.

James felt the polished wood of the desk on his face before he opened his eyes. He was getting used to dreaming as Freyr at this point. Skin sticking to the smooth surface, he peeled his face from the wood and looked to the doorway, where Angela stood looking at him.

She gave him a concerned half-smile. "You alright?"

A half-empty pack of cigarettes sat at the edge of the desktop, next to about a swallow of whiskey left in his glass. He downed the swallow and screwed a cigarette into his lips. "Fine." Looking at her, he wasn't sure that was true. "Are you having dreams about Freya?"

Angela sat down on the other side of his desk and took a cigarette from his pack. "I haven't dreamed about anything since we've been here. Have you?"

He nodded.

"Want to talk about it?"

He shook his head.

She looked at him for a moment, then picked up the lighter and lit her cigarette. "Andrew says that Vanaheim is your home, if you're really Freyr." She smiled. "He said you're going to have trouble leaving."

James thought of Freya's blue-tinged, frosted lips. He pictured Angela fighting frost giants, gathering her mouth to the side in disapproval as she cut the throat of some terrifying creature. Looking at her, he could feel doubt emptying from his mind. She was Freya, whether she liked it or not. And he couldn't figure out how to save her from what was coming. It was also very possible that he was going insane.

"Want a drink?" he said, pulling the bourbon from the bottom drawer of his desk. He had pushed the revolver that shared a drawer with it all the way to the back. It was loaded.

"Of course," Angela said. "If the world ends, I'd prefer to be drunk. It's how I intended it when I was arrested in the first place."

He nodded and poured them both a full glass. She took hers and sipped it as James shook the bottle, mourning the fact that it was starting to run low. It had only been a week since they had escaped from the prison, and he was almost ready to march back inside and demand another bottle of liquor from Loki. Maybe he would also give him the finger.

"I'm don't mind leaving," James said. "I just don't have anywhere to go."

Angela nodded. "I don't either. The closest thing I had to family is gone."

James smiled. "I'll be honest with you, though. I do like

it here. If we weren't still a fucking stone's throw away from Loki and his prison, I'd consider making this place home."

They clinked glasses and sat in silence.

\*\*\*

Perseus lowered his eyes as Odin left the small-roofed structure, little more than a shed. The god carried a small bag slung over his shoulder by a strap, which jingled faintly with every other step. He made notes in a small book as he walked, hardly looking up from them as he slowed to a stop in front of Perseus.

"For Odin," Perseus said. Then he said a silent prayer, hoping it was not cowardly to do so. If it was, Odin might kill him with a snap of his fingers.

Odin didn't look up. "I'm finished with it. Please return our friend safely to his tribe."

Perseus nodded. "For Odin."

The god looked at him for what seemed like years. Perseus kept his eyes lowered as Odin's face split in a wide, angular grin. After a few moments, Odin nodded and Perseus said a prayer of thanks when he went.

Sigurd and Aeneas approached silently and Perseus nodded at them. "For Odin," both of them said solemnly.

"For Odin," Perseus agreed.

"What orders?"

"The prisoner is to be returned to his people."

They nodded and opened the shed slowly. Perseus had lost most of his sensitivity to the smell of blood while doing Odin's bidding, but the dank and fetid smell of sweat hung thick in the air and contained a subtle, metallic tinge. The room was dimly lit and silent.

The man inside was unconscious and half-stuffed into a large bag. His hair was cut short and Odin had stripped him of his warrior's uniform. In His wisdom, Odin had left no visible wounds on the man.

The scouting sword that had brought the soldier to the shed as a trap had been cast aside in the ensuing struggle and Perseus picked it up. He tucked it into his belt and they finished helping the man into the bag before carrying him out. As they nearly finished zipping the bag, the soldier shouted.

"Coke!"

They stared at him. His eyes were still closed and his eyebrows furrowed. "Coke!"

Perseus took the scouting sword from his belt and battered the man's forehead once with the hilt. The soldier was quiet.

They closed the bag and quietly dragged the soldier from the shed. Soft music played in the distance, a single string instrument that tangled notes like threads of a gentle noose. Perseus found the ambiance pleasant as they lifted the soldier and carried him across the forest floor. Fallen leaves occasionally crumpled under their feet, but they worked in silence otherwise.

A low growl emerged from the foliage. They turned and were greeted with wide, yellow eyes set in a dark gray face. Almost-white teeth jutted from strangely immaculate, pink gums. The wolf's growl vibrated and grew, cut to silence for a moment, and crackled to life again as it drew closer with its head held low.

Sigurd and Aeneas drew their rifles. Perseus tried to stay them with a gesture, but it was too late. They opened fire and the wolf toppled. Perseus dropped to his knees.

"He who would save his life will lose it," Perseus recited. It was the first commandment, the call to boldness that Loki, God of gods, had handed down from his sacred seat. "We have failed, Odin. We deserve not your mercy and we do not ask it. May your punishment be swift. May it be cruel. May it reforge us into the weapons that suit your purposes perfectly, if we are given the honor of rebirth."

Sigurd and Aeneas fell to their knees as well and prayed similarly. In the distance, men marched toward them through the trees. They wore forest camouflage and carried rifles, and several of them shouted something at the scouts in a language they didn't understand. Odin surely had this information. The master of war had granted them swift punishment and they thanked him for it.

Perseus smiled as the soldiers approached. He didn't even attempt to use the scouting sword to escape.

***

Jeremy stood on the cliff and stared out over the camp and into the forest. It was the only place that he could get away from members of the Royal Army, whose incessant mantra was beyond obnoxious. Every time Jeremy heard one of them boldly shout "For Heimdall," or whisper it reverently as he passed, he cringed. He was starting to think that Loki was just using that creepy, two-word devotional to annoy him.

Gordon hadn't left his office in days. Scouts constantly entered and left the barracks, bringing news and carrying handwritten orders out with them. Some left through the scouting grounds. Three scouts had left this morning through the forest instead, each carrying a rifle and a scouting sword. Jeremy didn't agree with the decision to send them out with rifles, since they had already lost three guns to the Vanaheim tribes in an ambush the previous morning.

That left seven guns, and Gordon had allowed three more to leave the camp. Odin was supposed to be a brilliant strategist. Jeremy was sure that he had his reasons for what he was doing.

He heard gunfire and his eyes darted to its location deep within the forest. It must have been miles away, and he saw it as if through a telescope. The three scouts opened fire on a large wolf near a recently-constructed shed, then knelt and waited to be captured by men carrying the same rifles as those found in Loki's prison. Fenris's soldiers were venturing closer, and those three guns were gone.

The sheds were nasty business. Gordon had his reasons.

Jeremy pulled the scouting sword and was transported to the scouting grounds. He slid the sword into his belt and nodded to the prison soldier, who pointed one of their four remaining rifles at him. He couldn't tell if it was Heracles or one of the other two, whose names Gordon had revealed to be Alexander and Anansi. The soldier didn't nod back at him, and Jeremy gave him a wide berth as he made his way into the barracks.

When he got to Gordon's office, a member of the Royal Army nearly ran into him. The man was leaving in a hurry, and whispered "For Heimdall" as he passed with eyes plastered to the floor. It was amazing how many things could be said by changing the intonation of those two words, and every single combination made Jeremy want to smash the speaker's face.

Gordon was moving a small pile of pebbles on his map. He slid them about an inch away from the lion and toward the escapee camp. Other piles were scattered around the map, forming a wavy sort of polygon that enclosed Loki's prison and their group. Gordon studied the map and scratched the back of his head so feverishly that it looked like he was having a seizure.

A scout ran into the office and whispered in Gordon's ear. Gordon moved another pile of pebbles east on the map, closer to the camp and Loki's prison. He wrote out an order and handed it to the scout.

When the scout was gone, the old man slammed his fist on the table with a solid thud, rattling the pebbles. "It doesn't make any sense."

Jeremy shook his head. "We just lost three more rifles."

Gordon lifted his face and stared at him. "What?"

"The scouts guarding your torture shed near the ruins of the bear tribe," Jeremy said. "I just saw Fenris's army capture them."

Another scout came and whispered in Gordon's ear.

Then another, immediately following. Gordon moved a few more piles of pebbles toward the camp.

The old man gave him a flat stare. "The bear is Russian, and I don't know what you're talking about beyond that. I didn't order anyone to take rifles out of the camp. And I don't know what you mean by *torture shed*."

Jeremy was silent. Gordon maintained his stare and his eyes widened.

"No, no, NO!" Gordon grabbed a corner of the map and swung his arm, partially ripping the corner and sending the rest of the map gliding into the wall. Pebbles scattered and Jeremy could see Gordon's rifle leaning against the table next to his chair. The other three were still being carried by the prison soldiers.

The shadow laughed.

Jeremy's heart sank. Gordon couldn't hear the shadow, but Jeremy wished the old man could. Jeremy should have said something when he saw the men leave. Trying to find the words for an apology, his lips wrestled with each other until he could only say one word. "Loki."

"*For* Loki, you mean." Gordon stared at him. "The tribes of Vanaheim are coming for us. You thought I was torturing them and didn't even think to mention it. Whatever joke Loki is playing on you, it's coming out."

Jeremy's face flushed.

Gordon shook his head. "We have four rifles, with less than a dozen rounds left in each clip. The Royal Army is down to fifteen warriors, and Loki can take control of them again just by clapping his hands. There are six of us that aren't loyal to the trickster god, and if Loki has been impersonating me, he could be impersonating anyone. If we don't figure out what he wants from all of this, we're going to die."

The last words barely registered. "Five of us," Jeremy said. "Damien left to find Fenris a few days ago. He said he told you he was leaving."

Gordon's silence gave Jeremy a chill. If it weren't for that shadow consistently hanging around, he'd have been terrified that anything could be a trick. Because of the shadow, however, he was comfortable in the knowledge that Loki couldn't let a joke go on too long without getting to the punchline. He was too proud of his tricks.

"Let's hear it then," the shadow said.

Jeremy refused to look at it. Out of the corner of his eye, he could see the shadow leap across the wall, trying to get his attention. "Why would Loki give us an army, let us escape, send us supplies and scouting swords, and then sit back and watch the Vanaheim tribes massacre us? I don't see the humor in it."

The shadow cackled. "You're getting there, Heimdall."

Gordon shook his head. His gaze was hollow. "I thought I was free from him this time. I really did."

"Maybe this isn't the way he wanted us to escape," Jeremy said.

The shadow was silent.

Jeremy continued. His heart beat faster as he spoke. "Maybe there's another gate inside the prison."

The old man stood up and picked up the map, tossing it

onto the desk in a loose, crumpled ball. "That's insanity."

Jeremy shook his head. "Is it? How many prisoners have you fought in the arena, and how many have you seen again? Loki set this whole prison up to mess with the beliefs of the prisoners, right?"

"Right."

"Then they have to escape to complete his game. They have to get back to society and bring back whatever he's put in their heads. Otherwise, he's just playing in a sandbox that resets itself every time he kills a mass of escaping prisoners."

The shadow clapped. "I'm impressed, Heimdall."

"There's no way I'm walking back into that prison," Gordon said.

Jeremy nodded. "Then you're welcome to die here. If the tribes are coming for us, I don't see another way."

Gordon stared at the surface of his desk. His eyes took on a hint of red. "I think you're right."

"FOR ODIN!"

"For Thor!"

"For Freya!"

There was gunfire outside.

Jeremy stood up. "Fenris's army is here."

"No," Gordon said. "His army is still getting into position. They've cut off our scouts so we can't get behind their lines, but they haven't leaped over miles of forest in five minutes."

"Not unless they all have scouting swords," Jeremy said.

A scout ran inside and fell to his knees. "Forgive us,

Odin. The attack is coming from within the prison. We were unprepared, but I assure you that there are no cowards among the men. Each of us is ready to die, but we are but stupid—"

"Enough of that," Gordon said. "Is the Royal Army engaging?"

"Yes, Odin."

"All fifteen of them?"

The man hesitated. "All nine, Odin."

Jeremy stared. It was the first time he had heard a member of the Royal Army use sentences since they had escaped. For some reason, he wanted to punch the man even more.

"We can't afford that," Gordon said. "Come on. We have to stop them."

Jeremy plunged his scouting sword into the floor of Gordon's office and stood on the cliff, looking down at the battle. Nine men ran toward the prison with their arena swords held high. From the entrance to the prison, a group of twenty charged past the sign warning them to lay down their weapons. The space between them was closing.

With hardly a thought, Jeremy ripped the scouting sword from the ground and jabbed it back again.

"For Heimdall!"

Jeremy stood between the two armies. For a moment, the cold feeling overtook his chest again as he thought he was about to die. He wasn't sure what standing here was going to accomplish, but his instinct had been to join the battle and he hadn't had time to think it through.

Gunfire stopped and the army charging out of the prison slowed its charge. The nine members remaining of the Royal Army also slowed. Jeremy could hear the groans of a few men nursing bullet wounds behind him. The silence hung over the two groups and Jeremy thought there was every chance that he was still going to be shot.

In the silence, he could hear a violin playing softly in the distance.

A man from the opposing army left the ranks and walked out to meet him, a strange smile on his face.

Jeremy looked at Lance Hunter and couldn't help a smile of his own. The man wore a prison soldier's armor with a rifle slung across his back. He held a cleaver in one hand and a sword in the other, and set them both on the ground without breaking eye contact.

"It's good to see you again, Jeremy."

"You as well, Lance. I thought you were dead."

The members of Lance's group were slowly laying their weapons down as well, shooting appropriately distrustful looks at the Royal Army.

Lance shook his head. His eyes were a much brighter blue than Jeremy remembered, but this was also the first time he had seen his cellmate in sunlight. "It's Beowulf, now. My survival depended on it."

Jeremy raised an eyebrow. At least the man wasn't muttering "For Heimdall."

"You're kind of an idiot," Lance said, "appearing out of nowhere in the middle of a crossfire."

Jeremy's smile deepened. "And you're more of an

asshole than I remember." He paused, feeling that coldness grow despite seeing the familiar face. "In any case, I don't think dying would get us away from Loki. Let's talk in private."

Lance gestured to the group behind him. "These men and women are hungry. If you'll feed us, you and I can talk and then we'll be on our way."

"Your group can share our food," Jeremy said, "but I don't recommend venturing into the forest. Loki has been playing as many games out there as he did in the prison."

Lance stared out over the camp, then nodded slowly. They made their way to the camp. As they walked, one of the men in Lance's army whispered "For Beowulf."

***

When they got to Jeremy's office, he narrowed his eyes and leaned back in his chair. "How did you survive that long with no food or water?"

Lance spoke around a mouthful of rehydrated rice and beans. "We found a food storage room, ate what we could at the time and carried the rest for rations." He paused, his face darkening. "As for water, I imagine you know there was plenty."

Jeremy imagined drinking from the water that filled a prison stairwell. He wondered if the waterlogged bodies decomposing at the bottom would make the water poisonous. By the absolutely straight look on Lance's face, he imagined it wasn't a curiosity to the man.

"Any more encounters with guards? Has Loki been keeping the prison running?"

Lance shook his head. "A few scuffles, but only with other prisoners. People are still starving to death in there."

They met gazes and Jeremy nodded. "I'm sure you must have lost many men. I'm sorry about that."

Lace nodded. "So Loki set this place up for you?"

"Yep."

"And you're sleeping in it?"

"Yep."

Lance looked around. "So it's a better-looking prison."

Jeremy smiled. "Yep."

The man had changed quite a bit since Jeremy had last seen him. And those pale blue eyes weren't just brighter because of the change in lighting. Even inside the barracks, those eyes reminded Jeremy of a Siberian Husky.

Lance shrugged. "Did he leave you anything in the drawers?"

"A joke, according to him. Check this out."

Lance moved around the desk and Jeremy opened bottom drawer to reveal nine perfect copies of his wedding ring. Lance's eyes opened wide and he reached out to touch them.

"I would really not do that," Jeremy said. "Loki's playing some kind of game with them. There was just one when I got here, and a few nights ago the other eight showed up."

Lance pulled his hand back. "Have you told Gordon?"

"I don't want him trying to use the rings to his advantage, since I think that's what Loki wants." Jeremy turned his wedding ring on his finger, reminding himself that it was the real one. "If I can kill his fun just a little by leaving this joke where it is, I'm going to do that."

Lance nodded, still staring at the rings with a strange intensity.

Jeremy closed the drawer. "We're going back into the prison."

The man's stare ended and his eyes widened again. "You can't be serious."

"The people who already live out in that forest are coming to kill us. We don't have any choice but to go back inside and play Loki's games one last time."

Lance looked at him and set his bowl on the table. "That can't be true."

Jeremy shrugged. "Believe me when I say I'm not eager for it. Unless we find a better option, that's our next move."

They sat in silence for a moment. Jeremy felt a certain amount of pity for his cellmate. He had finally made it out of the prison, and they were either going to die or go back inside.

"We're not turning around and going right back inside that fucking prison," Lance said finally. "We'll take our chances out here."

Jeremy nodded. "If you want the rings, you can have them. I just don't want them near me, so don't tell Gordon or anyone else about them."

Lance went back to the other side of the desk and took a seat. They sat in silence for several minutes.

"I found my wife," Lance said. "She's dead."

"Jesus, I'm sorry. In the prison?"

Lance nodded. "Loki flooded one of the wings and I found her body when we got the water to drain."

Jeremy thought about their experience during the escape. He hadn't bothered to check the bodies he had come across, just to make sure none of them were Beth. Maybe that was something you only did if it took you a whole week to make your way out. Cold spread through Jeremy's chest one more time.

"I'm sorry," he said again. It sounded hollow and was probably taken that way.

"It's probably for the best," Lance said.

"Well, that's, err, no—"

"Jeremy, how many people have you killed since you got to the prison?"

"Permanently?"

"Period."

Jeremy shook his head. "I really don't remember at this point."

Lance's gaze leveled on him. "I don't either. Does that bother you?"

It really didn't. Jeremy thought about it and wondered what that said about him. Then he realized that, whatever it said about him, it didn't make any difference. His mission was to find Beth, and anything else just didn't matter.

"After everything," Jeremy finally said, "no, it really doesn't. You?"

Lance shook his head slowly.

"Yeah." Jeremy tapped his fingers on the desk. "I want to ask you something now."

"Go for it."

"I know why the Royal Army stopped when I showed up. I'm one of the people Loki told them to follow. But why did your group stop as well? There were nine on my side, and yours was the only side shooting rifles. You could easily have killed us."

Lance raised an eyebrow. "They're terrified of you."

Jeremy cracked off a burst of laughter that made Lance's eyebrows dash with the intention of hitting the ceiling. It was a short, mad laughter that would very much have concerned Jeremy if what Lance said wasn't so funny, and he cut it off as quickly as he could.

"No one is afraid of me," Jeremy said.

"They saw you sitting right next to Loki on that throne. They saw you in the arena. They saw you beat Loki right before the escape. Some did, anyway."

Jeremy shook his head again. "I didn't beat Loki."

"You fought him and he let you go. That seems like winning to most of the prisoners. In any case, when you appeared out of nowhere like a god, how many people did you really expect to run out into the middle to fight you?"

Silence hung between them again. Finally, Jeremy nodded.

"I can tell you one thing," Lance said. "You saved all of those people from death in another meaningless battle. If we meet again, they won't forget it."

"If you aren't coming with us," Jeremy said, "I don't

think any of you will survive."

***

Jeremy watched from the cliff, his hand on the scouting sword as he stood in his usual position. Gordon had the nine remaining members of the Royal Army gathered around him. Jeremy's vision was continuing to sharpen, and he could see Gordon's mouth forming a grim explanation. James, Angela, and Andrew stood behind the army, expressions blank. James was smoking another cigarette. Looking at them, Jeremy felt a flash of anger. They seemed to have been sitting around the fire this entire time, doing nothing at all while Loki pulled the strings that forced them all back into the prison for whatever else he had planned. They hadn't even looked concerned by the near-catastrophe as Lance's group escaped from the prison.

Lance had taken the rings and disappeared into the forest with his small army. Jeremy, unable to let the man simply march to his death after the horrors of the prison, had given him a scouting sword. There wasn't time for lessons, but Jeremy had given him a description of their use and he hoped Lance got the hang of it quickly on his own. If so, maybe he could find a way through the thousands of Vanaheim warriors who surrounded them.

He supposed he should be calling the man Beowulf if that's what he wanted. Despite his ever-lengthening sight and everyone's insistence, Jeremy still thought of himself as Jeremy. None of them were going by their mythological names, even though everyone seemed to accept it as fact at this point. He wanted to blame Loki for something about that, though he couldn't figure out what.

Over the plateaus, Jeremy caught sight of movement on the horizon. Flags marched through the forest toward the camp, proudly flying various animals and colors that he was sure marked concepts more deeply-held than he could see. Jeremy hoped that they held those symbols dearly, because he smiled at the thought of them worshiping what was essentially a high school mascot. He hated them, mascots and all, and he hoped they and their beliefs died horribly.

As far as he was concerned, those mascots were synonymous with Loki.

His eyes refocused on Gordon and their dwindling army. His wrinkled mouth turned downward as he further explained their fate. The tribes of Vanaheim had turned against them because of Loki's tricks. Then they had started trapping and killing Gordon's most far-reaching scouts, effectively cutting off any means of traveling behind them. Once this was done, it was only a matter of time before they closed in.

A slow, sad song on a string instrument played in the distance, wrenching into a dissonant, mock-cheerful dance that ripped across the strings.

They were not equipped to fight the thousands of warriors marching in their direction, especially the ones from Fenris's army who carried modern guns. With their enemies closing in, their only option was to give Loki what he wanted. They were going to go back into the prison to look for a gate there.

The violin struck a harsh chord and then played it over and over again in different articulations. The waterfall gurgled into the mouth of Loki' prison, the god's giant monument to himself in black stone.

Gordon stepped out of the center and the nine warriors dispersed without argument. Their faces held a placidity that was absolutely disturbing, as if they had expected this all along. Jeremy watched as Angela and Andrew exchanged a wordless nod, and James took a deep drag of his cigarette. Jeremy saw the mass of smoke rise in the air and flow complacently in the direction of the prison. He twisted his wedding ring around his finger.

"Whatever it takes," he said aloud as he pulled the scouting sword from the ground.

# Chapter 13

## A ROYAL FLUSH

James wrapped what was left of the cigarette carton in one of the plastic bags that once held freeze-dried food and put it in a sack he had taken from Gordon's office. He leaned back in his chair and twirled an unlit cigarette across his fingers.

"You alright?" Angela said. She and Andrew walked inside and sat down in the chairs on the other side of the desk.

"Fine." James set out the crystal glasses and filled each with bourbon. He lifted a glass, the texture of it strange against the prison soldier's gloves he wore. "To the weirdest thing that's ever happened to me."

"Probably not," Andrew said.

Angela and James shared a sour grin. Then Andrew lifted his glass and they drank. The shot was bigger than James had intended, and the burn was welcome. He poured another, depleting the bourbon, and they drank it.

He lit a cigarette and the others lit pipes. Andrew had found some material to make the stem of the pipe he had been carving, and he had given the pipe to Angela. She looked more fictional than real while she smoked from it. She held the pipe in the corner of her mouth and held the bowl between her thumb and index finger, breathing the smoke into her lungs despite Andrew's warnings against that. She didn't cough.

James took the revolver from the drawer, loaded it, and tucked it into the back of his belt. He slung the bag over his back along with one of the scouting swords. Gordon's prison soldiers held three of the remaining rifles. Gordon kept the last for himself.

They made their way to the prison entrance. As the three walked, the few remaining members of the Royal Army didn't say "For Freyr." They didn't look at him at all. Instead, they looked straight forward with a creepy, placid look on their faces. They looked like they were pleased to go back into the prison. The Royal Army stood behind James and the others, while the three prison soldiers took the front with their rifles pointed.

He bit the end of another cigarette and lit it, holding up a hand to shield the flame against a breeze that was getting colder by the hour.

As they marched across the clearing and toward the prison, James could see movement on one of the large boulders sticking up from the water. As they marched closer, James could see the toga-wearing Loki plucking strings on a violin with Alex's fingers and sawing across the instrument with warped bow. James looked at Gordon, who refused to look at the boulder. With every sawing motion of Loki's bow, Gordon's forehead crinkled just enough that James could see it from his place a few feet away.

There was no man with a bow tie and lobotomy smile to greet them. The abandoned ticket booths sat in eerie silence, winking at him in the strange light of the mist above and welcoming them back for what could easily be the last time. The onion sweat and sour meat smell of the hallways made him think of emptying his stomach, but the consideration passed and the reality fell on him that it smelled as much like home as Vanaheim.

As they walked, James saw the glowing mist above them ripple as if a breeze was blowing through it. He watched as the mist seemed to roll and fold itself into its center and the light dimmed. Finally, it disappeared, taking the light with it.

In the dark, James heard Loki clap his hands.

He drew his scouting sword and braced himself against the wall, crouching because he thought it would make him a more difficult target. He listened for scuffs of footsteps that would indicate the Royal Army was attacking them. What he heard was silence.

He thought of Loki's prison soldiers, their eyes black and their minds pulled out of their heads, leaving nothing but obedience behind. Staring into the blanket of darkness that surrounded him, he couldn't help but imagine some of that smothering black seeping into his irises. He clung to the wall and pushed forward alone as the familiar rush of water made its way to his ears.

\*\*\*

Jeremy stumbled through the darkness with Gordon. Silence blanketed the hallway beyond the eternal background of rushing water and his heart tapped out a rough approximation of a pop song, loud enough that he was sure it could be heard through the rock.

"Still with me?" Gordon said.

"Yeah, I'm fine. Just keep that gun pointed ahead of us."

Jeremy felt for the scouting sword on his belt, only to discover that it was gone. He held an arena sword pointed in front of him, ready to jab at whatever might lunge toward him in the dark. He thought about tigers. He thought about masked prisoners and those in the Royal Army, happily taking Loki's orders and cutting Jeremy into pieces with their blades.

In the dark, they were at Loki's mercy. Calm washed over Jeremy.

"He's afraid of you," Gordon said. "Heimdall and Loki kill each other. I don't know how, but I don't think Loki knows either. Whatever he does, with a single wrong move he can set off the whole chain reaction that plunges us into Ragnarok and brings about his own death."

Jeremy heard echoes of the shadow's laughter in the distance and he felt his lips curl backward over his teeth in a grin. One way or another, he would be rid of that shadow. Then he would find Beth, no matter what had happened to her. His grip tightened on the hilt of his sword.

The mist above him shifted and released a dim light. A shadow tapped its way through a dance against the far wall, twirling an ethereal cane and tipping a top hat in acknowledgment of its audience. Gordon fired the rifle at it and laughter echoed again as the shadow continued its dance. Water began to drift slowly across the floor, a lacquered sheet that spread in Jeremy's direction from its origin at the end of the hallway.

Gordon could see the shadow. Relief at the thought that he wasn't entirely insane was quickly replaced with dread.

The shadow leaped down the hallway, passing them as its throaty cackle pounded into Jeremy's ears. He turned and saw a woman slowly rise from a crouch. She wore the brown shirt and pants of the prison uniform, her blonde curls draped delicately over the dark cloth. As she lifted her face and stared at him with black eyes just like Loki's prison soldiers, Jeremy's heightened vision focused on every freckle and pore of her skin.

He traced the sculpted pout of her lips with his eyes and his breath caught as he traced the scar that slashed from the left corner of her mouth all the way up to her scalp. Another scar broke the smooth skin of her throat as it puckered across her wind pipe. Jeremy's mind flashed to the brutal decapitation again, picturing the arena fighter holding Beth's head high while the crowd cheered. His heart froze.

Beth's face was placid as Gordon pointed the rifle at her and pulled the trigger. By the time Jeremy pulled himself away from the sight of her and realized what was happening, the bullet had ripped through her chest and Gordon fired two more.

Without thinking, he turned and plunged the sword into Gordon's throat. The old man's eyes widened and he dropped the rifle, cupping his hands around the edges of the sword as crimson poured from his neck. Jeremy felt nothing as he gripped the hilt of the sword and yanked it free, leaving the old man sputtering on the black stone floor. Jeremy ran to his wife.

Her face didn't change expression. She held that placid look, her eyes glossy and doll-like, and he could barely even tell when she stopped breathing. His mind darted from thought to thought, desperately searching for a way to stop this from happening. He found none. As he held her, Gordon's body sank into the floor and disappeared. Beth's body did the same.

The numbness in Jeremy's chest blotted everything else out. Sadness and fear fell away, swallowed by a darkness that was growing inside of him. The underworld was a real place, and Jeremy had already seen the goddess who ruled it. He would find Hel, and he would make things right. He would bring Beth back from the dead. He told himself all of this, but he felt nothing.

The shadow chuckled behind him. "I don't think there's time for that, Heimdall. I have something else to keep you busy. You're going to guard the next round of prisoners."

It grabbed him by the shirt and held him in the air over a giant maw that opened in the floor below. The shadow grinned at Jeremy and tossed him into the pit. That grin dripped a thin string of mad drool that followed Jeremy into the abyss below.

Jeremy writhed in the fluid darkness that consumed him. He couldn't feel his limbs anymore. He couldn't see beyond the hazy black, and only a part of him was sure that he was plummeting through space.

Loki wanted belief. Jeremy could give him that, if that's what it would take to survive. "Praise be to Loki, God of gods."

"Oh Heimdall," Loki said, "it's not about that when it comes to you. Your praise is worthless to me."

The voice felt breathy against his ear and he sprawled to the side, throwing punches at nothing in the direction of the sound. Something fluid slowed his movements just like water, but he could breathe. He felt whatever it was push hard against his skin and his ears popped.

His mind reeling, Jeremy burned with anger as he saw Beth's black eyes again in his mind. Loki had taken everything from her. He tried to use Heimdall's sight through the darkness. If he could be a threat to Loki, if Loki was really afraid of him, he could bargain for Beth's life.

"Well, that's just silly," Loki said. "You can't bargain away the inevitable. And make no mistake, Heimdall. I *am* the inevitable."

A wave of pressure ground Jeremy's mind against itself until he thought it would burst. Then something opened and he felt as if his mind was spilling out into that blackness, covering his existence in sticky consciousness.

"Please," Jeremy said, "please make it stop."

"It's almost finished. It takes a little more finesse with you. You're something much older than Beth was."

Jeremy writhed at Loki's use of her name. The world shifted and Jeremy's skull cracked. Something stirred in the lobes of his brain, picking through gyri and worming its way around neurons, poking into memories and fears and a vain hope that his story didn't have an ending.

Whatever it takes. Jeremy prayed silently to Loki, hoping that he could think of something else before it was too late, something that would stop all of this.

The voice laughed. "That's never been what this was about."

The liquid dark around him became ice cold, sucking heat from Jeremy's bones like a vacuum. Jeremy felt darkness swell in his mind, blotting out his anger and fear and leaving something dirty behind. He cried out as he felt that swell press against his identity, then twist around his mind and pull until everything that he was ripped solidly in two, each half screaming at the other to, by *God*, do something.

When the pressure finally released, he felt himself floating slowly away. The laughter of the voice faded and the largest part of him believed he was dead.

***

James made his way down the corkscrew stairs, only aware of their shape by the curve of the wall. Although some instinct told him to keep track of his path, the greater part of him knew it didn't matter. He expected the stairway to fill with water, or for soldiers to follow him down with guns cracking off shots.

The corkscrew stairway stopped at the solid steel of a door, which James opened by feeling for the panel and pressing his glove against it. He stepped inside, remembering the last time he had stepped into a room without thinking, and had to shield his eyes from the light of a dozen chandeliers hanging from a blur of darkness above.

"Oh," Loki said with Alex's mouth. "Thank God you're alright. I was really starting to get worried."

Loki sat and smiled at James from the head of a long banquet table, wearing his toga and laurel crown. The table was set with a massive roast, with an accompaniment of side dishes that James didn't recognize. He could see steam rising from the dishes. Pitchers of wine and cauldrons of spiced drinks occupied nearly the rest of the space. There was no aroma wafting from the table, just like there was apparently nothing holding up the chandeliers.

"Tell me where Angela is," James said.

Loki shook his head. "You've done something interesting, old friend. I initially thought you would slip back into Freyr and forget about all of this James shit, but you haven't. You keep planting roots in this life, attaching yourself to all of these people, and you're blending the two identities. And who the hell is Alex anyway?"

James stared at him. "Fuck you."

"Wait, wait," Loki said. "Let me guess. Is it—" He leaned back on the table and tilted Alex's hips, spreading his legs in a feminine, beckoning way. He puffed his lips and regarded James with a weighing, cat-like glare. His eyebrows jerked upward twice and he purred. "I'll be your tiger."

James crossed the space between them, dug into his pocket, and yanked two cigarettes from his pack. He held one up for Loki and the man bent his neck to take it with his lips. James lit his first and then held the lighter for Loki's first drag. He stared into Alex's eyes and Loki stared back as an oddly insecure expression crossed his face.

James smiled at him and stepped back again, taking a long drag and billowing smoke upward. The gust of lazy, swirling gray rose until it disappeared beyond the light of the chandeliers. "Tell me what needs to be done to save Freya, if you care so much about me being Freyr."

Loki howled in amusement. "You're dreaming about the seasons, moron. I played that trick on you half an eternity ago." He closed his mouth and eyes and breathed two plumes of smoke through his nostrils. "The gods find a way to wake her every time, if you don't mind the spoiler to that story. This time is different, though."

The trickster god gestured with Alex's arms and James turned around to see a table sprout from the floor. Angela lay on the table, her skin blue-tinged and frosted, exactly the way Freya had looked. She wore Freya's crimson battle gown, but her hands rested on a green sash around her waist, made from the dress she had worn in her first arena battle.

"It's been too long for anyone to remember her real name, you know. None of us remember our real names. They become meaningless over time and people start calling us something else. The two of you always stick together, though. As long as I have her, I have you."

Thin tendrils of water began to make their way across the floor from the dark edges of the room. Loki smiled down at them and took a goblet from the table, putting it to his lips. Then he tossed it over his shoulder, coinciding the crash and splash of it hitting the ground with an upward turn of his finger as if conducting a small, succinct orchestra. The water rose, soaking James's shoes and tickling his ankles.

"Is this how you start Fimbulwinter?"

The trickster god cracked off a loud cackle, throwing his head back and dropping the laurel crown from his stringy, dark hair. "There's *nothing* that can stop Fimbulwinter. I needed Gordon to think there was something he could do about it, to keep him fighting, so I lied."

Loki snapped his fingers and the banquet flew from the table and into the shadows beyond the chandeliers' light with a crash. A bottle of bourbon grew from the table like a weed, followed close behind by two glasses. Loki poured the whiskey and handed a glass to James, who took it in silence.

"I don't need to take your mind away to make you work for me," Loki said. "Odin and Heimdall were easy to turn. Thor is a little less so, but I'm working on that as we speak. You, on the other hand, are a lot more useful to me if you can actually think."

James dropped the glass, shattering it on the floor, and drew the revolver from his belt. He took a long drag on his cigarette and smiled at Loki.

The trickster god steepled his fingertips against pursed lips and clapped them together. "I don't know what you think that's going to accomplish."

James put the muzzle of the revolver to his own head and Loki frowned. They stood there, staring at each other for a moment. Loki seemed puzzled, digging his thumb and middle finger into the corners of Alex's mouth and dragging them across his lower lip. James thought for a moment that Loki would reach up and pull the trigger himself, and his skin prickled against the cold steel in unwelcome anticipation.

Loki shrugged. "I'll just have Hel put you back together again."

"And if I do it again? You've got her chained in here like an animal, against her will. How long do you think she's going to keep bailing you out? Sooner or later, something is going to go wrong. How long do you think the prophecies give you after I bite it for good?"

Loki shook his head and poured himself a glass of whiskey that James couldn't help but trace with his eyes. "I'll just empty your mind and have you stand guard over the prison, then. I can black out your whole world and do whatever I like."

James set the revolver on the table and poured himself another glass of whiskey. "Yeah, but where's the fun in that?"

Loki was silent.

James shook his head. "That's the problem. It's no fun that way. So here's the new deal. If you want to play the game, stop changing the rules. Send us back to Midgard."

"That's a heavy demand," Loki said.

Without a word, James glared into Alex's eyes. He watched those dark gems skate back and forth, studying James's face for signs of bluffing.

"I'll need to reverse some of what I've already done to the others," Loki said.

James smiled. "And Angela survives until Ragnarok is over."

Loki threw his head back and laughed. "I actually like that. I can only guarantee her safety until the world burns."

"That will be long enough."

Loki's grin was genuinely delighted, his eyes on fire. "Deal." He extended Alex's arms outward in a grand gesture. "Why not have me raise your teenage boy toy while we're at it?"

It was an effort for James not to pick up the gun and blast Loki's skull apart. He crossed himself sarcastically, forehead to crotch and nipple to nipple. "Alex never really wanted to be here in the first place. If you bring him back, you can be sure I'll ruin any fun you could possibly have until you die."

"That's sweet."

"It really isn't."

Loki's smile deepened and he sipped his whiskey again. "So let it be written. I've missed you, Freyr."

They clinked glasses and James blew an opaque bar of gray smoke into Loki's face. Alex's left eye twitched and watered, and Loki scowled as he rubbed his fingertips against his irritated tear ducts. "Fuck you, man."

The walls, if there were walls, fell to nothing and water crashed in on them from all sides.

# Epilogue

Jeremy gasped as his face burst from the frigid water's surface and he tasted salt. His legs strained, freezing cold as they were, to kick hard enough to keep his head above the waves. Icicles were already starting to form on his hair and eyebrows as he struggled for air. As he sank under again, he felt a large hand grab him by his shirt and drag him through the icy water.

Andrew carried him over his shoulder across a frozen beach, with palm trees encased in ice as they reached upward to a dark, gray sky. Snow crunched under the mountain man's feet and Jeremy's dizzy mind danced to the sound of those footsteps. He closed his eyes and let himself be carried, numb and barely conscious, to the far end of the beach where the rest of the group waited for him.

When they came to a stop, he opened his eyes again and

looked into the faces of James and Angela, hugging themselves in a vain attempt to regain warmth. Their prison uniforms clung to their bodies, soaked in slowly-freezing water. Their skin had a gray coloring that made them look like corpses. Gordon wasn't with them, and Jeremy couldn't remember why.

"We need to move," Andrew said. "We'll freeze to death without a fire and dry clothes."

Jeremy tried to move his fingers, but his clenched fists only trembled. The edges of his fingers were turning black, and Jeremy tried to remember if that meant he would lose them. He couldn't summon any fear over the prospect. He barely had the energy for the thought itself.

He lifted his head as Andrew carried him. Though the others didn't seem to notice, there was a figure standing alone on the beach, looking out over the freezing water as if watching vigilantly for a threat. The figure had long, golden hair and skin inlaid with gold flecks that shimmered in the moonlight. As they walked, the figure turned and regarded Jeremy with piercing, golden eyes.

"Where are we?" Jeremy said.

James pointed to the line of hotels and man-made pools along the beach. "We're in Florida. That's Miami."

"It *was* Miami," Andrew said. "Fimbulwinter is upon us. Ragnarok has begun."

From The Author

Thank you very much for purchasing and reading this book. I truly hope that you enjoyed it, and if you did, please take the time to review it on Amazon and share it on social media like Facebook and Twitter. Even the briefest of reviews or blurbs is massively appreciated. If you would like to contact me directly, I respond regularly to comments and messages sent to the following Facebook page:

www.facebook.com/TheWolvesOfRagnarok

Be sure to 'like' the above page for information on the next installment of the series.

Thank you again!

Sincerely,
Nick Steuver

Made in the USA
Lexington, KY
10 April 2015